THE TARTARUS HOUSE ON CRAB

THE TARTARUS HOUSE ON CRAB

GEORGE SZANTO

BRINDLE & GLASS

Copyright © 2011 George Szanto

All rights reserved. No part of this publication may be reproduced, stored in a retrieval system, or transmitted in any form or by any means—electronic, mechanical, recording, or otherwise—without the prior written consent of the publisher or a licence from The Canadian Copyright Licensing Agency (ACCESS Copyright). For a copyright licence, visit www.accesscopyright.ca.

Brindle & Glass Publishing Ltd.
www.brindleandglass.com

LIBRARY AND ARCHIVES CANADA CATALOGUING IN PUBLICATION
Szanto, George, 1940–
The Tartarus house on Crab / George Szanto.

Print format: ISBN 978-1-897142-53-0
Electronic monograph in PDF format: ISBN 978-1-897142-59-2
Electronic monograph in HTML format: ISBN 978-1-897142-60-8

I. Title.

PS8587.Z3T37 2011   C813'.54   C2010-906358-9

Editor: Lynne Van Luven
Proofreader: Heather Sangster, Strong Finish
Design: Pete Kohut
Front cover illustration: Pete Kohut

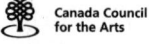

Brindle & Glass is pleased to acknowledge the financial support for its publishing program from the Government of Canada through the Canada Book Fund, Canada Council for the Arts, and the Province of British Columbia through the British Columbia Arts Council and the Book Publishing Tax Credit.

The interior pages of this book have been printed on 100% post-consumer recycled paper, processed chlorine free, and printed with vegetable-based inks.

This book is a work of fiction. Names, characters, places, and incidents are either products of the author's imagination or are used fictitiously. Any resemblance to actual events or locales or persons, living or dead, is entirely coincidental.

1 2 3 4 5 14 13 12 11

PRINTED IN CANADA

For Marie-Christine Leps
&
Robert Barsky
For decades of friendship

Tartarus, Jack

TARTARUS.
That place as far below Hades as heaven is above the earth. Home of the rebellious Titans.

JACK.
A pet name, probably the most common, for John.
In the *Oxford English Dictionary* there are more than eighty uses and compounds for Jack as a common noun.

The Tartarus house, two storeys high, white clapboard siding, sits empty. Pea-green shutters cover the windows. The metal roof, pitched front and back, is grass-green. Facing the drive in, two dormer windows extrude through the roof-line, two more adorn the back. A covered veranda skirts the whole of the house. Wooden pillars, painted white, four to a side, support the veranda roof. Thin wooden arabesque lacework softens the corners where pillar meets overhang. Along the west side, a dry stream bed. Some thirty metres to the east, an unattached garage. The land about it has been cleared, fifty metres on three sides. The meadow to the east extends a hundred-eighty metres. Beyond the clearing, dense woods. The house dominates the land.

Where is the house? Down a drive through the woods, a forgotten house. But strong bones, healthy timbers. No broken glass. Local kids have thought about forcing their way in. The house has scared them away.

ONE: Jack Tartarus and the House

Tartarus forced the longer teeth of the wrecking bar a couple of millimetres upward, beneath a length of white clapboard siding. The board wouldn't budge. Push up, pull forward. Again. It took the best part of a minute to work the teeth in five centimetres. He let go of the bar. It hung in place, chest-high. Good. He pushed down on the handle. The wood held tight. He leaned over the bar, forcing his weight downward. He heard a crack. Harder. Another crack, more pressure, and the wood tore, releasing the bar. A ten-centimetre splinter, faded white paint on the flat side, hung to the wall by a sliver. Okay, the destruction begins.

The clerk at Crab Hardware, a fellow named Turtle if his tag spoke true, had sold him the wrecking bar, a Fulton. "Fulton's way better than your standard gooseneck bar, bigger teeth for the crude work, the little ones when the job gets more subtle."

Tartarus had rubbed its two longer teeth against the pad of his thumb. Not blade-sharp but tough-sharp. He'd used it to scratch his right cheek through his thick curly beard, as if shaving with the Fulton bar. "Okay, I'll take it. I think it'll work."

"Yep," said the clerk, "Fulton gives any job a kind of class."

Jack Tartarus felt no class, not physical nor any other. A tool of destruction, he thought. Probably as fine in its own way as the tool of a builder. But this would be a less than classy project. "Just so's it gets the job done."

"Right. Need the right tool for the job," the clerk had noted, adding, "and you got to be working the right job." He gave Tartarus what might have passed for a salute and turned away.

Back in April, Tartarus had considered hiring somebody: bring an excavator in, half a day, flatten the house. Or pay a guy to work with him. But that'd make the job easy, both options missing the point. He hadn't come back to contract the work out. Tearing the place down by

1

hand, his own hand, was what he had to do. Besides, bringing someone in would call for explanations.

He stared at the torn wood. Starting, the first difficulty. Though middling and finishing wasn't going to be so easy either. He reached for the hanging splinter, gripped it, yanked. It held. Another pull. Still wouldn't give. He twisted the bar, and again. Tough little chunk, he thought at it. Typical. Nearly ripped away but still holding on. How much of the house would be this recalcitrant? A defiant house. A titanic house. In size and challenge. With his left thumb he again tested the teeth, the larger set, the smaller. He slammed down on the hanging chunk and at last it dropped. That clerk, Turtle, sure had liked the Fulton, a hammerhead, sharp on both edges of the hammer. Now Tartarus worked the shorter teeth in laterally where the chip had been. They penetrated more easily but less deep. He leaned weight against it, felt it give, then crack. Another splinter, half as big as the first. "It's you or me, house, and you're going to lose."

On the drive north he'd committed himself to this method: pry the siding loose. He'd pull off the outer layers, get down to the struts, cut through them one by one by one. With enough supports gone the whole thing would come crashing down, right on top of his old low-ceilinged basement studio. He wouldn't go down into it again, nothing there for him anymore.

He breathed in deeply. And out quickly, so he could breathe in again more slowly, tasting the dry air. A scent. Again a deep breath. Something? No. Maybe. He closed his eyes and saw her striding across the meadow, twirling, humming so softly he couldn't hear unless he held her by the waist and swirled with her, Maureen dancing on the grass, long red hair flying around, around. He breathed in again and for a moment it had to be her scent—then nothing. On a windy November day he'd sprinkled her ashes over the meadow, as she had asked him to. He opened his eyes. No wind. No scent. Her scent long gone.

He worked the bar under again, now the big teeth, and broke off another splinter, longer and narrower. Whatever perfection the house might once have known, he'd just destroyed it. He felt okay about that, pretty good. Except the house had lost its primal perfection years ago.

More than lost. It had been stained, debased. "Misery of a house," he said to it.

Green shutters covered all the windows. Simply pull them off? He'd painted them once, the summer after his first year at university, raw wood then, ready to be hung. So, no, not a starting point, they weren't original to the house. He had to make a great hole in the wall. A new hole. Not simply breaking a window in, any vandal could shatter a window. Tearing down a house is no vandalism.

He'd thought of starting with the garage. The real culprit. He couldn't see the garage door from where he stood. Then he'd realized, no, not the garage. Without the house the garage would bear no blame. The house had to come down first, he believed this. Some might find such a belief unreasonable, he understood this. Couldn't be helped.

The house would be shattered. Not out of hate but from vengeance. Terminate it, as much pain as possible. Was he starting at the right point, though? He stepped back on the veranda and turned left, past the siding with the missing splinters on around to the back of the house. He passed the big dining room window, saw only the backing of the drapes. He stopped at the door to the kitchen. The top half of the door, though glass, allowed no view inside because the blind was pulled down. The house, hiding itself away. Across from the door were more steps down, here to the woodshed. He glanced at it. Just about empty. Not his problem. He walked on, all the way around the veranda, to the front door. No, nowhere better. Any point as good as any other.

Back to work. He grabbed the bar, tested its heft. His two big hands on the leverage end, large teeth under the siding, tearing out a chunk of wood. Another chunk, defiant as before.

"Hey!"

He turned. Twenty metres away, running toward him from the drive, a woman. Who the hell? Some kind of blue top and a faded patterned skirt down to ankle boots, near to tripping over her hem. Hair in tangles to her shoulders. A scarf over it.

"What the hell you think you're doing!" She stopped between his car and the railing. "You crazy or something?" She pulled a backpack off her left shoulder and dropped it to the ground. "Get away from that house!"

He held the Fulton bar, one hand on the handle and the other on the pry. "What d'you want?"

"Cut that out!"

He squinted and got a better sense of her face. Narrow, hair raggy brown, small nose and larger mouth, overlarge eyes. Mid-thirties, he guessed. "Who are you?"

"Stop wrecking the siding, for shitsake!"

"Why?"

She glared at him. "Are you crazy?"

"Crazy?" He grinned at her, his best crazy smile. "Nope."

"Then why're you tearing away at the siding?"

"I am pulling the house asunder."

"You're what?"

"I'm razing the house."

"But why?"

"What's it to you?"

"You better get out of here. Or I'll call the cops."

"Yeah? And tell them what?"

"That you—that you're destroying a perfectly good house."

He shook his head. "That's where you're wrong. It's not."

"Not—"

"Any good."

She shook her head once, twice, then jerked herself still, chin up, as if interrupted by something beyond her. "You're completely nuts."

"Wrong." He took a step toward her, bar in hand.

"Hey, easy!" She flinched and stepped back.

"I'm not going to hurt you." He lowered the bar again. "I'm not dangerous."

She stared at the bar, then at his face. "I bet the house wouldn't agree with you."

He shook his head. "The house doesn't get a say."

Her glance moved from his hands, down to his feet, up again. "Only you get a say?"

"That's right. And now if you'll excuse me." He turned from her, worked the teeth between two boards.

She was up on the veranda now, the fingers of one hand grabbing his right arm, the other hand trying to undo his grip on the bar, shaking it.

"Hey!" Her nails had dug into the skin of his forearm. He grabbed two fingers. "Stop it!" She was strong, but he pried her fingers up one at a time, got them all loose, grabbed her wrist. She broke his hold, clenched his upper arm, and sunk her nails in again, bent forward with open mouth, bit into his wrist. "Ow! Okay! Okay! Stop, for godsake!"

"You stop!" Her throat growled from behind the teeth in his arm.

"Okay, okay!" With his left shoulder, he pushed at her hard. Her teeth and fingers let go and she fell butt-first against the side of the house. Her legs buckled and she crumbled toward him. He caught her arm, dropped the bar, and reached for her shoulder. Already she was shrugging his hands away. Not much meat there, lot of strength for somebody so skinny. He knelt down to her level. Her eyes, lots of white beside grey-green irises, white above and below too, lids blinking hard, looked as if they were about to cry. No tears came. A strange face, then a sudden nagging familiarity. He stared at her for a fraction of a second. No, no recognition. "You all right?"

She nodded. She raised her head a little. "You?"

He rolled up his sleeve, making much of examining his right arm, elbow to wrist. Her incisors had drawn blood. Not her nails, though. But double red marks on the arm, likely two bruises coming. "I'll live. Unless your fangs are poisonous." And she smelled too—no bath in a while.

She glowered. For a moment her brow wrinkled. She squeezed her eyes shut.

"Why're you so worried about the house?"

Her eyes opened. "You don't destroy houses. People need houses."

"I don't need this one."

"Someone else might."

"Someone else can need some other house. This one's mine, and I don't want it to exist."

She stared at him and slowly stood. "It's your house?"

He got up too, and his sleeve dropped to his wrist. "Course. I don't go around destroying other people's property."

She brought her right hand to her lips and her gaze searched his face, her huge eyes fearful. Her hand dropped away. Her mouth opened to speak. No words came.

"What's the matter?"

"Nothing." She looked away, to her left through the railing. "Oh my god." She shrivelled, decided, turned and headed for the steps. Glanced over her shoulder. "Please. Don't destroy it."

He sighed. "You want to pay the insurance?"

"Huh?"

"The insurance. On the house."

"What you talking about?"

"I-am-getting-rid-of-the-house-because-I-don't-want-to-pay-the-insurance."

Her mouth fell open. "Now I know you're crazy."

"Look. I haven't lived here for ten years. I don't want the house. I don't want to be liable for anything that happens to it. Or to anybody who goes in. And I won't pay the insurance."

"But to tear it down . . . Couldn't you sell it?"

"Can't stand somebody else owning it." No need to tell her anything.

"Well then, rent it or something."

"Did that. Eight years. While trying to decide what to do with it. Now I've decided."

"To tear it down."

"Yep." He picked up the bar, hefted it, turned to the house, tapped the bar against intact siding. He could hear feet on gravel. He glanced her way. She'd picked up her backpack and was stalking off, up the drive she'd come along. Again he worked the big teeth in, levered, tore out another nugget of wood, smaller. Two more times, three. He looked down the path. Nobody there. He rolled up his sleeve again. The bite looked angry.

Who was she? Could she have heard the bar tearing at wood? All the way from the road beyond the thick brush, off around the curve, quarter of a kilometre away? Why did she come down the drive? Anyway, she was gone. He pictured her, those immense eyes. Something familiar about her. But no, he'd never seen eyes like that.

He examined his work. The energy he'd felt by beginning the job had fled. He looked at his wrist. Little spots of blood, still oozing. Damn better not have anything communicable.

The small wood chips lay on the veranda. Despite his weariness, they deserved celebration. The six-pack in the car would still be cold. "Where'd they move the liquor store to?" he'd asked the hardware store clerk. The clerk pointed left. "'Bout a hundred metres down that way, 'cross the street." Maybe better to keep the pack intact to bring over to Don's? No, he wanted one right now, the August sun hot. Hell, he deserved one. He hung the bar on the rail, walked down the wooden steps. He kicked at the gravel on the path to the drive, opened the dark green Buick's back door, plucked an IPA from six-pack, screwed it open, took a swallow.

He stared at the house. Was he kidding himself? Tear it all down by hand? From eight metres, he could barely tell where he'd yanked the wood away. The place seemed immense, a huge white box with green trim, the skirt of veranda along the four sides adding to its enormity.

He stared at the beer bottle. He poured a little of the thin alcohol onto the bite marks. It stung. He whipped his arm up and down to dry it off. Now he stank of beer.

Maybe he should just douse a bit of it with gasoline, the front door say, symbolic, and toss a match at it. Be ready with his cameras, maybe a helicopter to get it from above. He'd thought about fire a couple of times some months ago, fire being, after all, his metier. A lot of softwood in that house, it'd go quickly. He'd have to get a burning permit. What, while the forest fire warning gauges all screamed Extreme? He scratched at his scalp through his thick hair. No, he'd come here for this, to tear it down. Fire was for his work, which was pleasure. Tearing down the house was a responsibility. Tartarus took his responsibilities seriously.

Her bite wound itched, ached a bit too. He released the catch to the trunk, went around, found his medical kit. He took out a small bottle of hydrogen peroxide, opened it, poured some liquid into the cap, let it seep onto the bite; instant foaming. He put the kit away. He opened a stiff leather camera pack. Right now he needed the little digital Sony. Back up the steps, and he found the image he wanted. Two shots of the slashed siding from a couple of metres, four more angled close-ups. Not for a history of the house's demise, this was hardly a project. Just a few particulars for himself, for later. He put the camera back into the pack and wedged it between his suitcase and his sleeping bag.

He stood up straight and sniffed the air, drawing it up his nostrils. He tasted it, first on his tongue, then in his lungs. Another sniff. Fir and grass and his own drying sweat. Nothing else.

Time to go. He sat behind the wheel, reached for the door handle—Someone calling? He listened. Nothing. He got out, looked around. Nobody. The woman, coming back to harangue him some more? Hiding in the woods? He listened hard. Nothing. The first person to wonder at his eccentric actions. He sipped beer. Still cool, but it didn't taste right. Not flat, just off. Why had that woman come down the drive? A hint of familiarity, as if her chin and nose were a transformed version of features once known. Then gone. He smiled. Like the scent of Maureen on the air. A day for hallucinations.

On his cellphone he spoke to Don, said he'd be there in ten or fifteen minutes. He looked forward to seeing Don again. He got back in and drove from the house, leaving the cleared area behind. Scrub starting to grow there, alders already seven-eight-ten feet tall, salal, the grass high and desiccated. "Ten weeks, no rain," the hardware store clerk had said, "and that's against the rules." Only a couple of years that the house had been empty and already nature was taking the land back. Get a chainsaw, heavy-duty mower, clear all that stuff out... But why? He'd bring the house down. And the earth could reclaim its own.

The road reached the heavy brush. He checked the rear-view mirror. The house stood back there, shadowed, white and green, outwardly in peace. At the first curve he slowed to a crawl. He watched the house recede, a third of it already hidden by foliage, a half, most of it, then all gone. His glance returned to the driveway ahead. Large firs, second growth but reaching a foot and a half in girth, a hundred and ten feet tall. Fifty-two years since the acreage had been clear-cut. A grove of cedar where the land lay low, probably a couple hundred trees, rainwater collected there in the late winter, in the spring. Twenty seconds and he reached Scott Road.

The house in the woods where his father had built it. A forgotten house, increasingly lost in the overgrowth. Still, in its way, in good condition. And behind the shutters, heavy drapes. Where had the woman come from, why had she come down the drive?

Jack Tartarus arrived just at seven. He and Don sat on bar stools in the kitchen drinking beer. Don's father, Frank, clasping his beer, stood a metre away. Once again Jack felt a sense of awe, of privilege, staring out at the wide drift of ocean beyond the big window. As a young man he'd often watched from here as mighty storms smashed the land, three-metre waves cresting and breaking on the shale beach. This evening, tiny waves tickled over the stone, the water near mirror-flat all the way over to the shores of Vancouver Island, the big island. He'd loved this view when he was eighteen. The windows had been small then, the rooms tiny. When Don moved in, he'd broken down walls, taken off the roof, built out and up. Six hundred eighty square feet became nearly seventeen hundred, about half of it the new second floor. A beach cabin, transformed into an elegant waterfront home. A pair of two-metre sliding-glass doors framed the sea.

Don asked the appropriate questions about the trip, easy drive, any problem at the borders? Jack gave suitable answers. Frank made a point of ignoring them, his only comment a grunt. At Jack's question, "So how you been doin', Frank?" Frank had said, "Fine, fine," and when Jack responded, "Glad to hear it," Frank raised his bottle, drank, and ignored him and Don. Eight minutes, two irritated complaints to Don and restrained impoliteness to Jack, and three of the five IPAs were empty. Frank glommed on to the last two.

"My good-for-nothing son always gets me Coors pisswater. Your mother wouldn't've treated me like this. You two drink the piss, me I'm takin' this stuff." Frank strode off, letting out a braying fart—his kind of rejection of the world, Jack figured. Or just of Don. Frank's cane led

9

the way through the doorway, around the corner to his chair in front of the den TV. "Call me when that bilge you're cooking's ready."

Don's tight lips opened and he puffed out a sigh. He slid from the barstool. "I buy beer that's more or less taste-free so Pa doesn't drink so much. He'll give me a hard time later. You got to tell him the IPA comes from some place below the border, far away so I can't get there."

Jack figured Don had lived with Frank's surliness for so long this backing off came to him not naturally but with resignation. Poor damn overgenerous guy. "Does he never stop?"

"Sometimes when he's asleep." For a moment Don's mind went elsewhere. "Want a scotch? Vodka?"

"Got any bourbon?"

A grin. "Elbert Simpson okay? Ten-year-old mash."

"You get that around here?"

"I have my sources."

"Good hostelry."

Don reached up to a cabinet over the fridge, took down a bottle near to full, and two tumblers. He poured two fingers of hazel-brown liquid into each and filled a jug with water. "Let's get comfortable before supper. Grab a glass." He led the way to the living room, as far from the sound of the TV as they could get. He set the jug and his tumbler on a low table between two large chairs. Beyond the glass doors the strait lay peaceful, little grey-blue waves barely breaking.

Jack sat at the edge of a brown chair and poured a smidgen of water into his Elbert. Then he sprawled back in the chair. "Good to see you, Donnie." He meant it, from deep down.

"You too, Jack." He raised his glass. "Glad you came back."

They drank. Couple of sips for Jack, a full finger gone from Don's. "He always treat you like that?"

"Nope. Sometimes he gets angry too."

"How can you . . ."

"I've been handling this for a long time. I deal with him."

"Why?"

"Because I can."

"Does he have friends? Cronies?"

"No more."

"Drinking buddies?"

"Guys he used to play cards with, fish with, the last two died last year. One after the other, March and April. That was it for Frank."

"So it's just you."

"Yep."

"Must be hell to live with. Let alone look after."

"And he resents it too." Don shook his head. "But I can't throw him out on the street."

Why not, Tartarus said in the silence of his head. The cold dark street, yeah. Leave him out there till he sees how lucky he is, being taken care of. "What about some kind of home?"

"No." Don sipped. "We tried that. He hated it."

"And you don't hate this?"

"Like I said. I can handle it. Him."

"By taking the guff."

"Least I can hear it. When I blow a little, his ears don't let him hear me."

"You don't deserve it. He doesn't deserve you."

"I'm all he's got."

"And what have you got?"

Don smiled. "I guess I got Frank."

Jack took a moment before saying, "And nobody else."

Don said nothing.

"Not Natalia."

"No." Don suddenly looked toward the den, to a sound like a roar.

"He okay?"

"Just pissed off at something on the TV." His attention came back to the room. "And you? Still no one?"

"Oh, somebody here, somebody there. But nothing to compare. Ever."

"Not even in one of those wonderful distant places?"

Jack shook his head.

"Somebody to take care of you."

"I take care of myself." He took a large swallow of bourbon, as if bracing himself. "So. You want me to call Natalia? Ask her to come over?"

Don said nothing.

"Or you could call her. Tell her I've arrived. Don't know why you haven't called her long ago. Or maybe you did."

"No. No, I couldn't."

"Just push the buttons on your phone. Remember her number?"

"Isn't she, I mean, I would've thought, a woman like Natalia . . ."

"She likes being on her own. Always has. Well, after Stan died. Except for you."

"How is she?" Don spoke quietly. "You've seen her?"

"We talk maybe once a month. I call her. Easier than her finding me, wherever I am."

He finished his Elbert. "She's still in the old house?"

"She loves the neighbourhood."

From the den, a strangled cry. Don got up. "I better deal with him. And with supper. And get myself another drink. Freshen yours?" He reached for Jack's glass.

"I'll do it. Go cope." He followed Don as far as the kitchen. He stopped at the bottle of Elbert Simpson. He poured another couple of fingers. Be a shame to add water again. But better for his stomach—and his head—if he added water. He sipped. Hell of a shame to add water.

He'd never been easy with Don's father, even while Don's much admired mother, Sylvia, was still alive. Frank Bonner hadn't liked Jack Tartarus much either, not after he'd grown up. But Don, Tartarus realized years ago, was his mother's son. He figured the only way his parents and Don's could have been such good friends was because of Sylvia.

Don was the good guy of the Bonner men. He'd come back to the island weekends for his mother, then nursed her over her last twenty months, Frank out of the house much of the time—had to work to pay Sylvia's bills, he'd shout. Letting Don do irregular caregiving. Don should've had kids. One of the few men Tartarus knew who'd have been a great father.

He glanced about the kitchen. He remembered it well, its shapes anyway. Now new appliances, new cabinets and floor, but familiar for all that. A comfortable place when Don's mother was chatelaine here. Its cleanliness, the shine of the sink, all in its place. He glanced about, through thirty-year-old filters. Don had taken on his mother's orderliness. Which, it hit Tartarus, now made him a mite uneasy. The sameness, the legacy. Mrs. Bonner's tradition, alive though she was long in her grave. Tartarus felt a small claustrophobia take his gut. For a few seconds he felt trapped by the kitchen, trapped three decades back and not able to return to the present. In the space of those seconds, the comfort of the kitchen had turned into a domination by the kitchen. Then just as quickly its sway flattened and dispersed. And what was that all about?

Should he step into his own house, stand in his kitchen? Would it say anything to him?

The kitchen of the Tartarus house had been his sister, Natalia's, favourite place. There she talked with her mother for hours as Hannah prepared meals, cooked treats, repaired clothes. Jack would join them in the kitchen, often not speaking, his mother and Natalia bringing the life of conversation into the room. He'd enjoyed this, listening in silence, understanding their unity.

Jack had adored his little sister. He loved her still, but back then she was his weakness, near as he could remember, had been since she was born: letting her take his finger, wiping drool and cough-up from her chin, toting her around though barely old enough not to want to be carried himself. Through elementary school he saw himself as her protector—not that his tomboy sister needed a lot of help. He was her shield, from a small distance. Years later when her husband, Stan, died—a man Tartarus had never warmed to—Jack spent six weeks with her and Justine, his niece, in their pretty house in the Berkeley Hills to help her bring to a conclusion Stan's financial life and whatever domesticity there'd been in her marriage.

More shouting from Frank, and Don was back. "One of his difficult evenings. He figures I've got a hoard of IPAs hidden somewhere, won't drink anything else, and won't eat his supper till he has one more. 'Just one more, Donnie, just one.' He does that too sometimes, whines."

"So let him starve."

Don shook his head. "Can't do that." He took one of the empty IPA bottles from the counter, ran the faucet, rinsed the bottle. From the fridge he took a Coors, twisted it open, carefully poured the beer into the IPA bottle.

"Won't he taste the difference?"

"After two he can't tell. Taste buds aren't what they used to be. Eighty-one-year-old taste buds." He paused. "And it's more than that. He forgets a lot, these days."

"Ah." Don, taking care of it. Family relations. Jack didn't understand families, hadn't even understood the two he knew from close up, his parents' and his sister's. He and Maureen had been lovers, a mutually adoring couple. Not a family. They tried to conceive a child, gave themselves over to the pleasure of trying, tried many times. No child had joined them.

Don took the beer to Frank. Jack heard a low argument, ongoing nattering. Don came back. "I'll set his dinner up in front of the TV. He won't come out, he does that sometimes."

"Doesn't much like me."

"It's not that. He gets embarrassed, how much of an old cuss he's become. Doesn't like to be around people when he's acted badly. And sometimes he acts badly 'cause he can't hear what people are saying. Sometimes he won't have dinner even with me."

"Okay. But if I'm complicating things . . ."

"I'll let you know. He can eat by himself. Way easier for us to talk, him not around."

Jack agreed. Don left him in the living room. Tartarus sipped bourbon. Yes, he'd call Natalia. She'd learn he'd arrived, some of their parents' friends still lived here, any busybody might call her. He'd told her he'd be coming back, though not exactly when. She knew why.

When their parents died, he'd let Natalia choose, their old home in Vancouver or their place on the island. The first choice was hers, he'd always allowed that. He had figured—hoped, really—she wouldn't want the Crab house. Before her decision became final, he'd had moments of worry that she'd pick this house after all. Maybe rekindle all she'd had with Don—that would've been good. But she opted for Vancouver, the big family house, a new home for herself and Justine. She loved the city. Good choice financially too, with real estate going through the roof.

But not a choice that would bring her and Don together. Tartarus had wanted them together, the sister he loved and his long-ago best friend. When, three or four years back, she'd come over to the island to live for a while, he'd thought she and Don would commit to each other. She'd rented out the Vancouver home for that year, one year only, so she could go back if that's how things turned out. But, she'd said, she did want, actively, to be on the island again. Tartarus hadn't seen either her or Don much that year, he'd been in Sicily shooting his Etna series. He knew she and Don spent time with each other whenever Don could get away from Frank. She'd borrowed the island house from Jack for an open-ended period. She left when the year was up. Why did she return to Vancouver? Tartarus didn't know.

Don came back. "He's eating, and some reality show's got all his attention."

"Good, I guess."

"Very good. And the food's ready. We can sup in the kitchen, okay?"

Don brought out roast chicken and potatoes, carrots, bread, salad, wine.

Jack figured, better ask Don one more time. "You know, I don't have to stay here..."

"Where else? Your house?" Don shook his head.

"Why not. Till it comes down."

Don shook his head. "It wouldn't let you sleep. You'd dream about it."

Jack laughed. "I could pitch a tent."

"With running water, toilet, fridge, stove?"

"Well..."

"Forget it. You're staying here."

They sat at the table. Jack took a bite of chicken. "Mmm, first-rate."

"Thanks." Don raised his glass. "Cheers." He sipped.

They talked through arrangements, how Jack would keep out of Don's way—no, Jack had to make himself at home. Maybe Jack could do some cooking, some shopping—better not, taking Frank to the

15

market was one of the old man's few chances to get out, part of Don's pattern. Okay, Jack would cook two days a week. He didn't know how long it took to tear a house down.

"You're really doing it."

"Yep."

"But why?"

"So I don't have to pay the insurance."

"Stop being ridiculous."

"Okay."

"It's crazy, you know. It's a fine house."

"Was."

"Tearing it down, Jack, that's pretty damn irrational."

"Maybe." He grinned. "I'm not always rational."

"Okay, tell me irrationally why you're doing it."

Jack picked up his glass, made a show of seeing it empty, reached it to Don who filled it. Jack sat back, and sipped. "Because the house is responsible for the deaths of my parents."

"What? Why?"

"If I tell you, I'll no longer be irrational."

"But, Jack, you have to—"

"Have to only when I'm being rational. But my irrational reason is a good reason."

"More than irrational. Like the house has demonized you."

"It could. It's a demon."

"Jack . . ."

"It's coming down, Donnie." Jack allowed a mirthless smile.

His tone chilled Don. "I don't get it."

"Do you have to get it?"

"I don't know." Don poured wine into his glass. "Get much of a start today?"

"Not a lot." He remembered the frenzied woman in the long skirt. "Strange thing happened, soon after I began. This woman comes tearing down the drive, all pissed 'cause I was taking the wrecking bar to the house. She attacked me." He rolled up his sleeve. "Bit me."

"Jeesus!"

"If she's got septic teeth or AIDS, I'm damned."

"Just came at you—"

"Out of nowhere. Any idea who she might be?"

Don rubbed his nose. "What'd she look like?"

Jack described her: maybe thirty-five, thin, the long skirt, those big eyes.

"Brown hair to about her shoulders?"

"Yeah, I think so. Hair covered with a scarf. Despite the heat."

"And her eyes—big, you said. Sort of greenish?"

"Yeah."

"What, like the lids pulled back? Bug-eyed? Irises dilated?"

He tried to remember. "No. Just—round. A lot of white. And lots of blinking."

"Lots of white." He nodded. "Remember the Rixtons—Rick, I think it was. Wife's name was—Mary?" Don thought and took a bite of chicken. "Midgie? Madgie."

"I think I remember a Rick close by." Jack felt a chill take his spine. "They had a place, came mainly in the summer?"

"Right. Just up the road from you. An older couple. He was probably in his seventies."

"Yeah, they had a kid, a daughter, was it?" This was not good.

"Right. Rick was in his late fifties when they conceived the kid, Madgie forty. Word was she'd had a lot of miscarriages but kept on trying. Finally made it. Ginny, they called the girl."

"Ginny." Ginny. He closed his eyes. He could picture her . . .

"I'd guess it was Ginny who attacked you."

"Is she crazy?"

"Don't know. Haven't heard anything like that."

"She still there, in her parents' place?"

"Back there. The girl came back after she finished school. Rick's gone, oh, fifteen years. Ginny's been here a while."

"I think I remember her." He opened his eyes again. "A good-looking young woman."

"Actually, drop-dead gorgeous. And wild, they said. I don't know her story, something about being engaged, going on a binge before

17

the wedding, week-long binge with her girlfriends. She came back and something was wrong, joints wouldn't work right. Some talk about rheumatoid arthritis; anyway, the engagement ended. And five-six months on she was okay again. And then she'd be gone for a while, here for a while. Here off and on."

"Don't know about rheumatoid arthritis. She ran at me pretty well."

"Well, that was a while back."

"And I wouldn't call this woman gorgeous."

"Yeah, she never got back to being a stunner, like before."

"But you think it was this Ginny."

"What'd she actually say?"

"Mmm. Just that I should leave the house alone. That she'd call the cops if I didn't stop."

"You tell her it was your place?"

"Yep." Jack thought for a couple of seconds. It would make sense. "She acted like she was, what? maybe the caretaker. Proprietary, sort of."

"Like she knew the house."

"Maybe. Worried about it, anyway."

"See, this Ginny spent time there, with your parents. They were good to her, I remember. And she'd help them along."

"During that year—"

"Yeah. But before too."

Jack pushed away from the table. Just over a decade ago, when they died. The year he couldn't be here. One of the years he couldn't be here. No, that wasn't for tonight.

Don said, "Tell me about the new show, Jackie."

Jackie. Nobody'd called him that in years. Decades. Maureen sometimes. His parents. Natalia too. Don. Don now. "The new show," Jack repeated.

"I hear it made a lot of waves."

He was more than happy to change the subject. No, Don had shifted it. "My part in it's done. It's out in the world. That's the best thing."

"You really got a lot of coverage."

"Yeah, it did well."

"World class, they call Tartarus." Don laughed a little. "And I knew you when."

"When?"

"Your first camera. You made me jump around so you could get action shots."

Jack laughed too. "I did, didn't I."

"How's it feel, everybody knowing your work?"

"Hardly everybody, Don. In fact, hardly anybody."

"I mean in the field. And those who follow you."

He shook his head. "It's just a hell of a big production setting up the installation and then making it go right. Listen, I've got a copy for you, DVD."

"I got a player a couple of years ago. So Frank could watch the new movies." Don paused for a moment. "Will you watch it when I do? Then I can ask you about it."

"Whenever you want."

They washed the dishes. Don set the table for breakfast. Jack drank a last Elbert. At ten-thirty Don helped Frank to bed.

Not the end of Don's evening, Tartarus knew. At eleven, three nights a week, usually Tuesdays, Wednesdays, Thursdays, Don made the rounds of the seven cafés and restaurants on the island. These places had agreed that FITN, the Friends in the Night committee, would send someone to pass by, pick up food that couldn't be saved because it might go bad. He'd be gone from about eleven till nearly one, he told Jack. "See you in the morning."

"And if Frank wakes up?"

"He's old enough to take care of himself." Don found his van keys and headed out. Tartarus followed, stopped at his leased Buick, and opened his trunk. He grabbed his cameras and suitcase and brought them inside. In his bedroom, Don's study, he opened the case and took out a packet of DVDs. A good man, Don. Donnie and Jackie. Long ago. These days it wasn't even Jack. Professionally he'd dropped Jack. Tartarus was the artist. Nobody needed to know more.

Back in the living room he inserted a DVD into the player and

19

started the machine. The screen read, *FIRE AND THE PHOENIX*. He worked through the menu and watched.

At the beginning the flickers of flame are small. Patterns of flame. Licking slowly over the surface, colouring the surface, possessing the surface. And into the surface, the surface spreading and deepening. Slowly. Fire starts tiny, a spark. The spark finds thin fuel—a dry leaf, a crumb of dead wood. The wood glows, warm. Hot. It touches its neighbour leaves, chips, branches. It spreads into the softest most parched among them, catching them, warming them, becoming them. Flames become fire. It burns. Many surfaces. Deeper. Wider.

Slowly too was how to take a house apart, a chip, a splinter, a chunk. Soon the unconstructing will speed up as more and more of the house is laid bare. Slowly at first, like fire. The house will come down like this. First a chip of siding. Next, a chunk of siding. The space where the splinter, the chunk, had been, grows like a fire, searching for wall, finding wall, the wall falls and soon where the wall had been there's open space, wall becomes empty space. The space spreads, up, left, right. Uprights appear, and joists. And then disappear, become mere wood, cast onto the ground far from the house, to be burned. On the house, once supports, they become space.

Tartarus watched the screen and thought, The fire burns, burns away. Fire is not rational. Fire leaves space. Ash remains. Wind blows the ash away. Tartarus thought, Ginny. Damn.

TWO: Don Bonner and Friends in the Night

Most stops on Don's rounds were predictable. There'd be someone from the eatery ready to hand Don the supplies of the evening, or the offering would be placed in a storage box out back, locked to stop raccoons from stealing the food—took more than a latch to keep the bandits out. Don had keys to three boxes: Ocean Spray Grille, Oyster's, and The Arbutus. The Dock Pub, Carleton's, and Fisherman's Rest-or-Rant would still be open, or just closing. The seventh, Eating Thyme, the vegetarian café, closed around nine. Etain lived in the apartment above. She'd be waiting for him.

He stepped into his Westphalia through the rear doorway. Shelves lined both sides, a half-metre aisle between them. Eight empty wine boxes for raw and cooked produce sat on the bottom level. The small propane fridge that he'd started before dinner would get turned off after his delivery. A plastic fruit box held a dozen bungee cords. What he gathered he dropped off at Island Kitchen, the food bank and soup kitchen. On some days he got little from the restaurants. Then he'd raid his own pantry for fruits and vegetables he had grown over the summer and preserved in the fall, as well as three kinds of potatoes, four of garlic. He always grew too much. The first summer he hadn't realized this, just planted all he could get in to reduce household food expenses because his small investment income and minimal pension barely hacked it. He'd preserved more than he and Frank could eat. In the spring when new vegetables came in, he gave away his jars and cans. It was a lesson well learned so now he purposely grew too much, to give it to the more needy. Earlier in the evening he'd loaded a dozen jars of green beans and six of peaches into the van. Just in case.

Ready to go. He glanced back at the house. He wished his father were less difficult. At the same time, he knew the old cuss would get ever cussier over the next years. He'd always been a little hard to live with. The only one who'd been able to handle him was Don's mother.

Sylvia had smoothed his rough edges daily, but by the next morning he'd grown new ones. She could tease them flat, gentle them, scold them, and he never resented her. Don remembered only the effect; he had not the least memory of her tactics. He wished he could pull open some drawer and find a list made by his mother: how to handle Frank, with specific details.

He edged up to the front of the van, sat, fired the ignition. The engine came smoothly alive. Nineteen years old, over six hundred and fifty thousand kilometres, purring like a pussycat. An oil change every four thousand kilometres keeps an engine clean. He'd known a cabbie in Vancouver, Parmjit, who told him about the four thousand kilometre oil change. At that time Parmjit's cab, a twenty-two-year-old Cadillac in vintage condition, had 3.8 million kilometres on it. Make sure engine's clean, Parmjit delighted in explaining, change your filters and belts, a good machine'll last forever. Just before hitting 5 million the Caddy got sideswiped, a drunk in a delivery truck. The alignment was never the same, a tendency to swerve, to skid on dry pavement. Parmjit no longer trusted his Caddy to transport fares. Don had sat with Parmjit as he mourned.

Now Don turned on the headlights and drove off. Jack was still Jack, Jackie, would be forever. No matter how famous. Only change this time around was the beard, short curly red-grey hair on his cheeks, lip, and chin. The curly hair on top had greyed, but he still stood his full six feet, no stooping yet; unlike Don. The penetrating brown eyes and elongated nose remained as ever, and still didn't go with his small round ears. All these part of a body covering a single-willed determination for whatever project he took on. Like tearing down a house piece by piece. Strange, but pure Jack—like the evolution of Jack's work, his ongoing inquisition into the nature of fire. Four major shows over the last seven years. Don had seen the Mount Etna series, the others he'd viewed only in magazine reproduction. The new one he'd not seen at all.

Tearing down the house saddened Don in another way. If the house were no longer there, what would tie Jackie to Crab? He'd still own the property, but would he build another house there? Vengeance, he'd said. Maybe he had gone just a little crazy.

More immediately, would Jack ask Natalia to come over? Don knew she still lived inside him. But he didn't want to see her. Not now anyway. Like Jack, Natalia would be Natalia forever. There had been a moment when he'd planned to speak to her of the closeness between them, and maybe of marriage. A world historic day, and so a private moment that never happened: dinner with Natalia on September 11, that September 11. Instead of dinner out, they stayed home with Frank and watched the horrors parade by on the television screen. First love, only love? Sometimes he felt this. Usually he kept himself from thinking about Natalia.

He turned north on West Road, toward the village, Oyster's his first stop. Titus, the owner, made it clear: for his guests, only fresh daily seafood and vegetables, nothing frozen. He bought his supply every morning in Nanaimo except for Sunday and Monday, couldn't get fish fresh those days so the restaurant was closed. He'd been one of the founders of Friends in the Night because, as he explained to Don and the others, though he bought as much as he figured he'd need that day, often enough he erred on the side of generosity and there'd be fish left over, vegetables too. He'd never freeze the fish. Sometimes he'd run out, which he prided himself on as it would prove to customers that his ingredients were only the freshest.

Don drove into Oyster's parking lot and over to the delivery area in back. He opened the van door to turn on the light, found the right key, reached behind and grabbed a cardboard container. He unlocked the restaurant's wooden box: couple of heads of lettuce, seven tomatoes, a small bag of Portobello mushrooms and two bunches of carrots on the right, a cooler on the left. Inside, resting on ice, a couple of rockfish filets, a large ling cod filet, and four sockeye steaks. Excellent. Excellent for Friends in the Night, too bad for Titus. Though Titus did keep an inventory of what he provided Friends with. At the end of each month he'd send an itemized note totalling his wholesale costs, for which he got a charitable donation receipt. As did all the others.

Fish in the van's fridge, box on the rack, and on to The Arbutus. Adam and Martine Cleer hadn't been eager to participate in FITN but had gone along because they didn't want people on the island, customers, to know they'd refused. So The Arbutus lay on Don's designated rounds, but he'd find food in the box only once or twice a week. Today? Some root vegetables that had seen better days. Root vegetables in June? Don took it all—Island Kitchen had two cooks capable of revivifying weary rutabagas, turnips, onions, transforming them into rich soups.

On to the village, past the ferry dock, and westward to Fisherman's Rest-or-Rant. He stopped, went in by the front door, found Steve Deaver stripping dinner tablecloths and setting up for breakfast. Only bare tables in the morning. "Hey, Steve."

Steve looked up, a scowl on his face. The scowl was permanent, even when Steve laughed. "Don. How you doin'?"

"Ready to go to bed."

"Yeah? Where?"

Don chuckled. "Probably in my van if I don't get on with my rounds."

Steve nodded, his frown wise. "Good, good." He pointed back toward the kitchen. "There's some hamburger, it's in the fridge. And potatoes. And a couple dozen cans that're coming close to maturity date you better take."

"Thanks, Steve." The Rest-or-Rant always made food available for Friends. Steve, born on Crab, had trucked to the mainland in his twenties where he found more booze and drugs than his brain could handle. He'd been homeless for a couple of years. He made his comeback, clean and dry, but he knew the other side, had logged enough time feeling the shame of begging, of handouts. He empathized easily with the hungry of Crab Island; single mothers eking it out on welfare and women abused by some man in or near their household, of these the island had its share. Don found the potatoes and cans. He took the hamburger from the refrigerator—felt like two-three kilos. Steve's ongoing generosity. Don headed to the door. "Take care. G'night."

"Hey. Got time for a cool one?"

Don made a play of looking at his watch. "Don't think so. It's getting late."

"Yeah, I know, and you want to get to bed."

"You know it." Don would have sworn Steve's scowl shifted to neutral. He dealt okay with this kind of kidding, mostly good-natured, because it was the tease of an equal. Over the years he'd made himself part of the island. Even natives like Steve came to accept him.

On to The Dock, the island's pub. Shelagh who knew everyone, and everyone's business, stood behind the bar chatting with two regulars who must've been on their seventh rounds. "Hey, Don," she called, "how they hangin'," her greeting this time of night to both men and women.

"Hiya, Shelagh." He nodded to the men. "Ben. Turtle."

"The man who takes cold food," said Turtle, who clerked at Crab Hardware.

"You betcha," said Don and turned to Shelagh. "Anything for Friends?"

"Pizza slices didn't do great. Two-thirds of three big ones, nobody wanted vegetarian."

"Go figure," said Ben, volunteer coach for sixth and seventh graders in basketball and baseball, according to the season. "And it sounds so-o-o-o good."

Turtle laughed. Shelagh handed Don four pizza boxes, tied together. "Good thing we've got that new microwave," he said.

"Old," said Turtle. Shelagh had given it to the Kitchen. She needed a faster one.

"Kids'll love the pizza for lunch tomorrow. And some of the moms too."

"Hey, Don." Shelagh squinted at him. "Did I hear, your buddy Jack's back on the island?"

"And where'd you hear that?"

She glanced at Turtle. "Turtle said he came in. True?"

Don didn't know why he had to deny it. Jack wasn't hiding. Just wanted a little privacy. "Yep. Arrived today." On islands, even light travels slower than information.

"He over at his place?"

"Staying with me."

"Oh yeah?" This from Turtle.

25

"Yep."

"Bought himself a crowbar," Turtle went on. "A Fulton."

"Could be," said Don.

"Yeah, guess I can see that, not staying at his place."

A couple of seconds of silence, till Don said, "Gotta be going." He waved. "See ya, Shelagh. Turtle. Ben. And thanks."

The pizza into the fridge, and across the street to Carleton's. Edgar Carleton was nearly as cheap as Martine at The Arbutus but wouldn't let himself come at the bottom of any list. He often made a play when Don arrived, so late diners could hear him, about the fine soups and meats he was donating. No clients tonight, so it was sliced turkey breast, sausages that looked like they'd been at the bottom of the freezer for months, and four cardboard cartons of milk, best before tomorrow. No commentary from Edgar tonight.

"Thanks, this is great," said Don and left.

Now came the usual dilemma. Island Kitchen was halfway along North Road to Ocean Spray, Eating Thyme another four kilometres beyond. Head over to Ocean Spray, pick up their offerings and double back to the Kitchen to drop off his collected packages? Or stop at the Kitchen on the way westward? Ocean Spray had made a large donation last night, likely they'd have less tonight. So to the Kitchen first. The kinds of things he got from Etain—quiches, thick vegetable soups, the makings for wraps—would keep in the van fridge till the next day's delivery. A good, satisfactory evening. Even generous.

He parked in front, a small house willed to FITN, run by volunteers. Taxes and upkeep were paid out of the proceeds of annual fundraising events—raffles, charity concerts, silent auctions, space rental for special events. The Kitchen had a kitchen and a living room/meeting room on the first floor, two small rooms and a bathroom upstairs. Don unlocked the front door and brought the food in, logged in the items and their source on the Donations sheet.

Second to last stop, Ocean Spray, across the road from the marina. In the box, a note: *Sorry, Don, nothing tonight. We'll do better for you tomorrow, I hope. And fear.*

Don sighed. Ocean Spray was the only eatery near the marina, a draw, but it seemed ever on the brink of failure. Annabelle and Harriet worked hard, meant well, but the boating diners preferred the island's other establishments. Even little Eating Thyme was a more popular choice.

Back in the van, on to Etain's. Some evenings she gave him tea, and they talked. Other times one of them would take their friendship further. They had an easy code. The one whose desire had reached its level would mention wine. Don: I brought a bottle of wine. Etain: I just bought some wine, like a glass? Questions that could be answered simply. Yes, No. Or more complexly: It's a highly recommended wine, I'd like to try a glass. Or, It's been a long day, I think it'd do me good. And maybe you too. To which the answer might be, Oh, all right. Or, No, I'm too tired for wine, tea will do me. They played their game three nights a week. Wine entered the picture every few times. Etain introduced the wine maybe fifty percent more often than Don.

Outside of Etain's little living room, wine for him had no erotic connotation. He'd not brought a bottle, his thoughts had turned to Etain only in the last few minutes, to her ease at understanding him and to her lovely breasts and sweet round bum and firm full lips. He parked behind the restaurant beside Etain's twelve-year-old Toyota. A used-books store, the recycling centre, and Eating Thyme shared a parking lot in front, but even at 11:45 PM Don preferred discretion. He stepped out. The back door of the café opened. Etain stood in the doorway, light from inside offering her in slender silhouette: shoulder-length hair so dark it looked black till the sun burnished it deep brown, tank top over small bosom, petite waist in jeans, bare arms and feet. She must've been waiting, seen the van's lights pull in. He felt suddenly pleased. "Hi."

She stood still until he reached the doorway, then reached out to him, arms around his back, head against his chest. Gently he held her in return. They stayed together for half a minute, his hand stroking her back. She dropped her hands, took his right in her right, and drew him into the back of the café. She locked the door and looked at him. "Glad you're here."

"Me too. And glad you're here too."

She nodded.

She might be glad, Don thought, but she'd not smiled yet. "Is everything okay?"

"Let's go upstairs."

"Something happened today."

"Today was okay."

"What'd you do?"

"The usual. Then after school Patrick and I went out to the Point for an hour. And Batiste. There was another dog and they both went crazy up there. Batiste thought it was glorious."

"And you did too."

"Out there, always. Come on." The staircase was narrow and steep. At the top they entered the living room—a couch, couple of chairs, throw rugs, TV and CD player, table with two kitchen chairs. The walls were covered with water colours and lithographs, presents from artist friends on the island. To the right, her tiny kitchen. To the left, two doors, Etain's bedroom and eight-year-old Patrick's bedroom. Patrick's door was closed. Not a lot of room, but all that was necessary for herself and her boy, she'd long ago explained. If she needed more cooking space there was the kitchen downstairs. On the table, two tea candles in ceramic pots, a bottle of red wine already uncorked, and two glasses. A brown dog, Batiste, rose from the carpet and walked slowly to Don, who stroked his head. The dog went back to his place and lay down.

"Patrick's asleep?"

"He was tired."

Don marvelled at Etain, single-mothering from birth on, running a successful restaurant, still having time for life. And for Don. He liked the boy, a bright kid, talkative, inquisitive. Sometimes Don took him for an afternoon, give Etain an hour or three to herself. Don found it easy talking with Patrick, just eight but with a talent for words, trying out strange combinations; Patrick called it making meanings. "I could pick him up from school. Sometime next week."

"He'd like that." She took his hand again. "How are you?"

"Pretty much okay."

"Your friend Jack arrived?"

"Yep. We had a good talk over supper."

"He'll stay with you, definitely."

"Said he would."

"It's better."

"Yeah. Though he's lived rough on some of his projects. And Crab is hardly rough."

Her eyes, in the candlelight flickering grey-blue, sought his. "Still, it's better. Right?"

"You just don't like that place."

She shrugged, fell silent for a few seconds, then said, "And he is going to tear it down?"

"He bought a crowbar. At the Hardware."

"Odd. He really must hate the place."

"I think so." Don took her hand. "It's a place of death, he says."

"Shh." Laying her head against his chest again, she whispered, "Like a glass of wine?"

He held her to him. He felt her heartbeat through her skin. "Yes." An echo, her confirming everything as okay, in its way, tickled his memory. "How about a cup of tea first?"

Some seconds later she said, "Good," and drew back from him, smiled up, and stepped into the kitchen.

A sad smile. Yes, something had happened. He heard water running and followed her to the sink. He waited till she filled the kettle, set it on the stove, and turned the burner to high. Then, her arms free, her back still to him, he brought his hands around her waist and pulled her to him. They stood together and watched the element slowly brighten to red. She took his hands and raised them to her breasts. He held her, drawing her tighter to him. He felt her breathe deep and exhale a jagged sigh. He waited as she breathed in again, out more easily. "What?" he said.

"My mother."

He knew little about Etain's family, only a sketch of her childhood. She'd left home, small-town Quebec, the summer she was sixteen. Her father, Irish by birth, had been dead three years, she the youngest of four daughters. She'd hitched across the country with a friend, 1980, close to the last moment in North American history when one could hitchhike the breadth of a continent in relative safety. They'd heard fruit-picking jobs were easy to find in a part of British Columbia called the Okanagan. They made money. Her friend took the bus back home, Etain stayed. She'd met someone, lived with him, later they got married, something happened, they divorced. She left the Okanagan, the winters unbearable, crashed on a couple of Gulf Islands, Pender, Thetis, with picker friends from the fruit orchards. No work, so she headed up to Cortez, another picker friend, and made out at low-level jobs for a couple of years. Twice, by bus, she returned to Nantierville to see her mother, the Québecoise part of her heritage. Two years ago when she and Patrick had gone back they'd actually flown across the country. Now something was wrong. "Your mother," Don said. "What?"

"Adèle called. Last night. Maman's gotten worse. Lots worse."

"The eyes?"

"And her ears too. And her bladder. She really can't do anything for herself anymore."

"What're you going to do?"

She turned to face him. "Adèle says we have to put her in a home. Adèle can't deal with her, the way she's become."

He drew her to him again. "Etain. I'm sorry."

"And Giselle and Marie-Louise agree."

"You don't."

"I'm not there. I ran away from them."

"You didn't run from, Etain. You know that. You ran to. A different place."

"Maybe. Hasn't stopped me from feeling guilty all day."

Don nodded, his chin stroking the top of her head, shining hair soft on his skin. The kettle went from wheeze to scream, commenting on their conversation. She lifted it from the stove.

"I know what you mean," he said. "But it doesn't help. Will you go east?"

"I've thought about it." She sighed. "Not much I can do there now. I'll go in the fall."

"As you planned," he said. "What we do for parents."

"You're much better at it than I am."

He chuckled. "Hardly."

"Braver."

"No."

"Yes. You're right there."

"Or more of a coward because I don't change things."

"A coward? Come off it."

"'Cause I don't try to live any other life."

"You don't want another life."

He heard it as halfway between a question and a statement of fact. He shook his head. "I just continue as I've been going. No job, no need for a job, no nothing."

She said, as she'd said before, "You volunteer your time. That's not nothing." He lived on very little, small stock investments, committed to quitting early his forever high-school teaching job. He'd shifted to bonds just months before the dot-com market began its crash. No foreknowledge, just a lucky accident. But after working only twenty years his pension was small. For ten years now he'd been near to fulltime taking care of his father. At the start Frank had been less cranky but just as needy. She drew back. "Tea?"

Don closed his eyes and laughed a little. "I think I'm ready for some wine."

"Good." She stood on her toes and kissed his lips, lightly. He bent toward her and kissed her, a little harder. She whisked his lips with her tongue and stepped away, took his hand and led him to the table. They sat. She poured. Each glass of the deep red liquid reflected two little flickers of candlelight.

He raised his glass and smiled at her eyes. "To mothers and fathers."

She raised hers, smiled back, and they clinked. "One of each for each of us."

They sipped. "Nice."

"Yes." She studied his face, then stared beyond him. "They had their children."

"And still have them."

"What will we do, when we become like them."

"We won't become like them."

She caught his eye again and laughed. "Who can say."

They studied each other's faces. Don self-consciously combed his lank whitening blond hair off his forehead. She stood, came around to Don's chair, knelt, put her head on his lap. He stroked her cheek, her hair. "We aren't them yet." With her hand at his thigh he felt himself stiffen. He lowered his head, their lips met. She brought herself to standing, with her other hand raising him to his feet, her left hand now sliding toward his crotch and finding him hard.

"Thank you for being a Friend in the Night," she said.

He chuckled. "And does Eating Thyme have anything for me today?"

"Eating Thyme has lots for you. And so do I." She kissed him open-mouthed, quickly, pulled back. She handed him his wine and reached for her own. They drained their glasses. She led him to her little bedroom, one dim light teasing out images of a chest of drawers, a night table, a closet, a chair covered with clothes. They undressed each other slowly, savouring each glimpse of the other's skin. Naked, she reached for his pointing cock and held it as they walked together to the bed. He brushed her lips with his as she reached down to pull the covers back. They slid onto the sheets and he entered her, a soft wet passage, both of them ready, yet in no rush. They held each other, unmoving as long as they could stand it. Then gave to each other all the tenderness they could find in themselves.

They lay together afterwards, on their sides, still connected. He ought to leave, not fall asleep here. And Etain should get some rest. But he didn't go.

She stroked his cheek. "What're you thinking?"

He told her his last thought, truthfully. "Like I said before, I'm not brave at all."

Her head shook slightly. "That's not the question."

"What is?"

"I wish I knew."

They lay in silence for a while. He said, "And what are you thinking?"

After a few seconds she said, "Being a parent. Being my mother's daughter. Having a kid."

"You're good at it."

"I worry about Patrick. When he's away from me."

"What do you mean?"

"All the dangers in the world."

"That's true for all of us."

For a while she lay silent. Then she said, "Your friend."

"Jack."

"Tearing down a house."

"Yeah," he said. "Jack can be strange. He does strange art."

"I think I'm afraid for him."

"You don't know him."

"Still."

"What do you mean, afraid?"

"Like, he's someone in danger."

Somehow this irritated Don. "That doesn't make sense."

"I know."

"What makes you say it?"

"I wish I knew. I just feel it."

"Danger from what?"

"I don't know that either." She thought for a moment. "Maybe, his house."

Don said nothing. Danger from his house. Houses aren't dangerous, no logic there. He should go. Frank would be pissed off if he woke and found only Jack at home with him. Worse than Frank waking up alone. But he wouldn't wake, he rarely did, getting mean but at least nothing wrong with his prostate, thank all the gods for that, no peeing six times a night. Yet. Still he should be there when Frank woke in the morning, when Jack woke. Or he could stay, get up with the sun in four-five hours, be back before Jack headed off with the wrecking bar. Jack's house dangerous? Ridiculous. Anyway it would soon be rubble. And Jackie was staying with Don. And Frank. Because—Because Don had insisted. Why? Because—the house wouldn't let Jack sleep. Don had said this. The house would make him dream about itself. Why had he said this?

33

"Staying?"

Don kissed her eyelid. "Want me to?"

"Please."

He closed his eyes. "Okay." He could feel her relax. He'd not realized there'd been any tension left in her, but in the moment after her "Please" she slackened yet further. He held her as her breathing, barely discernible before, softened little by little. He still lay inside her, but her grasp of him, seemingly pressure-free before, relaxed till he was merely beside her, wet, warm, and soft. For her each intake of air lengthened. Six-eight-nine times, and she was asleep. Good.

In the three years he'd known her he'd spent the night with her maybe a couple of dozen times. Actually he'd known her longer, more or less since she'd started at the Thyme; she was there whenever he came in for lunch or coffee. But he'd only begun to notice her, and she him for that matter, because of Frank.

A bone-dry summer afternoon, 2004. Crab Village, where West Road met North Road—four eating places, the Credit Union, Crab Hardware, a small supermarket, the Regional District office, two clothing stores, a crafts shop, the real estate office, the dental centre—Frank Bonner in his 1997 Mercury Grand Marquis mistook reverse for forward, the gas pedal for the brake, and at thirty-four kilometres per hour smashed loud into one of the island's three fire hydrants, sending it careening into the front window of the real estate office. The Grand Marquis came to a stop twenty metres away at the far end of the flower beds, the centre of Crab Village. Where the hydrant had stood, the stream of a mighty fountain climbed high into the air, the water returning to earth in a perfect circle to drench parked cars, desiccated bushes, and slow-moving pedestrians. At the realty office only the receptionist was in but two minutes earlier she'd gone to the kitchenette for a cup of coffee, so no injuries. It took the fire department the best part of an hour to cut the flow, but by then a fifth of what water remained in the island's little reservoir had been drained. Crab Island was furious with Frank Bonner. Crab Island pitied Frank Bonner. The Crab Island RCMP took away Frank Bonner's driver's licence.

How to get around on an island when everybody knows you and you have no driver's licence? If you drive without one, any inquisitorial citizen will report you. And there's no public transportation. Without a car, it's like somebody's cut off your legs. You need a son. He has to drive you wherever you insist on going.

Not that Frank felt like going anywhere. Why hang around people who pitied him? So? Sit in the living room, stare out at the sea? The fuckin' eternal sea. Frank's private eternity was approaching. But damn if he'd make it easy for them, those who pitied him.

So Don drove him everywhere, to one part of the island or another, nearly every day. Retired at forty-four after twenty-three years of teaching, nothing more important for Don to do in life but drive his pa around. Not in the stupid van but in Frank's Grand Marquis. Which had got repaired for under eighteen hundred bucks, little dint in the trunk. Stupid fire hydrant made out of tin, couldn't stand up to even the Merc's feather-touch of impact.

The days of the week became the basis of their driving ritual. Mondays, Wednesdays, and Fridays, ten in the morning, to the market for a newspaper and supplies. Saturday in the summer past the Farmers' Market and all the people who despised him so he could sneer silently. Winter Saturdays a drive around the island, maybe stopping at the beach or up on the cliffs or out on the southwest peninsula to Lighthouse, then along West Road and home. Whatever the season, a stop for lunch at Ocean Spray. Why Don chose that place Frank couldn't say, but it was okay, enough off-islanders so nobody to pity him. Tuesdays the library so he could get himself a weekly book he rarely read, and then a drive along the interior roads of the island, to see what houses were newly up for sale, what lots had been cleared, where trees had come down after storms, how badly the roads had deteriorated. On the seventh day, Frank remarked each week, he liked to rest.

All day Thursday and the afternoons belonged to Don. In the spring, summer, and fall he gardened; in the fall he canned, bottled, and froze his vegetables and fruits. He enjoyed this, both the act of preserving and the pleasure of eating his own produce all winter and into the spring and, important enough, it cut his expenses way down.

In the winter—in the other seasons too when his garden allowed him time off—he would walk the wooded trails of the island, usually alone, occasionally with Trevor, his only real male friend on Crab. If there was deepish snow, a rarity, he'd get out his cross-country skis and head for the fields, the woods never getting snowy enough to use the trails. Some Thursdays he headed off to the big island, up to Courtney or down to Nanaimo, and took in a movie, again by himself. When Natalia had been here she'd gone with him sometimes. Etain had walked with him several times this summer.

A couple of years of their weekly driving pattern and Frank decided he needed a change. "Saturday we try another restaurant."

"Which one? Carleton's? The Arbutus? The Rest-or-Rant?"

"Naw." Everybody there in the village would know him, stare at him from behind, laugh at him from back of their menus. "Don't like those places."

"Or we can go just down the road, Oyster's."

"What?"

"Oy-sters." Don produced the word with clinky clarity.

"Practically next door. That's no outing."

"You're narrowing the possibilities. Maybe we should stick to Ocean Spray."

"I don't like lezzie food."

"For chrissake, Pa—"

"Okay, I give up. No lunch on Saturday."

"There's that vegetarian place. Ea-ting-Thyme."

"Dumb name. God, there's nowhere to eat."

"We can try it once."

"It's terrible food."

"Yeah? You been there?" It was the farthest away, the longest drive.

"Sure, I was there just a little while ago."

"Yeah? When?"

"Just after Sylvia . . . left us."

"Frank, Ma died nearly fifteen years ago." Don shook his head. "I have lunch there sometimes. It's okay. And places do change, you know." He stared at his father.

"Still vegetarian, right?"

"I think I just said that."

"Vegetables don't change."

Enough for Don. "Okay, Saturdays we don't go out for lunch, we stay here, I'll open a can of soup for you."

For a few seconds Frank remained silent. Then: "Okay, that Thyme place."

Eating Thyme, Saturdays at 1:00 PM, was a popular choice. The single waitress, a woman with dark hair, a warm smile, and a scoop-necked, straight-skirted brown dress, a tie at the waist, told them they'd have to wait a few minutes till she got a table clear. Frank couldn't hear what she'd said. Don explained.

Frank said, "Let's go."

Don turned to the waitress. "He's a little hard of hearing and..." She was smiling. She touched Frank on the shoulder and said, enunciating carefully, "We'll have you seated in no time. I think you'll enjoy our food."

Her touch perhaps, or the clarity of her words, caught Frank's favour. He actually returned her smile. Still he growled, "I hope so."

With a nod she turned and left. Don glanced around. He'd been here often enough, at times with Trevor, once with Natalia. He liked the decor. Half a dozen booths, five tables. The walls were hung with dried herbs, onions, garlic, and dry flowers. And water colours, all labelled, for sale. Eating Thyme did four exhibits a year, local artists. Now a pleasant scent was coming from the kitchen, mixed odours, shallots cooking, hint of curry? Less easy for Frank to deal with, Don could already tell, was the rumble of voices in the room. Part of Frank's hearing difficulty was background noise. One of the advantages of Ocean Spray was its lack of noontime popularity, so you could lunch in relative stillness. Well, they'd try here.

In less than five minutes the waitress, true to her word, returned bearing menus. She leaned close to Frank's ear. "I'll put you just around the corner. The quietest place." Again her words came to him with measured ease. She led the way. Each slender hip rose as she walked and her hair glowed, black as coal except deep brown where

37

light touched it. Don could see a small smile on his father's lips. She seated them, holding Frank's chair, and handed him the menu. "We don't have specials here. All our food is special."

Quieter perhaps, but still a lot of sound. They made their choices, curried carrot and celery soup for each. Organic onion-avocado-pickled olives on seven-grain bread for Frank—"Seven grains?" A Portobello mushroom-arugula-tomato-chive wrap for Don. And a sleeve of beer. Organic, but to his father Don said only, "Never tried it. It's not Coors."

"Good choices," said the waitress and again touched Frank lightly on the shoulder, a commendation for the excellence of his selection.

They tried to talk, but Don found he had to shout for Frank to hear. Frank in turn shouted back, he could barely hear his own words when he spoke normally. Their voices added to the roar of the room. Food came quickly—maybe just the one waitress but at least a couple of cooks in the kitchen. The waitress set the plates down and again leaned toward Frank as she said, "I hope you enjoy your meal."

What Frank at the moment enjoyed most was a view of the waitress's cleavage and the hint of small round breasts. She stood up and Frank's pleasure was reduced to memory. They both watched her as she walked from the table, hips again swaying. And then as sometimes happens in a loud room, people simultaneously stopped speaking for a couple of seconds and through the silence Frank's gruff clear voice thundered, "Nice boobs and ass on that young woman." The roar of voices returned, a few faces glanced toward their table, the waitress did not turn around. Don's face had gone bright red.

They ate in silence. The waitress returned. Did they want dessert? Don stammered no. Frank wanted ice cream and chocolate cake. The waitress didn't seem exactly distant, but her earlier coziness had departed. They finished dessert. Frank headed to the men's room. Don waited for the bill. When the waitress brought it he said, "Look, I have to apologize for my father, it's his hearing, he doesn't realize . . ."

"No problem, you know." She gave Don a wry smile. "And you have to admit, he's got great taste."

A laugh exploded from Don's throat. The waitress chuckled. Don said, "Thank you. And the meal was delicious. We'll be back. At least my father will."

"She raised her eyebrows. "You too, I hope."

"My name's Don."

"I'm Etain."

With Etain peaceful beside him, her breath barely discernible, Don sank slowly toward sleep. He had never said to her that he loved her but felt he did. He'd never spoken the words for fear of changing things between them, maybe scaring her away. His next to last thought, not new: Do I want this, more of this, more of Etain? His very last: Will Natalia visit Jack while he tears the house down? Don would not be able to cope with her.

Don dreamt of Frank as he looked today, a little old man, thin grey hair, a dried out chin. Of his mother, Sylvia, as she'd been when she died, scolding Frank for unwashed hands, for making a rude noise, the two of them and Jackie and his parents at an unfamiliar train station, Don not ready to leave, the contents of his bags strewn on the floor, the train's arrival announced by a bell, a harsh bell that wouldn't stop ringing till a woman's voice said, "Yes? Hello?" and he felt Etain's hand on his shoulder. "Yes, he is, just a moment." She handed Don the phone.

Don took it. "Yes? What?"

On the other end: "Don, it's Jack. Sorry about this, man."

"Frank?"

"Yeah. He's sitting on his bed, he's howling. I can't understand a word now."

"Is he hurt?"

"I don't know. Not as in wounded. It's more like—a howl of rage. Or fear."

"I'll be right there."

THREE: Jack and the Island

Don and Frank slept on. A rough night for both of them. Less bad for Tartarus. Just a pain in the ears.

Frank had wailed on after Don returned, five minutes at least. Don force-fed him two tablets. The wail weakened to sobs, moaned for a long moment, drifted to a whimper, died away. Before, between Tartarus calling Don and his return, Tartarus had tried to talk to the old man. But Frank heard nothing, or faked not hearing. The clearly articulated questions, You want some water? Can you tell me what's wrong? What can I get you? only increased the wail's intensity. Finally, worry for Frank in his head and fury at Frank in his gut, Tartarus had shouted, "Shut the fuck up!" That didn't work either.

Don sat with Frank. Blessed silence. Jack made a pot of tea and waited in the living room. A quarter-hour passed. Don found Jack sitting on the couch, dozing. "He's asleep," Don said. "You better get to bed."

Jack squeezed his eyes tight closed, then blink-squinted them open. "Is he okay?"

"Okay as he's going to get."

"This happen often?"

"Four times till now. This was the fifth. Over a couple of years. Last was four-five weeks ago, though."

"He's been checked? Any medical assessment?"

"That's where the pills come from."

"Nothing else?"

"He should be talking to a psychologist. He refuses."

Can't blame him, Jack thought. "Want some tea?"

"What? Oh. No, no. Thanks."

Jack sipped tea.

"How'd you know how to find me?"

"That's how he started, before the howling. He was sitting there, shouting numbers-eight-four-six-three, eight-four-six-three. I asked him what was he going on about, but he wouldn't tell me. Took me a couple of minutes, maybe it was a number to call. I checked your phone. It's keyed in. Who's Etain?"

Don glanced at the teapot, took another cup, and poured it half full. "She's a good friend." He sipped. "She owns one of the places on my food round."

"And?"

"I stop there last."

"The place by the marina?"

"No, after that."

"Etain's place, that's your last pick-up."

"We talk for a while."

"Yeah?"

"I don't usually stay. Tonight she didn't want to be alone."

"How'd Frank know where you'd be?"

Don's smile seemed sad. "I think he's jealous."

"Of her taking your time?"

"Of me."

Jack said, "That's almost funny."

They sipped their tea. Don excused himself and made a phone call, a brief conversation. He said goodnight to Jack and retired to his room.

Etain, a friend. Now what's that about? Tartarus would think it over in the morning. And about the woman with the big eyes. Couldn't be Ginny.

He slept for a couple of hours, woke as daylight began its yellowing drift between the curtains, got up, washed and dressed. He half-filled a bowl with dry cereal, spooned it down. He filled his water bottle. He brought out his camera cases and set them in the trunk. Already at five-fifteen the dry air was warm. He backed out of Don's driveway and headed south.

For a kilometre the road passed along the strait, houses on both sides. In front of one of them, a sign: FENCING FOILS EPEES SABRES. Across the strait the hills of the big island glowed purple in the horizontal stream of sunrise. Houses but fewer as the road cut inland. At the Y he turned left, all rural again here, an occasional farmhouse. One of these mornings he'd go the other way, Point Road, to the lighthouse at the tip of the peninsula. One of Maureen's perfect places, the land that birthed the day. For Jack, the site of his first musings about light and fire. Not today. Today he had to get on with demolishing the Tartarus house.

He no longer thought of it as *my* house. He owned it, in that technical sense, but it was easier for him to think, my car, though the Buick was his only by long-term lease. As a thing of substance, my house, the house didn't exist.

Long ago it had been his house, his and Natalia's. His parents' house, Samuel's and Hannah's. In those days he called the house his island home. Now he felt at home when he arrived on the island, but the house was no centre of life, could never be again. The Bonner place, back when he'd been young, was an alternate home for Jack. Don's mother, Sylvia, had made it so. Different days, those, before she got sick. Now, in spite of its orderliness, in spite even of Frank, it still felt way more like a home than the Tartarus house. But now with Mrs. Bonner gone and Frank heading toward loony, possibly already there, the house felt reduced. Maybe too because of the layout of the kitchen, grown from Don's renovations. Or, another way of thinking about it, the house itself hadn't changed, but something in Tartarus had.

Could he bear the next weeks watching Frank mangle Don? Maybe he should in fact get a tent, pitch it on the meadow, live on the job site. Or find a B&B, stay there for whatever time it took. Money wasn't the issue. He wondered if money was a growing problem for Don. And Frank.

More than before, anyway. The Bonner family had arrived onto the island before Tartarus's parents, back in February 1969. They'd bought their oceanfront lot, a hundred feet of shoreline, a two-hundred-foot depth, twenty-five dollars down and twenty-five dollars a month for five years, one thousand five hundred and twenty-five dollars all told. A man on the island built them, right up by the water, a cabin—two little bedrooms, a kitchen that extended into a living room. A dining table divided the two spaces. Mrs. Bonner and Don passed the summer there, Frank Bonner leaving his dental supply factory mid-Friday afternoon to catch the ferry from the city over to the big island, Vancouver Island, the half-hour drive to the much smaller ferry for Crab, the little island. One weekend in July, again in August, Jack, his sister, and parents spent a couple of nights there, Don's bedroom given to Sam and Hannah, Natalia on the couch, Don and Jack with sleeping bags in a tent pitched beside the driveway. The two young men, then sixteen, the whole outside world to themselves, spoke out loud in the darkness what they wouldn't admit to each other by light of day, mainly about girls. What Jack had done with Sue, what Don had nearly done with Gail, what Sue wouldn't let Jack do with her. When the cabin door opened they'd fall silent as someone headed for the outhouse up the drive.

    South Road passed along the third-highest point on the island, the rim of the cliffs. Up here the constant blowing wind had turned wild rose bushes and ocean spray a grey-brown. Even the salal and Oregon grape had gone a bit desiccated. Ahead the road wound down to the beach. Tartarus drew off at the viewpoint, killed the engine, and got out. The ruddy sun had risen to six of its diameters above the horizon. Already it gave off dry heat. The island would be hottest away from shore breezes. Like at the house. Most of the time he enjoyed the heat, it was his environment. Far below, small rollers broke first over a reef just above the surface, then played themselves out with a foamy hiss on small crags twenty-thirty metres from the cliff base. To the south lay an expanse of ocean dotted with Gulf Islands fir green-black against the bluing sea. Vancouver Island stretched to his right, the mainland mountains to the east across Georgia Strait. Serious smog over Vancouver. The cliff rim had not been one of Maureen's spots. She preferred herself on a level with the sea—beaches, shorelines, rowing her dinghy. But the rim was one of Natalia's good places. She loved perspective, she liked to say. He would call her today.

    Thinking back to the first summer they'd stayed at the Bonner cabin, Tartarus couldn't remember Don having any interest in Natalia. Maybe he did but wouldn't say, not to Natalia's brother anyway. That happened the next summer. Maybe Natalia seemed as curvelessly plain to Don as she looked in her pictures. A year later, all had changed. Wondrous how much changed.

One day that fall Samuel Tartarus announced he too had bought land on Crab Island, not by the shore where Frank and Sylvia lived but inland, eighty acres of second-growth fir, cedar, and hemlock, and some still cleared land. He and Hannah would build a house there. He sited the house back from where forest met meadow, where in late winter the trickling stream became a mid-size torrent. The stream was the heart of the land, Sam had said. Maybe he'd farm the land. Or put in an orchard, that could be profitable. He might get a horse, ride across the terrain, the first Jewish country squire of his generation. Or run cattle. Tartarus remembered Frank scoff at Sam's foolishness, twenty-six hundred dollars for a chunk of land you couldn't even see the ocean from. Why bother living on an island if you can't hear the waves, can't swim right from your back door.

Jack wished he could remember how his mother had felt about Sam buying the land. Had she been delighted? Complained? No memory. Could the melancholy have touched her already then, seducing her with its malign tendrils? Jack believed his father loved his mother deeply. Had he bought the land for her? So she could turn it into—what? The perfect garden? A place to live in nature's beauty? A peace-filled home for the two of them, all four of them when "the children" came to visit? How did they think, Sam and Hannah . . .

Questions never asked, answers never heard. Growing older and wiser was unfair when you can't use the insights you discover. As it was unfair of Sam and Hannah not to be around: now they'd never be able to give Jack the details he needed. Sam should be celebrating his eighty-fifth birthday, easily possible these days. And Hannah her seventy-eighth.

He glanced at his watch. Nearing six. He'd been up here almost half an hour. Back into the car, back on the road. It curved downhill to the public beach, Siloe Provincial Park. Domingo Siloe as an ensign had sailed with Galiano in the Spanish exploration of Georgia Strait. It was known from the ship's log that during a storm he had fallen from the rigging and was presumed drowned. Early the next morning a party of sailors came ashore in search of fresh water and discovered Domingo asleep in a driftwood shelter he'd pulled around himself. They chided him, why hadn't he been up on the cliff signalling to them? Too tired, he told them. They named the beach after him. On early charts, it's known as Playa de Siloe, pronounced see low-ch, though on Crab known as sigh-low. Jack didn't stop at the park, another of Maureen's favourites.

At Arbutus Way he made a left; after two kilometres, a right on Scott; another four kilometres and left down the drive through the stand of big firs to the house. It had given him pleasure that Sam had built the house so far back from the road, just short of half a kilometre. The distance had lent the place a kind of grandeur, a reserved majesty, a private space removed from those who didn't belong there. And yet the woman, maybe Ginny, had walked in, nearly five hundred metres from the road. Why? He'd have to think about that. And about her. Later. Now he drove out of the trees and passed by the brush. The house sat in front of him. Despite himself, despite the malicious house, he admired both his father's dream and its fulfilment. The covered veranda running on all four sides, the tall white pillars with lacework corners where pillar met overhanging roof, the out-thrust windows of its second floor, all together had given the house both serenity and magnitude. Malignant magnitude now.

Its shadow leaned toward him, longer than wide. Two floors' worth of shade. A huge house. He would tear it down piece by piece as his father had built it up piece by piece. He had wanted to be an architect, two years of schooling, had to drop out, couldn't afford it. He became a draftsman. Now it was a house to stay out of. The inside was filled with memories, images, ghosts. He did not need to confront them again, not his parents, not Maureen. Not even a living one, Natalia, as she'd been when they would come here, younger, young. He'd seen buildings he knew razed to the ground. In a week, a month, the rubble cleared away, bare ground, the image of what had once stood there dimmed, it faded, faded to gone. And all gone was where the Tartarus house had to be.

He parked in its shade, got out, opened the trunk, grabbed his Fulton, found his work gloves, and headed for the veranda. Taped to the front door, a sheet of white paper. Computer-printed, heavy black letters. He pulled it loose.

NOTICE
ALL DEMOLITION ON CRAB ISLAND MUST BE
SANCTIONED BY OFFICIAL LICENCE. PLEASE CONTACT
THE ISLAND'S TRUST OFFICE IN THE VILLAGE.
Dominic Toussaint

Toussaint's signature followed his name.

Bastards. Tartarus considered the sheet of paper. Not on official letterhead, yet not scrawled. The work of the woman yesterday? Though likely half the island knew what he'd come back to do. On islands you get a lot of privacy but very little secrecy. He'd told no one but Don. Don needed to tell only one person, and anybody could know. Or maybe the woman—Shit.

Dominic had said please. Fuck him. Sure, Tartarus would meet with him. Later. Much later. He checked his watch: six-twenty. Dominic would not be able to protect this house.

Dominic was a small man. Even if he stood six-foot-seven or weighed two hundred and eighty pounds, he'd be a small man. Small men hid in the dim corners of daily life, by blind habit meandering out onto the great avenues of other people's fancy, setting themselves in the way of eruptive creation. On Tartarus's most recent project, there'd been two small men who reappeared like a Greek chorus chanting their litanies, you cannot, you must not, not now, not here.

Trouble was, something in Tartarus's constitution made it impossible for him to ignore the small men. They had to be eliminated, but in the appropriate way. They must understand the purpose of their obliteration. For the last seven years when Tartarus worked with fire, there'd always be a small man or a dozen of them, in overalls or suits or disguised as women, who challenged Tartarus's work-in-progress, thrusting the local Fire Regulations in his face. Fire Regulations exist only for their own burning.

Dominic Toussaint. Excellent name for him: Allholy. Dominic, possessor of Sanctified Demolition Regulations. Jack Tartarus would stamp on Dominic Allholy's brain.

Some thought Tartarus tended to become irrational about small men. This was incorrect. Crushing small men was the most rational act in the world. Irrationality was for greater things. Such as fire. Fire, like a paradoxical imagination capable both of containing itself and then surpassing its containment, was fully irrational. The mind wandered without reason, to where its images took it. As did fire, its ability to devour whatever lay in its track brought on only through its instinct, its intuition. Tartarus had learned this, and found the means to show it to others.

He lay the Fulton bar on the veranda deck, slipped fingers into gloves. The splinters lay on the veranda deck below the bare scars in the siding, yesterday's tiny beginning. He worked the large teeth under a piece of clapboard below the gouges. He hauled against restraint. A twelve-centimetre splinter came loose. He pulled it free with his gloved hand. Again teeth under siding. He held it there, in place. Stared. For a couple of seconds. With his full weight he pushed down. Another splinter, hanging on. He tore it away, dropped it to the deck. Bar under. He stared. It hung in place, ready for its work. He held it with his right hand. Slowly he pulled the teeth out from under. He held the bar with both hands. He loathed this house.

Dominic had, just for this morning, beaten Tartarus. Despite the certainty that Dominic Allholy was a very small man. Ready for combustion. When his office opened. A little flare-up.

What to do till then. He stared about. The meadow, rusty grey from the summer of drought, was bounded by tall green firs and angled arbutus. When Sam had bought the land, he'd found deer trails through the woods and widened them into paths. He had riddled the forest with paths, to the pinnacle and the Big Tree, to the rock slide, to the spring where the stream began. The spring was the source of the land's vitality, he claimed, the womb where life was born.

In his twenties Jack learned from a logger friend how to use a belt and boot spurs to climb hundred-ten-foot firs. He'd clambered to the crown of the Big Tree. It stood on the highest point on the island and gave him a full-circle view, land meeting water on all sides. From that perspective—glancing at maps it had never occurred to him—the island's name made full sense, Crab from the shape. Not from the wealth of a good crab fishery but because of its outline as it rose from the sea. Point Road out to the lighthouse was the long pincer like on a fiddler crab for battling other males during mating season, the broader peninsula east of Siloe Park the lesser pincer. The Big Tree rose from the centre of its carapace, the land extensions north of the village on the west and by the marina to the east its flattened rear legs for swimming down the strait. Remarkable! From up in the tree, the five little islands and two reefs north of Crab, the Guardian Group, had glimmered like a mailed shield. He'd told his father of this discovery. Sam had immediately sped off to Frank's cabin to tell him: Sam's property looked out at ocean not in one direction but in three hundred sixty! Frank had growled, You still can't swim right out your back door. He'd forgotten, it now occurred to Tartarus, that already back then Frank was a growler. Sam had thought for a while about digging out the stream bed and damming it below to make a swimming hole. He never did. Why not? One more question Jack would never get an answer to.

Explore the trails? Tartarus wanted food first, and coffee. It'd be close to seven by the time he got to the village. Something should be open by then.

Back to the car, out to the road, to the village. Where to go. The Arbutus Restaurant showed no sign of life. He turned south, searching for cars parked by any of the other eateries. He noted the Co-op a block up and passed by. A new location. Bigger too. And with a gas station now. He'd have to buy food, his contribution to Don and Frank's household. Later. Back over to West Road. The Pub looked closed, appropriate at seven in the morning. A few cars around Carleton's, twice as many beside a place called Fisherman's Rest-or-Rant, which hadn't been there the last time he'd been on the island. Terrible name but the locals must figure it better than Carleton's if they voted with their appetites. Also he'd never much liked Steve who owned the place, and he didn't in principle care for people who named restaurants after themselves. The Fisherman's, then. Or? He remembered a place at the marina. Pleasant to sit watching boats bobbing on the tide. He headed eastward, past Crab Hardware and the liquor store along North Road. It followed the shoreline. Out across the water lay the Guardians, blocking the winds from the northwest, making the whole of the north shore a natural harbour.

Here the land was thickly populated, summer cabins on half-acre lots, many transformed into year-round homes, some larger houses dating back to before his parents' arrival here. Too cheek-to-jowl for Tartarus's taste but, he had to admit, well-kept. The changes had started before, in the mid-1980s when he and Maureen had lived here. She'd loved Crab, her private paradise, a place to inhabit, to grow old. They'd been here six years. Grand years. The last five, anyway.

Tartarus passed a small house on his right, away from the water side, with a minimal sign saying, ISLAND KITCHEN. The FITN place. What had Don said, his final stop? Tartarus vaguely remembered an eatery after the marina restaurant. He drove on, couple of kilometres, still along the water, fewer homes till he approached the marina. The sea between Crab and the Guardians lay near to flat. Sailboats sat at anchor, no sway to their masts. Then Guardian Bay Marina, the docks bristling with sail and power boats. A smell of bacon frying. Thick and greasy. Delicious.

The smell didn't come from Ocean Spray. He parked. The sign on the restaurant door said, OPEN 11:00 TO 9:00. With all those boats anchored there, the place would be losing out on some good business. Couple of boats had their barbecues going, he saw wisps of smoke. His appetite quadrupled. Okay, back to village. Or the place Don had mentioned? Couldn't be far, nobody'd set up a business along East Road, too much out of the way. He drove on, past the road running to the northeast tip, Haggerty Point. At a parking lot in front of three attached cedar-sided businesses he stopped and got out. No other cars. On the left a used-books store, Hopalong. Then a place called CIRCE, which turned out to be Crab Island Recycling Centre Enterprises. On the right a modest restaurant, Eating Thyme. Three windows along the front allowed glimpses in. On the door a sign, CLOSED. Hours daily except Monday 11:00 AM to 9:00 PM. Normal?

He tried the door anyway. It opened. He stepped inside. Tables and booths, the walls painted an earthy orange. Dried fruit, vegetables, and flowers the primary decor. Also paintings, rural and seacoast scenes, tags with titles and prices. He heard a voice, "Sorry, we're not open yet." A woman appeared. "I guess I forgot to lock up last night."

"Oh, I thought you might be open anyway." Liar. You wanted to see her, didn't you? Hear what she sounded like.

"No, my lunch supplies don't come in till nine. And I don't do breakfasts."

He nodded, taking her in: five or six inches shorter than Tartarus, likely late thirties, black-brown hair pulled back and shining in morning light angling in through a side window, face without makeup, grey eyes hinting blue, full lips, ears pierced but without rings, blue oversized logo-free T-shirt, jeans over long legs, sandals revealing red-painted toes, which he noted as a couple of nods of fake disappointment led his glance downward. "Well I'm sorry about that. Smells good in here." He smiled. "Looks like a pleasant place."

She returned his smile and it warmed the room. "Why don't you come back for lunch."

"I just might." He glanced about. "Or maybe dinner. You're open in the evening, I see."

"We are."

He considered asking, and decided. "You're Etain."

"I am." For the first time she took him in seriously.

"My name's Jack Tartarus. I'm Don's friend."

"Oh," she said.

He would not apologize for waking her last night. "I'm pleased to meet you."

A tinge of blush came into her cheeks. "Is he all right this morning? Frank?"

"Sleeping like a baby when I left. But that was a couple of hours ago."

"Good. I'm relieved."

"So was Don."

"It's . . . hard for him."

"Yes."

Then neither spoke for a few seconds, then both at the same time: "I better be going." "Would you like some coffee?"

They laughed. Tartarus said, "No, I'm starving, I need to eat."

Etain said, "I wish I could offer you something. But I do have to go out. Buy my breads and eggs and veggies. I'm just waiting for my off-island supply truck."

"Eggs. I thought this was a vegetarian restaurant."

"I hate being pure."

"Good."

"But I do have coffee. Organic fair-trade, shade-grown, bird-friendly."

Tartarus made a point of sniffing the air, though the scent of recently brewed coffee had been there since he came in. "Smells good." But what would Don think of his being here. "Maybe a rain check. My appetite is beating out my need for caffeine."

She chuckled. "Some people are like that."

And what did that mean? He reached out his hand. "Nice meeting you, Etain."

She took his hand in a firm grip. "And you."

"Sorry to burst in before you opened. The door . . ." He shrugged.

"Glad it was open. Glad you came in. I've heard a lot about you."

"You have to know, Don exaggerates." He dropped her hand.

"Not only from Don. Reading about you too."

"Well," he said, "I'll be going."

"Come back with Don. And Frank. They eat here Saturdays. Lunch."

"I'll do that. If they want my company. Goodbye."

"See you." She stepped to the door in front of him, as if leading the way.

He stepped outside and heard the door close. He turned to wave. She waved back. He got in his car and drove toward the village and the Fisherman's place. Etain. Yes, he could see it, Don and Etain. He didn't like it, but he figured it made sense for Don. Or almost. He parked and walked in. A standard oceanfront family restaurant, air-conditioned, laminated wooden tables and chairs, no tablecloths, anchors and ship's wheels the decor, the ceiling draped with a massive white-and-blue lined sail. Most of the tables were occupied, several by three-four people, men outnumbering women two to one. The sign said, PLEASE WAIT TO BE SEATED. He waited. Etain. Damn. After a few seconds, a tall, skinny young woman bearing menus asked, "One?"

"Yes please." His usual number.

She led him to a table beside the window, a plate with yellow egg stains on it, a coffee cup with a napkin stuffed inside. "I'll get this wiped up," she said, set a menu on a clean section of table top, and walked away. Three people at one table, two at another, were watching him. He caught a pair of eyes, another. They turned back to their meal. Only a man sitting alone still stared. Tartarus thought he recognized him. Couldn't place him. Quickly a kid, maybe seventeen, appeared with a tray and a rag, "Hi, how you doin' this morning," and began loading.

"Fine." Fine like most mornings at a table for one with the work of the day ahead of him.

"The waitress will be with you in a moment." The kid wiped. Tartarus read the menu. The kid was back with a tray: a glass, a pitcher of water, a coffee cup, and a thermos. "Water?"

"Sure."

The kid poured, each into each.

"Thanks." The kid left. He glanced again at the breakfast options and closed the menu.

Within seconds a waitress appeared. "Now, what will we be having this morning."

A pert thing, short blonde hair and an unfailing smile. "I don't know what you'll be having, but I'd like the Rant Special."

"Sorry, that's how they tell us to ask. Usually it's okay." The last hinted of small worries.

"That's fine." He watched her walk away, less sprightly now. Beyond her, the man he nearly recognized dug into his breakfast. He looked up, caught Tartarus's eye, nodded. An acknowledgement? The man turned away and held his coffee cup before him with two hands.

Tartarus sipped his coffee. Nearly rich enough, not quite there. He knew the restaurant too, he'd eaten in hundreds of them in the last years. Expect adequate food and you won't be disappointed, except ten percent of the time you will. Another ten percent something unusual appeared, something happily delicious. He hoped staying on at Don's worked out. A home breakfast before house razing could be a small ongoing pleasure. He scanned the room again. Again a couple of glances his way. Gone when he noted them. The man alone glanced at his watch, stood, left some change on the table, and walked past Tartarus, giving him a small salute.

Etain. Attractive and, if Don cared for her, probably a woman of charm and decency, her electricity second nature. Not someone Tartarus would choose for female companionship, but the kind of woman who could grow on a man. As clearly she had on Don. Last night, had he told Don that Natalia might be coming over? Don hadn't said not to call. Tartarus drew the cellphone from his pocket, opened it, pressed Natalia's number. No one looking his way now. Except—by the door, the almost recognizable man. A clear smile from him now. Tartarus knew who he was. The man at the hardware store, the wrecking bar man. Turtle. He heard the phone connecting, a ring at Natalia's end. No. He cut the connection. After breakfast. Outside.

The eggs, bacon, hash browns breakfast proved to be a member of the middle eighty percent, the sliced strawberry garni adding a dash of textured red cardboard. The bill, three dollars above average, proved that hostess, busboy, and waitress made for a weight of overhead. He paid, left, and wandered down to the docks. He found a bench in the sun and stared out to sea.

All those boats—motor yachts, Boston whalers, two-masters, dinghies, a tug—how would each look set afire. The wood, the paint, the plastic, the creosote, the sails, the traces of gasoline left in the tank. The colours and shapes could be glorious. He'd do one at a time, harder to get good angles from a Zodiac. Fire was the most damned difficult element to shoot, always had been, with water a distant second. Difficult was the reason fire fascinated him, the technical problems ever new. Fire lived without reason, fire danced and soared, fire thundered and died away. The event so short, the challenge immense.

But nobody'd front him the cash to buy cabin cruisers and sailboats, to burn them down.

He took out the cell again and pressed Natalia's number code. Nine in the morning none of her students would have arrived yet. It rang, again, six times.

"Hello?"

"Natalia. It's Jack."

"Jack! Where are you? Are you here yet?"

"I'm on the island."

"Are you okay? Are you at the house?"

"I'm staying with Don."

A moment of silence. "Good. Is he okay?"

"He's well. I think he'd like to see you again."

"Oh Jack, stop. He doesn't want that."

"I talked to him last night. Quite a while." He waited, she said nothing. "I think you should come over."

"No no, that wouldn't be right."

"Right?"

"We've gone through all this, Jack. That was long ago."

"Well, I'd like to see you."

"Come to Vancouver. Justine would love to see you too."

"How is she?"

A second of silence. "Broody again. Sometimes. We had dinner last week. She brought me half a dozen reviews of FIRE AND THE PHOENIX. Unanimous raves."

"Must've selected carefully."

"From the *Times* and the *Post* to *Art Forum* and *Photography Today*. Impressive, Jack."

"I enjoyed it."

"Do you have a disk of the show? With you?"

"Yes to both."

"Bring it when you come over. I've seen photos. Just got a big high-definition screen."

"I'll see how the time goes."

She waited before she said, "What will you be doing?"

"Everything I intended."

"Oh Jack . . ."

"That's why I came back."

"I guess I only quarter believed you."

"Oh you of little faith."

"I should have taken you at your word." She sighed. "Do you have to . . ."

"'Fraid so, Nat."

"If—If I can get over for a couple of days, would you wait till I got there?"

He considered that. He wondered how long a demolition permit would take. "I was going to start this morning," he lied. "When could you come?"

"I have some summer students. But one cancelled for tomorrow morning—let me look." He heard what could have been a page turning. "No, it's okay, just that one and she won't be coming, and nobody on the weekend. I could get the ten-thirty from Horseshoe Bay and if it's on time is there still a one-forty to Crab?"

He didn't know but said, "Yes." If there wasn't he'd call her back.

"Okay. We'll have dinner. I'll bring stuff and we can warm it up in the kitchen."

"Natalia . . ."

"In the kitchen, Jack." She waited. "Okay?"

"We'll see."

"In the kitchen. You don't do anything till I get there."

Whose house is it anyway, lady? But he said only, "Okay."

"I'll bring a sleeping bag."

He closed his eyes and felt the clarity of all that his mind had organized slip away. "Natalia. I haven't been inside."

"Well go in, get the place ready for me. Okay?" She heard only silence. "Jack?"

"I guess."

"Thanks. We'll talk." More silence. "You'll see." She waited. "Love you, Jack."

"Love you too, Nat," he said with reluctance. Not because he didn't. But her affection sometimes undermined him. Had when she was tiny, still did.

"See you tomorrow. Bye."

"Bye." He stared at boats. He'd never get a chance to burn them. He walked to the Islands Trust office, three blocks away. He arrived just after nine-thirty. They opened at ten. He sat on a bench. He didn't want Natalia in the house. He hadn't thought about that before he called. He should have finished the job, then contacted her. He'd wanted her to be with Don, for them to get back to each other before this Etain person became a serious block. He'd never been a fool, subsection matchmaker, not even with Don and Natalia. But her sense of too late and his of the attractions of Etain—Don referred to her as a friend. Okay. Except now Tartarus had met her. She could be a woman for Don. Except Tartarus knew better than either Don or Natalia who should be, should have been long ago, with whom.

A car drove into the Trust lot. A man and a woman got out. They walked to the entryway. Tartarus waited till they disappeared, then followed. He opened the door. Ahead, a bright little room with a counter, the woman seated behind it, an open door in back of her. "I'd like to see Mr. All—uhm, Toussaint."

"He just came in, he's getting organized. A couple of minutes. Please take a seat."

Tartarus did, in a folding chair. The only thing that'd be just around here was just getting justice done by receiving a demolition order in just the time it took to crank it out of the computer.

Fifteen long minutes later the woman called to him, "Mr. Toussaint can see you now. This way please." She gestured to the doorway behind her.

Toussaint's office contained one window, a bookshelf heavy with files lying flat, a small table holding a large coffee maker and several cups, a desk and chair, a kitchen table with four chairs, and Dominic Toussaint. The small man stood four inches taller than Tartarus, wore jeans, a white shirt, and of all perverse things on an island, a bow tie. Grey hair and a good tan covered round cheeks. Small nose, sad, dumb eyes.

"How can I help you, Mr.—?"

"Tartarus. Jack Tartarus."

"Ah, of course. I was expecting you, Jack." He gestured to the table. "Please. Sit."

"I'll stand. This shouldn't take long, Dom."

"There are some forms—"

"Look, all I want is to tear down a house I don't want on my land. Okay?"

"Perfectly okay. But it has to be done properly."

"What, with an excavator? A backhoe?"

"With a demolition permit."

"But for crapsake, why?"

"To legally destroy it."

"Listen, it's my house, I can do what I want with it."

"Not anymore, Jack."

"When my father built it, *Dominic*, he didn't even have a construction permit."

"But if it gets torn down without a permit, you might try to collect the insurance."

"It isn't insured. I just want to get rid of it. Get what I'm saying?"

"Now don't let's be angry. You want to tear down a house, you need a permit."

"Why?"

"It's the law."

"Why is it the law?"

A squint across the whole of Dominic Toussaint's face told Tartarus that Mister Allholy had never heard such a question in his life. "It's the law, Jack, because destroying a house without a permit is illegal. That's why it's the law."

Tartarus puffed out a sigh. "And if I tear it down anyway?"

"I'm afraid you could be arrested and charged with destroying private property."

"Even if it's my private property."

"In the eyes of the Trust, on this island all property is part of the Trust. Even if a piece is owned by a private individual. The Trust is responsible for all properties on the island, be they dwellings, businesses, or land."

"You mean I couldn't even log my land without your permission."

"Oh you could. But we wouldn't like it."

"Would it be illegal?"

Dominic considered this. "No."

Demolition orders. A money-making racket for the Trust? "How long would it take to get a demolition order?"

"Hard to say. Possibly a day, possibly a week, possibly longer?"

"A month. A year."

Small Allholy shrugged and shook his head. "Nothing like that."

"Who gets to say?"

"My superiors. The trustees."

"Aren't you a trustee?"

Dominic raised his head, haughty. "Do I look like a trustee."

Tartarus had no idea what trustees looked like. Maybe not like small men. "How do I apply for one of these orders?" Maybe trustees were honourable.

Dominic smiled. Another tamed citizen. "Miss Chance will take care of you." He reached his hand over to Tartarus. "Good of you to come by."

Tartarus did not take Dominic's hand. "Thanks." He turned and left the office. He said to Miss Chance, "You're supposed to give me . . ."

"Yes, here." She handed him two sheets of paper. "You may fill them out here."

Tartarus did. Name, address, phone, address of place to be demolished. A statement noting he took full responsibility for demolition. A signature. "Here you are. When will the approval be ready?"

"Check back middle of next week."

He shrugged. What else to do? The request would be approved. How could they not? He'd start as soon as Natalia left. "How'd you know I'm planning this demolition?"

Miss Chance neither smiled nor frowned. "We hear about impending changes."

"I'll come back next week. Early."

"Any time, Mr. Tartarus."

He left. Any time he'd get the order. In the meantime . . .

Had it been the woman with the big eyes? Ginny. Couldn't be Ginny. He headed back to his car, grabbed the handle—Closed his eyes. Rick, the father. Last name Rixton. He decided, turned, back into the restaurant. He found the thin hostess and asked for the Crab phone book. She brought it. Rixton. Yes, on Scott between his land and West Road. Back to the car. Drive to her land, knock at her door . . . And say what? Ginny, this isn't any of your business. Maybe whoever opened the door wouldn't be Ginny.

He yanked the car door closed and started the engine. He opened all the windows to let hot outside air replace the baked oxygen-wanting vapour. He turned the key and gave gas hard. The tires skidded on gravel and dirt, then thrust the big Buick forward. He let up on the pedal, no sense screaming through the village. Windows closed, air-conditioning on. He drove two kilometres under the speed limit, back as he'd come, past the marina and Eating Thyme and up West Road. He would be calm. He was already calm. Four kilometres and onto Scott. Less than three kilometres, a driveway on the left, a sign, RIXTON. He stopped, decided, and turned in. The house was immediately visible, two storeys, cedar-sided, a carport right of a gravel court, a work-shed to its right. The nearest trees were maybe fifty metres away. The house seemed lonely, a thing all by itself. He'd seen houses like this mostly on the prairies, desolate houses. Here the main reasons people cut down garden trees was to keep them from falling on houses in windstorms or to sell them for lumber or firewood.

Beside the carport sat a battered station wagon, early eighties vintage, a true island beater. In front of the house, a couple of tended flower beds—roses, lilies, cosmos. He stopped, got out, walked up some steps to the house door and knocked. A hollow echo, no answer. He tried again. The house in fact felt empty. He glanced around. Someone lived here, the place looked neat enough, fencing in order, no grass or weeds amid the gravel. "Hello!" Silence.

Okay, he'd made the attempt. Back to the Buick, a three-point turn, and out onto Scott. His place, and he turned right. He rolled down the drive, thinking, Why am I here?

He parked as he had earlier and stared at the house. It was staring back. Contesting his actions: the law is on my side, stay away. Take your Fulton bar and go.

Would he in fact allow Natalia to stay here? Sleep here. Cook here, in the house's kitchen? The house had been closed for two years. What, hire cleaners to sweep up dust and vacuum away spiderwebs? Vacuum? With what electricity? A week before he tore it all down? A dirty house tears down more easily than a clean house.

He had promised himself he wouldn't go inside, not till the sides were stripped to the struts, the walls reduced to skeletons. Time to break that promise.

He got out. Hot and getting hotter. Just the way he liked it. He clicked the trunk open, found the key in a side pocket of the camera pack. On a ring with other keys. To open what? He couldn't remember. This ring of keys had always been The House Keys. All those years when others rented here, when Tartarus was away, Natalia the on-call person would have The House Keys. She'd come over four times a year to inspect the house. And between rentals Natalia would organize the cleaning, any needed repairs. A key circled in green fitted the front door lock. Should he do this? He should wait till Natalia arrived. They'd go into the house together. And she'd laugh at him, tell him he'd gotten loony, fame no excuse for this new nuttiness, not entering his own house. What a mess, Jack! she'd say. Spider poop all over the place, she'd say. Sow beetle corpses. And everything, ceiling to furniture, every corner and each window, laced with cobwebs. Mouse-shit, Jack. You preparing for Halloween?

He'd go in, clear away the worst of it. In the trunk he found his flashlight. Key into keyhole. It turned easily. The handle too turned as it should. He pushed the door open. He stood outside and peered in. Dark, despite the bright day. Shutters over windows, right. And, inside, the drapes would be drawn. He stepped in, the air several degrees cooler now. His fingers found the light switch, a motion of habit. Nothing happened. He pointed his flash up. The entryway remained dark. As it should, he'd had the power turned off when he closed the place down. He played the beam around the entry, spasmodic illumination of the area, about three metres square. The bench for sitting while putting on shoes, the coat closet, the polished wooden floor, the throw rug he stood on, the rosette wallpaper: all as he'd left it near two years ago. On his right the stairs led up. In front of him lay the hallway to the dining room, the door there open, and the arch to the living room ahead on the left. The kitchen door across from the living room stood closed. Everything normal. No, not. He sensed a presence in the house, some kind of being, as if he were not alone. Impossible.

And not normal too in a more mundane way. Because here inside it looked precisely as it had two years ago. Clean. The floor shone. As if a cleaning woman had just spent a couple of days here. He walked along the hall playing the beam off the wall, across the floor. No cobwebs, not old and tattered, not new and functioning. To the left of the dining room doorway he found the switch and clicked it on. Of course no light. He played the beam about the room. Here too all seemed spotless. The glass cabinets shone, the teardrops on the little chandelier centred above the table twinkled when the flash passed over them, the eight chairs stood square around the oak table, its white tablecloth immaculate. Two silver candlesticks, no tarnish, held long white tapers. Had he left the candles in place? They rose straight and true from their holders. No cobwebs anywhere, no dead insects, the whole room sterile.

Not sterile. He again felt a contamination, that presence, some kind of intrusion. He walked around the table. As if someone were forever one room ahead of him, cleaning and vacuuming, tidying and polishing, preparing for his arrival. He pulled aside the drapes over the window between the cabinets. No light, just the inside of shutters. The big window at the back had no shutters. He drew aside the drape on the left a metre or so. Bright morning light flooded in from the southeast, as his father had intended. He pulled the drape open all the way, and the other one as well. The dining room glowed in sunlight. The green-tinted glass on the double sliding doors to the living room sparkled. Where bugs and dust would normally have laid claim, he saw only spotless surfaces, ledges, and corners. And the presence of—what?

He walked toward the kitchen entry, a pocket door, and slid it into its slot. Daylight from the dining room spilled into the kitchen, enough so he didn't need his flash. Again, all as he remembered—the cabinets to his left, ahead the dishwasher and sink, on the right the stove and refrigerator. At the sink he turned the faucet. Nothing. Of course not. Two years ago he'd turned the water off and drained the pipes; with nobody in the house they'd have frozen over the winter. The door to the downstairs bedroom stood ajar. He pushed it open and shone his light around. The mattress protected by a blanket, the chest, the dresser, all in place. The door to the basement stairs stood closed. Down below, his one-time studio. There his art had been born, in a space cramped and low-ceilinged but with much wall-display space. Never enough. In the bedroom he sensed less of an intrusion. He retreated and turned back to the other kitchen door, the one out to the hallway. On his left, the downstairs bathroom. He pushed the door open and shone his light about. Again, spotless. He shook his head. Incomprehensible. At least he wouldn't have to clean the place before Natalia arrived. No, that was it! She'd already been here. Come over and cleaned the house. Or hired someone to do it.

He crossed the hallway and stepped through the arch to the living room. Dim light from the dining room came through tinted windows on the sliding door. On the dining room side his mother would thrust it open, announcing to guests, Dinner is served. Jack smiled, then shuddered, the words were that clear. He played the beam past the sliding doors to the dark window across from him. To the left of the window, between it and the fireplace, there on the outside would be the clapboard he'd been chipping away at. He should go upstairs, see if the rooms gleamed as much as these down here. He passed the beam from the window on to the fireplace, past the big hearth chair, to the couch . . .

Back to the chair, hand and light quivering. Someone. A person. Or the shape of a person. He held the light steady. The woman from yesterday, her blinking eyes immense.

"You mustn't tear down the house."

"Are you . . . Ginny?"

"For your parents' sake."

FOUR: Natalia Tartarus Golden and, Her Daughter, Justine

Call Justine. But she didn't want to. But she had to. If she held off now, it'd be worse afterward. Justine would not forgive her. And Natalia didn't need more weeks of an unforgiving daughter. During and after their argument Monday—it should have been such an easy relaxed lunch—there'd been reproach aplenty. On both sides, Natalia had to admit.

Call Justine, tell her what? The simple truth—just that blatant?—that her uncle had begun tearing down the house on Crab? Find a way to pass on this information in little-by-little phrases? No words came to her. Did words, phrases, exist for situations like this?

Natalia glanced at her watch. Ten minutes till her first student was due. Okay. She poured a second cup of coffee, picked up the phone, brought up the autodial phonebook, and pressed 1. Three rings, four...

"Hello, Mom."

"Hiya." She hated caller display. "How are you?"

"Okay."

Well, she'd called. But she wasn't prepared. "Uhmm—come to any conclusions?"

"Since Monday? The same."

"There's still time to reconsider."

"Look, Mom, it's not like I'm going to stop playing, you know that."

"I can't believe it. I just can't."

"Can I say this one last time? I do not want to be a professional cellist. Okay?"

"I can't make you."

"Good. And how are you?"

"Okay." And she didn't mention Justine's other crazy idea, learning a trade. Plumbing.

"What's up?"

No getting away from it. "Jack's come back."

"Hey! Great! Is he with you?"

"No."

"On the island?"

"Yeah."

"He coming over here?"

"I don't know. I'm going there."

Justine waited. "Mom. Am I missing something?"

"He's got a project. There."

"And?"

"And I'm going to Crab to convince him not to . . . not to continue with his project."

"Okay. I'll bite. What's the project."

"The house." Just say it. "He's going to tear it down."

A couple of seconds of silence from Justine. "Did you say, tear the house down?"

"Yes."

"His house? Gran and Granpop's house?"

"Yes."

"But . . . but he can't."

"It seems he can, and he will. But he'll wait till I get there."

"But why?"

"Justine, I don't know."

"But what about . . . what about Gran and Granpop?"

"We can remember them without the house."

"No." A pause. "No, he can't do this. I won't let him. It's just a thing he's saying."

Natalia had to tell her. She'd find out anyway. "He's planned this for a while."

"What?! You're telling me in that calm voice he's going to . . . to get rid of the house."

"I'm not calm, Justine. I'm sad."

"Oh very good, you're sad." She waited. "What do you mean, planned it for a while?"

"Since the spring."

"Mom. Did you know this? Since spring?"

Natalia nodded, then said, "Yes."

"And you never mentioned it to me."

"I didn't think he was serious." But she did know he'd grown more serious.

"You could have told me! I love the house! I love—everything in it. He can't do this!"

"I'm going to talk to him. Try to talk him out of it."

"I'm coming with you. He'll listen to me."

"He might." Or maybe not, Natalia thought. Jack liked Justine, but a few years back she'd gotten at his nerve endings and he hadn't forgotten. "But I think he's not listening to anybody."

"He adores me. He'll listen. When are you going?"

The doorbell rang. "There's my ten o'clock. I'll call you back."

"He can't do that, not to Gran and Granpop!"

"Forty-five minutes." Natalia disconnected and went to the door.

The girl came in, they spoke pleasantries, she sat at the piano and played for her teacher.

Natalia's mind wandered. To Justine, this insane refusal to continue with her music, turning down the scholarship. To Jack, how to deal with him. To Don, forever on the island. She, like Justine, felt close to the house on Crab, near to intimate. If it were gone, a part of herself too would disappear. She'd spent a lot of time there; two times, significant periods. In '89 after Stan died she went over regularly with Justine, Justine from six to ten, to sift through her mourning time for Stan, the healing for herself and Justine. Then four years ago she'd lived there alone, Justine at university, rooming with a friend. Justine had already proven herself a fine cellist, the lush urbane tone she brought from her instrument, her authority of wrist and forearm. Natalia could not abide it, her daughter walking away from her cello. No, just away from the possibility of becoming one of the great cellists of her generation. No, don't go there, not now.

The house on Crab. With Stan's death her own life shattered. She'd stopped performing, both on the classical stage and at the little clubs where she at the keyboard, Lester on drums, Cy's guitar, and Patsy on bass delighted patrons with evenings of forties and fifties jazz. She did continue the lessons, that was her income. Visiting Jack and Maureen on Crab with Justine was the best of what held her together. More: the year after Stan died, Don's mother too had passed on—that would have been her phrase—wonderful Sylvia, and Don came to Crab to live. She spent time with Don, not precisely dating, too soon for that, but spending hours together, easy together. Could they have gone on? Not then. Justine, just ten, wanted to live in the city. Weekends are for being with my friends, Mom! She had started the cello at seven and was playing well, a devoted student, had gone beyond the only possible teachers on Crab. She needed a strong mentor. Jack and Maureen weren't there anymore, they'd left soon after Maureen was diagnosed. In addition, Sam and Hannah decided they should live on Crab full-time, they needed to get out of Vancouver, especially Hannah. The city was driving her crazy.

The music stopped.

"Most of that was well done," said Natalia. "Except for the scherzo. Try it again. Sprightly this time. Sprightly." The girl played.

Don. Had it been too early, too soon after Stan's death? A year after she graduated from Berkeley she'd married Stan, they stayed around, lived and worked in the Bay area; four years later Justine was born. Justine turned seven a month before Stan was killed, a car accident. His brakes failed. No one could explain why, metal fatigue the best of several inadequate explanations. And then Don. Again.

Long before, in the early seventies when she was fifteen, sixteen, seventeen, eighteen, Natalia and Don had been a close couple. Easy together, funny together, loving together; as much in love as a fifteen-year-old could be with a seventeen-year-old. And, it seemed, at eighteen and twenty. Except then Natalia went away, left Vancouver for her university degree, off to California. Don had already been at UBC for two years, she'd seen his UBC and wanted more. Don needed her to come back, be with him again. She finished her degree at Berkeley.

For eleven months, 2001–2002, Natalia had lived on the island alone. She and Don were together as much as they could be, if Don could leave Frank. When she and Don had been in their teens Frank had liked Natalia well enough, pleased she was his son's pretty girlfriend. But in those days Frank had Sylvia to take care of him, then more recently only Don. So Frank had come to like Natalia less, possibly out of fear Natalia would take Don from him.

The music stopped. Sprightly seemed absent from the girl's repertoire. "You'll have to give that a bit more work. When you practise, set your metronome faster. Let it push you. Now let me hear the Brahms." The girl arched her back, stretched her fingers, addressed the keyboard.

Natalia had arrived on Crab on September 8. Don helped her settle in, pick up provisions, wood for the stove. They did a well check; low but passable till it poured again. The rainwater cistern had gone dry, buy a tanker truck of water? No, let the garden survive as it would. On the eleventh she and Don had planned an evening by themselves, dinner at Oyster's, see where it led, both unsure. But in the morning Don called, asked if she'd heard. He knew her cable wasn't connected yet. What? The Twin Towers in New York, the planes. She must come to his house. No restaurant, he'd cook, it would help divert him. Right now he couldn't tear himself from the television. She spent the morning listening to the radio. In the afternoon she drove to the cliffs and walked along the rim. She stared out at the ocean for a long time, haggard breakers foaming against jagged rock below. Despite the planes, the sea hadn't changed, not for her.

She arrived at the Bonner house in the late afternoon. Don opened the door. She saw his face, drained of colour, grey lines at the edges of his eyes. She hugged him, held him to her tight. His hug in return felt soft, tired. He closed the door. "It's awful." He only nodded. Arm around her waist, led her to the TV room. Frank in his chair stared at the image, the mayor of New York striding toward the camera, officials and reporters at his side, the commentator speaking over sirens and static. Frank, staring so undivided it seemed a physical line connected his eyes to the screen. "Hello, Frank." She spoke only loud enough to carry over the cacophony from New York. Frank seemed not to have heard. She stepped to his side. He turned to her, saw her. He stood up. She reached out to hug him but he stepped back. He glared at her. "You!" A harsh whisper. "You and your damned country! Look what you've done. Look at yourself! What you've done, all this—what you've done. Go back to California." He shook his head and walked from the room.

She glanced at Don. "What?"

"It's the planes. He's scared."

"Of the planes?"

"That I might have been on one of them."

"What?"

"An American plane, it crashes, and he's all alone."

"Oh, Don." She hung her head, understanding the weight of Frank's fear, its irrationality, she hadn't realized till then . . .

"Mrs. Golden? Are you all right, Mrs. Golden?"

Natalia raised her head. A girl sat there, at the piano, staring at her. Oh. "I'm sorry, I'm just a little tired. The Brahms sounded fine. Now for next week . . ."

Better not let that happen again. They arranged the assignment, the girl wrote it in her notebook, paid and left. In the bathroom Natalia soaked the washcloth with cold water and held it to her face. Another student in twelve minutes. She picked up the phone and again pressed 1.

A couple of rings. "Hello, Mother."

Anger there. "Hi, J."

"You had your lesson."

"Yep."

"I've decided. I'm not going to Crab with you after all."

"If you're okay with that . . ."

"No, goddamn it, I'm not okay! I just can't bear to go."

"J, what's the matter?"

"What do you mean, what's the matter. He's going to destroy the house!"

Justine was shouting. Even on Monday when their argument about her cello career, the scholarship, plumbing for godsake! reached its most acrimonious, Justine's voice had remained composed. Justine's anger rarely reached for clamour. Natalia spoke softly. "So far he's only saying he'll raze it. I'll try to stop him." Natalia's uncertainty—better if Justine comes along to Crab or try to keep her away?—had settled out: Justine not going over would be a major mistake, the house gone without her attempt to save it the source of heavy new guilt for a long time to come. "You should be there. You maybe could convince him better than I."

"I can't do it, Mom. I know Jack. If he's decided, we won't be able to change his mind."

"You said it, he adores you. If you explain how much the house means to you..."

"He doesn't adore me. He used to adore me."

"He loves you very much."

"He holds back. Like he doesn't want to be close enough to talk to, let alone hug me."

It was more than that, Natalia figured. But Justine seemed to be talking about something else. "Justine, what's this really about?"

"About Uncle Jack tearing down the house, Gran and Granpop's house. I can't stand it."

"Jack loves you every bit as much as he ever did, and maybe he'll listen to you."

"Well I'm not going."

When Justine made her decisions there was no moving her. Okay. Once Natalia had talked to Jack, maybe stalled his intentions, Justine could come over and reinforce her effort. "But if you change your mind, call. I'll be taking the ten-thirty tomorrow."

"I won't change my mind. He's going to tear the house down and if I go over he'll probably wreck it right in front of me."

"Why would he do that?"

"I don't know. But he would. And anyway I can't bear—to say goodbye to the house before—before it goes either!"

Natalia heard a quiet sobbing. "I agree, Justine. I'd find it hard to say goodbye too."

"To the house." A moment of silence. "And—and everything inside."

"We can take out whatever we want. We can bring it here."

"No we can't!"

"If Jack won't back down, we'll rent a van and move out those things we care about."

69

"Oh Mother, you just don't know."

"What? What don't I know?"

A deep sigh, a dismissive sigh. "We can't take *them* out. They're part of the house. As much as the walls and the windows."

"Them?"

"Them."

"Who them?"

A sniff from Justine. "Gran and Granpop."

Oh dear. "They're with us, J. In our minds."

"And in their house."

"Yes, we feel our memories more sharply over there. And I'll be sorry not to have that. But if we take some of their favourite things, Granpop's big clock, his rocking chair . . ."

"Then Granpop won't have his clock or his chair any longer."

"Justine . . ."

"You know they're there. You can feel them too." Justine waited a moment before adding, "You just don't talk to them."

This again. "Yes, I know. You used to talk with them, after they died." Justine would accompany Natalia to the house on her caretaking duties. Justine would disappear, usually to her grandparents' bedroom. Hours later Natalia would find her, chatting away to her Gran and Granpop as if they were sitting on the chairs in the room as Justine lay on their bed. A wonderful fantasy for the girl, Natalia had thought, a lovely way to remember Sam and Hannah. Justine had always followed these fantasies, always been good at concocting scenarios. Even as a child she'd made up stories about people she knew well, stories that often proved to be nearly true, extrapolated from a very few details. Usually on the ferry home from Crab Justine would tell Natalia what Sam or Hannah had said, stories of Crab when they'd been alive, advice to Justine about her music, about boyfriends. "But you were younger then, that was when you were a kid."

"But, Mom, later too."

"Later."

"When Jack didn't rent the house out. The years it's been empty."

"The years it's been locked tight?"

"I have my key."

"Justine? You've been going over there, breaking in, spending your time..."

"Didn't you hear me? I didn't break in. I have my key."

The doorbell rang.

"What—what did you do at the house?"

"Talked to them. Played my cello for them."

A chill took Natalia, back and shoulders. All she could say was, "Oh."

From Justine too a long silence. Then she said, "So you see why I couldn't handle being there. While he destroys the house. When he takes their home away."

"Justine..." Suddenly Natalia was frightened for Justine. The doorbell rang again. "My eleven o'clock," she said. "I'll call you back when he's gone." She started to take the phone from next to her ear, stopped, and added. "I love you, J."

"Thanks, Mom. I love you too."

The eleven o'clock was a professor of mathematics in his forties, using his sabbatical to learn to play the piano. He wasn't bad. Neither was he very good. They chatted for a couple of minutes. He played his assignments, a short Mendelssohn piece, a longer Ravel, a sonata that he'd been practising for three months, two Schubert *Lieder*. Again Natalia's mind wandered.

The love she felt for Justine. A force so powerful Natalia had no language to explain it, even explore it. The darkest and the lightest forces conspired in her chest each time her mind led her to an image of her daughter, fear for her, pride for her. This full person who had once been a part of her. The tiny being she'd suckled, become now a full woman, a force in the world yet still as much tied to her—and perhaps she to Justine, Natalia sometimes thought—as in the moment she was born. She rarely allowed her mind to wander to impending death but Justine's talk of her grandparents now brought on the terrible power of one of those What-if kinds of questions, What if Justine were suddenly no longer there? So terrible for a child to die before her parents. Which happened often enough, wars eat up the children, the son or daughter gone to battle and then simply no longer there.

The hinted pain of such a sense of loss now filled Natalia with pure knowledge of the depth of her love for Justine: if she were no longer there, it would be an end to things, the largest part of Natalia taken away. Her parents' deaths: Natalia just as purely tied to her mother as Justine to Natalia. Parents who had brought her along paths of daily life with them at all her sides, even if she knew nothing of it. One day Sam and Hannah Tartarus had been in the world, the day after gone. At first she had blamed them, bitterly, Hannah afraid of the world and its people, Sam disappearing slowly, Hannah when lucidity came back wanting to end it. Sam insisting he had no place in the world, on the island, in their house, without her. So they had left, together. The shield protecting Jack and Natalia from their own mortality had disappeared. Now she had nowhere to lay her love for them. A world devoid of the protection of parents—not economic or even domestic, she and Jack were out in the world, on their own as cliché might have it but not at all on their own, the living ghosts of their parents with them until the moment of their suicides. Then only dead ghosts remained.

With whom—Natalia had great difficulty here—Justine would commune. Play for them. Last year? The year before? Explained her life to them? As she rarely did these days to Natalia. Love for her grandparents in a house Jack now plotted to destroy. Then came a thought: Had Sam and Hannah participated in Justine's decision to leave behind a career in music, to take up a trade? Plumbing, the craziness Justine was drawn to. Natalia could see Sam helping her plot such a decision. Which was mad, because even if Justine talked to her grandparents, they did not, did not, did not! speak to Justine.

Though someone was speaking to Natalia. Her student. "Yes," Natalia said, "that was very good. A great improvement over last week." Was it? How could she know? She hadn't heard a thing. "Now would you play the Beethoven sonata?"

"Uh—Natalia? I just did."

"Yes. I enjoyed it. I'd like to hear it again. Now that I know what you're doing with it I can be more specific in my suggestions." When he nodded, she smiled in relief. For the next fifteen minutes she listened hard, fought back her meandering sense of love for her family—didn't even consider Jack, where he was in her affections. No, not now. Concentrate on the sonata.

The forty-five minutes over, the professor gone, Natalia poured the cold coffee down the drain and called Justine back. "Hi."

"I don't know what's wrong with me, Mom. My brain's just clicking in all directions and I keep disagreeing with myself. I'm going to go with you to the island. Okay?"

"Sure. Okay."

"Or . . . Your students, right? So you're not heading off till tomorrow. So maybe I should go today, get the next ferry. Just in case Jack decides he doesn't want to wait till you get there."

"Hmm." But Justine should not confront Jack alone. Needing to explain why but without suggesting that she didn't trust Justine, that Justine and Jack could hurt each other. That Justine could hurt Jack more than he her. It was good that Justine hadn't been in ongoing contact with him these last years. "I think you should wait. Let your anger at him subside, let it get filtered."

"Filtered."

"You know, like thinking through what you want to say to him. And how."

"Mother. I think I know what I think."

Natalia made herself chuckle. "You know that what you think now isn't the same as what you thought fifty minutes ago. Which was different from what you thought an hour before then."

A couple of seconds of silence, and Justine giggled. "You're right."

Cement her assent into a schedule. "I'll pick you up at nine-fifteen. Traffic should be okay." Natalia lived up near UBC, Justine off Commercial Drive. On the way to the ferry.

"I'll be ready. Call me when you're five minutes away and I'll be downstairs."

"Good." Should she suggest this? "And, J?"

"Yes?"

"Bring your cello."

Silence for a couple of seconds. "Why?"

When it cost nothing, best to be on Justine's side. "To play for them."

Another silence. "Okay."

"See you tomorrow."

"Yeah. Tomorrow."

Natalia put the phone down. She glanced at her watch. She closed her eyes. Going to Crab again. Inevitably, Don again. But why. She could go to the island, stay at the house, talk—argue—with Jack, convince him or not. And leave. Without seeing Don.

She knew she couldn't. If she avoided Don, he'd be hurt. So even if she didn't want it, Jack would arrange some sort of rendezvous. She'd call Don. When she arrived. Better than he calling her. She would set the tone. In their early years he had set the tone. And the direction. There was an early summer evening, the sky at last gone dark, she sixteen, Jack and Don eighteen. Don had graduated high school, she had two years to go. She loved him, she knew. Had said so to him. And Don loved her. They were all staying at the Bonner house by the water, she, her parents, Jack, Frank and Sylvia Bonner, Don. She, Jack, and Don had swum till the sun dropped into the sea, the gold on the wavelets ashimmer, a blinding beauty. After, they sat on the deck with the parents. Then she and Don took a walk along the dark road. They held hands, they held each other, they kissed. They knew they should return to the house, so they did.

Natalia shook her head. They had been such good kids. So decent.

The parents were already in their rooms. Jack must have gone to the tent though he hadn't called out to them as they'd passed. They kissed again, and Don went to join Jack. She wished she could be with them, talk into the night and fall asleep between them. This would be as close as she could let herself get to the other thing. She both wanted and was scared. To sleep with, as in make love with, Don. They had not talked about it. She sensed Don felt as she did, but the discussion hadn't happened, as if by speaking the words, desire, penetration, intercourse, loss of virginity, something holy between them would die. While the late 1960s had been their moment of falling in love, in comparison to their friends they each discovered they were conservative, puritan even, compared to most other kids. Natalia changed into her pyjamas and lay on the couch, made into a bed for her. Sleep rejected her. A large moon flooded doubly into the living room, down from the sky and up from the sea. She got up, put on slippers and a bathrobe, and stood on the deck. The world stretched away in silence. The water lay flat, the moon buried on its surface an unbroken circle, her private moon. She decided. She walked around the cabin as if heading for the privy. She stared down at her feet, willing them to make no noise. She approached the tent and heard a voice. Don. She couldn't make out the words. She stepped closer. Jack was speaking now. She caught only intermittent words, heard "... drive-in ... pizza ... Lauren ... hair ... September ... so-so ..." Jack was dating Lauren. This was the talk Natalia wanted to hear, how her brother feels, what was living inside him. The things he never told her. She took a few steps, around to the side of the tent, still a couple of metres away. The window had been tied open. She could hear better now. She glanced down. A stump. She sat on it.

Don was saying, "Well I think Lauren's great."

"But there's nowhere to go with it," Jack said. "I'm going away, there's two months left. I don't think it'd be fair."

"Yeah, but she knows that."

"She does and she doesn't. I can say it and she hears it, but inside her head there's something telling her I'm not really going away. Or if I do I'll be back, and I'll be back for her."

"She'll know when you go. And she'll know that you're gone. But in the meantime she just likes being with you. And you with her. You've said so."

"I do. You're right. But you're wrong about spending my summer dating time with her."

"Yeah? Why?"

"She's getting, I don't know—intenser."

"Intenser."

One of the two giggled, Natalia couldn't tell who. She held her breath.

"Sounds pretty good to me." That was Don. Then a silence. "Jack? I never asked you, figured it wasn't my business, you'd tell me if you wanted to brag on it, but—are you and Lauren making it?"

And a silence from Jack. "Yeah," he said at last.

Natalia, unmoving till now, turned to stone. She must have known. She could see from the way they grinned at each other, a private exchange. From how Lauren touched him, a possessive kind of secret contact.

She heard Don say, "That's great, man."

"Yeah."

"Except you don't sound real happy."

"I am. I mean, it's terrific."

"But."

"But—it's like, every time we do it, it's like she owns a bit more of me."

"Hey, listen, you're going away."

"That's what I mean."

"Long as she doesn't get pregnant, you can walk away. Hey, she on the pill?"

"Yeah. And I always use a rubber. Just to be sure."

"Well hell, Jack."

And silence. As if they had fallen asleep. Natalia needed to move, to breathe aloud. She slowly rose to her feet. She heard Don say, "Jack."

"Yeah?"

"Something I want to talk to you about. Okay?"

"Talk, man."

"Natalia. And me."

"You and Natalia, you go great together."

"More than that, Jack."

"More."

"I—I feel like I've got to say this."

"Okay."

"Ask you this."

"Get to it, Donnie."

"Natalia and me, I—I want to make love to her. With her."

"You mean you're not?"

Natalia, half standing, flushed hot down her neck and sank back onto the stump.

"You thought we were?"

"I didn't know."

"Jack—I wouldn't. Not without talking to you first."

"Have you talked with her?"

"Not—directly. But I think she wants to too."

"So what're you saying?"

"I want to be sure it's okay with you."

"Don—you asking for my permission, for catsake?"

"No, not your permission, just, well, like I said, that if Natalia and I made it together, I wouldn't want you all pissed off at me."

"Look, she's my sister. I think she's wonderful. I'd do anything to keep her from getting hurt. But first of all she's Natalia Tartarus, all by herself. If she wants you like you want her, I think that's great. But if you hurt her, yeah, then I'll be pissed off. Yeah."

Natalia was scared of hearing anything more. She couldn't move.

"I never would. I'll be here even if I'm at the university, I'm not going away."

A bit of a nasal laugh from Jack. "Even if she gets intense?"

"She will be intense. I'll be intense. God, Jack, I love her."

"Well good on you, man."

"Thanks, Jack."

"Maybe one day the two of you'll get married. Then we'd be brothers-in-law."

Now it was Don who laughed a little. "That'd be good."

A silence. Then Jack said, "I don't know if she's on the pill."

Another silence. "Neither do I."

"Talk to her about it. All of it."

"Yeah," said Don. "Yeah." Natalia waited, still frozen in silence. She heard Don say a third time, "Yeah."

"I'm quittin', man," said Jack.

"Yeah. Me too."

Natalia waited maybe two or three minutes. It felt like an hour. She rose slowly from the stump, her legs stiff. She took a small step, another, a third—bashed her toe against a rock, stifled a yelp, walked on very slowly, a few metres from the tent. Then more quickly, reached the side of the house, ran around to the deck, and sat on one of the chairs, staring out to sea. Don and Jack. She loved them both so so much. Wonderful. Jack thought she was wonderful. And she felt the same about Jack, irritating as he sometimes could get. But Don not only loved her, he wanted her for himself and forever. And she wanted exactly the same.

Such a long time ago. She tried to recall her body, its glow and tingle. She knew she'd felt those things. But now they were only words, no longer a part of her. Except in memory. She would have to call Don. With Don she had become a being, no longer a daughter or sister merely, but a private entity. A lovely little paradox, that one needs the love of another to become a unique part of the world.

And no, Don never did hurt her. It was she who'd gone away, at eighteen, to California, Berkeley. He had wanted her to be with him at UBC, desperately wanted her, he even proposed marriage. But she'd left. She'd been like Jack. She knew she had to leave, to try living somewhere else. Outside of Vancouver. Outside of Canada. Not because she didn't care for her country. Because she had to know what else was out there. And so she'd hurt Don, deeply wounded him. From the moment Berkeley accepted her, the letter arriving on a Monday in April, she knew she'd be going. The last five months with Don were grievous, and sweet. Though she'd be living in the Bay area didn't mean they wouldn't be together, she'd be back and he'd visit her there. But she knew, like Jack had known two years earlier, that something had come to an end, or to a new beginning.

She took some leftover soup from the fridge, poured it into a pot, and heated it.

The loves of her life. And then there was Stan. A tall, gentle man with, already before thirty, light yellow hair, balding, his eyes bright blue, ever-sparkling. She met him in her last year, he doing a master's degree in chemical engineering but taking a piano course for the pleasure of it. With Natalia for a teacher, she with a teaching fellowship to help pay her way. Only after the course was over, after she'd graduated, would she date him. He charmed her, he dazzled her, she was besotted with him, not since the first years with Don had she been so smitten. They lived together for two years, they married, they were inseparable. They had a child, they loved the child as they loved each other, each of the three part of the others. Nine years of marriage. Until one rainy afternoon the brakes of Stan's car didn't hold, the guardrail gave way, the car tumbled down, and all future years were hacked away. Clean. In one moment life, in the next none. Justine had been seven. She says she remembers her father. Maybe. After fifteen years, he is only frozen memories for Natalia.

She took the soup off the stove, poured it into a mug, picked up the phone, and dialled Don's cellphone number. She didn't need to look it up.

FIVE: Jack Tartarus and Ginny Rixton

Her eyes reflected his flashlight. For a man rarely caught unawares, Tartarus didn't know what to say. None of the obvious questions, How did you get in? Why are you here?
She spoke. "Please."
The word broke through. "Please what, for catsake."
"Go away. Leave the house alone."
"You are Ginny, aren't you."
She breathed out as if she'd been holding all her breath. "Yes. Ginny. Rixton."
He played the light over her, forehead to toes. No ragged long skirt, but jeans, a white shirt, running shoes. Her hair, brushed smooth. Only the large eyes remained familiar, more green than grey in the beam. He drew the sliding doors open. Sunlight filled the living room. The face was suddenly too familiar. Don was right, she'd lost that mesmerizing beauty. But the small nose, full lips, sloping cheeks, though they'd doubled in age, were Ginny's. Not the eyes. He closed the memory down. It no longer had a place. He switched off his flashlight. "How'd you get in?"
"I have a key."
Impossible. "From where?"
She waited, as if deciding what to say. "You probably won't believe me."
"Try me."
Her lips turned up, a tiny twist at the edges. "Sam gave it to me."
Not possible. "You're right. I don't believe you."
"You don't have to. But it's true."
"He gave it to you? Why? When?"
"Before he died." Her smile broadened, her cheeks filled.
"Why?"
"So I could get in. When he wasn't here."

His father somehow involved with—her? Not in a million years. "It makes no sense."

"Have it your way."

"Anyway, what are you doing here?"

"Waiting for you."

"You could've waited outside. This is breaking and entering."

"Entering, sure. But not breaking. Like, I have the key, remember."

"Here without permission of the owner."

"The owner doesn't want the house. What does it matter to the owner?"

He shook his head. "Just tell me, why are you here?"

"I have told you. To keep you from pulling this house apart."

"I could have you arrested."

She laughed.

"What's funny?"

"You sound so pompous."

He jerked his head to the door. "Come on. Get out."

"Not yet."

"What are you . . . ?"

"Don't take the house down. Your father built the house. Your mother felt so much a part of it. It's not yours to tear down. I mean that."

He didn't like it, this so intimate sense of his parents. "Did you sic the Trust on me?"

"Jack. Please don't destroy the house."

Was her non-answer as good as a yes? He took a step toward her. "Ginny. Go away."

"You're going to throw me out."

"If I have to."

"Be careful. I bite."

"I know. Out."

She stood. "I'm sorry about that yesterday. Really."

"So am I." She still looked good in jeans. Not a lot of change in her there. Her face looked good too. Except the strange eyes, their constant blinking. "Come on, out of the house."

81

"No."

"And give me the key."

"It's mine. Sam gave it to me. It's not yours. You weren't around, remember."

He wasn't going to follow her there. "Okay. Why did my father give you the key?"

She sighed. "So I could take care of Hannah."

Tartarus shook his head. "You wouldn't have needed a key. They never locked up."

"He did." Her eyes, dark irises surrounded by white, didn't move from his face. Still that ongoing blinking, every second or two. "If he had to be away."

"Away."

"The village. The big island. He ran his errands."

"My mother would've gone with him."

Ginny shook her head. "At first. Not later."

"Later? When later?"

She turned her head and looked beyond the sliding doors. "The last six months or so."

Damn her. His mother had had more time than six months, way more. If he'd known she—they—would give themselves only six months, he'd have been here. He said nothing.

"Sam had to lock her in. Or she'd wander away." A small, sad smile took Ginny's lips. "I appreciated that, her wandering." The smile fell away. "But for her it was dangerous. She wandered enough in her mind."

Tartarus said at last, "He trusted you? With the key?"

"With her."

"You came to see her? When Sam was away?"

"He'd let me know when he was leaving. And when he came back. And if he missed the ferry. He'd become a great believer in his cell-phone."

That jarred Tartarus. His father had mocked just about all the technology he'd not grown up with. "So you were her—what? Her minder?"

"Her friend. And Sam's." She stared hard at Tartarus. "I came other times too. For either or both of them. To visit."

He could not see his parents befriending this woman. "I don't get it."

"What?"

"Them. And you." She'd had the key for more than ten years . . .

She turned back to him, studying his face. "Shall I show you something?"

"What?"

"Come with me." She reached down beside the hearth chair, pulled up the backpack she'd been carrying yesterday, drew out a sealed beam light and a litre bottle of water. She drank several swallows, put it back in the pack, strode over to the archway, and turned down the hall.

"Where you going?"

"You'll see." Toward the front door, but she turned left, switched on her beam, and headed up the stairs.

At least not to the basement. Just dark, empty space now, his equipment long removed. He flicked the flashlight back on and followed to the landing where the door to his one-time bedroom, directly ahead, stood ajar. She walked past it, on through the narrow hallway by the bathroom at the left, to the door of his parents' bedroom. She played her beam on the handle, grabbed it, and opened the door. Aside from the merest suggestion of light at the windows ahead and left, the room was dark behind drapes and outer closed shutters.

She shot her beam across to the far wall, marched toward the single drape, and pulled it aside. Edges of light marked the contour of the shutters. She unlocked the window, raised it, with one hand held it in place. She picked up a two-by-four leaning on the floor and propped the window open. With a hand on each shutter she drifted them apart. Light streamed into the room.

Ahead of him and halfway across the room stood the big bed that had been his parents', back where it used to be after the renters had replaced it with their own. In place too the nightstands, dresser, and table that he'd left there when he rented the house out. The shelves against the wall to his left, now empty of books. No paintings or lithographs on the walls; he hadn't brought them back. On the table in the far corner, between the two windows, stood four photographs in thin frames. He walked toward them. Three he recognized immediately.

Natalia after her graduation from Berkeley, late-1970s, her brown hair still long, her sparkly eyes and her lips laughing. Himself maybe ten years later, long before the beard and moustache, long before any of his hair had gone grey. His nose already too long, and those tiny ears poking out from under his shag of curling hair. His parents together, his favourite picture of them, both in their fifties, on the dark-blue couch in their Vancouver living room, his mother smiling a bit up at the camera—at their son, Jack, taking the picture, he kneeling across the coffee table from them on the evening of their thirty-fifth wedding anniversary. Hannah wore her brown-grey hair short, a no-nonsense cut that Jack had admired but Sam found harsh. She also wore the dangling earrings she affected, these ones large red cubes hanging eight centimetres down. And an emerald V-neck cashmere sweater that even after twenty years still shone bright in the light of his flash. Tartarus felt a small shudder along his spine. Sam was wearing one of his dozen tweed jackets, a white shirt and a red tie—even when relaxed his father insisted on wearing a tie in the company of others. His hair had already thinned, greying like his weak goatee. Sam's glance was turned not to the camera but at Hannah, a look so filled with conscious veneration that Jack found himself recalling the precise moment of snapping the photo. The instant before the lens opened something must have flicked in Sam's mind and he'd turned to Hannah, the need to tell her right then that he loved her suddenly having become a universe more important than getting his picture taken. Tartarus squeezed his eyes shut.

And opened them. The fourth was a photo he didn't know: facing the camera, his parents much as they'd been the last time he'd seen them alive. On the right, Hannah, her face heavily lined across the brow and at the eyes, sitting at a picnic table bending forward toward the camera. Sam on the left, grown narrow in the shoulders, head straight up, hair and beard thinner but longer than Tartarus remembered, now fully white. Between them, Ginny. She had one arm on Hannah's shoulders, the other on Sam's. Ginny's smile filled her face. His father's smile seemed weary and sad. His mother looked as if she'd learned to smile only recently, the upward twist on her lips a sign of success over earlier ignorance. She looked tired, more lines rising and descending from her mouth, lateraling from its edges. Ginny dominated the photo, pleased with her place between these two. He looked away, picked up the anniversary picture and studied it, hoping for a sense of proximity to them. And to reject the picture of them with Ginny.

He felt her come to his side. He stared harder at the photo.

"Are you okay?"

"What? Oh, sure."

"They were lovely people, both of them."

Tartarus said, "I took this picture."

She said, "I know."

"Who took the one with you?"

"I did," she said. "A timer, and a tripod."

"So. You're still a photographer."

"No. I take pictures. I don't make them."

Tartarus had to keep himself from smiling. "Hmm," he said. "They cared about you."

She waited before saying, "I think so."

He stepped over to the window. The view fell to the southwest, to catch the longest light the year around. Both his parents had craved light. Why why why had they rejected the light!

"How did you meet them?"

She laughed in silence. "They found me."

"Found? How?"

"Here. Sitting on the steps up to your veranda."

"What were you doing there?"

She shook her head. "I don't know."

"I'm sorry?"

"I must have wandered there."

"Wandered."

"I didn't know I was there. Not till I heard Hannah's voice."

"You're not making sense."

She sighed. "Let's go downstairs." She stepped by him, pulled the shutters closed, reversed her window-opening project, and drew the drapes. With his light on again Tartarus led the way, past Natalia's room that she'd always kept locked, no one allowed in unless she were in residence. "What're you doing in there, Natalia?" Jack always called as he passed by.

Back in the living room, Ginny again on the hearth chair took a long drink of water.

Tartarus sat on the couch. What had this woman become since the last time he'd seen her? Why was she important to his parents—if indeed she was? Still an attractive woman. In the years when his parents knew her would she have been a younger version of herself now? Or different? Why had his parents taken to her? Had they? "Okay," he said. "You wandered in."

"I wandered. I don't know if 'in' is right."

Tartarus waited.

"For about three years, a long time ago, I'd find myself in strange places, no idea how I got there. Like I'd been sleepwalking, except I was awake." She stared at the ground and waited.

"Go on."

"Maybe I should start back earlier."

The photo of her with his parents—yes, and the key. They were to blame. Otherwise he'd have said he didn't care where she started, just finish and leave. "If you want."

"Before those three years I—came down with a creepy syndrome. I got very stiff in my joints." When he said nothing she went on, "Stiff, and dry—dry wherever I was supposed to be wet. My saliva glands got inflamed and went dry. My gums dried out. The inside of my nose got so desiccated I'd get nosebleeds two or three times a day. And at night. My eyes couldn't produce tears, and sometimes the corneas were so dry and they itched terribly, I kept scratching them all the time." She raised her head and faced him. "Have you noticed my eyes?"

Larger and rounder. Why was she telling him all this. He said, "They seem—big."

"They look big. It's all the white around the iris. Know why they're like that?"

He shook his head.

"I need eye drops. I've used eye drops, stronger ones all the time, for the last dozen years. Ever since this started. I can keep most everything else damp by drinking a lot of water. But for my eyes I have these drops. They make my eyes look big. Really big. Some people find my eyes scary. Others find them attractive. What do you think of my eyes, Jack?"

What did he think? "They're very—dramatic."

"Good." She laughed a little. "Dramatic."

"Look, Ginny, I've got things to do. What do your eyes have to do with my parents?"

She looked in that moment as rejected as Tartarus had intended her to be. "Nothing. It's the other part, the wandering. When I started to dry out, I began to wander. I have something called Sjögren's syndrome. That's the drying-out part. It's an autoimmune disease. Which means my body is, like, doing this to itself, drying out. Drying out is what happens to most people who have it, dry on surfaces where they should be damp, dry in the joints too. Except with me, I began to wander too. Nobody's ever said that was part of Sjögren's. But for me it was."

"And you wandered. Here to this house."

She nodded.

Hannah had come out the front door and found Ginny sitting on the steps. It was a cool day in early fall. Ginny wore only a light blouse, shorts, and sandals. Hannah did not say, What are you doing there, or, Get away from here. Hannah sat down beside Ginny and said, "Hello."

Ginny said, "Hello. Who are you?"

"I'm Hannah. I live here."

"Oh."

"Where do you live? Nearby?"

"I—I don't know. Where am I?"

"You're at a house on Scott Road."

"Scott?"

"On Crab Island."

"I live on Scott Road."

"See? Then you're close to home."

Ginny shivered. "Oh."

"Would you like to come inside?"

Ginny took a moment before answering, "Yes. Please."

"Would you like some hot soup?"

"Yes. I think so. And, please—a glass of water."

Hannah stood. So did Ginny. Ginny looked at Hannah for the first time. Short grey hair, warm brown eyes, as tall as Ginny. Broad around the middle. She wore a sweatshirt, baggy blue jeans, and running shoes. "Well come in then," said Hannah.

They passed through the doorway down a hall into a kitchen. "You're kind," said Ginny.

"You're cold. This'll warm you up." Hannah went to the stove, took a burbling pot off the heat, in a cabinet found a small bowl, filled it with broth, gave Ginny a spoon, and said, "Eat."

"Are you going to have some?"

"When my husband comes back." She filled a glass with water and handed it to Ginny.

"Oh. Good." She took a spoonful of steaming soup, blew on it, sipped. "This is delicious. Thank you. You have a husband."

"Yes."

"Why?"

"Why do I have a husband? Because—because I live with him. I have for a long time."

"Oh." For that moment the answer satisfied Ginny. She sipped another spoonful.

"Do you have a husband, my dear? Or maybe you're too young. A boyfriend."

"No." And at this moment her world re-entered Ginny. "No," she said again. "I would have." She blew on the soup, took a spoonful from around the edge, and swallowed it. Another spoonful. A third. She added, "Except I don't. Can't. Anymore."

"I'm sure you will."

"No. No." She sipped more soup. "It's too late."

"Of course it's not. You're a young woman. You'll see."

"Who could want me? I'm useless."

"You're lovely. Anyone can see that."

Ginny glanced down at herself, her blouse over braless breasts, her skinny hands, her pale legs coming out of the shorts. "You're wrong," she said. "You can't know." If she could have produced tears, she would have cried.

Hannah waited before asking, "Do you like the soup?"

"Yes. Thank you."

"Do you—do you like my house?"

Ginny glanced about. A plain, practical kitchen. "Yes, I do."

"My house is very wise."

"Wise."

"It suits me. It knows me. It knows me well."

"And you know your house?"

Hannah smiled. "I do. I know it. But my house actually understands me."

The door opened. A man with a kind face came in. "Hello," he said.

"Sam," said Hannah. "I didn't hear the car."

"And who is this?"

"Oh. She's a neighbour. She lives on Scott too." She watched as Ginny took four quick spoonfuls of soup.

"And does she have a name?"

Hannah looked at Ginny. "Do you have a name?"

"Oh. I'm sorry. This is terrible. My name's Ginny. Ginny Rixton."

"Oh. Then Madge is your—?"

"Yes. My mother. Madge."

"We don't know her well. Just to say hello."

Ginny finished the soup. "I should go back. She'll wonder where I am."

"Yes, of course. Sam will drive you."

"I can walk. I think I know where I am."

"It's cold. He'll drive you. Sam, will you?"

"Of course. Would you like to go now, Ginny?"

"Yes. Thank you," she said to Hannah. "I finished my soup." She got up. "It was good."

"Wait a minute," said Hannah. "You'll be cold." She rushed from the kitchen.

89

"Yes, you live close by," said Sam.

"Yes."

"I don't think I've seen you before. Have you been here long? Here, on the island?"

"I think—for a while. With my mother."

"Well then, we'll likely see more of you."

Ginny smiled, suddenly shy. "That'll be nice."

Hannah returned, carrying a coat. "Here, put this on. It'll keep you warm." She held the coat open for Ginny. It was Persian wool, grey tightly wrapped curls. "It's yours," Hannah said.

"Mine?"

"I won't need it anymore."

"No. I—I can't take that."

"Of course you can. Come on now, right arm first." She brought it closer to Ginny.

Ginny put it on and pulled it closed. "It's warm. Thank you. I'll leave it in the car."

"That would make me sad," said Hannah.

"Why?"

"Because then no one would want it."

Slowly Ginny nodded. Sam walked to the door.

Ginny remained quiet for a long time, maybe fifteen seconds. At last she said, "I kept the coat. I could see she'd loved it, once. I could see it wasn't part of her any longer. Like, shedding the parts of her that didn't help her anymore."

Tartarus remembered the coat. Sam had given it to her, a birthday present. Which birthday? What did it matter. "She was like that. Generous, I mean." He sighed.

"Very. With her soup. With her coat. With herself."

He still wanted Ginny to leave. But the story had touched Jack, in that part of him where he kept old memories. "You saw them again."

"Yes. Very soon. And often. They were my friends."

Friends. Ginny, fifteen or so years younger than Tartarus. Could Tartarus ever have said, Hannah and Sam are my friends? Loved his parents, of course. Intimately tied to them. In his own way, responsible to them. But friends? He could tell himself he didn't know. Which would be a lie. They might have become his friends. He'd always enjoyed their company. Friends. If he had allowed it to happen. He hadn't made the time. "They saw you as a friend too?"

"I hope so." She sipped from her bottle. "I think so."

He stood. "You should go now, Ginny."

She looked him square in the eyes. "I'm upsetting you. I'm sorry."

"You're not upsetting me!" He shook his head. "You're not upsetting me."

"You asked me why I came into the house. I said. But why did you?"

"It's my house—"

"But you didn't come in before. Yesterday, you stayed outside."

"Were you watching me?"

"Of course."

"Why?"

"To protect the house. As much as I could." She paused. "Jack?"

"Yes?"

"Wanting to tear down the house—does it have something to do with your parents?"

He studied her face. She was staring directly at him. Then, for the first time Jack had seen, not a blink, not for several seconds. For an instant, her face looked normal. Then the big eyes again, blinking. At last he said, "Of course it does. It was their house."

She nodded. "And why'd you go inside today?"

Tartarus sighed. "My sister is coming. To the island."

"Natalia."

This woman knew his family too well. "Yes."

"That's her picture upstairs."

"Yes. I came into the house to clean away the cobwebs, and the dust. To make up a bed for her." He squinted at her, realizing. "You've been keeping the house clean. Tidy."

"For them."

"Well, that's—generous of you."

"Hannah was always so neat. Even in the last months. There was a lot she'd forget. But she always remembered to keep the house in tip-top shape. That was her phrase for it. Tip-top."

"I remember that." He had kept his room neither clean nor neat, nowhere near his mother's standards. Now he should make up a bed for Natalia, have it ready for her when she arrived. He smiled: Or his mother would be disappointed in him.

"First time I've seen you smile. What's up?"

He shook his head.

"I'll help you make up the bed."

"Hey. I can make a bed."

"Lots easier for two. Besides, I bet you don't know where the linens are."

"In the closet..."

"Wrong."

"That's where I left them two years ago—"

"And where I moved them from."

"Where'd you put them."

"There's an old chest." She grinned. "In the basement. The linens are closed up tight, wrapped in plastic. Against damp and insects."

The basement. Where he'd once had his studio. Tartarus shrugged. "Okay, let's get it."

"You'll need some lamps if anybody's staying here. And at least a little water for the toilet, for your sister. You can pee in the field. We've got lamps at the house I can lend you. You'll have to buy drinking water. Or at least water containers."

She was too damn organized. Had she been planning? "There's the well..."

"Electricity, Jack?"

"Oh. Right."

"Want to borrow a generator? Plug in the well."

She had crossed the line somehow, from antagonist to collaborator. He didn't need this. Crossing lines was a dangerous business. But he followed her.

One reached the basement through a door in the first-floor bedroom. Steps led down. A space barely five and a half feet high where the beams crossed. Tartarus crouched slightly, his usual posture down in the ex-studio. In the early days he'd bashed his head often enough. But it had been his space, his own. The chest sat on six two-by-fours held up by cement blocks. Ginny opened it, picked up a parcel wrapped in plastic, took it out. Similar parcels lay below it. She checked inside the parcel. "This'll do," she announced and led the way to the stairs.

Yes, quickly leave the basement. Tartarus too climbed the stairs.

In the downstairs bedroom Ginny said, "You should have Natalia stay here. No need for her to battle stairs in the dark."

Here, in the guest bed. But Ginny was right. Without light the climb to the second floor could be treacherous, the landing black.

Ginny pulled the curtain aside, opened the window, unlatched the shutters, and pulled them wide. Suddenly the room was bright. The yellow walls looked near to golden even without direct sunlight. They pulled the protective blanket off the bed, wrestled a cover onto the mattress, bottom and top sheet, pillow cases, the blanket on over. Ginny stood back and admired their handiwork. "Pretty good, I'd say. For a house where nobody's slept in two years."

A domestic scene, Tartarus thought. "Yep."

"Except me."

"What?"

"I've slept here."

"When?" Shit. "Why?"

"A few times. To be close to Sam and Hannah."

"Close?"

"I think they like it when I'm here. This is the room I use." She laughed a little. "I take the sheets home and wash them. Every time."

Tartarus shook his head. This then was why Ginny didn't want him to tear the house down. Well, too bad. "I see," was all he said.

"Come on, let's go buy some water. We can stop to pick up the lamps. You should get a little gas burner. And a canister of propane. A little one. Does Natalia drink coffee? Beer?"

"You mean you don't know?"

Ginny giggled and shook her head.

"Both."

"Let's go pick up what we need."

Like they were playing house. Insinuating herself into his day just as she'd keyed her way into the house. Who gave her the right to say *we*? *What we need.* Tartarus had to wonder, Did she think he himself had? "Look, I can get all that stuff myself."

"You don't need to buy lamps, I can lend you those. So I have to come with you. I can lend you a generator too. We don't use it in the summer. We'll get your well going."

"I can buy lamps."

"No need. I have lamps. You won't need extra lamps. Come on. Leave the window open—the room should be aired." She headed for the hallway as if floating and out the front door.

Lock up? Yes. They never used to when they lived here. And why no extra lamps? Bad idea, her driving around town with him. She was the adversary, she'd told the Trust about his plans. He followed her outside. She had already opened the passenger door. "Hey!"

She waved, got in, and closed the door.

He marched to her side of the car, grabbed the handle—She'd locked the door. He glared at her through the glass. She was grinning. He jerked his thumb away, a get-out gesture. She ignored him. He tapped on the window, repeated the thumb sign. "Ginny. Out."

She turned away from him and with her index finger pointed at the driver's seat, jagging her hand up and down, her own imperative: You sit here and drive.

He shook his head, more in exasperation than negation, came around and got in. "Don't you have anything better to do than get on my nerves?"

"Yep," she said. "Organize your house for Natalia the way Sam and Hannah would, if they could themselves. That's why I'm here."

He was also tired of her using his parents as her ongoing trump card. "And you don't think I can do that myself."

"I know you can't. You were a messy kid."

"What?!"

"Hannah told me. 'Once untidy, always untidy,' she said." She gave him a sudden wicked small grin, turned and stared out the window.

Tartarus worked it out: best way to get rid of her, let her sit in the car while he picked up supplies for Natalia. Then they'd come back, when there was nothing else left to do. She'd go away. "Okay," he said, "let's go shopping."

"My house first. The lamps." She opened her bottle and drank more water.

He started the car. Untidy? He drove through the open land to the brush and in among the trees and she said nothing. He would be silent too, whatever she said. At the road he turned left.

She said, "You know the way?"

"Yes." He speeded up, four minutes later turned onto the drive of the house he'd checked out earlier. Unchanged from a couple of hours ago. Was the mother here?

"Drive over to the work-shed."

He did and stopped.

Ginny got out and headed for the shed door. Follow? She had already disappeared inside. He stood in the doorway. She carried three propane lamps and a couple of kerosene lanterns. "My mother's gone down to Victoria for a few days." As if she'd heard his silent question. "Here, get these." She handed him the lamps. "Hold 'em upright, they're full of fuel. We keep them like that. Don't want to fiddle with kerosene when the lights go out." She found a cardboard box, led the way back to the car, and waited at the trunk for him to open it. The box in first, then they wedged the lamps into it standing. "Almost forgot, the generator. Easier if you drive over to the house. There." She pointed to a bulkhead along the side. She walked, he drove. She opened the bulkhead doors and crouched to get in under the house. He got out and followed her. The ground sloped where it led into the crawl space, dark ahead, earth floor near as he could tell. Boxes and pieces of machinery, stacks of lumber, cobwebs new and old everywhere. "Watch your head!" she called. He had to, with the four-foot ceiling. "Here it is." He joined her. The generator, though heavy, had wheels on its feet. They rolled it along the dirt floor to the ramp, up and out, and to the car. They raised it slowly onto the back seat. Clumsy thing. "Okay. Let's go."

95

"Wait." Once more into the shed and she returned with a red twenty-litre gasoline canister. "We'll get gas in the village."

"You don't run that thing from under the house, do you?"

"You crazy? You want us to breathe in the fumes?"

Back into the car. Tartarus said, "Well. Thank you."

"Welcome."

He pointed to the beater parked beside the carport. "That yours?"

"Yep."

"How'd you get to my place?"

"Walked."

"It's a ways."

"Yep."

Okay, onward in silence. And her monosyllables. He headed back as he'd come, past his drive, toward the village. No words till the Co-op. He parked along the side.

"By the door," she said. "Water's heavy."

He moved the car. In the Co-op he ground two hundred grams of dark roast coffee, sacked it, and dropped it into his carriage, followed by two twelve-packs of bottled water, a couple of boxes of crackers, tortilla chips, a jar of salsa. He and Natalia would eat meals out. He paid, they loaded the purchases onto the back seat, and got in.

"Hardware store. It's down—"

"I know where it is." He parked in front. By the door, a notice board. Aikido. Fencing. Pilates. Intro to Water Painting. Find Your Voice. Belly Dancing. He went inside.

Ginny followed him in and strode toward the back. The clerk, Turtle but today without his name badge, nodded at Tartarus and stared at Ginny, Tartarus watching as the clerk's eyes followed her. When he asked Turtle where he could find propane burners, the clerk jerked his head toward Tartarus as if he'd been pulled out of deep thought. Tartarus found the burners, chose one, and took a small canister of propane. He checked out non-electric coffee makers.

"There's one in the house," said Ginny, suddenly appearing.

He paid the clerk. "No name tag today?"

"Nope. Free ride. How's that Fulton working out?"

How indeed. "Not getting as much action as I'd wish right now."

"Yep, that's it."

As if he knows something I don't, Tartarus thought. About the bar, Ginny, the house, me. As they reached the door, Tartarus turned and Turtle quickly looked away. The purchases went into the trunk. Though it was close, they drove to the liquor store. He got out, she followed. A near to silent shadow. Inside he bought two six-packs of pale ale and a sack of ice.

"There's a cooler at the house."

He remembered. In the garage.

She bought a bottle of Merlot. "For when we get back."

Like hell it is. But he said nothing.

They returned to the car, the beer in the trunk beside the produce.

"And now we can stop playing our non-talking games," she said. The sweet, evil smile again. "And because I've been such a great help, you can buy me lunch."

"We're going back." He started the car.

"You don't have food at the house. And you're not going to open the salsa till Natalia gets here. It'll turn bad without a fridge. Let's go to Carleton's."

Why he acceded, Tartarus would never figure out. Maybe because her smile got to him. The tiny malice to it.

She pulled her pack onto her shoulder and they stepped in. Early for lunch, barely noon, and Carleton's was near to empty. Another restaurant with no character. They should have gone to that restaurant past the harbour, Don's friend's place. Now from a window table they could see the dock. The ferry, broad and chunky yet graceful gliding across the water, had just left. Too late for that escape, he thought, and smiled privately at his foolishness. They ordered, clam chowder for him, a burger and fries for Ginny. And a large glass of water.

"Okay," said Tartarus, "the price of this meal includes the answer to my question. Did you tell the Islands Trust I was tearing down my house?"

Ginny leaned back in her seat. That smile again. "Of course," she said.

He'd not expected to get the answer this easily. "Because, as a law-abiding citizen of Crab, you had to."

"Because, as a friend of Sam and Hannah, I had to."

Her damn trump again. "I don't get it. I can maybe see you as their friend. But why does the house itself matter so much?"

She shook her head. "You're not understanding. Let's talk about something else." Before she could head in another direction, the waitress brought Ginny's water. Ginny picked up the glass, a twenty-ounce beer stein with ice cubes, and drank it down in a single quaff.

"Thirsty?"

She squeezed her eyes shut tight. "The cold gets behind my eyes." She pressed the heels of her palms against her eye sockets. "I need to drink water." She lowered her hands.

He nodded. "You told me."

"You know what the worst is about this Sjögren's syndrome?"

"What?"

"I mean, aside from having your beloved fiancé saying he can't handle it, he's gone, and he disappears overnight."

"That happened to you?"

"A long time ago, a long long time ago." She laughed lightly. "So long ago I've forgotten what he looked like. No, that wasn't the worst thing."

He waited. She would tell him.

"All that dryness. All over. Especially my vagina. It gets so terribly dry."

"Ginny." Tartarus sat back. Not a good direction. "Why are you telling me all this?"

She giggled. "I'm impetuous, don't you remember?"

He would keep himself from remembering. It's not worth remembering. He has kept himself from remembering all morning long. He will not remember . . .

Too late.

Maureen had gone away, that was the problem. Gone to be with her sister Elinor. Elinor was pregnant, a difficult pregnancy, and Elinor's husband, Zach, an oil consultant, had been seconded for two years to his firm's office in the United Arab Emirates. They'd not wanted the baby to be born in the UAE. Tartarus didn't like Elinor, nor she him. It was Elinor, a couple of years before, who had introduced Maureen to a man, Karl. Maureen and Karl had a sexual interlude. It lasted seven months. Jack didn't know until it was over. Maureen told him, Maureen full of guilt. But she blamed Jack too, Jack never home, Jack more devoted to photography than to her. Untrue, Jack had ever maintained. His job at the junior college, Jesperton, four courses a term teaching photography, fifty hours a week. A tiny bit of time stolen on weekends, some evenings, for his own photography, and she begrudged him this. So she punished him, he said to her, with Karl.

Maureen and Jack threw blame at each other, argued with little aim, agreed to see a counsellor. Got through the counselling. They would make a change, leave Vancouver. The house on Crab was empty most of the time. If Maureen and Jack wanted it, could put up with Hannah and Sam on some weekends, it was theirs for the interim. Jack would work on his photography. Maureen's homeopathy would be in demand wherever she lived. They moved to Crab, a new start for Jack and Maureen.

They lived quietly on Crab for more than a year. They referred rarely to Maureen's affair. She had gone beyond it. Had Jack? He wasn't sure. Likely. It didn't matter.

It mattered. It remained an itch, small enough and only occasional. Elinor asked Maureen to help in her latter stage of pregnancy. Maureen said she had to go, Elinor truly needed her. Jack dreaded Maureen being in Vancouver, her sister's influence, and likely Karl still on the scene.

"That's long dead," Maureen insisted. "I know you don't like Elinor, for reasons before Karl. I know all that. But she is my sister. I have to go."

"And my show?" In a couple of weeks Jack's first showing, work completed since he'd left Vancouver, new directions he was pleased with, would be presented to the community.

Maureen promised to be back for the show.

The morning of the show she called. Elinor had gone into premature labour. Maureen couldn't leave. The doctors feared for the baby. Implicitly, for the mother as well. Maureen would come to Crab as soon as Elinor was out of danger. A day, a few days, she didn't know.

So no Maureen on Crab.

The show was a success. Friends, slight acquaintances, strangers too, talked to him, told him what he already knew, that he had a wonderful eye. Seven of the twenty-two photographs, a couple of little ones but five of the big ones also, sold that evening. Jack was exhausted. He'd built the frames too, each integral to the image it contained, and hung the show all that day. No, he wouldn't join friends for a beer. He apologized again for Maureen, and explained about Elinor. He again thanked Martin, who ran the gallery, CrabArt, and stepped out into a thin evening rain, unusual for early in September. He marched to his car.

A woman with a scarf over her head intercepted him. "Jack?"

"Yes?" He recognized her. She'd been one of the last to leave, someone he'd not met before, noticed but not part of any group he knew.

"I'd like to talk to you. About your photography."

"Look, I'm wiped. It's been a long day."

"That's fine." She gave him a twisted little smile. "Can I come visit your studio?"

He laughed. "My basement. You'd have to watch your head."

She smiled. "I can do that."

He looked at her face. Quite pretty. Young. Cheeks wet, from the rain. "Sure. Come by."

"Tomorrow?"

"Yeah. Why not. Mid-afternoon? I live on Scott, number—"

"I know. See you then." She smiled again. "You're very good." She walked away.

He didn't even know her name. That was okay. She knew him. At home he poured himself a beer. It would knock him out quickly. He was doing his photography. What he wanted, what he felt he had to be doing. They'd moved to Crab for this, and it was working out. At only thirty-three he could call himself a photographer, the kind who sold his work for real money. Nearly two thousand dollars' worth that evening, half of which went to CrabArt. That was fine.

He checked the answering machine. No messages. He called Maureen. No one home at Elinor's. He told her answering machine about the show. She should call him in the morning.

In the morning they talked. Maureen made congratulatory noises but sounded distant. Elinor had delivered a three-and-a-half-pound boy by Caesarean section. The baby was in intensive care. They had found three cysts in various stages of infection beside the womb. Elinor was very weak, on antibiotics, she wouldn't be able to leave the hospital for a couple of weeks. So Maureen's distraction seemed fair enough, given everything. Still it would have been so good if she'd been there yesterday. He didn't say this. They'd talk again tomorrow.

Three-thirty, a knock on the front door, and he remembered the young woman. He glanced out the living room window. He'd not heard a car. He saw no one, but yesterday's rain had given way to clear blue sky. The firs and cedars were shimmering green. He opened the door. The slender young woman who stood there wore a simple white blouse that left her arms bare, tight khakis, and sandals. Her extraordinary face—pronounced cheekbones beneath eyes in which grey and green flashed against each other, a full smiling mouth, and a little nose—was crowned with thick waving chestnut hair that gleamed deep red-brown.

"I'm Ginny." When he said nothing, she added, "Last night? You said I could come by? To talk about your pictures."

"Oh yes, of course, I'm sorry." He glanced beyond her. "Did you park on the road?"

"No no, I walked. I'm your neighbour. I'm Madge and Rick's daughter."

"Oh. Yes. Of course." Madge and Rick. Maureen knew them a little, Jack less. "Please. Come in." He stepped aside and she entered. The scent of something lightly sweet but heady passed by his nose. "We can sit in the living room. To the left."

She glanced around. Her brow wrinkled. "You don't have your own pictures up?"

He was impressed. The walls were covered with the work of others. His heroes. "You think these aren't mine."

She giggled. "I saw your work yesterday. No, they're not."

"An earlier phase?"

She glanced at his favourite Edwards, at a good Mathier. "Nope."

"You're right. My work's downstairs." She was making him a bit uncomfortable. Yet it pleased him she was here. "Please, sit. I should've brought some of it up."

"That's okay. Wherever it is."

They sat, she on the chair by the fireplace, the sunlight from the window stroking her hair, he on the couch. "I'm sorry, Ginny, I'm being rude. Would you like something to drink?"

An impish smile took her lips. "Like what?"

"Well I can give you coffee, or tea, or some juice."

She closed her eyes and laughed again. "Tea." She looked at him and said, her voice full of sincerity, "Did you know that's what they called pot in the fifties?"

"I did. Tea. Pot. Euphemisms by association?"

"Something like that. I'd like a glass of water, please."

In the kitchen he took down two tumblers. What an extraordinary face. He had to photograph it. Capture that merry fire in her eyes with black and white? Or would he have to compromise by using colour. He filled the glasses. Today he wouldn't have to simulate sunlight.

"Thank you," she said and reached for one of the glasses. Her hand touched his as she took it from him. She turned and glanced around the kitchen. "No pictures here either," she said.

"No, I told you, they're downstairs."

"So." Again that smile, at once off-putting and beckoning. "What are we waiting for?"

"Let's go." She couldn't be twenty, yet had the composure of a woman much older. He led the way. Their silence was suddenly an embarrassment to him, as if he were somehow inadequate. "Do you study photography?"

"Not yet," she said. "But I might."

"Oh. Where? Not here on the island, surely." If she did he'd have seen her before, even if she wasn't actually taking lessons. The photography subculture was small. He entered a ground floor bedroom, passed around the bed to a door. She followed. He stopped.

"I'm off to college at the end of the week. Grantner, down in Seattle. I don't know what they offer in photography. It'll be my first year." For a moment she seemed delicate, vulnerable even. Then she raised her head and the outer maturity returned.

He opened the door. "Wait, I'll turn on the light." He reached around into the space and flicked a switch. Bright light streamed up. Through the door, a wooden stairway down. "Be careful, the steps are narrow. There's a rail." He headed down. "And watch your head. The beams can be deadly."

They stood on the floor. She looked about. Here every surface—wall space, the wooden supports, the sides of the beams—all was covered with photographs, from snapshots to Polaroids to metre-high portraits to a landscape triptych two metres wide. Black and white, coloured, tinted, several daguerreotypes, even two X-rays of hands.

"You've been busy."

He grinned. "You sure all these are mine?"

"There're some that look like they were part of the series in the show. Ones you didn't use. For whatever reason."

He nodded. "You're right. And the rest?"

She reached up and touched a beam with her fingers. She set her head against it. The bottom caught her forehead below the hairline. She stepped back and turned slowly, the full three hundred sixty degrees. Five times her glance came to rest for a couple of seconds. She spent over a minute doing this. At last she stood facing him, took a step in his direction, and said quietly, "Possibly a dozen or so aren't. The rest are. I don't know about the X-rays."

"You have a remarkable eye. You should, you know. Make photographs."

"I may." She turned away.

Had he said something wrong? He needed her to trust her eyes. He said, not realizing why, "You want to see what I'm thinking about working on next?" He'd not shown this material to anyone, not even

Martin. He'd mentioned it to Maureen only once. He hunched his head and shoulders and walked over to the light table. He heard her following. He took an eighteen by twenty-four portfolio from a rack, lay it on the table, opened it. On the first page four black and white photos, six by eights. He moved to one side. She stood beside him and bent down to examine them. The heady scent, light but pervasive, now seemed to surround her. He bent as well, their shoulders near to touching.

The two top photos showed four terraces, in stone. "That's here on the island," he said. "Up by the cliffs. Wind and water and salt have done that. Just wind, water, salt. The sandstone and shale would have been layered millions of years ago when this was all covered with water. Then the land rose and the rock became exposed. So the layers eroded, each at its own pace. And this is the result, nature's homemade terraces."

She studied them carefully and nodded slowly, her right shoulder brushing against his left. "And you saw them. Like that. Up by the cliffs."

"The light was right. I was lucky."

"I've been there many times and I've never seen that." She stood up quickly, too quickly, and the side of her head scraped against a beam. "Aghh!" She staggered a little.

His left hand caught her arm and held it, to keep her from falling. Her face seemed suddenly flushed. "Hey! You okay?"

She squeezed her eyes shut, open, shut, open. "I . . . yeah, I think so." She took his right arm with her left hand, steadying herself. "I think so." She raised her head, half a metre from his face, stared then smiled at him. "Thank you."

He could not take his eyes from her face. The green in her eyes, dominant here in the artificial light, penetrated his skin, his skull, slid into his mind. It pained him, yet the pain brought with it a kind of joy and even, it felt like, hope. Where had this creature come from, how did she get here? He felt her grip on his arm loosen. He released his as well. He said, stupidly, "You're sure?" He, he sensed, was something other than okay.

"I'm fine." She stroked her head. "Will you show me some more?"

"Okay." He would rather look at her than at the photos. But they bent over the table. The two lower photos also looked like terraces. "Have you ever seen, on dirt driveways that slope a little, especially in the fall when millions of fir needles have come down, after heavy rain the needles get pushed along in small bunches till the bunches get too heavy and the water can't push them farther, they became a kind of ridge, and there's flat dirt behind the ridge, and below the ridge the water's gone along and pushed more needles down till they also get too heavy, and on and on down the hill. You get a series of terraces. Fir needle terraces. They're magical."

She stared at the photos. Just as he had described. Terraces. Formed by water and fir needles. "Jack, that's fantastic." She turned her head to face his. "You're amazing."

For easily ten seconds they studied each other's faces. He no longer wanted merely to photograph her face, he needed to touch it, to assure himself it was real. He allowed his hand to reach toward her. He touched her hair. Soft and warm. He let his fingertips glide to her cheek. She remained motionless. He raised his other hand to her face as well. She turned her head a few degrees and her lips brushed his index finger. She brought her hand to his and laid all his fingers over her lips. She began to lift her head, quickly glanced up, no beam, and continued raising her head with his two hands holding her. He too unbent, slowly, following her. They stood. In one move their faces came together, his fingers withdrew from her lips, her lips slanted up to meet his mouth. They kissed, lips stroking lips, his hands again on her cheeks, her right hand now at the back of his head, pulling his mouth hard against hers. Her teeth parted, her tongue flicked his lips, again, till his mouth too opened and their tongues met, hands pulling heads toward each other, tongues conjoining in the same warm space. He realized her eyes were open, which told him his must be too. He wanted, needed, to see everything about her face. Now his arm dropped to her waist and he pulled her tight to him just as she did precisely the same. He felt her breasts firm against his chest, warm through the white blouse, just as he figured she must be feeling his erection tight against her belly. He closed his eyes and pulled her yet tighter to him as if to join with her here in his basement, his studio, his . . .

He was crazy. This was just a kid. A remarkable woman-to-be, now only a kid. Stop it, Jack! Slowly he released his grip on her waist, on her head.

She followed his lead, stepped back, opened her eyes. Saw his face. "Jack? Are you all right?" Concern in her voice, a little fear as well.

"Ginny. I'm sorry. I don't know what came over me."

She grinned. "I know. Me. And you. Us."

"No, I mean, that wasn't fair. Of me."

"Or me. But we did it. And we don't have to stop."

"Ginny. We do. I can't take . . . take that kind of advantage of you."

"Listen, Jack. No advantage." She took his hands and leaned back, her head barely missing a beam. "Hey. I'm eighteen. Haven't been jail bait for five months." She stepped forward again, arms around his back, she leaned her head against his chest.

"Why, Ginny?"

"Why what?"

"Why are you doing this?"

"Why? 'Cause I'm impetuous. Anyway, it's not me doing this. It's us."

His arm went about her as well. He held her for a minute, two. Her scent filled his brain. Had there been scent all the time they'd kissed? Couldn't remember. Should he do this? Could he? Her hand had dropped to his crotch. She pressed her palm against his cock. Just eighteen. Much older. She turned her cheek from his chest, leaned up, and kissed his chin. She turned around, now pressed her bum against his cock and brought his hands up to her breasts. He'd been right, no bra. He kissed the top of her head.

"Let's go," she whispered. She took his hand and not waiting for him to answer led him to the stairs and up to the bedroom. She turned out the lights in the basement studio. He closed the door. They stood facing each other. She reached up and undid the top button of his shirt. And the next. The next.

He let his hands follow her example, more slowly. She had his shirt open by the time his fingers reached her last button. He undid it and let his hands slide underneath. He cupped each young breast and closed his eyes. He could feel her hands on his belt, she undid the clasp, reached for his zipper with one hand, and let her other slide into his pants behind the zipper. What care she took. Where had she learned all this? His pants loosened, fell to his knees. He knelt now and brought his face up to her breasts. He licked them, one by one. They tasted of sweet alien fruit, the source of her scent. Her nipples stood hard, each a little brown pebble crowning a rust-topped hill. He kissed the one, the other. His hands dropped to her jeans. No belt, he undid the zipper, slid his hands round to her bum, and pulled the jeans down. No panties. He marvelled. Her pants were down now. He kissed her, from navel to pubis to navel. She knelt, was pulling his underpants off, sliding them down, now one hand held his cock and squeezed it hard, kneaded it. His loafers came off, and his socks. Her jeans, her sandals. She steered him by his cock to the bed. She sat him on the bed, turned him, leaned over him and took him in her mouth, squeezed, released him, lowered him back, opened herself and slid him in.

They worked each other slowly. And as they worked they recognized each other. Slowly. Then more quickly. And then with all the speed they could bear. They came moments apart. They held each other tight.

He had remembered. The whole of it.

SIX: Frank Bonner and His Beer, and Justine

For the third time since Don went out the door, Frank glanced at his watch. Yes, today is Thursday. Yes, Don has left him alone on the island. Last night Frank had figured it this way, today would be Thursday and Don would go away, off on his lonesome. And he wasn't coming back, not for a while. Frank took the last bite of the sandwich Don had left him, egg salad. Not enough pepper. Don always stinched on the pepper. Frank opened the thermos and poured himself a second cup of tea. Still hot. Good. At least Donnie hadn't screwed up the last of the tea. After the tea had settled, after he'd pissed out some of it, he would get himself a beer. He wondered if Don knew he took a beer every Thursday. No, Don wasn't that observant. Or paranoid. Frank grinned. Or maybe Don did know, just allowed it. No way Frank would ever find that out, sure wasn't about to ask Don.

Jack Tartarus was gone for the day too. Tearing down the house. Good god, what an asshole Jackie had become. A nice kid at ten, even in his teenaged-years. Till he went off to that university. He'd gotten lost there, somewhere. A photographer, what kind of life was that? And not around when Sam and Hannah needed him. Bastard. Come back to tear the house down. Sam had built that house, built it from a good design. Better house than Frank had built, he had to admit it. A good house now after Don renovated it, but till then the place was a shack. He had to give Don that, he'd made the house comfortable. Attractive too. But Sam's house had been comfortable from the start. Still was, Frank figured. And here was Jack, back from wherever the hell he'd gone to, to destroy it, for pissake! What right did Jack have to tear down Sam Tartarus's house? Somebody had to stop him. Maybe Don. No, didn't have the gumption. Who else? Call Gary, Gary'd get his Land Rover out, head over to Scott Road, keep Jack from destroying Sam's great house. Not much of a view, but a fine house. Yeah, get Gary and his Land Rover. Frank headed for the phone, picked it up, stared at it.

No cord? Who'd torn the cord from the phone! Oh. Yeah. The new one, Don brought it home. You could walk anywhere and talk, yeah that's right. The buttons, in the receiver. Nuts how they made phones now.

Call Gary. What the hell was his number. Four-two-three... Had to start with four-two-three, all Crab numbers started with four-two-three. Frank shook his head. Ridiculous, he'd known Gary since coming to the island, couldn't remember the number. When was the last time he'd phoned Gary. Frank couldn't recall. Have to look him up. He found the island phone book, at least he knew where that was. Gary. Gary—Goddamn it Gary! Gary Damiano, there, he remembered. He opened the book, not much of a book but every name on the island was in it, all thirty-one hundred names. Well, not the kids or the wives. Damiano... Frank could see the capital D, not the little letters. Where'd he leave his glasses. In the TV room, there. He ambled to the TV room. Yes, over by the show guide. He put them on and headed back to the phone book. D. Dallaway, Dalmanski, Daniels, Dante. No Damiano? Had to be a Damiano, had to...

Frank felt his knees go weak. He backed to a chair and dropped his backside onto it. No Damiano. No Gary. Goddamn it, no Gary. Of course not. No Gary, no Land Rover. The Land Rover went before Gary did. They'd buried Gary, he and Stretch and Larry and the others, buried him. How could he have forgotten that? No Land Rover. What was it he wanted the Land Rover for? Go for a ride with Gary—No no no—The house, that was it. Sam's house. To stop Jack from destroying the Tartarus house. What a terrible thing, to destroy a house. Ess-oh-bee.

Sylvia would have known what to do. Sylvia, best wife a man could have. She went before Gary did. Long before. She could've stopped Jackie. Jackie would've listened to her. Jackie had liked Sylvia, and she'd been good to him, she understood him. Frank sure didn't understand him. Who could understand a man who'd destroy a perfectly good strong house. And Don had invited this man, invited him into Frank's house. To sleep in the room next to Frank's bedroom. Don's study. Don had his stuff so organized. Don got upset when anybody went into that study. Even Frank. But he'd brought in Jack, he who demolished houses, put him in the study. What if Jack had messed up Don's stuff? Frank knew exactly what. Don, who couldn't see any problems with Jack tearing down Sam's house, would blame Frank for any mess in the study.

Frank stood. Better check out the study, make sure everything's okay. Afterwards he'd see what was on TV, Sportsnet could be okay, they'd have something. In the kitchen he opened the door on the left. A small room, even smaller with the futon turned into a bed. The bed was made up, all the corners tight. To its right Don's desk, a roll top, once Frank's father's, stood closed. The drawers on the three tall filing cabinets, closed also. Long ago Don had kept his teaching materials there. The closet door was closed, the window three inches open. On the left, the stuff that didn't belong in the room, Jack's suitcase and a couple of mid-sized container boxes. On top of one of the boxes lay a CD, out of its case. That was messy. Frank poked at the CD with his cane. It slid to the floor. He bent, picked it up. A picture of a fire. Actually, just some flames. It said, in block letters, *FIRE AND THE PHOENIX*, and in regular letters, Tartarus. It also said, DVD. Aha! A movie. Made by Jack—A dangerous movie about tearing down houses? Maybe about torching houses. He should watch it, see if it was dangerous. Just take it? This was his house, he could take anything. Flames. Red and sort of brown and some yellow and a wiggly line like copper. He'd never thought of that before, that fire came in different colours.

In the living room he turned on the TV, shifted it over to the DVD player, dropped the disk on the deck, watched the deck disappear into the machine. A rectangle on the screen now held the words *FIRE AND THE PHOENIX*. Like on the jacket. Underneath it said, FOR MAUREEN. Frank clicked. Two more rectangles: 1. The film. 2. An interview with Tartarus. Frank didn't need any more talk from Jackie, he'd heard enough of that prattle. He pressed 1. More words on the screen. Wasn't this supposed to be a movie? He read what it said.

Phoenix unites death and childhood, pyre and candle.
Old age fills with phoenixical dreams. One dies afire with one's memories; and yet, because one keeps on loving even as one

burns, one grows worthy once more of the eternal love of one's experience.

Jean Bachelard

Huh?

At the bottom, another rectangle: 1. Begin. Frank pressed 1.

For forty minutes Frank heard music he later couldn't recall while watching more flames than he'd seen in his life, tiny candle flames growing huge, fearful crackling flames cutting across dry grasslands, flames face-on through glass and flames from above, flames all the colours of the spectrum—green flames growing purple, orange flames blackening, fire of a hundred descriptions. He tried to make out what in fact was burning but almost never could. The grass, yes, and maybe one sequence of a forest fire, for a moment something that looked like a tree flare, but he couldn't be sure. Small fires first, flames growing in intensity, burning whatever lay before or beside them, leaving nothing behind. Except, sometimes, ash. It didn't make sense, fire was dangerous, destructive, evil sometimes, but he was fascinated, had to be an evil film but he couldn't figure out why. He'd forgotten how much he'd loved sitting in front of a fire when he'd been a kid, a campfire but also a couple of times at home, flames dancing around, no way of predicting where a flame would go next. This was before television, and he'd loved the flames. Here they'd had a regular fireplace when he and Sylvia built the place but Don replaced it with a gas fire and those weren't real flames. He remembered a small boy, a sick small boy, little Frank. Chicken pox was what it was, and his father had taken him from his bed and brought him into the den to be in front of the fireplace. They rarely made a fire in there, his mother thought it could be dangerous. But that day, when Frank had all those red, itchy blotches on his skin, his father made up a bed on the couch and started a fire for Frank to stare at. Frank thought, my father made that fire and the chicken pox faded away. Burned away, he could almost say. Burned right off his skin, a cool fire taking away his chicken pox. On the TV the fire burned softly, the flames swept across the screen, edges of flame danced lightly at the top of the screen as if trying to escape from inside the monitor. Slowly the flames decreased in size and intensity, leaving behind glowing coals, red and black, and he still couldn't tell what had been burning. Slowly the coals shrank to darkness except for a tiny dot of flame at the middle of the screen, a bright red spot in the centre of black. Then the black brightened into a grey, a grey-blue, a bright blue, an intense blue sky, and at its centre the spot evolved into a flame, a single yellow flame from a tiny candle. The candle grew, increasing in breadth and height, expanding yet more quickly. Then the screen swept up to the flame, a huge yellow-red flame tall and broad as the whole screen, the screen in front of Frank's eyes burning, Frank's eyes themselves burning, the screen ever redder, deep rose red—And nothing. A white screen. It slowly darkened and became black.

Frank stared. He felt as if he'd been hypnotized. Blinded. He wiped his eyes. He saw the flames on the inside of his eyelids. On the black screen the credits ran in red. He squeezed his eyes shut, opened them wide, shut again. Red and orange flames burned the underside of his lids. He breathed deeply and opened his eyes again. A blank screen now. Okay.

He suddenly thought of Sylvia. Sylvia would have said something smart about the movie. She'd say what she thought, she'd think whatever she thought was just a normal thing to say. No big deal. She'd know why Jack Tartarus's movie was dangerous. She used to make Frank feel smart too, just by having her beside him. She was his wife, he'd chosen her. And she'd chosen him. They'd not only been husband and wife, they'd been friends. Friends who planned things. They'd planned Donnie, for a long time they planned Donnie. They'd spent long evenings together, he telling Sylvia about the new machine he needed to buy, speed up making casts by fifty percent, or about the dentist he supplied out in Richmond, the one who tried to cheat him till Frank figured a way to cheat him back. And Sylvia would laugh, or help him work a problem through. Big problems, little problems. Your biggest problem, Frank, she'd say, is you. Trouble was he knew this, he'd been embarrassed by it. He got angry easily. So many things to be angry about, the world was full of ess-oh-bees. All around him things went wrong, would grow wronger next week. He'd go into a funk. Only Sylvia could pull him out of it. He'd loved her, so much. Hell, he still loved her. His wife, his friend. She knew all the holes he dug for himself. Like any good friend. Like Sam and Hannah. The four of them, friends. That didn't happen much, where each of four people liked the other three. He'd not thought about that before. But it didn't seem like much of a new thought. Sylvia and Hannah were friends, good friends. He and Sam too. Sam, Hannah, Sylvia. And Frank, the only one left. Oh dear god.

Sam and Don, friends too. Don was still here. But not today. Today Frank was alone.

Sometimes Frank enjoyed being alone. Like now. Some things Frank couldn't do so easily when Don was around. Frank blasted out a fart. Like that. Don hated it when Frank farted. Frank giggled. Like get a beer for himself in the middle of the day. Get a beer before peeing out the tea. He headed for the kitchen. From the fridge he stole a beer, Coors. He didn't mind Coors that much, just told Don he hated it. Had to keep Donnie on his toes. Donnie was a good kid, he admitted that. Mostly to himself. Only to himself. Maybe he should say that to Donnie, Don, I like you a lot, you're a good kid. And Donnie was good to him, took him around, protected him. Still it was important to keep Donnie on his toes. Frank liked that, Donnie on his toes.

He headed out onto the deck. A bit of sea breeze but the sun was hot. He liked that too, a cold wet beer on a hot dry day. The sea swells broke into froth when they reached the shore, the tide high enough to catch the boulders below the house. He sipped beer. Not great. Not bad. His throat had gone dry. Parched, you might say. Must've been that terrible movie, all those flames going right to his throat. He sipped, stared at the sea, sipped, listened to the waves.

He liked drinking beer by himself but he preferred drinking in company. Just one other person was enough. Even Donnie. They'd have a beer together, out here on the deck at the end of the day, or in the winter in the living room by the fire. Yesterday, was it only yesterday? he didn't have a beer with Don because Jackie was here. Jack had brought the pale ale, damn that was good. Except they wouldn't give him any. Not more than one. Had to take the others for himself. Jack would have drunk it all. No IPA for Frank. Frank didn't want to drink with Jack because Jack was pulling down Sam and Hannah's house. Son of a bitch. He used to like to drink a beer with Sam, sitting on the deck with Sam and Hannah and Sylvia, listening to the waves lap the shore. Now there was just Donnie left. And Donnie would stay. Not go to what's her name, Jack's sister, over there in Vancouver. Stay right here on Crab. Didn't have the gumption to leave Crab. Yeah, good thing too. Because in the end, Frank knew, he depended on Donnie. Well, for some things. Anyway, Donnie was staying. Frank could see that.

He sipped but the bottle was empty. They put less and less in these damn bottles all the time. He belched. He needed to pee. He went to pee. He brought the bottle to the sink and rinsed it. Don would know he'd stolen a beer if there was old beer smell in one of the bottles because Don always rinsed the bottles before taking them back. Perfect, neat Don. He wanted another beer, but Don would notice. One beer could disappear but not two. Sometimes he'd have a beer with Sam at The Pub. Hey! He could go to The Pub now, have another beer.

One late afternoon, early August, they were at The Pub. Sam had called Frank. "Come to The Pub, need to talk to you." Frank remembered, clear as if it'd been yesterday. Sam was already there, and Frank walked in. "Hey, Sam."

"Frank." Sam had a table by the window looking out at the ferry dock. No ferry, just cars waiting. Sam's pint of beer was a third gone.

Frank ordered a pint and drank a third of it soon as it arrived. "Now we're even."

"No we're not." Sam drank another third.

"I'll wait. What's up?"

"Nothing new."

"Same old."

"Same old same old and I'm more worried. More and more worried."

"Something changing?"

"More of the same. Except..."

"Except."

"Little things. Like, she goes to bed right after supper."

"Maybe she's tired."

"Not tired like that."

"Worn out, she says."

"Come on. Hannah's not worn out. She's sixty-five, for shitsake. Just barely old enough to travel the ferries for free."

"Say what you want. It worries me."

"It's just a phase, Sam."

"Adolescents have phases. Not Hannah."

Frank sipped beer. "I've caught up with you."

"And her hips aren't getting any better."

"She should get on a list."

"She's not going to have any replacement, she says."

"I know she says it. She should still get on the list. She'll want one, one day."

"She says no."

"I'll talk to her. Invite me to dinner, I'll convince her."

"You don't need an invitation. Just drop by."

"Make it a formal thing. Invite me."

"Formal schmormal. You're invited."

"Talk to Hannah about inviting me."

"She'll think it's peculiar, inviting."

"Let her. Tell her it's a special occasion."

"What's the special part?"

"Me convincing her to get her hips on a list."

"It won't work."

"And why not?"

"She's got one answer. Her brain's going, she says. Who needs new hips when you don't have a brain. She says, 'Give me a brain transplant.'"

"A brain transplant, that'd be good. If the government paid."

"She's scared of her brain."

"She should be scared about her hips. Get her on the list. I'll convince her." Frank drained his beer. "Gotta take a piss." He left Sam at the table. How clear it all comes back, Sam sitting at the table, himself going for a piss. Then Frank was back at the table, but Sam was following the waiter to the bar. Now Sam was talking on the phone. Frank

115

couldn't hear. But right away Sam came back. "It's Hannah," he said. "We've got to go." Sam was already going.

Frank jumped up, left some cash by the beer mugs, followed. "What about Hannah?"

"The girl, young woman, few houses away. She found Hannah, can of gasoline, spreading it." He leapt into his little Nissan truck. "Tell you when we get there."

They roared down South Road, onto Arbutus, doubling speed limits. Fastest speed ever driven on Arbutus by a man in his seventies, Frank figured. Two-tire banking turns on Scott and down the Tartarus drive to the front of the house. An old Pontiac station wagon to one side. Sitting on the front steps, the girl Ginny and Hannah. A pile of singed blankets beside the girl.

Sam, leaping from his Volvo. Ginny, her arm about Hannah. "Ginny! What happened?"

Frank arriving in time to hear, ". . . how Hannah was doing, a visit, a cup of tea. She'd gotten out somehow. The gasoline, lucky the canister was nearly empty, she'd spread all there was on the grass, over there." Ginny pointed. Burnt grass, a patch eight-ten metres in diameter. Unburnt dry grass around it, ready for fire. "I grabbed some blankets from the closet, spread them on the fire, it was creeping into the dry grass. I got Hannah to come with me, we jumped on the blankets at the edges of the fire. It's out, but the blankets are a mess."

Sam said, "Ginny, thank you." To Hannah, "Are you all right?" Hannah said nothing. "Please?" He sat beside her and brought her head to his shoulder. They sat still.

Frank stared at the blankets. He went over to them, picked up one, folded it. Then Ginny was beside him, she picked up another, folded it. Four blankets in all. "I can take them," said Frank, "I'll dispose of them." Ginny nodded. Frank said to Hannah, "Your hips must be getting better, Hannah, putting out the fire like that."

Hannah said, "I don't know why."

"What don't you know why?" asked Sam.

"I don't know. I just don't know."

Frank hadn't convinced her about her hips. He'd only drunk a beer with Sam at The Pub. Later too he never convinced her. Too late, too late.

Yes. He'd have a beer at The Pub again. Not with Sam. He could head down there. Could he? Course he could. Cane? There by his chair in the living room. He marched to the front door, out—Where was his Grand Marquis? Somebody's stolen the Grand Marquis! Nothing there except Don's van, that VW thing with some kind of German name. That goddamn Jack Tartarus, stolen his Merc! Don would know where Tartarus had hidden it, he'd ask Don . . .

    He stopped. He smiled. He knew where the Merc was. With Don. Don drove it these days. Don took it. Then and there Frank decided he didn't approve of Don driving his Merc. First, the Merc was Frank's. Second, it left him without transportation. Or—maybe not. The van. If he wanted to take it for a spin, who'd stop him. Don was far away, out by his lonesome.

    Back to the kitchen. Yep, keys hanging right where they ought to be, Don put things back where they belonged. Now, what else. Wallet, better take the wallet. He headed for his room. Where the hell was the wallet. Right in the place he put it. But where was that? When did he last see it? Must've been the day he and Don went to lunch, Saturday that'd be. Wait, Don paid, Don took him to lunch. Maybe he hadn't taken the wallet on Saturday. Then where was it? He checked the pockets of his pants hanging in the closet. Nope. Under the bed. Not there. His chest of drawers? Top shelf, just junk. Underpants in the middle. Socks and T-shirts in the bottom. He started to slide the drawer closed and stopped. Reached in. Beneath the T-shirt pile. Yep! Well hidden, no robber'd ever find it. He looked inside the billfold. Forty-five dollars. What else? Keys, wallet, that's it. He took his cane and headed for the van. Westphalia. Yep, German.

    He got in behind the wheel. The seat seemed low, hard to see above the dash. Raise the seat? He reached under, found a lever, yanked. Nothing happened. Old piece of junk. He went back to the house and came out with a pillow. He sat on it. Okay, perfect. He rolled down the window, slid the key into the ignition, and turned. The van leapt forward. The engine sputtered, died. What, Don leaving the van in gear? Frank grinned. Gears, there's the trick. The van had a stick shift! Long time since he'd shifted gears. But that's something you don't forget, shifting up and down. Like riding a bicycle, you always know how not to fall off. Clutch must be down there someplace. He felt around with his foot. Yep, there it was, the third pedal. Left foot. He could do that. Clutch in, stick shift into neutral. Neutral's in the middle, middle of the H. He found the middle, left right left right, lots of space there. He stepped on the clutch again, just to be sure, and turned the key. Ignition, and the van stayed in place. Slowly he released the clutch. Still no movement. Good. Now into first. Down on the clutch. Should be up and left, upper left arm of the H. Easy, he released the clutch. The van rolled forward. He swung the wheel hard to the right but the van's turning radius was for shit and he braked inches from the cosmos bed. Into neutral again. Where was reverse? Used to be a hard push to the right at the middle of the H, then down along an extension of the H. He shoved, the stick moved—but wouldn't go down. Wait, there's a trick here. Something about ramming the stick into the belly of the van. He tried. There it went. He eased off the clutch and backed away from the cosmos, and swung the wheel left. Stopped. Okay. Plenty of room now. Impressed with himself, he was. Long time since he'd done that.

He shifted into second, no more experiments till the road. There he slowed and turned right. Along West Road now, into third and picking up speed. Fourth, and he hit seventy kilometres. But at sixty the van was already vibrating, piece of shit. Slower, sixty was the limit anyhow. Didn't want to get a ticket, heehee. He leaned his left arm out the window. The hot air felt good. He could practically taste that beer. He drove past Oyster's. Maybe Don could take him there Saturday. No, Don liked that Thyme place, liked having his time with—with what's-her-name. Frank liked looking at her. Danger lay that way. No, think positive, positive.

Yeah, great to be behind the wheel again, even this rattletrap. Make sure Don takes his own damn van from now on, leave the Grand Marquis to its rightful owner. That beer was going to be effin' good.

Ahead, the village. Past the Arbutus, sure as hell not going there.

The village centre looked strange, back on Saturday everything was normal. Maybe his unusual position, higher than ordinary. And in the driver's seat. Yeah, that'd be it. Now down to the ferry dock, The Dock Pub. He slowed. He wanted that beer, wanted it bad. To get to the beer, he'd have to walk into The Pub. He hadn't been to The Pub in years, ever since . . . Ever since. Who would he find there? Probably wouldn't know anybody, have to drink his beer alone. Or maybe he'd know—people. Each and every one of them. They'd all know him, bet on it, know about the—the—the—something he'd done. He knew about the hydrant. The van engine coughed, began to stall. He shoved in the clutch. Ten kilometres an hour in fourth, not good, into first. The van crawled past The Pub. At the corner he turned. Ridiculous, just park. Walk in. He circled the block and returned to The Pub. He pulled into its parking lot, killed the engine. Sat behind the wheel. Thought about his beer. He reached for the door handle. He touched it, held it. He stared ahead, through the windshield, toward the ferry dock. He released the handle. He stepped on the clutch, turned the key. Into reverse—A huge blast of a horn, he slammed on the brake. No bash of metal, no sickly crunch. Into neutral. He checked the side mirror. A beater, an old Ford, pulled past, passenger window open. A fat-faced girl leaned out and gave him the finger, yelled, "Asshole!" and sped away.

He breathed deep, in, out. He didn't need that again. Slowly into reverse, check each mirror, nobody, and he backed out. He realized both hands on the wheel were sweating and the wheel was slippery. Into first. He drove forward, away from The Pub. He pulled to the side of the road. Stopped. A hundred metres from the temptation of The Pub. Goddamn, he wanted that beer.

But there's other ways in the world of getting a beer, right? Don brought beer home, that pisswater Coors. Don had to have bought the beer here. At the liquor store. Over there, just off to the right. Okay, he'd do it. Buy a six-pack, take it home, drink it on the deck, and listen to the waves. He cut the engine, got out, felt in his pants for his wallet, took his stick, and marched real slow down the road. He could have driven. Now he'd have to carry the beer back. What the hell, what does a six-pack weigh? He went in, found the beer section. And look at that!

Half a dozen brands of pale ale. Oh Donnie, how could you do that? All these years, nothing but Coors.

He pulled a six-pack of some green-labelled bottles of pale ale off the shelf. Paid for it. Yes, he did want a bag. He walked out, stick in one hand, his own personal, private beer in the other. He opened the door, got in, six-pack on the seat beside him, started the van as if he'd been starting this van all his life. He headed back, past the ferry landing, past the big sign FIRE HAZARD TODAY with the arrow pointing to EXTREME. Fire everywhere today. Creepy movie. Dangerous. Staying at Frank's home. Son of a bitch Jack. Shouting at Frank in the middle of the night. Shut the fuck up! that's what he'd yelled. At Frank. In his own house. His own bed. Goddamn, he'd been scared. Terrible dream. Terrible. Monster creatures, they had Donnie, come over him out of nowhere, dragging him. Goddamn. And then Jack, shouting.

Soon he'd be home. He reached over to the six-pack, touched the bag. Cold, like the beer inside. Wonderful. He could if he wanted stop right here on the verge, have one right now. No, not smart, best to drink in the privacy of his house. Before Don came back. Don, who never bought good beer, no fair of Don. But now Frank knew about the good beer, he'd make Don . . .

Fuck. How would Don know you could get pale ale at the liquor store? Somebody'd have to tell him. Which had to be, well, Frank. And admit he'd gone to the liquor store and bought beer. Which he couldn't do. Shit, piss, and corruption! In fact he mustn't bring the beer to the house, what would he do with the bottles, throw them into the ocean? If Don got a whiff about something like that . . . He'd have to find somewhere. Some public place but not too public, don't want to get caught drinking beer in public. Not the beach, with this heat too many people there. Or the cliffs, way too public. Maybe out at the lighthouse. Did people go there in the summer? Good idea, down to Lighthouse Point.

South Road ahead, he could see the yellow triangle with the T and the stop sign. He stopped and looked both ways, a law-abiding driver. Probably first time anyone ever actually stopped at that sign. He turned right, down along Point Road, the land heavily treed here through winding hilly country, second growth nearly fifty years old, he remembered Don saying. He didn't remember the curves as so sharp so he took it slower. Goddamn van banked like a hearse. Three-four kilometres of this and the landscape opened up. Logged? Maybe burned off, he couldn't remember. Maybe just too rocky to grow trees. He'd always liked the peninsula, first part of it high above the sea, sea ahead, sea left and right. You could come here really only in the summer, in the heat. Rest of the year the wind would blast through you.

Get off the road before the lighthouse. A few cars at the end, none here. He parked. The land sloped down, toward the cliff edge. He pulled the handbrake tight. Fine view, looking across the strait to the Coast Range. Same as from the house looking to the mainland but from home he hadn't noticed, not much snowpack over there this year. Same view was good, he could pretend he was sitting on his deck, drinking beer at home. Get out? He rolled down the passenger window. The breeze blew through the van. No need to leave his privacy. Open the bag, take a bottle from the pack. And . . . No bottle opener. Damn! Damn, damn, damn! Maybe screw it off? He checked the top. Threads in the glass? Looked like. He found a rag under the seat to protect his hand and tried to turn the cap. Didn't budge. Again. Nothing. Maybe a different bottle? Same thing. What, go home, find a bottle opener, come back? He wanted his damn beer now.

Tailgate parties! Incredible, his brain working overtime this afternoon. Football games, the tailgate of somebody's station wagon down, a case of beer. Friends. Sylvia. No opener. He'd figured out how to use the wagon's back-door lock as a churchkey. Impressing Sylvia no end. He grabbed a bottle, got out, marched around to the rear, and pulled the doors open. All kinds of shelves in there, and boxes. Hey, a little refrigerator. Maybe Don kept beer in the fridge, wouldn't that be the irony of ironies. No, Frank couldn't take one, Don would notice. But Frank could put his six-pack in, keep it cold. After, on the way back.

He checked the lock. Not configured the way he remembered. On a station wagon the tailgate opened down, nice and horizontal, not like these right and left doors. Maybe angling the lid against the place where the latch went in. He caught the cap against it, yanked at the bottle, the bottle pulled free. Another yank . . . Yes! Beer fuzzed from the bottle top. He put his mouth around it and sucked in the foam. Delicious, delicious. He held the bottle before him and toasted the sea below. To life! To life and love. Well, to a little lust anyway. Not that he could ever do anything about it. Well maybe his body could, his many-year-old body. Had to be over eighty, he remembered, he'd had an eightieth. Four score years, Donnie had pronounced. And what good did they do this body that he could maybe still fuck with but who could there ever be again who'd want to join him. Four score. And he'd never score again. Ah well.

He sat on the ground and took a deep swallow. Pale ale, his greatest pleasure these days. End of scoring. Donnie scored with her, with... with... Frank pushed his brain hard, the restaurant, Thyme, Eating Thyme, sounded like eating, eating... Etain. With her. And here was Jack Tartarus. Tartarus and his fire film. Was that how Jack scored these days, with fire? Long ago Jack had scored with... with another what's-her-name. He'd find it, today was turning into a good day for remembering. Pretty little thing, if he recollected. Long hair, that seemed right. Yes, that red hair, copper. Like those flames in the movie. He could almost see her face.

Only the girls had cried with him, he remembered that too. They'd brought him to Sam's house. Sam and Hannah. Jack and... He sipped beer and squeezed his eyes shut... Jack and... her, his wife, red-haired wife. Donnie and... and Jack's sister. The sister, the wife, they'd cried. Donnie? He cried later, not then. Had Hannah cried? Frank had cried for Hannah. For Sam too, he remembered that. But that was later. That afternoon after Sylvia's funeral? No, after the wake, down at the Arbutus, fifty-sixty people. Then they brought him to the Tartarus house. They talked about Sylvia, nothing but Sylvia. And the girls had cried, he could see their faces. Natalia! That was Jack's sister. Don's—friend. Goddamn it, she always showed up when her brother was on Crab. Always. And she showed up at Frank's and Don's house. She'd take Don off for... walks, that's what she called them. Ha! Frank knew. She was luring Don away from Frank. With her allures. Now here was Jackie again. So she'd be here again. Goddamn.

But back then she'd sat with him on the couch, they'd stared into the fire. She'd put her arm around him and leaned her head on his shoulder, they'd both cried, together they'd cried and people told stories about Sylvia. Then Natalia was gone and Jack's wife sat beside him, held his hand. He hadn't wanted to cry but he couldn't stop himself, and she cried too, Jack's wife... name... name... He took a large swallow of beer. Very pretty, she was. Lots of red hair, if he remembered right.

Maybe still pretty. But he didn't think so. He stood. What a day, a fine day. All those memories. Not to mention the beer. Except for that movie. Did Jack want to burn down Crab? Frank raised the bottle to his lips. Nothing left. Better have another. What, two beers in the middle of the day? He glanced at his watch. The middle no longer. Over an hour since the first. One more, couldn't hurt. Up front, another bottle, back to the rear, cap in. Cap didn't want to catch. Come on, cap, again. Nope, won't catch. He checked the latch hold. It didn't look right, like it had pulled away or something. He ran his fingers on it. Nothing there for a bottle cap to grip on to. Funny, it had worked before. Try the front? The passenger door, yep, similar catch. Bottle cap in, yank... Try again. In. Yank. Success. Again he slurped foam. The very best day.

A walk? Why not. Bottle in one hand, stick in the other. A sip. Just fine. To the rim of the cliff. Someone had placed a bench there. Just for him. A commemorative plaque, some name. Given by... He couldn't make it out. He stared down at the ocean below, not much spray on the rocks. He sat on the bench. Maybe in honour of someone who'd fallen off here. Or jumped. Killed himself. Herself. Maybe two of them. People did that. Damn you, Sam. And Hannah. How... No. He sipped his beer. Good beer, a fine day...

Maureen! The wife's name, Jack's wife. She'd held his hand, she'd cried with him. He'd never realized they'd been such good friends, Maureen and Sylvia. She'd been powerfully shaken, Maureen had. Frank breathed hard. He belched hard. He could smell the beer on his breath. Still tasted good, second time across the tongue. Not as good as the first. He took a long swallow. Nothing like it in the world. Maureen. Why hadn't she come back to Crab with Jack? Didn't want her here when he tore down the house? Yeah, she wouldn't want to watch the house come down. No woman in her right mind would. Not something to have happen to a house she'd loved so much. Or maybe she wasn't just left behind, had he divorced her? Heehee, or maybe she'd divorced him. But that didn't feel right. They hadn't divorced. He took a swallow of beer. Last he remembered, they'd been very close. Loved each other, Don always said, Jack and Maureen loved each other as no two other people he knew. Did Jack and Maureen have kids? Frank couldn't remember. No, she'd gotten sick, that was it. What kind of sick? Real sick and she left the island, left the Tartarus house, off to Vancouver, he seemed to recall. Never came back. Jack had come back, a few times. And his sister. Walking with Don. Not Maureen. She'd stayed . . . stayed away. Did she die? Maybe she died. He drank down a deep swallow. Maybe she died. He stared at the beer bottle, its green label. First-rate beer. He looked at his watch. Nearly four. When did Don say he'd be back? Hadn't mentioned it, if Frank remembered right. Usually returned around—well, before evening. Time to get back. Had to hide the empty bottles. He laughed aloud. Time to hide the full ones too.

Up to the van. Empty bottles in with the full ones. Shut the back doors. Slam. The right door bounced open. He grabbed the handle, pushed the door tight, turned the handle. The lock didn't bite. Tried again. Nope. He'd done something. Wouldn't tell Donnie. Maybe Don wouldn't notice. Something must've happened, Donnie.

Behind the wheel. He reached over to the passenger door handle and yanked it shut. It didn't close. He got out, twisted the handle, pushed the door to, but some kind of blockage kept it from closing. Damn, if he'd messed up that lock too . . . He let the door swing open and he ran his finger against the lock-catch. Maybe he'd pulled something away with the beer cap. Maybe the catch was tin, or plastic. Goddamn, this van, what a piece of shit. Used to be able to open a hundred bottles on a lock, a thousand. He checked his watch. Getting on, time to head back. He climbed in again, seat belt on. He automatically reached toward the passenger door, but the belt held him in place. He released it, reached again for the passenger door, grabbed it, and pulled it closed. It slid open. Just a little open. It'd be fine, leave it, get going. He stepped on the clutch, turned the key. The engine turned over. Into gear, gas, the engine roared, the van stayed in place. Shit, what now. Back into neutral. Gear shift fine, everything fine except the door. He saw it then, the handbrake. He laughed a little. Just concentrate. He released the brake, again into gear. The van inched forward, toward the cliff edge. He slammed on the brake and the engine died. He must have missed reverse. Okay, one more time. Neutral, start, clutch, reverse aaalllll the way to the right, then down hard. He released the clutch with extreme care. The van rolled backward up the slope, out onto the road, and the passenger door opened wide. From his open window he could see a couple of cars coming from the Point, but they were far away. The wind pressure would keep the door closed while he was driving. He clasped the seat belt tight. He'd be fine. A one-point turn and he was headed home.

A first-class day. Couple of beers, a real treat. They didn't hurt him one bit. And the door was staying shut. He shifted into third, checked his watch. Maybe too long a good time. What if Don was already back when Frank returned? Only thing to do, tell Don what he'd done and take it like a man. Don would be mad. Well, Frank could handle that. Couple of days of Don mad. And then no more, Don didn't stay mad for too long.

He left open land behind and wound into the forest. Hurry. Into fourth, heavy on the gas. Sixty, seventy, the van vibrating again, better slow down, curve coming. He felt for the brake, stepped on it hard, and the truck surged ahead. Damn! Where the hell's the brake? Foot off the gas, but it was a downhill slope to the curve and the van wouldn't slow, and the wheel was wet like his hands and it wouldn't turn. A brilliant thought: into neutral and yank the handbrake! The van crossed the centre line and hit the left verge, sloped into a ditch, the left-front tire caught and threw the van forward rear over front and onto the farther bank, the back door flew open, boxes and a small refrigerator bounced out. The van slid along its passenger side and stopped against two large firs.

The drivers of both cars behind the van had seen it leave the road. Both braked hard at the curve, Etain's Toyota the second car there.

"Stay here!" she shouted at Patrick in the back with the dog. She knew the van so very well. She leapt from the car, she screamed, "Don! Don!"

The driver of the first car, a man in his thirties, had reached the van and was peering through the shattered windshield. Etain caught up. "Don!" she shouted again. "Can you see anyone? Is he all right?"

"Just the driver."

"Is he moving?"

"I . . . I can't tell. There's lots of glass. And I think blood."

"No, no . . ."

"You know him?"

"I—I know the van. Can we get to him?"

"Maybe the passenger door . . ." The man stared at the van on its side. At the underside. "Maybe," he said. He stepped on the left-front tire, found a foothold on the axle, pulled himself up by grabbing the right-front tire.

Don oh Don oh Don. What was he doing, what had he done? If she lost him here . . . She thought, Can I lose him without having him? No. But she knew, instantly, she might be losing him. Therefore, with the logic of fear, she must already have him. She knelt beside the spider-webbed windshield and tried to make out the face. The head was lying on its cheek, on the ground, spattered with grass and leaves.

"Hey, can you give me a hand?"

She stood. The man had reached the passenger door, had it open. "What?"

"Get a heavy stick, pass it to me. There's a couple of branches over there." He pointed to the trees.

She ran for them, picked one up. It shattered. Rotten. Another. Solid. She broke of a few side twigs, ran back, reached it up.

The man wedged the door open with the branch. "I'm going to lower myself down, see how he is. Go to my car, there's a cellphone in the glove compartment. Call 911, the cops, and get back here."

"Okay, yes. Is he alive?"

"Can't tell from here."

"Just tell me, can you describe him?"

For a moment he screwed his forehead tight, then glanced down.

"Oldish guy, maybe seventy-eighty, maybe older," the words came muffled, "thin grey hair, can't really tell more. Stinks of beer in here."

She could feel herself coming alive again. She felt her eyes fill with tears. "Thank you. I think his name is Frank." She ran across the street. She saw Patrick and Batiste standing beside her Toyota. "Get back in the car!" She didn't wait to see what the boy and the dog did. She rushed to the man's car and found his cellphone. Oh Don oh Don oh Don. Oh Frank, you poor stupid man, you've done it now.

No way would Justine let Jack tear down the house. He had no right. Maybe legally it was his house, but in reality it belonged to all the Tartaruses. Even if she was only half a Tartarus, she had a say in what should happen to the house. A house belongs to those who love it, that simple. And there was no one, no one at all who loved that house more than she. Damn you, Jack!

Justine hadn't seen him much over the years she'd been an undergraduate: she was tied to her cello, her rehearsal studios, her performances. And he'd been away, making art, travelling, commissions, lectureships. She'd seen him maybe three or four times over those years. Always at her mother's place. He hadn't had any time for her, like he used to when she was younger.

After her mother's calls she'd dithered in her apartment, then taken a bus to Stanley Park for a long walk, thinking through reasonable tactics for stopping him. Aside from pleading, breaking down in tears, she couldn't find any rational way to make him give up on the stupidity, the folly, of harming the house. Having no reasonable notions forced irrational ones on her. How far could she go? Even after all these years she felt, well, a bit intimidated by unreasoned tactics. No, more than intimidated, more like fear of being caught out trying to be irrational.

Just as well her mother had doused her idea of going over to Crab this afternoon. She had her appointment at five with Professor Tomlinson. Hart, he'd said to call him now; with BFA in hand she'd graduated also to first-name basis. She could of course have postponed the meeting. But the larger part of her wanted to get it over with, the coming session, the scholarship. She glanced at her watch.

Not too early to head out, the bus could be slow coming. She had an hour. They'd agreed to meet at the Faculty Club, which meant he was buying. Good. The scholarship had shocked her a little and pleased her a lot. Whatever else it suggested, she knew it was a major statement of approval. Three weeks back the department was told it'd won the large grant it had applied for, including three MFA fellowships to be given out. One they awarded her; another went to Reg Wu, a dazzling pianist, well deserved; the third to a guy she didn't know, supposedly a brilliant young composer, a coup for the department, lured away from the Berklee College of Music. There they thought they'd had him sewn up.

She changed from tank top, jeans, and running shoes to blouse, short skirt, and sandals. More appropriate for the Faculty Club. She grabbed her purse and left the apartment. A hot dry wind brushed her bare skin. She waited twelve minutes for the bus, glad she'd given herself extra time. Though if she'd left the house ten minutes later she'd only have had to wait two minutes. She enjoyed playing little what-if-she'd-done-this-differently games. It approached living an alternative life. And it allowed her to exercise her mind, something she'd been doing as long as she could remember, making up different possibilities for herself and others.

Now, how to figure some way for making Jack consider the house in an alternative manner. She might cast one of her spells on him. Woodoo spells, she called them. She'd invented them. They didn't work. At least not like a real voodoo spell was supposed to. But it pleased her to think hard at someone and try to move them with her mind. Actually she shouldn't assume they didn't work. No way of knowing because whatever happened, the alternative didn't. Would he or she have acted differently without the spell? Impossible to say. The act of casting the spell did change one person. Herself. This she knew.

Her music satisfied her intensely, for similar reasons. Music was the only medium in which she could act as irrationally as her mind and fingers allowed. She knew the difference between playing in control and playing out of control. Except an out-of-control performance could never come about without her having mastered control, then broken through it. Her body told her when her performance was a triumph. Her alternative performance. In the music she could have it both ways. Many ways. All the alternatives her talent allowed. Irrational ones too.

She would cast a woodoo on Jack. In the dark of night, best time. If she was awake. She often would be, she liked to practise while the world slept. And tonight she could do this more easily than she might have yesterday. Because now she knew where Jack was. Always easier to cast a woodoo on a person in a known place. She tested her woodoo often, casting a spell on some guy she was attracted to, a guy she wanted to get to know. Sometimes it worked. Would he have noticed her without the woodoo? But why take the chance of not casting a woodoo.

She'd tried over the last two years to help her mother along, casting spells on three or four men. It hadn't worked, at least as far as her mother let on. And she'd cast woodoos on Don's father, Frank, send him to a nursing home, leave room in Don's life for his friend and one-time lover Natalia. That hadn't worked either. Yeah, she'd try casting a woodoo on her Uncle Jack. What was there to lose?

She didn't want to hurt Jack. Even if she hated him. At least hated what he wanted to do to the house. But saying to her mother that she cared for Jack, and keenly, was also true. As once he'd cared about her. No, way more than once. For a long time. They were alike in many ways, she and Jack, she'd always felt this. And was proud of it. It went beyond merely feeling their similarity when she first began to study his photography. Their art proved the two of them analogous, his work with fire, hers with her cello. They were travelling along equivalent roads. Fellow travellers. She smiled again. It shouldn't be that hard to make a fellow traveller change his mind. Not about something he should do but, easier, something not to do. Simpler not to do something than do it. Do not tear down the house, Jack! She would concentrate tonight, hard, on Jack at the house and cast a woodoo on him. For all the good it would do.

The door opened. She got off to transfer. Even hotter and dryer now than before. She waited. Uncle Jack, her fellow traveller. A notion strengthened even more by *FIRE AND THE PHOENIX*. Its passion and grandeur had engulfed her. She'd read the advance hype and knew she had to go to San Francisco for the opening. Through one of her professors who'd performed with the symphony there she'd finagled a ticket. She flew down in early June, two days before her graduation. Should she tell Jack she'd be there? She was torn. She would love sharing his glory. But if he was as standoffish as he'd been for the past several years, then that could hurt. She wouldn't tell him. But if he saw her? Not likely, with so many people present. But still, if he turned her way at the wrong moment—She'd disguise herself. She had always wanted jet-black hair. She bought a wig. How about that for living an alternative life! Yes!

The venue for the opening was the Orchestra's Louise Davies Hall. The orchestra played live, on stage. Beyond and above them, one vast and two smaller lateral screens. Raven-haired Justine sat in row L, trying to read her program through dark-lensed glasses. The Phoenix Fire Symphony had been composed by Cyrus Laing, the guest conductor this evening Lawrence Tennenbaum. Far as she could tell, all the orchestra seats were full, as well as the loges and boxes, the upper tiers too. A couple of thousand people had come to see Jack's work, to hear the music born of Jack's fire. Impressive. She wondered where Jack might be sitting.

The lights dimmed. Music preceded image, plucked violin strings, pinpricks of sound. Then on the large screen the fire began, two pixie flames bouncing as if on strings themselves about a taller flame, handsome and static, to their right. Closer to the senior flame, away again, closer, away, for the best part of a minute as whispering woodwinds and soft-spoken kettle drums joined the violins, the volume rising and dropping with pixie bounce. The little flames died away, the music barely audible. The tall flame grew suddenly higher, wider, then exploded across the screen, joined instantly by the full orchestra, sound filling all space, for a moment a furious cacophonic assault, then as the flames spread to the lateral screens and sorted themselves into lavish order the music turned rich, full, golden as the flame. Harmony swept dissonance away, flame like hands stroking flame like hair, flame like grasses strumming in the wind.

Through its every moment Justine sat enthralled. For forty minutes the screen burned with Jack's fiery passion, guiding the orchestra, flame dancing with sound, till an immense red flame devoured the three screens, the deepest red she had ever seen. Then it disappeared. The screen went white. No sound from the orchestra. The audience exploded to its four thousand feet with applause, bravos, hurrahs. Tears ran down faces. Now the orchestra members too were applauding. Then out came Jack onto the stage so handsome in black tux, one hand holding the fingers of the conductor, Tennenbaum, the other another man's hand, presumably the composer, Laing. The cheers doubled, tripled. Justine had never felt herself so possessed by total joy midst a throng of others equally inspired. The man who had wrought this was her uncle. Just plain Uncle Jack. For a moment she thought how ridiculous she must look, her dark glasses and glossy black hair, no way would she ever get close enough to Jack for him not to recognize her. How she admired the man. Her heart, she realized, was beating hard, pounding. As, she assumed, must everyone else's in the room. One day she would tell him she'd been there. He had enlisted a moment of normality that magnetized many, the fascination of watching flames in a fireplace, at a bonfire, and turned the normal into art.

The bus was taking forever. She glanced at her watch. Now she might be late. So Hart would have to wait. Nothing to be done. But that had been one remarkable evening. Jack, in all possible glory. Her fellow traveller. She wondered if he'd brought a DVD of the performance with him. Shame to see it on a small screen. Way better than never seeing it again.

Long ago he'd seemed like an older brother, whether on Crab or the times he came over to the city. She knew he was older than her mother, but he didn't look older. He always seemed younger than her father; she'd thought of her father as much older maybe because he was nearly bald. She didn't recall much about him. But Jack back then she remembered with intense clarity. One morning as her mother drove them onto the ferry, she'd said, "Mommy, can I go clamming with Uncle Jack?" and her mother had said, "If he has the time." Turned out Jack had the time, always plenty of time for Justine. She drove with him in his old truck to the clam beach, she beside him in the front seat. She'd gone clamming with him once before. He'd told her then she could take clams only if she'd eat a few. She'd never eaten clams before but promised to try. "We got fifty-seven clams!" she shouted as they'd come through the door with a small bucketful. Jack washed them, added oatmeal to their water to draw out residual sand, let them sit overnight. For lunch the next day they all had clams, her mother and Jack and Aunt Maureen and Justine. In a salty liquid. Jack watched as she took a steamed clam from its shell with her fingers and stared at it. She realized everyone was looking at her. She remembered she'd said, "This is all there is?" and he'd said, "That's it." So she popped it into her mouth, chewed it, swallowed. And said, "Kinda good." Laughter from everyone and Jack got up, lifted her by the waist, held her high, and said, "You're amazing, kiddo." After, when she remembered the lunch and asked her mother why everyone had laughed, her mother said it was because little kids usually don't like clams but Justine had eaten them as a matter of course. Even now, waiting for the bus, she could remember with stark clarity Jack throwing her up above his head, grinning at her, calling her kiddo.

Most of the time he had treated her as an equal. Well, for a while. They would go on walks around the property, to the big tree or along the stream and out to the spring, and she'd keep up with him, no problem. He'd take her hand and help her over the high bits. And along the way they'd stop, she'd sit on his lap and he'd tell her stories. Sometimes they walked side by side, equals, as he pointed out wildflowers and birds and strange rock formations.

Then Jack and Maureen left Crab. Justine would have been about eight. When she and her mom came to the house on the island, there'd be no one there. She'd see Jack and Maureen in the city sometimes, but he wasn't nearly so much fun. One day Maureen wasn't there. She'd gone away, her mother said, she died. Justine had never known someone who died. She didn't miss Maureen a lot. But Uncle Jack was different now. As if he'd gone away a bit too. Anyway, she was getting too old to sit on his lap. She'd missed that, she recalled, him reading stories to her, showing her bugs and stones and flowers on the ground. He used to sing to her too.

The bus came at last. Damn, she definitely would be late. Five minutes at least. No big deal. She sat back and closed her eyes, glad to be out of the sun. She'd not thought so extensively about Jack in a long time. Why had she waited to revisit these lovely memories till he'd come back to commit a dreadful act. All those wonderful days on the island, the house their base, and now he wants to destroy it. Just because he's famous he thinks he can do whatever he likes.

When she was twelve or thirteen, that was when he began to become famous. She saw his first fire show when she was fifteen, fifty photos in colour and twenty in black and white. THE MAJESTY OF FIRE the show was called, and the photos played with all that, princely flame and regal flame, noble flame and demonic flame, royal flames all. It was the first time she realized she wanted to be just like Jack, to use her cello to achieve, try to reach for, his majesty. Never had photographs spoken to her with such clarity. She told her best friend, The show was right there, dead centre of my wavelength. She told no one but herself that she wanted to be Jack's favourite person in the world, that one day he would dedicate his new show to her.

After the show, at the party, casual, she in blouse and skirt, Jack wearing slacks and a turtleneck, she told Jack she thought she and he shared a wavelength.

Jack had laughed. "Have you taken up photography then?"

She smiled at him, he now the younger brother, too naive to understand what she was talking about, he didn't get it. She had to explain. She shook her head. "My music. My cello."

"Ah, I see." With one arm he embraced her. A quick moment. "Keep it up, do it well."

She shuddered a little at the touch of his hand and laid her head lightly against his shoulder. She felt eight years old again; she felt like a woman. Then someone came over to congratulate him, he introduced the man to her and her to the man and became engrossed in conversation. She walked away. She turned, he making a point by forming a connected shape with thumb and index finger of both hands, then looking through the space he'd created, framing what he was seeing. A gorgeous man, her younger older brother uncle.

A gorgeous man intent on destroying the house she loved. A man who'd better prepare himself, late tonight she would cast her most powerful woodoo ever on him. The bus stopped at the campus terminal. Her watch told her she'd be ten minutes late. Her mind wandered back to Jack, to when she'd last spent time with him by herself. Her sixteenth birthday. Jack, in the city to complete a commission for Vancouver's centennial, said he would take her and Natalia to dinner Saturday evening to celebrate the birthday. The Coast Watch was a small but grand new restaurant, impossible to dine at without a reservation made three months earlier. Jack knew the owner well. From Monday on, Justine first let excitement take her over, then fought it down—dinner with Uncle Jack, no big deal even if the restaurant was, but the excitement rose again, again she restrained it, but upcoming moments snared her imagination. She would dress up for the evening. She searched through all her clothes. Nothing appropriate, nothing in the closet. She told her mother. Natalia agreed, she would take Justine shopping for the right dress. Justine recognized it the moment she saw it, deep purple, a scoop neck, short sleeves and straight skirt to the knees, a short matching jacket over. She tried it on. It was made for her. And three-inch black pumps. And purple pendant earrings. The excitement grew.

Unfortunately Friday night her mother slept badly, her body intermittently burning and freezing. By Saturday morning it was a miserable flu. Justine went back and forth between worry about her mother and fury at her mother: how could she destroy the best evening Justine could ever have? Her mother called Jack and explained. Jack said if Natalia would be okay by herself for the evening, he would take Justine anyway. She could be his date.

His date!

He arrived at seven. Natalia in her bathrobe, eyes red, shawl tight over her bathrobe, opened the door and led him to the living room. He saw Justine in her purple dress with the scoop neck. She could tell he was impressed.

"Excuse me, I'm looking for Justine. Is she here?"

It took a moment to get the tease. "Why, I have no idea where she is. She's not been around all day. I think she may be away."

"Oh," said Jack, "that's a shame. Because I have a small present for her."

"How very nice. For Justine."

"But if she's not here . . ."

"You could give it to me."

"Yes. Good idea." He handed her a small package wrapped in silver, with a gold ribbon.

She took it, hesitated a moment, slid off the ribbon. Inside, a little leather box. She opened it. Two deep red stones. Each on a short silver lead. Earrings. The red glimmered like magic flames. "Oh."

"But if Justine isn't here—"

"May I—may I try them on?"

"I think you should. We wouldn't want to waste them."

She removed the purple pendants from her ears and replaced them with the rubies. She held up her head, modelling them. The most wonderful moment.

"Yes, I think that works. They go well with your dress too. You look lovely."

"Thank you very very much for—uh, for letting me try them on."

"Now may I ask you something. As long as Justine isn't here, and I've got this dinner reservation, would you by any chance be available to join me?"

"Well, there's something I should do. But it's not important. Yes, I'd love to join you."

"Excellent. And since we'll be spending the evening together, what may I call you?"

"Hmm," as if in thought. "Please call me Justine."

It was not till they reached the door that she remembered her mother. She turned. Her mother was smiling. Her mother said, "Have a fine time."

Now Justine hurried across campus. Every minute of it so clear. It had gone on, a perfect dinner with Jack. They were shown to their table by the owner, a great fan of Jack's who made a pleasant fuss about the very beautiful young lady Jack had brought this evening. The candle at the edge of the table glimmered, its golden yellow reflecting in Jack's cinnamon eyes, his irises sparkling. She wondered what the candle did to her own eyes. She wished she could see her eyes. To see what she looked like in his eyes. Tonight she was Justine, yet only playing Justine. So not quite Justine. Almost another person, for this evening.

Jack had a martini before dinner, she something non-alcoholic. She asked if she could have a sip of his martini, she'd never had one. She sipped. She liked it. Sort of. They ordered. Funny, what they'd eaten was gone from her mind. Jack did order a bottle of wine. The waiter poured, a little for each, the liquid the colour of her earrings. She said this. He glanced at them and said yes, the candlelight is burning in them even more wildly than in the wine. She glanced at the wine. He was right. The wine drank in the candle's reflection. She said this too. He raised his glass and toasted her birthday. They both sipped. She'd had wine lots of times but never anything so smooth. They talked about his photography, her cello-playing. About Jack and Natalia, about Justine and Natalia. About Justine, her life. The most wonderful evening ever. And then it was over, the food and drink and talk done.

They got into his car. She remained Justine/not Justine. If she were not Justine, then Jack was not her uncle. Possibly the wine was speaking when she turned to him, raised her face to his. "May I tell you something?"

He grinned. "You have been all evening. I've enjoyed it. What else can you tell me?"

She smiled a small, sad smile. "I'm sweet sixteen and I've never been kissed."

He laughed. "I don't believe a word of it."

She leaned closer to him, her lips slightly apart. "It's true," she whispered. He shook his head and leaned her way, raised his lips to her forehead, and kissed her brow. "Now you have." He sat back in his seat, started the car, without turning her way again drove off.

And so the spell was broken. To his attempts at conversation on the way she had responded with monosyllables. At the house she opened the front door and they walked in. Natalia had made up a bed on the living room couch and was lying there reading.

Yes, a wonderful evening, yes the restaurant deserved its reputation. Jack said, "Good night to you both." To Justine he said, "And if Justine does come by, please give her the earrings. I'm sure they'd be lovely on her too."

She followed him to the door. All she could say was, "Thank you."

He leaned toward her and kissed her cheek. "There. Twice in one evening. Happy birthday." He left.

Now, she opened the door to the Faculty Club. Now she would talk to—Hart.

Then, in her bedroom, she'd wept. Long ago she'd come to understand what her sixteen-year-old self was feeling. But what had that child expected anyway?

TURTLE'S RESPONSIBILITIES

The cabin was all Turtle needed. The logging road through the ex-clearcut was overgrown, rarely used even as a walking trail. In back were the bedroom, its double bed rarely sleeping more than one, and a bathroom with toilet and sink. No shower because no water line came into the cabin. Turtle bathed sometimes at the hardware store, mostly at the boaters' shower at the marina. A bucket brought in water from a trickling hand-dug artesian well, just enough to wash dishes or flush the toilet. Electricity arrived by way of a line tapped into a transformer on East Road. It passed through a one-time pump hose and lay on the ground by the side of the logging road. Turtle checked it regularly. He figured the Hydro guys knew about it but let it be. The front room served his other requirements—cooking, eating, sitting, warming himself at the fireplace. Most important, it stored the tools of his work. His real work, not what he did at the hardware store. There he put in three days a week, enough income to cover expenses. Not that he didn't enjoy the job. The people of Crab came in to buy materials for making repairs, fixing, patching, mending, overhauling stuff that already existed, not starting over with a new piece of furniture or appliance but remaking the original, preserving the old. Turtle approved. His job was to help them.

The cabin had been built thirty-one years ago by Turtle, then age fifteen, and three friends. The land had been clear-cut five years before. Alders already then reaching thirty feet had taken it over. During the building process, the friends carted in what they needed with Larry's older brother's ancient beater of a truck, Larry, the only one old enough to drive. They brought in lumber, plywood, and drywall, pilfered a piece here and a board there at the worksites around the island, or picked up from CIRCE, the recycling depot, or borrowed and not returned. The cabin had begun with the one front room. It was their clubhouse. The three others left the island to seek whatever fortune might be out there. Turtle stayed. The place became his home.

These days he parked his 1968 Chevy Nova, best car ever built in North America, around the first curve of the logging road. He'd need a backhoe to clear the way to drive in farther. Anyway, from the car to the cabin was only a four-minute walk. He regularly left the house early in the morning since one of his real-work responsibilities began around five-thirty. About seven when it opened, he arrived at the Rest-or-Rant and joined the carpenters, plumbers, electricians, tilers, roofers, and the rest at the four tables they commandeered for their breakfasts, their stories, their gossip. The grouped assemblage knew the underside of every incident or decision, every illness and celebration, who had taken up with whoever, that occurred on Crab. So Turtle kept current. He drank his two cups of coffee and ate his two pieces of toast and listened, and sometimes contributed; sooner or later all his sources came through the hardware store. By eight-thirty, the group had dispersed to their several job sites.

At nine on mornings he didn't go to the hardware store, more work began. He had set himself in charge of assuring that the island's rules were respected and the island's balances maintained. Rules and balances were Turtle's bailiwick, not laws. He had little interest in laws. He left those to the Regional District office, to the Islands Trust people, and to the Mounties.

His one difficulty with the island was its white-bread ethnic nationalism, the implicit superiority of its citizens—and it was his duty to maintain the rules and balances they all had to live by. Crab the class-free, minority-less society. Or nearly so because the exceptions, like himself, were pretty much invisible. Class-free because the nearly new ones were all part of the same class, the clever ones who arrived when you could buy a house for a quarter of what it cost today. The luck of their purchase, which they referred to as astuteness regarding real estate. Yes, by gum, these were his people. Their lack of prejudice against Jews was as bold as they got.

Earlier this morning he'd been enforcing one of Crab's basic rules, that no one arrive at the ferry line-up for the 5:35 or the 6:40 more than ten minutes before departure. While the former rarely became an overload, the latter might be full. But it was unfair to have to race to the ferry early to line up half an hour early. Those who disobeyed were apprised of the rule. Crab people knew the rule well and would never dream of breaking it, but some visitors needed Turtle's special admonition. To those who didn't know, he would hand a small card that simply stated the rule: One does not show up for either of the first morning ferries more than fifteen minutes before departure. He rarely gave out more than six cards a week. Only twice did he find repeat offenders. These he dealt with by appropriate means.

He left the Rest-or-Rant for the dock, the incoming ferry just arriving. He parked so as to inspect the drivers and occasional passenger in incoming cars. Smoking on the ferry was illegal. Desperate smokers would light up the moment they crossed over to land. Turtle waited. A burning cigarette tip was easier to see in the winter in the dark, but Turtle had the good eye. Now he noted a lit cigarette, started illegally on the ferry. He followed. Most often the cigarette was smoked and the butt tamped into an ashtray. At times the butt would be thrown out the window, sometimes still burning. No telling what this woman would do. He followed her along North Road, law-abiding at sixty-two kilometres an hour. Just after the Island Kitchen she turned into the driveway of a house on the ocean, no butt thrown from the car. Good for her.

Half an hour till the next ferry. Time to grab a coffee at the Rant.

He could follow only one car per ferry. But that was fine. Over the months he'd spot his share of potential forest-fire starters. Only the 8:55, 10:05, and 11:15 ferries interested him, the largest loads. Today he followed another good citizen off the 10:05, but with the 11:15, he got lucky. Or rather, the passenger got unlucky. A couple of kilometres down West Road, a butt flew from the green Porsche's window on the driver's side. Turtle noted the licence plate number, slowed, stopped, found the lipsticked butt, stamped it dead, picked it up with tweezers, and dropped it into a baggy. He roared off in overspeed chase. He caught up with her a kilometre before Lighthouse Point Road, drew close behind her, flashed his headlights, honked his horn, gestured for her to stop. She did. He grabbed the baggy, got out, and walked up to her car.

She stuck her head out the window. "You got a problem?"

"No," said Turtle, "you do." He tossed her cigarette butt onto her lap. "You dropped this."

"I . . . What?"

"Good way to burn down an island, miss."

"I—I—"

"Try it again and you're in real trouble. Got it?"

"Uh—uh—yes."

"Good."

He saluted her lightly, walked back to his car, got in, and made a U-turn. He noted the Porsche hadn't moved. Maybe she was shaken. First-rate.

His trailing for the day was done. The next ferries, until the commuters returned, carried small loads. But commuters were island people, most of whom knew better than to toss burning butts from automobile windows. Occasionally he'd get information on a thrown butt from one of the guys at breakfast. They knew Turtle's job and often provided him with a licence number or an address. These folks Turtle would accost at their front doors with one of the many butts he'd picked off the road and kept stored in bottles on a shelf in his front room, present them with the tell-tale evidence, and chew them out. If he couldn't find the person, only the car, he'd leave the butt under the windshield wiper with his note: *Throw another butt from your car and you'll wish you hadn't.* Rarely would he find a repeat offender, but the three times it happened Turtle broke into their cars and burned three small holes in the driver's seat cover with a lit cigarette.

On days not at the hardware store Turtle got half his daily sleep in the afternoon, the other half from one to four in the morning. His basic working time, sunset to midnight, was given over to non-public responsibilities. Last night, like many others in the summer, he'd been resetting one of the island's balances. Crab had two public beaches, large signs pointing to them, parking available. And several dozen others, less easily reachable, much smaller. Summer residents and tourists often sought out these hidden bits of shoreline and overcrowd them. The Chamber of Commerce gave out maps that noted, approximately, where public access to a small beach was available. Often this would be a right-of-way through the woods a couple of feet wide between two properties. Loud off-islanders passed along such trails, dropping empty cans and shouting shrilly, to the dismay of the inhabitants. On the beaches the visitors' CD players blared music to drown out the crashing waves. Altogether wrong.

Turtle's role in rectifying this injustice consisted of obliterating any sign that public access paths existed. Last night he'd arrived at a North Road entry point just before eleven. No lights on in the houses on either side of the trail. He opened his trunk and pulled out three of the four large green plastic garbage bags. Four more lay on the back seat. Each he'd stuffed with brush—bushes and branches from the land around his cabin. At the entrance to the access trail up to four feet in he emptied the bags, the new dead undergrowth obscuring the way in. He stared at his work in the starlight. At first it'd been hard to tell if he'd done a thorough job so he'd come by again during the day to ensure it was okay. Now he knew right off if the path looked blocked and yep, this was a good job. It wouldn't close off access to the locals, they knew how to get around it, they'd approve of the new camouflage. Between eleven-thirty and twelve-thirty, he sealed off two more access places. A positive night.

Some of his work was seasonal, some monthly, some occasional. He took one day a month—likely be tomorrow night or the night after—to conserve those areas on the island where someone with a cellphone couldn't contact a server. For this job he needed an exceptionally dark night. He dressed in black and wore gloves. He brought with him his simple tools, a regular and a needle-nosed plier, and a plastic bottle of water. He drove to half a kilometre of the cellphone tower—it had come to Crab as a radio tower and within six months the server had strapped cellphone equipment to it—walked stealthily to the wire fence, clambered over, and climbed the tower. He adjusted each of the transmitters by a degree or three, then poured a little water on the connectors. And back down, the whole project taking less than five minutes. He knew the server's technicians would come over to Crab after enough complaints from clients, again mostly summer residents, though increasingly year-round people used cellphones. Then some other dark night Turtle would return and repeat his work. In six years, no one had caught him. Obviously high winds were responsible.

In one aspect of his work Turtle stayed an equal-opportunity supplier. He felt a loyalty to the deer of the island. They'd been unfairly treated by all islanders, regulars as well as visitors. Fences. Fences were wrong. The deer had lived on the island long before humans. They followed their trails today as they had of yore. Except, of course, when a trail was blocked. Turtle saw it as his responsibility to help the deer. He'd never cut a fence or tear it down—that'd be vandalism. But to create little gaps in the fencing, nothing wrong there. If a heavy branch fell on a fence—easier after a storm but broken branches did get hung up by heavy winds, only to fall months later—why, this was inherent in nature. If a small boulder made a rent in the fencing, who could say where it rolled from. If the base of a fencepost rotted out, well that happened, even with treated wood. And nobody knew how to treat and detreat wood better, how to drop a branch better, than Turtle. Again the deer could pass along the ancient trail, as was their inborn right.

Crab, mostly, was a worthwhile island. Where it deviated from its imperative, Turtle enjoyed helping it along, rebalancing its little aberrances. He felt good on Crab. He fit inside it easily, naturally. He wore the island like an old sweatsuit—he gave it both shape and life. Though, like unwashed sweats, Crab's inhabitants sometimes left him itchy and smelly.

SEVEN: Jack, Ginny, and the House

Ginny said to Tartarus, "You haven't heard a thing I said."
"What did you say?"
"Nothing for, like, the last ten-fifteen seconds."
He stared at her. Such a vivid recall that had been. He sensed the foreboding of senility: every moment with Ginny from nearly twenty years ago crystalline, and right now no short-term memory at all. "Sorry," was the best he could do.
"So. Where were you?"
"I remembered something."
"What?"
"Doesn't matter."
"I think it does."
"Maybe." He watched as she leaned across the table and stared at him, her eyes large and glowy. She was about to speak, but the waiter with his tray arrived: her burger and fries, his clam chowder. She had to withdraw, arms back, body back. She asked for more water.
The waiter left. She said, "Did my dry vagina send you to the far side of the world?"
"Ginny, don't."
"What? That was long ago, in a country far away, and besides the wench is much older."
"I said don't, okay? Eat your burger."
"Want a French fry?" She grinned.
He would not meet her glance but took two fries. "Thanks."
"You disappeared," she said.
"I guess I did."
"You know you did." With a napkin she wiped the grin from her mouth. "Three days before I left. And you didn't say goodbye. Hell, Jack, you never even told me you were going."
"You want an apology? I apologize."

She picked up her burger. "A small explanation would be nice."

He sighed. "Tell me, why did you seduce me?"

"You sure that's what happened?" The grin again. "Maybe you seduced me."

He shook his head. "We were both—attracted to each other. But you came to my show. The next day to my house. Why?"

She took a large bite of burger. With her mouth full she couldn't speak. The waiter brought another stein of water.

Jack slid his spoon into the chowder, brought it to his lips, blew at it, and slowly placed it in his mouth. She was still chewing. He took another spoonful. "A good burger?"

She swallowed. "Good."

"Want to answer before you bite into it again?"

She nodded. "I participated in our mutual seduction to . . . see if I could."

"Could."

"I was testing my sexuality. Could I get an older man? I was going off to university in a week, remember? I figured I'd try out my strengths. Before leaving home."

She had never mentioned such a thing, not a breath of it in the days they'd had. Days filled with arrant lust, feral and unqualified. They had taken each other half a dozen times in daylight, on the grass, against trees, in his car, on his desk, on the carpet; and as many in the darkness, each bed, the bath dry or wet, the shower, the dining room table, the couch, the washer-dryer. Maureen, from the moment after the first moment, was no longer part of the house. Jack and Ginny were alone together four straight days. They shared sensual food for sensuous purpose, their appetite for rutting the greatest of gifts, an appetite so commanding it might have grown from eons of starvation. An older man? He believed her. She had known she could. From the first moment. "Those were heavy-duty strengths you found," he said.

"You were a surprise. An older guy, such stunning revival ability."

Tartarus frowned at her. "I was only in my thirties, Ginny."

"Why did you go? You have to tell me."

To that he knew the answer. "It was enough."

"Of me?"

"Of those days."

"You went to her."

"I did."

"You loved her."

"I loved her."

"A sudden guilt."

He shook his head. "Guilt was nowhere in sight."

"It was instant, Jack. You were there. You were gone. No guilt?"

He stared at her. Her eyes gazed back, the grey now dominant over the green, blink blink blink. "Not guilt. Not then, not ever after. Maureen's husband wasn't in the house for those four days. It was someone else. Someone I've never been able to understand since. Or become again."

"Someone damn good."

"That may have been."

"It hurt, you disappearing."

He shrugged a little laugh. "You'd have disappeared, a few days later."

She blinked hard, three or four times in a couple of seconds, and nodded. She sipped water, picked up her burger, and took a smaller bite.

Another spoonful of chowder. Lukewarm. "Days outside of time. Out of place too. My house here, but a different house. Everything was raw, that I remember. Raw, like new, like I'd never seen it before. My house was another house."

"Another house?"

"A sort of parallel house. For a parallel state of existence. A kind of ecstatic state. Like what I'm told some people get from religion. Or drugs."

"You're funny." But she wasn't smiling.

"A parallel pleasure too. No—a pleasure beyond. Beyond the sex, I mean. A state of elated bliss." And no guilt, but he wouldn't repeat this now. In the few times he had allowed himself to think about the four days, he thought too of Maureen: that she should have been sharing this with him. Not the action, not then, not in any way. But sharing the pleasure beyond.

"Elated bliss," she repeated. "Four days of it. You and me."

"I've wondered. You never called home. In four days. You were eighteen."

"I'd told them when I left," she said. "I had to be away for a few days. By myself. Before becoming an organized undergraduate."

"But if I hadn't . . ."

She shook her head. "I knew."

"You knew. How?"

"I knew what I could do. I just wasn't sure I could handle an older guy."

"But why me?"

"I just said."

"An older guy? Lots of older guys around."

"You were far and away the most intriguing."

"An intriguing older man."

"Sounds wrong when you say it." She sniffed a giggle. "I should stop calling you that."

"It's what I am. And intriguing too. Hmm." But he'd not thought of himself as old, or older. He was a man who made photos, photos of ledges then, photos of flame now, and films of fire. He had no age. He'd had no age. Till now.

She took her backpack and left, to go to the bathroom. He'd been wondering about that: so much water, was her bladder infinite? He asked for the bill. She equated his kind of bliss with great sex. She'd not understood what he meant. She came back. "I filled my water bottle."

And why had she told him that. "Are you finished?"

She looked at her burger, mostly uneaten. "They're finished. I'm not hungry."

"Let's go then." He got up and paid at the counter.

She waited for him by the door. "Thank you."

"It wasn't very good."

"Not what I'm thanking you for." That smile again.

"I'll take you home."

"We need to set up the generator and—"

"I know how to set up a generator, Ginny. We used to have one."

"It's heavy."

"Thanks, but no." He headed for the car, opened the passenger door, got in behind the wheel. He noted, across the street, the hardware store clerk watching. The guy was everywhere.

She dropped into the seat beside him. "It works great, but it's got a pinprick leak."

"The generator?"

"The drip pan catches it. It seals up after a while."

"Okay." He started the car.

"You have to promise me."

"What?"

"To leave the house alone."

He U-turned. "The house is safe." He headed back. "Until I get the demolition order."

She said nothing till he turned onto Arbutus. Then, "Are you trying to punish them?"

"Who?"

"Sam and Hannah."

"What?"

"Hurt them. By taking away their house. Hurt them in your mind."

"Stop it, Ginny. You don't have any idea what you're talking about." He felt her shrug.

She drank water and went silent again. They approached her driveway. She said, "Maybe you were right, before."

"What?"

"That for our four days it was another house." Her voice had taken on new softness, though with a fine edge. "Well, it's yet another house now. A third house."

"Don't be silly."

"Not the other house we had. A different other house. It's not your house anymore."

"Now? It's the same goddamn house. Nothing different. The original house."

She shook her head.

He drove down her drive and stopped. The Rixton house sat there in the middle of the field, free-standing, a house in solitude. "Thanks for your help. And the lamps and generator."

Her smile was large and fake, the whites of her eyes huge, the irises green, as if mounted consciously on those high cheekbones. "And thank you this time for lunch." She got out.

He waited till she had the front door open. He drove off, opening the window wide. In the few seconds he'd been parked the car had heated up. She'd gotten to him with her third-house comment. How? Another trump card, turning his sense of the house against him? Or just her quiet feigned superiority.

He turned onto his drive, through the forest, the brush, and approached the house. Surrounded by its usual silence. He parked on the east side beside the garage to set up the generator where Tartarus-house generators had always been set up. He didn't want to go into the garage. He had to, to shift the house's power source from the main to the generator panel.

First the food. The cooler? In the garage. Anything not used daily got stored in the garage. Did Ginny have a key to the garage too? Must have. He got out, felt in his pocket for the key ring. The House Keys. Three. He stared at them. One would be for the garage. He walked to the garage door. Four horizontal panels. The second from top was small windows. He looked inside. Full of junk, as he'd left it two years ago. The door would glide upward. He tried the lock. The key turned, and he heard the tumbler click. He reached for the handle, rotated it. Stopped. He had not been inside, not since. Since they'd died. In here. Natalia had tracked him down, on that afternoon eleven years ago, called him:

"**Hi, Nat, how'd** you locate me?"
  "It doesn't matter. Jack . . ."
  "Hey, what's up?"
  "Sit down."
  "What?"

"Just sit." She waited. "It's Mom and Pop. They . . . They . . ."

"Nat! What?"

"They're . . . they're dead."

"No."

"I'm sorry, Jack."

"Please, no." Silence from Natalia. "How?" He could nearly hear her, her head nodding, or shaking. "Nat, for godsake . . ."

"At home. In the garage. They killed themselves."

Jack felt his legs weaken. He sat on the arm of the overstuffed chair. "No, Nat."

"They closed the door. They sat in the Volvo. Pop behind the wheel."

"That's not possible. There's too much junk in there. They never parked inside."

"They'd moved stuff around. Out. They made room. Pop himself, probably. She wouldn't have known what . . . wouldn't have . . . He drove in. He'd have started the engine. That's it."

"That's not it."

"What?"

"There must've been more."

"I don't know, Jack. I wasn't here. They called me."

"Who?"

"The RCMP. I was in the middle of a lesson. They called. Out of nowhere. The minute before everything was normal. The minute after everything had collapsed."

"Oh Nat, Nat . . ."

"Yeah." Silence for a couple of seconds. "Can you come?"

"Yes. Yes of course."

"They'd been dead . . . dead for . . . a couple of days."

"What?"

"Pop told Frank they were going to Vancouver over the weekend. But a neighbour came by. They always parked . . . outside like you said, the garage was too full. The neighbour didn't see the car two days in a row, just a lot of . . . stuff outside the garage. They hadn't told her anything about Vancouver. She saw the Volvo inside. She opened the door. It had begun to . . . to stink inside, Jack."

He heard her sobbing, slowly. "Nat, I'll be there soon as I can. First flight I can get."

He'd arrived the next day. The funeral was held in Vancouver. Over three hundred people came to the synagogue. A cremation followed. The ashes were brought back to Crab and strewn across the meadow. Joining Maureen's.

The garage door slid up, curved around, and rested overhead, horizontal. Inside, a smell of must and mildew. And stuff. The three mowers, garden tools, four barbecues, old lumber, three chainsaws, axes, mauls, hundreds of metres of heavy extension cord, broken bookshelves, the toboggan, skis, snowshoes, three red jerry cans probably half-full of old gas, window screens, empty wine bottles, his slingshots, three crab traps, fishing rods. More. The stuff the neighbour had seen outside. The neighbour. She. Ginny? Had Ginny found his parents? He shuddered.

Tartarus closed his eyes. He breathed in deeply. Shivered in the heat. Puffed the air out past tight lips. Opened his eyes. Get moving, man.

He located the cooler—two, one that didn't close properly—behind the crab traps, dragged out the good one, and carried it to the veranda. He opened the car trunk, took out the ale, the water. Still cold. The ice. To the house. He unlocked the door. To the kitchen, cooler first, then the drinks. He looked about the kitchen, the fridge and stove, the cabinets. The cabinets, all the way to the ceiling. As his mother had ordered, for her kitchen. He could practically hear her saying to Sam, Of course all the way. You think I'm going to climb a ladder to dust up there? Besides I want more storage space. Because one always needs more storage space, that's why. Enclosed space, keep my dishes and bowls from getting all dusty and greasy. The carpenter had built the cabinets high, to the ceiling. Though when he looked at Sam and Hannah, five-foot-nine and five-foot-five, he did ask, You people planning on growing some? Tartarus smiled and sighed. Suddenly felt the presence of his mother, as if her aura had remained in the kitchen, her best room. He closed his eyes and saw her when she had been well, a sprightly woman, grey hair never artificially tinged. Always ready with a comment, mostly complimentary. When you have done the best you can, she enjoyed saying, then you've done well. He'd loved his mother. He'd also liked her a great deal, enjoyed her company. He opened his eyes, nodded, agreeing with himself. He tore open one of the water bottle packages, stood them in the cooler, and all the ale. Ice on top. He brought in the crackers, chips, and salsa, left them on the counter beside the fridge.

Now the generator. Hellishly heavy, too much to lift. Maybe he should've let Ginny help. No, she'd never have gone away. He opened the car's back door and drew the generator toward him. It slid, got stuck on the seat back. He forced it, it came forward but tore into the seat cover. Damn. But it was half out, angling down. He worked it along the seat, its front-end wheels onto the residual running board, down but too quickly, landing with a bump. And scraping the paint. But the front end did sit solid on the ground, supporting the machine. He climbed in the other side and worked it out from behind, letting the wheels bear the weight. He eased the front bar down. It touched the ground. Sweat poured from his forehead, his armpits, down his chest.

He roll-dragged it to the garage, to a lattice-sided box with removable facade and roof, opened it top and front, plugged in the power-out cable. He worked the machine into the box, stepping it forward. It wasn't about to rain but inside the box was where generators belonged. He brought over the jerry can of fresh gasoline, filled the tank, found the safety, and turned it to on, opened the gas line, choke open, yanked hard at the starting cord. It caught, first try. Choke off, idle on. He switched the source breaker to GEN. He was in business. He hoped.

The generator powered the well pump, the cistern pump, three electric outlets, and the refrigerator. The fridge! He could have bought real food after all. He wiped his face in his sleeve. He couldn't hear the well pump a hundred-sixty feet down, wouldn't know if it was working till it'd had time to bring water up to the cistern under the garage. He'd give it fifteen minutes.

He checked the drip pan below. A hint of dampness. He rubbed his finger in it, brought it to his nose and sniffed. He'd watch it carefully.

Likely it was Ginny who found his parents. Why hadn't she told him?

He brought the lanterns and Coleman lamps inside. Chips and salsa into the cabinet. Yes, he was setting up house. Spend the night here?

Probably he would tomorrow after Nat arrived. Except Don thought it was not a good idea for him to be in the house. Well, damn it, neither did he. Stay in the house, sleep here, then three days later tear it down. It did seem obscene.

What more did Ginny know about his parents' suicides? Withholding information, another of her trumps. Damn her.

He opened the cooler. Beer or water? He wanted a beer. Fewer beers, more water. He twisted open a water bottle. Colder than when it went in. He drank down half. He thought, I wanted, in fact needed, that water. And yet I wasn't dry. Ginny says she gets dry, in her mouth and nose and eyes—and all about. Dryness is different from thirst. He recalled the picture of his mother and father, with Ginny between them. He found the flashlight, climbed the stairs, and went into his parents' room. He picked up the picture and brought it down, into the light. His mother's face: lines extended from the edges of her lips, also from the corners of her eyes, and across her forehead. Her face, drying out. She'd been aging, perfectly normal. We are all aging. Tartarus too, Ginny had made that clear enough. He stared at Sam in the photo. Not aging, not so's you'd notice. Not from what Tartarus remembered.

Enough. If Natalia slept here, and she would, he'd better open the house up. He went outside, unhooked and drew apart the shutters over the living room windows and the downstairs bedroom window. Inside he unlocked the living room windows and opened them. New air, baked though it was, refreshed the space. He sat on the couch. A blank space. No life here. He got up, went out again, checked his watch. Too early to go over to Don's. No desire to spend time with Frank. Nor here in the house. Too much death.

It hadn't always been so. He and Nat, his parents, lots of living there. Of course Maureen too. And the place where he'd come to master his photography, where he'd learned to make pictures. Down in the bowels of house, his private space, the little womb of his creative bursts, the hothouse where he had forged and freed his imagination. Lots of life there. Lots of life then.

He would go for a walk, see if the trails his father had blazed were still passable. Take along the chainsaw, cut through any deadfall. He started for the garage... No, illegal to use little gasoline-powered motors when the fire danger was extreme. He'd check out the forest unarmed.

The generator had a little gas-powered motor.

To hell with all the small men.

From the house he headed east across the meadow. The high dry grass, thickly matted, was hard to traverse. He stopped, raised his nose to the air like a hopeful rabbit, and sniffed. No scent, none. He broke through dogtail and brome. And timothy, his mother's favourite, she picked it in the fall, kept it in vases till midwinter, threw it out only after it was hung with spiderwebs like tinsel on the Christmas trees Maureen would bring into the house come December—and foxtail, bluejoint, quackgrass. By the edge of the wood he found salal and Oregon grape, the deep purple berries on the grape near to desiccated from lack of rain. The trail leading to the pinnacle, and the Big Tree he'd once climbed, lay this way. No treetop views for him today, but he wanted to see it again. Touch it. The trail was overgrown. Long ago it had been rigorously cleared. He could still distinguish its margins. It climbed steadily, the firs and alders, the arbutus, all newly familiar. Ten years since he'd passed this way. He remembered the curves of the trail.

Why had Ginny not mentioned she'd discovered his parents' bodies? How well had she really known them? Why did she suggest she knew more than she said? Did she? Was she in fact the one who found them?

Up higher, finally to the pinnacle. It remained near clear of growth. A shelf of shale lay a couple of centimetres beneath the topsoil—in reality not soil at all, just leaves, fir needles, small branches rotting to humus. Still, a few scrawny obstinate alders had grown to three feet, four, their roots horizontal under his feet, fixing nitrogen below the surface. Sam had cleared a little plateau here, had the highest firs and arbutus below the lip topped to provide a view of the centre of the island. The sea lay opposite. He'd left those trees as he found them, too many and too high to open up an ocean vista. Over a dozen years the topped trees had found their revenge by growing tall again. No view now.

But of course. Trees do tend to grow. Until they fall down. Had Sam thought he'd be able to see, from here, the house he'd built? Or the house Ginny lived in. Had Sam told her about this place, the pinnacle? Had she surveyed her house, and the Tartarus house, from here?

Turn south to the Big Tree. Or head north and west to the rockslide and the spring. The tree wouldn't be going anywhere. He started north. The undergrowth at the base of arbutus and spruce thickened, mostly salal grown wide, tall as his head, searching for light. He marvelled at the girth of some of the firs, second growth, some of their trunks nearing a couple of feet wide.

Here too, Tartarus realized, his father's handiwork had been undone. The forest floor, now a bed of mulch over the shale, allowed growth to any seed that could find protection, hidden from juncos and towhees. The one-time pathway was now barred. In earlier days he would've thought, I'll open up this trail again. But he never would, this job was for the land's next master.

Until this moment he hadn't considered selling the property. Getting rid of the house was the important thing. Instantly he felt a sale was inevitable: the house gone, the property goes on the market. Unless Natalia wanted to buy it. The land too, a collaborator in the deaths of their parents. A bit player but part of it all. Natalia wouldn't want the land. To a buyer, the land's role in Sam and Hannah's death would have no significance. But the house, yes. Who would buy a house in which two people had killed themselves?

Yes, the land was a collaborator. One of the many. Likely he himself as well. If he'd been around more often, been with them, understood their day-by-day attitudes and fears, he might have turned them from such an end. Collaboration by avoidance. It wasn't a large broad guilt he felt, just a small heavy piece of one, coming and going. He'd spoken it aloud, to himself one morning in the shower, If I had been there ... And realized his role in their suicide. Voicing it, he knew he'd long been feeling it, a burden occasionally weighty, often no more than a whisper. But since his little five-word soliloquy, its substance had lightened. He could handle it.

He headed back to the pinnacle. Would he be able to access the spring and the rockslide directly from the house? Or would one have to break new trails to them from that direction too? He headed across the plateau to the Big Tree, the going easier here, fifty or sixty metres of trail. The ground beneath the tree was free of undergrowth, the tree sucking up all the water around, leaving no nourishment even for salal. He stood at its base and looked up. Its branches began at about at about ninety feet. There they joined the green of neighbour cedar, arbutus, other fir. He searched the bark before him for spur scars, from when he'd climbed the tree. Yes, here, and here. The girth of the trunk was greater than he remembered. He touched the weathered marks in the bark. A long time since his spurs had dug in here. The outlook from up top, in sync with Sam's later delight at his full circle view, had been grand.

Natalia had shown him the note. It said, simply, *There is no more.* In Sam's handwriting.

Was Ginny the first to see the note? He didn't know. A lot he didn't know. He admitted to himself in irritation, Ginny knew more about his parents than he did. How to find out what she knew? Ask her, damn it.

So selfish of Sam and Hannah. So selfish.

Back to the house. In the kitchen, a choked roar. Water! From the little cistern, pouring out the faucet. Which he must have left open. Of course, to keep the water line from freezing. A good strong flow. He turned the tap closed. Okay now, go . . .

Natalia and Jack, alone in the house, sitting on the couch. A brilliant low May sun outside the living room window gave life—and therefore lie—to the bright, throbbing meadow and the lush firs, hemlock, and spruce at its periphery. Natalia's tears had dried. Jack had not yet begun to cry. They sat silently with their thoughts, far from each other. They sat for ten minutes, fifteen. Time passed but was not felt. Neither was prepared to spread the ashes. Not yet.

"Why, Nat?"

She said nothing.

"You don't know," he said. "Nobody knows."

Natalia spoke at last. "They knew."

A bitter, thin grunt rose from Jack's throat. "But shared none of it."

"Pop..." She stopped herself. "Maybe... Pop thought he did. I don't know."

"What?"

"We talked about it, once."

"You and he."

She nodded.

"He told you something."

"It was a strange evening. Four weeks ago. I was here, with them. Mom had gone to bed. It had been one of those dark April days. Grey, a week of fog. He said—he said that he and Mom—that they were no longer of any use. Any use to anybody."

"What?"

"No use. That was the phrase he used."

"That's crazy."

"Just about exactly what I told him. He said, 'Less crazy than most things.' I asked if he believed that, that he was of no use. He said, 'I'm pretty sure. Hannah is very sure.'"

"And that's dumb. At the very least he was of use to her—way more than of use. Absolutely necessary."

"Yes."

"And that's really what Pop said?" Jack leaned toward her. "That Mom was very sure."

"Yes."

"How could he listen to her? What made him say that?"

"Pop said, 'The house told her.'"

"What house."

"This house."

"Our house. Our house told her she was of no use."

"That's what he said."

"Oh god. Poor Mom. She really said..."

"I'm only the reporter here. Of what Pop said."

"That this house—Oh damn. Damn! She was really so far gone as to believe the house—"

"We talked. We were sitting right here. Staring into the fire. We wondered where you were, if you'd have liked to be sitting with us, by the fire. Then he said to me, 'Hannah speaks to the house. She talks to it from inside a room. Whichever room is most appropriate to what she wants to talk about. But mostly from the kitchen.' Pop said she believed her house was animate."

"Animate?"

"A living thing. And her interlocutor."

"She said the house told her she was useless."

"Of no use. The words she used."

"Her mind was going, Nat, we both know that. So maybe she'd come to believe this no-use business. And came up with a lot of nonsense about the house."

"Like I said, I'm just reporting."

Tartarus shuddered. "It's awful."

At sunset a strong breeze came up. They found the silver serving spoons, walked out to the meadow, opened the urn. With the spoons they fed their parents' ashes to the wind.

The year before his parents' suicide, his wife, Maureen, had died. Some months ago, April, Tartarus ended his mourning for her by finishing *FIRE AND THE PHOENIX*. The film, her final funeral pyre, burned away both the last of his grief and the thick curtain that had hidden his clear responsibility. And he'd seen what was next demanded of him: avenge his parents' deaths.

He knew this wasn't rational, vengeance against a house. But, sitting in San Francisco, in Louise Davies Hall, watching and listening to the premiere of *FIRE*, the flames on the screen reduced to ash any need for rationality as far as his parents' deaths were concerned. The city had been driving Hannah crazy. Did that mean she was already then moving toward her dementia? He hadn't understood. Well, nobody had. Treatment might have helped. But instead they moved to the secluded house on Crab Island. The speed of the dementia's onslaught increased. Jack hadn't realized how much of her the dementia had taken away. Hannah and Sam were in the house because they loved it, it had become part of them. So, in its way, the house was responsible for their suicides. A metaphoric responsibility, to be sure. And to take revenge on a house for metaphorical reasons was irrational, Jack knew this too. So he had tried not to explain himself to anyone. He could give out reasons: fear of liability, cost of insurance, and so on. Rational reasons to cover the necessarily irrational reason. He had taken the greatest leap forward in his work when he allowed himself to become irrational about fire. He trusted himself fully, in needing to destroy the house. It looked irrational to do so because it was irrational. His best work grew from refusing the rational. Nonsense to deal rationally with fire. Thus the breakthrough in his work. So too now: acting on an irrational urge made total sense.

For ten years he hadn't talked with Natalia about their conversation when she had told him that Hannah spoke to the house. In fact he had rarely allowed this information back to his consciousness. Not until April. He had then called Natalia to say he was coming to Crab, he had to commit a ritual act. "Don't be foolish," she'd said.

His plan had taken on various kinds of clarity. Among them, obviously, fire. Cameras set at four angles. The house ablaze, flames reaching high into the sky, ruddy flames and yellow flames . . . No. Fire would give the house grandeur, majesty, a legitimacy it had not the least right to. And fire was too quick. His parents had built their lives into the house slowly, plain hard work. Then the house had turned on them. In that same way, he had to destroy the house, slow and measured steps, a little at a time. And he had found the appropriate means of destruction.

Start now. Forget the damn demolition order, get on with it! Where was that bar? He couldn't find the damn bar! He strode the veranda the full three hundred and sixty degrees. There, where he'd been working, fallen off the deck. He picked it up. Stared at it. Slammed it sideways against the wall, a hard cracking noise, and it bounced off. Damn you, house, and damn you, Allholy! He threw the bar down and sat on the top step. He could be irrational about anything except disobeying regulations. He went inside and took a drink of water.

He checked his watch. Just after four. Into the car. Or walk, as she did. No. Car. Up her entry drive. Her station wagon in place by the carport. The left rear tire looked low. No wonder she walked. Hitchhiked too? He turned off the engine, got out, up the porch steps. He knocked on the door. Like last time, no answer. He knocked again. Was she never at home. Only her beater stayed home. Where the hell was she? He had to know, was she the woman who found his parents? To the left of the door, nearly at the end of the porch, was a window. He looked in. A small living room, nothing moving.

Sit on the steps and wait for her to come back? Nothing much else to do. He sat. The late-afternoon sun was still high but a bit of a breeze cooled the air, or maybe only the skin of his bare arms. The field before him and to the sides lay flat and brown. Did Ginny and her mother lease it out as pasture? When he and Maureen lived on Crab, Sam had asked Jack if he wanted to run some cows and a bull, milk or beef, a calf in the spring. Jack had answered, definitively, no. Strange to think of this now. As if his father, never having become a farmer or rancher or even squire, wanted to live such a life through Jack.

He sat for ten minutes, twenty. He sorted strategies: maybe start on the inside after all, plasterboard would come away more easily than wood. When to shatter the windows—or just take them out whole, maybe somebody could use them. And use the kitchen cabinets, the shutters? No, no part of the house should remain whole.

He didn't hear the front door open but suddenly behind his back he heard Ginny say, "All right. Come in." He turned. She passed back through the doorway.

He stood. "Hello." He followed her in.

They were immediately in the living room. The ceilings seemed high and the space felt roomy despite the petite dimensions. Hotter in here than outside in sunlight. A flowered couch, two deep-red chairs, a coffee table covered with magazines. A half-full bottle of water. A large bowl holding a rag. A fireplace, kindling to one side. And Ginny still in jeans and white shirt but now with a heavy shawl wound about her shoulders.

"Sit," she said.

He stared at her. The whites of her eyes, wide and large at the restaurant, were now immense. She seemed to shudder. "Are you okay?"

She glanced at him and then away. "Of course not."

"What's wrong?"

"Nothing."

"Doesn't look like nothing."

"All right. An attack." Again the shudder. Despite the heat. "A normal attack." She reached for the rag in the bowl, a facecloth. She rang water out of it and mopped her brow, cheeks, eyelids. "They happen."

"What do you mean, attack?"

"I told you. My constant companion. Who attacks me when I'm not looking."

"That—disease."

"My good buddy Sjögren. His syndrome."

"Worse than the—the dryness?"

"Yeah."

"It goes on—?"

She gave a bitter little laugh. "For very long moments. Right now my fingers are numb. Sometimes my skin goes so dry and my legs and arms tingle as if they were being poked with a million tiny pins. I'm chilled and dry at the same time."

"Is there something you can do?"

"Ha. I drink my water." She picked up the bottle and drained it. "I take my pills. My cyclosporine and pilocarpine. I'm a regular addict." She shivered, again wiped her brow. "Sometimes they help. Sometimes not. Not now." Again the dry laugh. "It's my immune system attacking me. All the damp external parts. Bit by bit. Even my skin. It's stinking hot today and I can't sweat. It's neurological. I'm doing it to myself. It'll let up."

"When? How long?"

She shook head. "An hour. A day. Three days, once."

"Can I do anything? Something to help."

"Yes."

"What's that?"

She lay the wet rag in the bowl. "Would you hold me?"

At least four reasons for saying no . . .

She noted his hesitation. "It's all in my immune system. I'm not contagious."

Well, that was one of the reasons. He stepped over to her. He put his arms about her shawl and the form inside it. Through the shawl he could feel only shape. No warmth. Her head rested on his shoulder. She smelled sweet, like summer grasses. He held her for some seconds, more seconds. He could feel her now, small tremors. And little dry nasal sniffs. Her ear was millimetres from his mouth. He whispered, "Easy. You needn't cry."

"I'm not crying." She drew her head back so he could see her face. "I can't cry."

Her eyes, the grey now dominant, stared at him as if she were seeing the inside of his head. "You really can't cry?"

"Not for many years."

He put his palm against the back of her head and pulled her face again to his shoulder. There had been times in his life when he'd not been able to cry. But his lack of tears was never neurological. "I'm sorry, Ginny. Do you want to cry?"

"Very much." She shivered.

"Now?" He felt her head nod. "Why now?"

The sniffs slowed. The tremors stayed. "No one..." She dropped her head so his shoulder hid her eyes, kept light from them. "No man... has held me, for a long time."

He stroked her hair.

"Many, many years."

He breathed out hard, a nasal sigh. He relaxed his embrace and took a small step back. He took her shawl with both hands, pulled it from around her, and dropped it on a chair. He again put his arms about her and enfolded her. And she clasped him. This time he could feel her, no longer a bulk, now a woman. He held her, she him. Two fingers of his right hand stroked the vertebrae along her back. He felt her shudder. They stayed in the embrace for perhaps a minute. He felt her arms loosen around his back, her head move off his shoulder. Their faces, a few centimetres apart. She brought her mouth to his. Her lips were warm. But dry, so dry. She kissed him softly. A parched but gentle kiss.

Quickly she pulled away. "Oh Jack. I'm sorry. I shouldn't..."

"Hush." He took her right hand and they sat on the couch. What the hell did he think he was doing?

"But—thank you."

"How you feeling? You want some more water?"

"Yes. In a minute."

"You want your shawl?" He started to stand.

She pulled him back down. "I'm—I think I'm—a bit better. I think the shivers are—less." She squeezed his hand. "Some of the numbness is gone." She flexed the fingers of her left hand. "Really. Thank you." She released his hand. "It goes like it comes."

Now he stood. "I'll get you more water, if you'd like."

She shivered again. "Yes, I would." She pointed. "The kitchen's back there."

Out through an archway, immediately into the kitchen. Glasses in the dish tray, they'd be clean. He ran cold water and filled a glass. This was crazy. He was here to tear down a house. Concentrate on that. She would do, was doing, all in her power to keep that from happening. And he was consorting with the enemy. Hugging and kissing the enemy. An attractive enemy, but that was not the point. A sick enemy, a weak enemy he could take advantage of. No, hardly weak. She was dangerous. Always had been. Give her the water and leave. He went back to the living room and handed her the glass. He noted the shawl over her shoulders again. But she was holding it looser about her.

She drank the water. "I'm glad you came. To visit. But—you want something."

"How'd you know?"

She smiled. "You stayed. You sat. On the steps."

He nodded. "I want to ask you. About—my parents."

"Okay. Will you sit? Next to me."

He considered this, let her see he was deciding. "Okay." He sat beside her.

"Sam and Hannah," she said.

"Yes. Ginny. Were you the one who found them?"

She said nothing. Then she turned to him. "Yes."

"In the garage."

She bit her upper lip. "I came by. Twice. The first time I knocked on the door, nobody answered. I had the key so I went inside. And everything looked normal. So I left. Anyway, the car wasn't there. That wasn't a big deal, Sam could have gone away, maybe taken Hannah to a doctor's appointment. Or somewhere. Except usually he would say to me he was going off. I told you that."

Tartarus nodded.

"I left, and only later that night I thought, Why was there so much stuff in front of the garage? So I came back in the morning. I knocked, again no answer. I went over to check the garage, you know, through the window in the door. And there was the car. I thought I could smell something abnormal, exhaust maybe. I raised the door open, it wasn't exhaust but like a dead, heavy weight inside, dry, it felt like it hit me in the chest. I was coughing, hacking really, I wasn't having an attack but it felt that way, whatever was in there dried me up. I thought I saw someone in the car but it felt so dry I couldn't go in. I went around back and opened the door. To get some cross-draft." She shook her head. "It took maybe ten minutes to clear the air out." She closed her eyes and breathed hard. "The police said the car was out of gas. Sam must have burned up the whole tank."

"Ginny—I'm sorry, this isn't, I mean, remembering—It must have been terrible."

"Yeah." She waited, then said, "There was, well, a smell too." She stopped, hard.

"I know. Natalia told me. Them. And the smell."

"They were starting to—to decay, Jack."

"And you could—smell that. Coming—from inside the car."

For some seconds she said nothing. Then, "The driver's door was open."

"Open."

"I didn't tell this to the police."

"What?"

"Hannah sat in the passenger seat, seatbelt on, ready to go somewhere. But her head drooped on her chest. And—and Sam was half

163

out of the car. His head was—hanging to the ground, and his feet were still behind the wheel. And—the seat belt was all askew."

"What do you mean?"

"I don't know. I can only guess. It looked like—like maybe at the last minute, he—he changed his mind."

"Changed?"

"Like he didn't want to die. Not right there. Not then."

"He didn't want to die . . ."

"But it would have been too late. He'd breathed in too much carbon monoxide, he had no strength or will or whatever left. He couldn't make it."

"Ginny. You called 911, right?"

"Of course. But not right away." She waited. "I—I lifted him back into the car. So he could be beside your mother. Just like her."

Tartarus stared at her. "So that—"

She found the facecloth and held it to the back of her neck. "So no one could suggest he'd tried to kill Hannah. And not himself."

"And you told nobody."

"Nobody. Except you. Now."

"Why?"

"He was your father. You would understand what he did. Whatever he did."

Tartarus saw her eyes, now more green than grey. He said only, "Hunnnhh."

She took his hand again. "Was I wrong?"

He thought for a moment. "No. You weren't wrong. Thank you."

"I'm sorry. I've upset you."

"No, no." But she had. And he knew she could see she had.

She waited a moment. "They were good people." She finished the water.

"Want some more?"

"I can get it. Now."

"Are you okay? Better?"

She soaked the facecloth, squeezed water out, lay it on her wrist. "I think so."

"Then I should be going. Don'll be expecting me."

"Okay."

He squeezed her hand and stood. Thought for a moment and said, "Get me a piece of paper and a pencil."

"Why?"

"I'll give you my cellphone number." She looked blank. "In case you have another attack."

Her head shook as if she couldn't fathom him. But she went to the kitchen and brought him paper and a pen. He put his number down. She took the paper, tore off a blank piece, wrote on it, and handed it back to him.

"What's this?"

"My number here. In case you need to ask me more questions."

Nothing else to say. He thanked her and started for the door.

She called to him, "You're going to your house first?"

"For a couple of minutes."

"Look at it, Jack. Look at it hard. It's a beautiful house. Sam's house. He and Hannah cared for it, cared profoundly."

Except, according to Natalia, Hannah believed the house told her she was useless. Though clearly the house never said anything to Hannah, Hannah believed the house had said this. And she told Sam. And Sam and Hannah died in the house's garage. Together.

"Let it go, Jack. Don't tear it down. Whatever your reason to tear it down . . ."

"No, Ginny, you let it go."

"What?"

"Saving the house. Your big self-absorbing cause."

She stared at her hands, now grasping each other. "I can only try. I won't win. You have all the power."

"Don's expecting me." He shrugged lightly. "You're sure you'll be . . ."

"I'm sure." She followed him to the door.

He opened it. She took his hand and squeezed it. He didn't squeeze back.

He drove to the house. He parked in front of the house. What had happened to Sam and Hannah's car. Oh yes, Natalia had sold it. She'd thought of keeping it, it had lots of good years on it. But she couldn't bring herself to drive it—to start the engine, to hear the exhaust. She didn't tell the buyer it was a suicide car. Jack remembered more: she had told the buyers the truth, it was her parents' car but they didn't drive anymore. He got out, up the steps, unlocked and went into the house.

He washed his face. The cooling cleansing power of water. He checked the refrigerator and freezer. Cold, and frozen. The bag of ice cubes into the freezer, the beer and water, the food, into the fridge. He checked his watch. Time to head off. Don said he'd be back by five. Fifteen minutes ago. He made a decision, took off his shirt and washed himself, armpits, then his chest. Better, if he was going to be social. He found a towel, dried, put his shirt back on—change it at Don's—and left the house. Drove away. Stopped before entering the wooded part of the drive. What had she said? The house was beautiful. He got out and looked back at it. Serene, yes. But just a building. Beauty was of no importance here. Even if it were, there is a beauty that poisons and kills.

He would not think of his father, possibly unwilling to die. He would not think of his mother, seat belt in place. He would not think, either, of Ginny. Whom he had held again, after nineteen years. Who had kissed him again. The kiss was chaste, it held no memories. He hadn't kissed her back. She had once embodied savage life, a primitive ferocity yet to be expended. How much of that was left inside her, and how deeply buried? Inside a shawl, clutched tight about her. He got back behind the wheel.

A red automobile roared down the drive toward him. It braked hard and stopped fifteen metres from his Buick. On the driver's side the door flew open and a woman leapt out. He recognized her. That restaurant, Don's friend—Etain. He again opened his door. "Etain! What is it?"

"Oh I'm glad I found you. Don—he's at the clinic. Frank had an accident. Off the road. He's in bad shape. Don said—find you."

"He should've called, I'd've . . ."

"Didn't have your cell number at the clinic."

"Come on. I'll back up, you can turn, get ahead of me. Lead the way."

EIGHT: Jack and Ginny, Now and Before

"**They said it'd be as** dangerous to move him down to Nanaimo."

"So they're keeping him here?"

"Till tomorrow anyway." Don's voice sounded controlled, matter-of-fact.

Tartarus heard it as a verbal mask. "How stable is he?"

Don's mouth lay flat. "I would guess not very. They aren't moving him."

Jack nodded. "How good is the staff?"

"They know their job."

Etain stood beside Don. She now put her arm about his waist. "Crab has a single intensive care bed, and Frank's in it."

"Impressive. New."

"And," she went on, "we've got two doctors here full-time. And a surgeon part-time, mostly retired but he's kept up his accreditation. Goes into Nanaimo twice a week. He was here today. Doctor Bandeen. Bandy, he's known as. He stopped Frank's internal bleeding and cast the bones. Much as he could do. And a couple of nurses, they're half-time too. Nancy's here today too. Frank's in good hands."

"What happened, Don?"

"He'd borrowed my van. Drove it off the road. Etain found him."

"He'd been drinking," Etain said. "The van stank of beer."

"Is he going to make it?"

"I don't know, Jack. I can't see the future."

And now he'd pissed Don off.

"I have to go to the restaurant. Terry can't handle it alone. I'll close up, emergency closure. Back soon as I can."

"Your regulars won't like it," Don said.

"They'll understand."

"Stay open, Etain. Nothing you can do here."

"I can be with you."

Jack heard it, a simple statement. Love. And great affection. She'd be back. Nothing could keep her away, not this evening. "I'll stay with Don in the meantime, Etain."

"Thanks, Jack." She gave him a little smile, Don a quick kiss, and was gone.

"So," said Don. "So begins the vigil."

"Is he conscious?"

"In spurts."

"Have you talked to him?"

"Just a few words. To let him know I'm here."

"He recognize you?"

"Sure. He croaked when he talked. But he asked for a beer. A good one." Don let a little smile come to his face. It twitched at the edges. As if holding back tears. And likely he was. But far back, very far.

"Come on," said Jack. "I'll buy you a coffee. Or a whisky."

Don shook his head. "I need to stay here."

Here was a six-chair waiting room in the Gladstone Clinic on Mustard Drive, just off North Road at the edge of the village. Aside from the intensive care space, the building held a consulting room, a rear storage room, and the common area they now stood in, all the gift of Harley Gladstone, a Crab Islander who had literally won the lottery. Dr. Bandy lived three minutes away. Nancy Dunbar sat in with Frank, monitoring his blood pressure, heartbeat, temperature, intravenous. Dr. Gastini was home with his family but on call. He too lived around a corner from the village core. Jack said, "I could go get you some coffee."

Don said without looking up, "That'd be good," waited a moment and added, "Jackie?"

Jack was already at the door. He turned. "Yes?"

"Uh, Natalia called me."

"She did. When?"

"Earlier. I was driving. She got me on my cell."

"She has your cellphone number."

"I leave it on when I'm away from the house. So Frank can reach me."

"What'd she say?"

"She's coming over to Crab. To talk some sense into you. And she wants to see me."

"What did you tell her?"

Don chuckled. "I said, of course. What else? Your sister's my friend, Jack. Always has been. And I hope always will be. You're the romantic in the group."

Jack said only, "I suppose." He reached for the door handle. "Black?"

"What?"

"Your coffee."

"Please."

Jack left. He'd told Etain he would stay with Don. The waiting room was claustrophobic. Now, at seven, the day had cooled, but the sun continued to desiccate the earth and leaves and grass. He would stick around till Etain returned. Then he'd leave the two of them—the three—to themselves. And what's to come of all this? If Frank survived—and maybe the old coot would in fact make it—would he return to the Bonner house, Don nursing Frank eternally? Or go to a, what was the phrase, mature care facility? Too many unknowns. And Don and Etain. A unit. Had they admitted this to themselves? Which meant that Natalia was, for Don, a person of the past. Don was right, he and Natalia were linked to each other only by Jack Tartarus's imagination.

But Natalia was for real arriving tomorrow. Call her, tell her about Frank's accident? Tartarus wondered suddenly, Was it in fact an accident? Had to be. Frank didn't have a suicidal bone in his body. Just some old broken ones, now. And how much of a suicidal bone had lived in Sam's body? Did his father at the bottom of his heart want to die, then, there?

Call Natalia, tell her? Didn't matter if she arrived on Crab tomorrow, she wouldn't be here to spend time with Don. She still had every reason to come over.

At North Road he turned left, walked past the liquor store, farther on the hardware store. In front, the clerk who had sold him the Fulton wrecking bar was sweeping twigs and leaves from the sidewalk into the gutter. Turtle. He said, "Nice evening."

"Sure is," said Tartarus.

"Work going okay?"

Tartarus stopped. "Okay as I can make it."

"Like it should be."

"Yep."

"Read about you." He leaned on his broom. "You and the fires, your movie."

"Yes, I made a movie."

Turtle nodded. "All those fires. Must've been hot."

Hot. Hot was one of Tartarus's central concerns. Make the viewer feel the heat coming at him. Electronically. "'Specially close up," he said. Photographing close to fire, close as possible, was where he felt most alive.

"Middle of the fire, eh." More nods. "Must've been something."

"Oh, it was. Say, where can I get coffee to go?"

"No problem. Co-op's always got coffee going."

"Thanks." Tartarus started off.

"He gonna make it? Frank, I mean?"

"We truly hope so."

Again Turtle nodded. "Take care."

Oddball. Every village needs one. On to the Co-op. Where he found coffee. He opened the spigot, drained one measure into a Styrofoam cup, sniffed it. Brewing since early morning. He covered it and took out his wallet. A piece of paper drifted to the floor. He picked it up. Ginny's phone number. He shoved it into his shirt pocket, paid, and headed back. Turtle had disappeared.

Don would be at the clinic all night. No, he wouldn't sleep at Don's tonight. Nothing to be done, he'd have to stay at the house. Didn't matter, he'd spend the night there tomorrow anyway. Might as well get used to it again, prepare himself for Natalia's invasion.

At the clinic he found Don and the nurse, Nancy, in consultation. They turned to him as he entered. "What's up?"

"Frank's awake. Sort of. He keeps repeating, 'Fire, Jack, fire, Jack, fire . . .'"

Jack grinned. "He wants to fire me?"

"I think he's talking about your film."

"I get it. But why?"

"Don't know."

"Would you mind going in?" Nancy asked. "He might recognize you."

"Does he recognize you?" Jack asked Don.

Don released a closed-lips sigh. "I don't know. But he keeps repeating your name."

"Sure. I'll go in." He handed Don the coffee. "Here." And to the nurse, "Sorry, I should've asked you if you wanted some."

"I don't use it." She gave Jack plastic gloves and a face mask. "Just a precaution."

He put them on, turned the handle, entered. Frank Bonner lay flat except for his head and shoulders, which were propped up by the mattress and a pillow. His eyes showed through tiny lid slits. Tubes connected his body to machines. Bandages covered his head, both shoulders, and right arm. Jack moved silently to his right side. "Frank, it's Jack."

For several seconds Frank didn't respond. Then his lids pulled back and the bloodshot whites suddenly grew large, ringed with a dark-red tinge, big enough to let Tartarus see fear. Frank's breath came and went, in-out, in-out, so shallow the air couldn't be reaching his lungs. No, not breaths at all but the attempt to say words which now he could make out, "Jack—fire—Jack—fire," Jack on the intake, fire on the outbreath. "Jack—fire—Jack—" And the fright in his eyes.

"It's okay, Frank, I'm here, take it easy." Though what good his being there could do . . .

"Jack—fire—Jack—fire—"

"Yeah, I made a movie about fire."

"Fire—fire—moo—moo—v—fire moov—""

"When you get out of here, I'll play it for you."

"Moo—moov—see—seen—" His words came out dry.

"You've seen the movie?"

"Seen—moov—see—"

"Well how about that. Did you like it?"

"Moov—fire—fire—fire—"

171

"I'll take that for a yes."

"No . . ."

He seemed out of breath. Or shallow breathing had taken over his attempts to speak. His upper lids dropped, not quite heavy enough to reach the lower, and the slits returned.

"Take care of yourself, Frank. For Don's sake."

No response from Frank.

Jack carefully backed away to the door. It was ajar. He stepped outside. Don stood by the entryway. Jack said, "I think he saw my fire film. Must've sneaked it from my pack."

"And he wanted to tell you?"

"Yeah. But he seemed scared at the same time."

"Scared."

"Like last night, when he woke up. Scared of something."

"I think he's scared of lots of things."

What that meant Tartarus didn't ask. He still didn't like Frank. But not liking Frank didn't mean he wanted Frank to shuffle off. Though Frank's departure would make Don's life a whole lot easier. Likely even Don knew that.

Etain returned. "All set. Nancy, you want to get yourself a sandwich? Or you want me to bring you something?"

Nancy considered this. "I'd better be in there with him."

"What would you . . ."

"Whatever they've got, without meat. Thanks." She returned to the intensive care room and closed the door.

Etain turned to leave. Don said, "I'll go. I'd like some air." He left.

Jack sat. "I won't stay. Only till Don comes back."

"Will you go to your house?"

He squinted at her. "How did you figure that?"

"It made sense."

He nodded. "I shouldn't be here. I'm irritating Don."

"No. He's upset. All by himself. He loves the old man. Sometimes neither of them like the other very much. But each one loves the other."

Not an original thought. But her words as she spoke sounded wise. "I guess you're right."

For several seconds, silence. Till Etain said, "May I ask you something?"

"Some things yes, some things no."

"Tartarus. Is it your real name? Or the name you use for your art?"

"Hhnnh. You never asked Don?"

"I didn't have to. Till I met you."

A mind that inquires only about the immediate? "Okay. It was my father's name."

"Then it is your name."

"It wasn't my grandfather's name. That was Tataraski. Otto Tataraski."

"And he changed it."

"They changed it for him. An immigration official did. When he arrived in Canada."

"Ah."

"My father was just six. In 1933. My grandparents left Germany when Hitler came in."

"They saw it all coming."

"They saw what was happening and they feared what could come."

"I see. They were Polish?"

"German-Polish." Tartarus chuckled. "My father tracked down the immigration guy who changed our name. Years later. An out-of-work high-school teacher of Greek and Latin. Turned my grandfather Tataraski, a sweet gentle man, into Tartarus. My father said to me—I'd started working with fire, just still photos back then—he said the ex-teacher proved how a little learning may not be dangerous but it can have ramifications for the generations ahead."

She smiled. "I looked him up."

"Him?"

"Tartarus. The original."

"Ah."

"'Spawned from primordial chaos,' it said. Deep in the underworld. He married Gaea and had a son named Typhoeus, a monster with a hundred legs."

"Yeah. Gaea, my eternal partner. Except I've spawned no one. With or without legs."

"Then we have two things in common."

"The other being?"

"The source of my name."

"Etain?"

"Etain, the beautiful wife of Mider, an Irish god. He too lived in the underworld. Though my mother would call it the otherworld."

"Your mother's Irish."

"Her family, long ago. When you grew up in Catholic Québec, everybody intermarries."

"Not you?"

"I haven't been Québecoise in many years."

Tartarus said nothing.

"And you. Are you Jewish?"

He waited before speaking. "Culturally, sometimes."

"No God."

"Definitely no God. And you?"

"I told you. Not for years."

"You said not Québecoise."

"More or less the same thing. In Québec we got rid of God pretty fast. Maybe as quickly as you did."

"I don't know," said Jack. "My father didn't have much of a God problem. If there'd been a God, we might all still be in Germany."

"Yes, and I in Québec. We disappeared God from there quick as we could."

"An ex-Catholic atheist."

"Perhaps more an ex-Catholic pantheist."

"God is everywhere?"

"Many gods everywhere."

Before Jack could respond, the door opened. Don came in carrying a brown bag. He glanced from one to the other. "Something happen?"

"What?"

"You both look deadly serious."

"Oh," said Etain. "We were discussing God."

"Maybe you both better leave."

"The absence of such a phenomenon," said Jack.

"I guess you can stay." Don tilted his head at the ICU door. "Any change?"

"All quiet."

Don nodded and tapped on the door. It opened, he spoke a few words to Nancy, handed her the sandwich, and closed the door. "No change, she says."

"I'll head off." Jack stood. "I'll pick up my stuff and sleep at the house tonight."

"You don't have to do that . . ."

"Is that a good idea?" Etain asked.

"It's fine. I want to." He paused for a moment before adding, "And I would have tomorrow night anyway. Natalia's coming over and she wants to sleep in the old house."

Neither spoke till Don said, "That'll be nice for you. A while since you've seen her?"

"A while." He noted Etain watching Don. "I'll check in with you tomorrow. See you both. Nice chatting, Etain."

"Nice," she said. They watched Jack close the door behind him. She waited a few seconds before asking, "Are you okay?"

"Sure." Don glanced at the ICU. "Except for Frank." He turned to Etain. "You?"

She got up and took his hand. "I think so."

"Good." He brought his arm around her. She lay her head on his shoulder. "I cancelled out of my food pick-ups for tonight. Trevor'll do them for me."

"You'll be forgiven."

With both Tartarus and Natalia at the house tomorrow, they'd need food. The Co-op might still be open.

It was. Jack bought more coffee, also milk, sugar, bread. A couple of small steaks, some potatoes, carrots, onions, garlic, tomatoes, lettuce. A small jar of vinaigrette. Steaks? The generator didn't power the stove. But in the old days they grilled steaks and burgers on the coal-fired hibachi. He bought a bag of briquettes. At the liquor store, a bottle of Okanagan Merlot.

He drove, on toward Don and Frank's. Would it ever again be Frank's home? How quickly all can shift. Were there people he could call about Frank's condition? He should have asked Don. Who were Frank's friends, after Sam and Hannah had killed themselves? Should he call Ginny? She'd been a regular at Hannah and Sam's, had she met Frank there? She might know if Frank had other friends. He pulled to the side of the road, found the slip of paper with her number, pressed it in. A dozen rings, no answer. Never at home. Or pretending not to be.

At the Bonner house he picked up his suitcase and the two container boxes. On top of one lay a casing for *FIRE AND THE PHOENIX*, but no disk. The old thief must have come in and taken it. Tartarus checked the tray of the DVD player. Yep, there it was. He started to pick it up, stopped, and turned on the machine. He skipped through the first ten minutes, stopped, let it play.

Fire in a fireplace, a single log. The flames rose, an undisciplined triangle of flame, non-cohesive, tickling the little log, teasing it into helping them grow tall, surge up as mighty flames, all red-black destruction. Suddenly no sound. Had Tartarus muted the sound away here? He didn't think so. But no whisper, let alone roar of flames. And no music in the background. He turned the sound up. Silence. Had Frank messed with the disk?

He put the suitcase and containers in his trunk and drove to the Tartarus house by way of the cliffs. He got out halfway along the cliff-top and leaned back against the car door. He faced south but to his right he could see the sun hanging a couple of its widths above the horizon. To the southwest the lighthouse blazed yellow-white in the low sun. Below him waves shattered into shadowy spray. Out over the strait three gulls sailed on invisible wind trails—hardly currents, he felt not a breeze. He stood up there alone, and that was just right.

He waited till the sun dropped from sight and suddenly felt gratified, fulfilled even. Frank might be dying, his parents had killed themselves, Natalia and Don were unlikely ever to be a unit, yet the world was okay. One day he might do a series, the sun at work. He had seen many a sunset more glorious, but the surge of satisfaction this evening, a sense of sweeping beneficence, more than hinted there might be a realm worth exploring in the sun rising and setting, the sun warming and hiding. Nothing original there, just that these patterns were renewed every day. Which in itself was marvellous.

He recalled that, in the beginning, he had considered fire just this way. Fire, a daily occurrence, no big deal. Until he began his study. And immediately every fire was different, each one a strange new action, a new demand on his imagination, and so on his cameras.

Fire, he'd discovered, gave him strength. Strength to, for example, raze the house. Before working with fire in motion he would never have thought of tearing it down. Tearing it down would cleanse the Tartarus land. Fire too could cleanse the land. Controlled fire. But today, tomorrow, the fear of burning down the whole of Crab hovered over him. It could never be a controlled fire, not now, not here. His hands-on tearing down of the house would, however, be a controlled act.

He drove into the twilight, back to the house, no lights needed yet, he wouldn't disrupt the transition between day and dark. He slowed into his drive and the minimal lingering daylight guided the car through. The house outlined against pale sky did, he had to concede, suggest a solid beauty. He parked by the front door and got out. There by the garage, another shape. A station wagon, ancient vintage. Goddamn her! He walked over, looked in. Empty.

He would not get angry, he would not get angry. As if all were normal, he unloaded the car, groceries and wine first, brought them to the veranda. Would she have locked the door behind her? Yes. He tried the door anyway. It held. He slid the key into the lock, turned it, then the handle, and pushed the door open. Groceries in, back for the suitcase and containers. A flashlight too. Leave the briquettes on the veranda. Meat into the fridge, its light shining bright. To the living room. The flashlight's beam found no one. Nor in the dining room. Up the stairs. On the landing he saw ahead, from under the door of his one-time bedroom, a bleed of light.

"Ginny," he said quietly.

"Hello, Jack," came her voice.

He pushed the door open. She lay, head on a propped-up pillow, on top of a sheet on his made-up bed, one of the battery lamps beside her. She stared at the ceiling.

"What now, Ginny?"

"Now?"

"You better leave. Please don't get me angry."

"Jack." She turned to face him. Again the eyes, that spread of white. Without light reflecting on them the irises were neither grey nor green. Simply large.

"What?"

"I think they're here, tonight."

"What? Who is?" But he knew what she would say.

"Your parents. Hannah and Sam. Both."

"Ginny, stop it."

"I think—I know—I can sense them."

"You can sense your overblown imagination."

"Much more. Much, much more."

"Come on, Ginny, time to go home."

"I think they're letting me know they're here—because you're here."

This was mad and she was madder. He took her by the forearm and pulled. "Let's go."

Slowly she shook her head. He pulled harder. It was as if she were nailed to the bed. Then a sudden grin from her, that hint of evil again. "Better let go, Jack. Remember what happened last time you grabbed my arm."

He wasn't afraid of being bitten, but he did know she wouldn't move unless he did more than pull so he released her. "Okay. Be reasonable. Sensible. You have to leave."

"Why?"

"Because I'm going to find something to eat and get some sleep."

She sat up, bounced off the bed on the far side, grabbed her backpack from the floor, and walked slowly toward him. She wore a white loose sundress and was barefoot. "Good! I'm starved. No food since lunch. Let's make supper together. Come on." She ran from him through the doorway into the dark hall, swinging the backpack, the skirt of her dress wisping behind her.

He grabbed the lamp and followed. A waif of a woman, he thought. No, too old for a waif. Which made Jack Tartarus an old, old man. She was already on the ground floor, taking the stairs in the darkness as if she'd been descending this dark passageway for years. Which likely she had. Make supper. With her. Ridiculous. Okay, what other social or even domestic events faced him tonight? He could sit alone in the house. Alone had been fine on the cliff as the sun took its slow diurnal dive. Alone would remain fine this evening. On the other hand, he had plenty of future time to be alone. So why not open the salsa and Tostitos, have a beer, and then she'd go home. Yes, damn it, home she'd go. In the morning he'd buy more salsa.

In the kitchen she'd turned on the other battery-powered lamps. Only ten watts of light each, but enough. The refrigerator door stood open. In one hand, the steak packages. "Jack! Steaks. Wonderful! Did you get briquettes? Or there's firewood in the shed, you'll have to split a log down, the hatchet's standing right there. And get the hibachi from the garage, the one with legs, we can set it up on the veranda and . . . What?" Because he was staring at her.

"You know everything about this house, don't you. Where everything is, what to do in any situation."

She dropped her glance to the floor. "I know the house. Yes."

"Making a fire. Now."

"Come on. A controlled fire. A tiny hibachi. You watching it all the time."

He sighed. Loud, making sure she heard. "I'll get the hibachi."

"And it's too late to bake the potatoes in the coals. So I'll just peel them, we can steam them on the propane stove. The steamer's in the third drawer, can you grab it for me."

Not a question. Just this was how it was going to be. He took the steaks and his flashlight, left the meat on the veranda rail, and headed for the garage. He felt as unprepared to enter the garage as the first time. But she had said bring the hibachi and because he had acquiesced to A, he needed to accede to B. He rolled up the garage door, beamed in the light, and scanned the dark space. The suicide scene. His father, partly out of the car. The door open. The hibachi. Who was it had brought all this junk back into the garage? Must've been him. Natalia. Ginny, maybe. Might have been Frank. Why Frank? Why anybody.

He lifted the hibachi, waltzed it over jerry cans and a lawn mower, carried it outside. Someone had not cleaned the grill after the last use. Maybe Jack Tartarus. He didn't think so. Maybe his father. The grease of his father's hamburger, still on the grill.

He wished she had not said she felt the presence of his parents. Because Tartarus did not feel his parents to be present. If they were, would he have sensed them? They had, after all, been his parents, not hers. He wondered what it would be like to feel his parents' presence, the ghosts of their presence. There was nothing. He remembered his father, standing over the grill, cursing the uneven heat, three hamburgers nearly black, four barely tinged. He could see the moment. But it no longer existed. More than vanished. Gone up in smoke. Literally.

He hefted the hibachi up onto the veranda. How to clean the grill. He didn't remember ever cleaning the grill. Not cleaning the grill suddenly wrenched another memory into the present: Sam Tartarus angry with himself, Why do I have to get old to be smart? Why did I have to do it the hard way so often before figuring out the easy way? He had said to his son, Why not let the flames clean the grill? Which they did, with red-hot precision. Firing the coals, preheating the grill, and all the fat and soot from the previous week's cookout burned away. A newly sterile grill. A quick whisk with a steel brush left the grill glowing, ready for the first piece of meat.

He opened the briquettes and dumped a batch onto the coal platform. Paper to start them. Gasoline. He found the jerry tank beside the generator, poured maybe fifty millilitres onto the coals, waited for it to soak in, then dropped a match into the mix. No flare of flame here, merely gasoline burning through the outer shell of briquette. When the briquettes glowed a bright red, the gasoline would long be burned away. He gave the fire a minute to be sure it was on its way, then placed the grill as close to the fire as the hibachi allowed.

The hibachi, with its open fire. But here at the house no wind, not even a breeze. Not a small man in sight. He blew on the little flames.

Through the open door from the house wafted a new scent. An intense familiarity. He knew it, onions and garlic frying in his mother's kitchen. He had fried onions and garlic himself, many times in many places. But the smell of onions and garlic from the kitchen here was different from the same combination frying anywhere else. From the kitchen and through the front hall something transformed the scent. It wafted on a wave of warm air that smoothed onion and garlic into a buttery ribbon of aromatic delight. This had been Hannah's private craft.

He followed the scent into the kitchen. She had opened the window behind the stove and sink. Important, with the propane stove on the table working full blast. A pot on one burner, a pan on the other. He glanced through the pot's glass cover: potatoes steaming, perspiring. In the pan onion slices were going transparent and small chunks of garlic had browned lightly. In a second pot on the table, sliced carrots waiting to be simmered. How about that. The first meal to be cooked, in many a year with a Tartarus present, in the house on Crab.

Ginny appeared from the dining room. "Would you mind opening the wine? The glasses are out on the table." She smiled.

Something about her seemed different. As if she'd combed her hair. But that wasn't it. She certainly looked better than earlier in the day, her syndrome in control.

"We can eat in the dining room," she said.

Dining room. She was playing House and Home. "The kitchen's not good enough?"

"A special occasion. A Tartarus is again in the Tartarus house. Celebration time!"

Uncanny. He'd said nothing. Or had he? No.

About not eating in the dining room he could insist. But, ridiculously, it all seemed to be giving her pleasure. She had made it clear enough, her life had been without much of that for a long time. How did she get along with her mother? he wondered. He'd asked her nothing. It would be the small talk at the dining table. "I suppose you know where the corkscrew is."

"Right beside the wine. Also on the table." She smiled again.

Whatever else, she seemed to be feeling mighty pleased with herself. Well, let her. He headed for the dining room. And was impressed. She had found a white tablecloth. She had set the table for two, with plates and napkins. Water glasses, wineglasses, water, and the Merlot he'd bought. The cutlery was his mother's silver plate—had he really left this in the house for tenants to use? She'd found candlesticks, the candles were burning brightly. As were the kerosene lamps. Almost enough light to see food by. She had done all this while he'd merely wrestled the hibachi to the veranda. He noted the wine set on a small dish to keep drips from staining the tablecloth. He uncorked the bottle, sniffed it. Not great, but okay. He should get the steaks on. Small steaks, luckily. He returned to the kitchen. "The wine is breathing."

"Would you bring me a half-glass? And you should have some too. Are the steaks on?"

"Waiting for the grill to be hot enough."

"The potatoes should be ready in ten minutes. Gauge yourself."

"I'll be close with the steaks." He returned to the veranda. Just as Sam Tartarus had promised, a clean grill. No idea where a steel brush might be, possibly the usual storage space. And he should wash the steaks but that would mean back to the kitchen and admit he'd gotten virtually nothing done. Let the fire burn away all impurities. No. He remembered the hose spigot at the edge of the garage. He opened the valve. A burst of air, a spurt of rusty water, hiccups of air and water, then the water ran clear and strong. He shut it off. Back for the steaks, tear off the wrapping, wash them, back to the rail, set them on the paper. To the garage. He flared its content with the flashlight. No obvious wire brush. He turned off the light, tried to think, to remember... Nothing. Nothing but silence and darkness. He listened. He thought he'd heard soft, strong laughter. The way his father had laughed. He remembered it, all so clear. He waited; nothing. The wire brush would be with the other hibachi, the rectangular one. He shone his light at it. Nothing visible. He went over to it and lifted the grill. One wire brush. Obvious.

He brushed the fired ashes into the flames and lay the steaks atop the grill. They sizzled, at first the water, then the red meat. He needed a spatula, a fork, a plate. He strode back to the hall. Coming his way was Ginny, bearing a fork and a spatula. He took them. "Thank you."

"Thought you might want them. A plate?"

"Two, please."

The flames spurted around the meat, scorching the underside. A particle of fat dropped into the fire, creating a volcanic jet of yellow-purple flame. The coals below glowed a dusky orange, each single coal alive with a hundred flamelets. Tartarus figured the meat for ready on the underside. He flipped both pieces, tested them with the tines of the fork. The surface had seared nicely, the meat beneath still red and tender. Two more minutes on this side and he was done. If she wanted it rare. Well that was how she'd get it. He worked each steak loose from the grill. She appeared, carrying two plates. He scooped a steak onto each, brought them in, and set them on the kitchen table. "Be right back." He glanced about, saw the potato pot in the sink, filled it with water, and returned to the hibachi. He poured the water over the coals. They sizzled, whooshed with steam, and their orange died.

In the bathroom he washed his hands. She'd put a towel out. When he returned to the dining room, he found himself standing beside a chair in front of a yellow plate bearing brown steak, orange onioned carrots, and a pale cream potato. Her wineglass, quarter full. Another glass, his, fuller than hers, and an equal setting.

She raised her glass. "You never brought me any. So I had to pour it for myself."

He took his place opposite.

"Thank you, Jack," she said, and her lips curled up.

A pretty smile, he thought. The former malice gone. "Nothing to thank me for. In fact, I should thank you. I'd have had crackers and beer and gone to bed."

She sat, and so did he. They ate. They complimented each other on the other's production. He told her about Frank, and the accident. She didn't know Frank at all but felt for Don, she'd met him a couple of times. She asked him about his fire art. He told her about some of his projects. At one point he said, "I've come a long way since my first show on Crab," and wished he hadn't mentioned that moment in his, in their, history.

She told him about living on Crab off and on in the last decade-plus, forays away for work, twice gone to the Grover Institute for treatment for the Sjögren's. "Nothing helped. It'll go away only when I die." She told him about her mother. "Madge is seventy-nine and fit as a horse. She's got a man-friend down in Victoria, she spends a couple of long weekends a month with him. He comes here once in a while but can't relax when I'm around. They sometimes like to get it on. I make him nervous." She giggled, the light laugh of a naughty schoolgirl who's gotten away with a small crime. She sipped wine, a very little. She had drunk barely a quarter of what she'd poured herself. Yes, with her medications, no more than half a glass a week. "And I'm drinking it all tonight." So Tartarus finished the rest of the bottle. Ginny drank water—two, three, four glasses. But when they left the table, it was she who appeared dizzy.

"You okay?"

She laughed, embarrassed. "It's not the wine."

"Looks like the wine."

"It's my cyclosporine—my medication. It doesn't like wine."

They washed the dishes together, in cold water and dim light, and joked about them being clean for Natalia. Tartarus dried. "Can't find a dish rack?"

"No idea where it is."

"I'm relieved."

They thanked each other again for a very pleasant meal.

Ginny said, "I should go, but . . ."

"I'll drive you." She might be too dizzy to drive.

She laughed. "You've had too much to drink. Way more than me. I won't let you drive."

"Ginny, I've driven with way more likker in me than this."

She laughed. She shook her head. "I'm staying here tonight."

"No, Ginny, you are not."

"First, I am. And secondly, I'm sleeping with you."

"Look, we've had a perfectly pleasant evening. We aren't enemies anymore. Antagonists maybe, but not enemies. And now the evening comes to an end."

"Listen to me, Jack. I didn't say I'm going to be fucking you. I said sleep. Sleep. I will not take off my clothes. You will not take off your clothes. We can lie side by side on your bed, and talk, and fall asleep. Because I am not driving home, and you are not driving me home."

"Shit, Ginny. Don't do this."

"It's my only choice."

"Okay, don't go home. Stay. I'll—we—will make up a bed for you on the couch."

"Make it up. But you'll see. I will lie beside you and we will fall asleep."

"What the hell for?"

"'Cuz I want to. I'll never find someone new to lie beside, not the way I am. You aren't new, and I'm not the way I was then, and we're friends now. Aren't we?"

Her voice seemed smaller but she wasn't begging. Tartarus found himself saying, "I'm crazy, Ginny. But okay."

She took his hand. "Thank you." She found her backpack and headed for the bathroom.

And true to her word, they lay side by side on his bed, shoes off, she on her back in her white sundress and he in khakis and shirt, on his back as well but lightly turned toward her, and she didn't touch him. She had set the ever-present bottle of water on the night table on her side. They talked little. But more than Tartarus wanted when she said, "I can feel them watching us."

"They?"

"I think they approve."

"Stop it."

She said nothing more. In a few minutes her breath grew steady. Tartarus was near to certain she'd fallen asleep. He felt too warm in his clothes. Nothing to be done.

He lay still by a woman with whom he'd once shared the most erotic days and nights of his life. She'd been little more than a girl. He lay beside her now and didn't touch her. He had touched her when she'd asked him to hold her. She had felt like a woman, she was definitively a woman. He knew he wanted to touch her again, hold her to him. Like earlier. To protect her, to keep her safe. From? Safe from her loneliness. It lay on her surface in plain sight. And from her conversation a deeper isolation lived inside, only part hidden. Safe too from her disease, this Sjögren's syndrome, which held her in its clutch—not completely, not always, but ever-threatening. Or so she said.

He hadn't moved since he'd lain down, but now he turned fully onto his left side, propped himself up on his elbow, and looked at her. Very little light, a half-moon tonight, shining on another side of the house. He watched her face, those large eyes now hidden behind lids. Her brow was smooth and her chin rounded, as if she had no worries. Beyond loneliness. Her hair lay unruffled against the side of her head—had she combed it in the bathroom? In the dim light he could make out two thin lines from the edges of each eye across to the curve of her temples. He smiled. We are each of us growing older, Ginny. The lips of her small mouth opened lightly as she breathed in, and when she exhaled the air came from her nose, her breathing shallow.

He lay still for ten minutes, maybe fifteen, watching her. Then, over two or three minutes her breathing sharpened, exhaling now from her mouth. The breathing quickened further, and little sounds came from her throat. Her left hand that had been flat by her side now wound up to her head, a loose fist scraping at her hair as if the knuckles were searching for her scalp. Was this part of her syndrome. She whispered, "Oo—oh—uhh," sighed deeply, shivered.

He had no idea, should he respond? Wake her? Did this happen every night? An unpleasant dream? The Sjögren's attacking her? He waited a minute, two. Calm took her again. Her hand remained by her hair, but her body lay still, her breathing shallow again. All normal? He twisted and lay flat on his back.

He closed his eyes. How unexpected. That he was lying on his bed again, the bed he and Maureen had shared. The bed they had tried, in the three-plus years before she had been diagnosed, to conceive a child in. That he was in the old house altogether, after he had sworn not to enter the front door. That the house did not yet have a gaping hole in its side. That small men existed in every corner of the universe. That, perversely, the local small man had been instructed by the woman now lying beside him. Less strange, he had obeyed the small man.

With his eyes shut he drifted, from the cliff overlooking the strait where Maureen preferred not to be, to the woman Etain and her independence in her restaurant and her bond to Don, to Natalia and Don . . . He was in shallow sleep when he felt an arm strike his hip and he heard again Ginny's "Ohh—ahhh—oo—ee." He opened his eyes and turned. Both her hands were scraping at her scalp. He reached out and took her near hand. It pulled away like a spring. His palm rested on her hair. He soothed her head. Her hair, sweaty and clumped. He raised himself to look at her, direct moonlight now striking her face. Her breath came fast, her arms now down along her thighs but her fists again clenching, unclenching, and her torso seemed rigid. He reached out and brought his right arm across her chest to her left shoulder, raising it lightly so her body turned toward him. The sound kept coming, lower now, from down in her throat, and he slid toward her. Her eyes remained closed, sleep still clasping her, but her body had relaxed, not yet supple but less tight. He brought her up against his chest and felt her muscles slacken. Her clenched fingers loosened and her breathing slowed. He held her to him, her right cheek now against his chest, his hand stroking her matted hair. She had gone silent and limp. He felt her breathing, the small rise and fall of her breast. He dropped his hand to her waist and spread his palm across the small of her back. He closed his eyes.

A part of him said, Tartarus, you are a fool. Another said, less harshly, And who is not. A third chided, Man, you are playing with fire. And a fourth, Yes, that is what I do.

They lay still together, she asleep, he floating into sleep, sleep taking him away. His drift was wide, to Yucatan, where he felt lost, to the highlands of central Mexico. He knew no one here and in his dream he fell into a deep sleep. He slept beside an old man, a very old man, but the old man reached over for him and took him in his arms, and held him. Jack didn't mind, in fact was pleased, because the old man was his father. He held on to his father as his father to him. They held each other for a day, another day, and said nothing to each other. Then with unfelt movement his father was gone. Jack felt only an easy joy because he knew his father loved him. He woke from the sleep inside his dream and felt a light pleasure, as if the difficulties of his days had been swept away. Slowly he pulled himself out of his dream and back onto his bed because he had to get up and pee.

He sat. He was alone on his bed, dressed as before, khakis and shirt, and his watch. He had been sweating because his shirt was soaked, back, chest, and armpits. In the morning he would take a long shower. No, short, a cold shower. She, Ginny, had disappeared. He called, "Ginny?" No answer. "Ginny?!" The house was empty of her, he felt his voice's echo tell him so. He got up in the dark and peed. He swept water over his face and dried it. He went back to his bedroom, stripped, threw his clothes into a pile, tossed the blanket from the bed, lifted the bedsheet, and lay flat. He had to assume she had gone home. He could check the other bedrooms, the couch. But he knew she was gone. Tomorrow he would go to ensure she'd gotten back okay.

Her words, that his parents were watching them. And that dream, already faded to lost, something about his father, somewhere in rural Mexico—Where he had shot most of *FIRE AND THE PHOENIX*. The midnight mind is strange.

He found his flashlight and checked his watch. Just after three. The mind is strange all night long, its wonderful irrationality ever present. He lay on his side and reached out to where she had been. A flat mattress. He closed his eyes against the moonlight. He fell into sleep . . .

. . . and knew abruptly he was no longer alone. He was being watched, he could feel eyes. He dared not open his, for fear of learning where his mind was leading. He could not tell whether there was a breathing in his ears or in his imagination. A slow, soft breath. Neither sweet nor aged, merely a movement in the air. He reached his hand out, under the sheet, very gently, for fear of losing—whatever was there. He extended his fingers. And touched something soft. Silky. He slid his body across, to follow his hand. Fingers took his fingers. Raised the whole of his hand. Lips kissed his fingertips. And she slid closer to him.

He opened his eyes. In the indirect moonlight he saw her, Ginny, back in his bed. He lowered his hand to her cheek, her neck. She slipped yet nearer, her legs reaching out to his. Their ankles touched, feet wound around legs. His hand eased across bare skin to her breast, draped in silk. Her hand touched his chest, gently stroked the hair. He slid his hand down her ribs to her waist, to her buttock, silk-cloaked all. Her lips found his and they breathed into each other's mouths. Into each other's core, each other's marrow. Her hand slipped farther down and found him crystal-hard, coal-hot.

She pulled her mouth from his. "Hello, Jack," she said.

"I wasn't expecting you," he said.

"I think you were."

"In all truth, no."

"Shall I leave?"

"I think you better not."

"If it's better, then I won't."

"Much better—" he felt her palm and fingers, squeezing, releasing, squeezing "—much—"

"You like my mouth?"

"Yes. Very."

"It's not dry. You notice?"

"No, no, not at all." He hadn't, and it wasn't.

"I'm ready. Almost."

She kissed him again, and then brought her arms up and embraced him, held him against her, drew him to her so tight she might have melted into him. He clasped her nearly as fast, but no embrace could be as firm as hers. Then her hold on him loosened, and his on her. He raised her head and slid the silken sheath up along her body. He kissed her breasts, small and round, and he let his lips slide around her nipples, left, right, left. She giggled.

He drew back. "Ginny."

"That's me. You got the right one."

"Are you—I mean, you said . . ."

She sang, "How dry my vagina can be."

"I guess."

"I'm prepared." She kissed him. "I'm organized." Another kiss. "Are you?"

"I guess."

"Losing your vocabulary?"

He laughed. "I guess."

"Okay." Again a kiss, long and deep. Till she pulled back, twisted on her bum and brought her mouth to his cock and held him there, wetting his shaft from glans to hair. She raised her head, "Here we go," and climbed on to him, lowered herself, and he slid inside her like hands on silk. They moved slowly against each other, holding each other. Slower and slower was richer, richer, slowness the privilege of age. An old, old man with a woman too old to be a waif, and even their delay proved too hasty as without toil they exploded within and about each other, through and through each other, only their mouths capable of searching deeper.

Somewhere in their post-coital moment he said, "Isn't this a little crazy. I'm an older man, right. Way too old for you."

She answered, "After a certain amount of suffering we're all the same age."

On they went, three more times, the last two with the assistance of vegetable oils, before they would admit to each other that the sun was high, the day bright, and the daughter of the Tartarus house on Crab would be arriving on the early afternoon ferry.

NINE: Natalia, Justine, and Ghosts

What did it mean, that Justine spoke to her grandparents in the house on Crab? That she was a loving granddaughter? Yes. That she had an overactive imagination? No question. That, maybe, there was something not quite right in her head. Natalia shuddered. Especially when combined with that plumbing apprenticeship nonsense.

She'd called as requested, Justine had said she'd be waiting down by the front door, but she wasn't there. Natalia, double-parked, turned off the engine and flicked on the hazard lights. A strong wind had come up overnight and now burst down the road, howling fierce between condos, whooshing through the leaves of tall bushes, desiccating the grasses. If Justine really believed she could talk to her dead grandparents—really believed, came to Crab on her own to play for them—then something more was going on than the make-believe games of a child. Did she need—what?—some kind of counselling?

Natalia had never tried to stop the so-called conversations between her daughter and the girl's grandparents. They'd not sounded in any way harmful. Actually, they'd seemed dear. Which could be understood as Natalia's encouragement of Justine to remember her grandparents in this way. But what is dear in a twelve-year old, could it not spell danger for a woman in her early twenties? On the third hand, Justine had always created dialogues in the stories she made up. And not out of whole cloth. Since childhood she'd done her homework—what Don had called, when Justine was maybe seven, her research. Asking as many questions as she could think of about other people. And then making up stories about them. Did she do research on her grandparents' lives before she made up conversations with them? Don's description: Justine will tell you more than you ever want to know.

And why, in truth, had Natalia suggested Justine bring her cello? A moment of love for Justine so great she'd been unable to censor herself? Or maybe something more devious. Could it happen that Justine, united with her cello in the house on Crab, would come to her senses and take the scholarship? Maybe hearing herself play in the house she loved, her plumbing decision, any decision other than her brilliant career as a cellist, would appear as the clear nonsense it was.

Find a parking place and go in? No, just wait. Till a cop or a car that needed to move made her drive off. She pushed the door open. Wind tore the handle from her grasp, slamming the door so hard against the hinge it grunted, missing by a couple of centimetres the car by the curb. She got out and stood between car and door. The wind slowed for a moment, then renewed itself. She looked up at a brilliant blue sky. What makes wind come out of nowhere?

Nine minutes. Justine appeared, shirt, shorts, and sandals, wielding her cello case, a pack on her back. Her long, loose blonde hair, her father's endowment, flew wildly about her head. Then the wind caught the case and shoved her sideways. She stumbled, caught herself, stood still. Natalia waved and called, "Point it into the wind!" She opened the trunk.

Justine did and reached the car. "No," she said, "the back seat."

"Okay." Natalia closed the trunk. Holding the handle tight she opened the back door.

Justine slid the case onto the seat, belted it in place, and got in up front. "What a wind!" she said and gave her mother a hug. "Hi."

"Hi. You okay?"

"Sure. Why?"

"Just asking." Because you were late, she thought but would not say. But it pleased her, Justine's care for the cello. Its protection mattered. Good.

They drove through downtown Vancouver and out by way of Stanley Park, Natalia catching up on Justine's recent details—the lives of her two apartment-mates, a new restaurant she'd discovered and liked. A guy she dated last week but probably would not see again; he'd come on too strong, not sexually, just about himself. They left the park and headed across the Lions Gate Bridge, three narrow lanes over False Narrows. They stared ahead at the supporting stanchions as they seemed to sway in the wind. "Amazing," Justine said.

Natalia's foot pressed harder on the accelerator: get off the bridge! She had never been on it in a blow like this. At last across. "That's better."

Justine probed at recent details in her mother's life—any interesting new students, couple of movies she'd seen. No, not dates! Each time with ancient friends. Yes, women. They climbed up into West Van and turned onto the highway toward the Horseshoe Bay Ferry. High up, the wind caught them again. "Going to be choppy, crossing over," Natalia said.

"You planning on seeing Don when we get there?"

"I—called him."

"You did? Great. How is he?"

"He sounded . . . okay."

"Better than usual? He should be, knowing you'd be there soon."

"I don't know if better than usual. We haven't talked in a long time."

"Yeah." Justine slumped back in her seat. "I know."

Natalia would not enter further into this conversation. Both Jack and Justine tended to get on her case about Don. She felt the car swerve as the wind blasted sideways against it, against all the cars on the road, and most of them too looked unsteady. Or did she imagine it.

At last, the ticket booths. "Line five. Ferry's an hour late," said the BC Ferries woman.

"The wind?"

"Yep."

Damn, thought Natalia. No rush, but she wanted to be there. They'd be lucky to make the last Crab ferry before shift change. Shift change meant a two-hour wait.

They lined up. They'd each brought a book. They read, chatting from time to time. Pleasant to be together. The ferry arrived and unloaded. They drove on, parked, climbed up to the passenger deck. They headed forward, their ever-preferred seats, first Natalia and her parents, then Natalia and Justine, for the trip to the big island and on to Crab.

But the front cabin with its normal panoramic view of the Horseshoe Bay cliffs and the strait was cordoned off, and the high windows had been covered with heavy plastic shutters. "Too bad," Natalia muttered. "Damn," said Justine. Natalia had seen this section closed only once before, when a snowstorm with heavy winds had lashed at the ferry going across. A precaution against the glass shattering after smashing into heavy waves, unlikely to happen but, the announcement had come over the public address system, better not to take chances. They found seats on the port side. Second best, they'd see the coastlines of some of the other islands on the way over. The ferry eased from its berth, now a full hour and twenty minutes late departing. For the first five minutes they sensed a gentle rocking. After ten, drawing up by Bowen Island, they could feel the roll. Past Bowen out in the open strait waves smashed into the ferry's starboard side. "Two-metre swells, easy," they heard a man in the seat in front say to his companion. Blasts of spray swept against the windows.

Justine got up. "I'm going down to check on my cello. I should've wedged it in."

"Be careful. We're really rolling."

"'And hold on to the railing,'" she quoted. "I will."

Because sometimes she was certain Justine could see what her mother was thinking, Natalia only now let herself wonder about what she would say to Don. And to Jack, but that was another matter. She hated thinking how nothing could have been, as long as Don was in effect married to Frank. She had loved Don, her discovery of love. The one full mature love, that was Stan. Yes, she'd loved Don again, perhaps could live with him, enjoy a life with him. But it would never be the wonderful absolute love of a sixteen-year-old. Was she interested? She didn't know. Wrong, she'd made no attempt to find out. Don was still committed elsewhere. So yes, they'd meet, talk, some spark might arise but would catch no tinder, no flame let alone fire, and they'd say goodbye. Probably as it should be.

She ought to call Jack. She fished her cellphone from her purse and turned to the window to muffle her voice. She poked in his number. She hated people speaking on cells in public places as if they and their interlocutors alone existed on the planet. She would say nothing about the house. She heard the ring, then his voice. "Hello, Jack, it's me, Natalia."

"Hi, Nat. Where are you?"

A clear connection. "On the ferry. Just left fifteen minutes ago. We're over an hour late."

"Doesn't matter. Lunch will keep."

"Sorry." Had she heard laughter in the background?

"Listen, Nat, there's something you should know." He told her about Frank's accident. "It doesn't look good. Nothing they can do for him in Nanaimo, they'd have to get him down to Victoria. But he won't let them—won't let Don give an okay."

"Oh Jack. Poor Don."

"Yeah."

"Is he holding up okay? Don, I mean."

"You know Don. Steady as ever."

"Yeah," said Natalia. "I know."

"Call again if you miss the connection. We'll turn lunch into early supper."

They said goodbye. Justine returned. Natalia asked, "The cello's okay?"

"Fine. But it sure is wild out there." She stared out the window. "Not even clouds." She sat back. "The car deck's soaked. And the car needs a wash. To get the salt off."

She explained she'd called Jack to say they'd be late and told her about Frank, and Don.

A nasty little laugh from Justine. "There goes the opposition."

"Justine..."

"Am I wrong?"

"A terrible thing to say." But it might be the beginning to a shift in things...

After a moment Justine said, "Okay, what are we going to say to Jack?"

"We tell him he mustn't."

"You think he'll listen?"

195

"He has to."

"It's his house."

"I don't know what to say to him, Justine. I think we have to play it by ear, see where his thinking is at when we arrive."

"No plan?"

"I can't think of one."

"We could camp out there, throw our bodies between the house and him. There's two of us, and he wouldn't hurt us."

"I have to teach on Monday."

"We could cry. I could go on a hunger strike."

Natalia smiled. "We'll think of something."

Justine shook her head and settled down to her book.

Terrible about Frank, but what did it mean? Don first had to deal with his father. Likely also second, fifth, and twenty-fifth. But then? Likely Frank would recover. Not to his old self. To a more decrepit, dependent self. Twenty-fifth and a hundred and fifth. She opened her book. Stared at the words. Couldn't concentrate. Closed her eyes. She realized, was horrified to realize, she hoped Frank would die. Soon. Now. Stop! She opened her eyes, stood, said to Justine, "Heading to the washroom." She trod slowly down to the stern, grasping seat backs to keep her balance against the rolls, slowly back up along the starboard side, slowly toward the stern again, studying faces to keep from thinking. Balancing. Distraction. Don't think. Finally to her seat.

"You okay?" Justine asked.

"Sure. Why?"

"You were gone a long time."

"I wanted to walk."

"Oh." She went back to her book.

Fifteen minutes and the announcement, Would all passengers please return to their vehicles. Approaching Departure Bay, Nanaimo, their destination. In the lee of Newcastle Island the sea was smoother. The ferry berthed. They roared up the coast to the little ferry for Crab. They entered the terminal parking lot as the last of the cars were boarding. Natalia and Justine drove on. The final foot passengers walked on. The gate swung closed behind them.

With Crab between the ferry and the open strait, the fourteen-minute crossing should have been smoother. But, attacked by swells more than a metre high, the much smaller ferry rolled as badly as had the big ferry from Horseshoe Bay. Here the cars stood on an open deck, huge blue sky above, sea spray exploding to port. But a short enough trip, and they disembarked.

They passed through the village. "Nothing seems to have changed," Natalia said.

A left on Arbutus. The wind blasted just as hard here despite the thickly wooded land on both sides of the road. The roadway, littered with twigs, as much green on the road surface as asphalt, acted as a wind tunnel. Twice Natalia had to drive on the shoulder to avoid four- and five-metre branches as big around as her upper arm. Left again, onto Scott. Seven tall firs standing together in a field swayed like poppies in the blow, fifteen degrees left, compensating degrees right. At last the drive to the house. Natalia slowed to ten kilometres, checking on familiar trees, the gully, rocks, bushes. Here too the ground was littered with twigs and a couple of avoidable branches. She rounded the curve—and slammed her foot down on the brake. Across the driveway, the trunk of a fir thirty-five centimetres in diameter.

"Wow," said Justine.

"End of the road."

They got out and examined the fallen tree. It lay half a metre above the drive, heavy branches supporting it. No way under, or across. "We'll leave our stuff here for now."

"Lock the car," said Justine.

"On Crab?"

"My cello."

"It'll be—Okay, sure." Natalia did.

The tree's root ball looked closer than its tip so they tramped through the brush and around. Branches and blackberry brambles caught at their clothes, scraping Justine's bare arms and legs and Natalia's arms. The tree had taken down with it three smaller firs. By the time they got back to the drive, both were sweating despite the wind. Onward. They reached the clearing.

The house before them shimmered in the early afternoon light. Glowing, Natalia thought.

Justine said, "Well, it's still there."

"Yep." Natalia had not expected her relief to be this great. The veranda, sheltered by its lid as she'd called the covering when she was eight, girded the house. On rainy days she would go for long walks around, many circumnavigations—circumlocutions she used to call them then—and never get wet. The pillars that held up the lid made the place look grand, stately even. How could Jack ever think of tearing it down! What would he do, smash the lacy wooden cornerwork that softened the attachment of pillar to roof, shatter it? No, Jack. No way. The wind howled through the veranda passageway and wheezed in the trees. She glanced up at the thrust windows. The shutters were open, fastened to the wall. Good, he'd prepared the house. Not the act of a man who would raze it. They headed for the front door.

The door opened and Jack appeared, barefoot, jeans, short-sleeved shirt, large grin. "Walked all the way, did you?" And to Justine, "Hey there, didn't expect you."

Hugs of greeting, warm and friendly. They told him about the tree across the driveway.

"Damn. I'll get it, but come in first. Hungry?"

They entered. Natalia headed through the hall to the kitchen, running two fingers along the wall as she went. He hadn't harmed it inside either, good sign. Ahead to the dining room, bright and pretty as she remembered. "The place looks good, Jack."

"It is what it is."

Whatever that meant, in this context. "Clean too. You bring in a cleaning lady?"

"In a manner of speaking. Now. Something to drink. Water? Beer? Want to wash up?"

"I need to wash off my scrapes," Justine said and headed for the bathroom.

"Just some water."

He turned into the kitchen. She followed. He took a bottle from the refrigerator, from the cabinet a glass, handed her both. "It's cold."

She squinted at him. "You got the generator going. I didn't know it was still here."

"The generator's working fine." He stared her up and down. "You look well, Nat."

"I'm okay."

For a moment he said nothing; then, casually, "How come Justine came over with you?"

"Same reason as me. Make you listen to reason."

"There'll be two different kinds of argument, I guess."

"To the same end."

He opened the fridge again. "Now about lunch. Cold cuts, couple of cheeses. Fresh bread, just picked it up this morning." He considered his words. "That tree must be recent. I got back barely an hour ago." He laughed. "Could've been a mess if the timing had been right. Wrong."

"For either of us. Does the old chainsaw still work?"

"Don't know. Haven't tried it."

Another moment of relief: he might have taken it to the house. "And how are you? Aside from the craziness in your head."

"As ever."

"Which tells me nothing. What's up, Jack?"

He grinned, as if getting the point of some private joke. "I'm having a good time."

"Here? On the island?"

"Right here."

"In the house. On the property."

"In the house."

"Then—have you changed your mind?"

"Nope."

They heard behind them, "Change it." Justine in the bathroom doorway, hands on hips.

"Some water, Justine. A beer?"

She came toward him. "Jack, don't do this. You're a good guy. You're my favourite uncle. You're . . ."

"I'm your only uncle."

"Don't be pedantic. And please, don't hurt this house."

He turned to Natalia. "About sleeping arrangements. You want your old room upstairs? I was going to put you downstairs but if you..."

"Downstairs is okay."

"And you, which room do you want? You can't have mine."

Justine clenched her teeth hard, which made her nostrils flare. "Don't change the subject. But okay, I'd like Gran and Granpop's room."

"I'll try the saw. If it starts I'll cut the drive open. If not—" He shrugged. "Either way I'll get your baggage. Take what you want from the fridge."

"You're going to listen to me, Jack."

"Of course I am."

"And stop being such a blockhead."

"And you stop talking to my brother that way." Natalia scowled at Justine. "Jack is a reasonable man. And intelligent. And he'll be both about this too. Here." She turned to Jack. "You'll need these." She took the keys from her jeans pocket, handed them over, and noted his frown. "We locked it. Justine's cello's on the back seat."

"I'll go with you."

He looked Justine up and down. "Put some jeans on. And a shirt with sleeves."

"They're in the car."

"Hold on." He went upstairs.

"I'll try to convince him. I'll talk to him while he's dealing with the tree."

"Don't be rude to him. And don't antagonize him."

"Mom, come on. We've got to do something. He doesn't listen."

"He might."

"Sure."

"I know Jack. I know that he'll..."

Justine held up her hand, waved it, put a finger to her lips.

"What's up?"

"In the dining room. Come on."

She marched, nearly ran, into the next room. She stood still, listening. Then she smiled. "Hi," she said.

Natalia came to stand beside her. "What?"

"They're here."

"Who's here?"

"Gran and Granpop."

"Justine, don't do this now . . ."

"Sshhh."

They waited. Silence. "Granpop is mad at Jack."

"What?"

But Justine was listening again. At last she said, "Granpop says there's no heaven. They just remain here. In the house. Until they're forgotten."

Natalia took her by the arm, but Justine pulled away and set a finger across her lips. Natalia watched her, fascinated by and fearful for her daughter.

"He says anybody who didn't know him and Gran can't sense them." She waited. "That's why they're mad at Jack. There could never have been a problem with renting the house."

"What?"

"No renters would ever sense them here."

Natalia held her upper arms tight against her breasts. "I don't understand." This was getting absurd.

A half minute of silence. Then Justine said, "Okay."

"What okay?"

"They simply wanted to add a hello. They'll be back later."

"Justine, for pity sakes, don't."

"I'm sorry, Mom."

"You should be."

"No, that you can't hear them."

"Justine!"

"Okay. All right."

Jack returned, carrying old jeans and a shirt. "They're too big but they'll protect you."

She took them and headed upstairs. To her grandparents' room, Natalia realized. She had best nip this ploy of Justine's right away. "Jack. There's something you should know."

"About?"

"Justine. And the house."

"I know. She already told me."

"No, something else." She released an audible breath. "The last two years. When the house stood empty. Justine would come here. Stay overnight sometimes."

Jack's eyes narrowed. "Why?"

"She came with her cello. She played it, here."

"She never asked. She never told me. I mean, it's fine but . . ."

"Jack, she says she . . . she played for an audience."

"She invited people in? Damn. Big reason for the place to come down."

"The audience—she says—were her grandparents."

"Okay." He frowned. "I can see that. Playing for the memory of people she loved, it could improve her performance. So she didn't bring people in. Good. I'm relieved."

"You're not listening to me. She says she didn't play for anyone in her memory. She played for them. Sam and Hannah Tartarus."

As he said, "That's crazy," she was certain she saw him wince. "You don't play your cello for ghosts. And anyway, there are no ghosts in this house."

"I agree. But while you were upstairs she said they're here now. She said she spoke to them. Here in the dining room. She said 'Hi' out loud while I was standing beside her. She said they said they wanted to say hello to her. Or maybe to us all is what she meant."

"This is nuts, Nat. Is Justine okay? Otherwise?"

"She's always made up stories, right?" Natalia walked to the window and stared out. "I—don't know if she's okay."

"What? Something else?"

She spoke to the outside. "She's been offered a full fellowship from the music school, tuition, living expenses, the whole thing, to get her MFA. She turned it down. She doesn't want to be a world-class cellist. She wants to apprentice. As a plumber."

Jack chuckled. "Going where the money is."

"I think she must've fallen and bashed her head and stepped into a parallel universe. Which'd be funny if it weren't funny at all."

"What's the relationship between wanting to become a plumber and talking to ghosts?"

Natalia shook her head. "Don't know. If it weren't all stupid, I'd think maybe she's following her grandfather's advice."

"Would Sam Tartarus suggest plumbing?"

"One side of him might."

"One side of who?" Justine stood tiny inside Jack's jeans and shirt.

"Your grandfather telling you to drop everything you're good at and become a plumber."

Justine backed away from Jack so quickly she lost her balance. Natalia grabbed her arm to keep her from falling. "Easy," she said, "easy."

He pulled a chair from the table, and another. "Justine, sit."

Natalia released her grip on Justine. Justine walked slowly to the chair and sat.

Jack sat opposite. "Justine. Listen to me. I'm not angry that you broke into my house to play your cello. But I am worried about you. I'm worried about your thinking there are ghosts in this house. Justine, the only remains around here of Sam and Hannah Tartarus are their ashes. And those ashes are all over that field. Wherever the wind carried them. Wherever the wind's still carrying them. Listen to it." He stopped. They listened. A long howling came to their ears. "Your grandparents are dead and gone. We all have great memories of them, maybe even some less than great memories. We treasure them whatever they are. And that's it. No ghosts, okay? Justine, look at me."

Slowly she raised her head.

"No ghosts. Right?"

She nodded, once. "Whatever you say."

"That's what I say. Because that is the case."

"Shall we go to the car now?"

"Yes." He got up. They went out together.

Natalia wondered if she should go too. And decided Jack and Justine would find their own best way of dealing with each other. The crush her daughter had on him at fifteen, sixteen, at times flirting with him flagrantly, at times hiding from him, that had long passed. And she'd not seen him in years, probably since she started university. They would cope, the two of them.

Natalia walked over to the kitchen. She closed her eyes and could nearly see Hannah standing by the sink, scrubbing potatoes to be baked in the fireplace, slicing cucumbers to marinate in oil and vinegar, kneading dough for that fabulous whole-wheat bread Natalia hadn't eaten in more than ten years. No bread since gave off the same smell or had just that taste. She opened her eyes. Nor would she ever encounter it again.

In a certain way it must be lovely for Justine, to imagine her grandparents so clearly it felt as if she could in fact speak to them, and imagine what their part of the conversation would be. Natalia wished she had that talent. She put her hand on the stove top, testing its feel. And the same with the refrigerator handle, sliding her fingers down it. A handle her mother had opened the fridge with, the stove she had cooked their meals on. She glanced into the bathroom. Where they had washed their hands. She smiled lightly, silently. Yes, and the same toilet her parents had peed into, shat into. So stop. They will not appear to you. They are dead.

Still she walked upstairs, to her parents' room. She opened the door and stepped inside. Hannah and Sam were not standing there. Just Justine's blouse and shorts on the bed. Her parents' bed. What had they talked about when they lay in that bed, in this house. What had they said to each other, in their early years here, in their later years? When last had they made love on this bed? Questions unanswerable. Because they were dead. Wrong. Even if they were living, right now, here, they would not answer these questions. Because Natalia could not ask them.

She sighed. She should go and see Frank. While he was still alive. And Don. Yes, while he too was still alive, anyone can die at any time. She said aloud because she had to, "Hello, Mom and Pop." She listened and heard only silence. Of course.

She went back downstairs. If they let her see Frank, he the last of the four of them still alive. She had sat with him after Sylvia had died. She and Maureen. Maureen, who had loved Jack with such intensity.

They so badly wanted a child, children. At first she couldn't conceive. She conceived and miscarried. Twice, if Natalia remembered correctly. Then she found the little lump in her right breast. The medical exam led to a mammogram, the mammogram was inconclusive. A biopsy. Not with a needle, the lump lay too deep. Oh Maureen, Maureen. Her thirty-sixth year. Jack was in agony, Maureen terrified. The excisional biopsy confirmed the worst, more lumps behind the felt lump, all positive. And on through her lymph nodes, on to her underarms. Classic. Chemo, radiation. A few months of normalcy, if Maureen could be considered normal without her red hair. It grew back in, slow and stubby. But in less than two years she was dead. Dead. You've never come back from that, have you, Jack?

She stepped out onto the veranda. The sound of wind in the trees multiplied, hot air blasting through branches. She realized, despite the heat of the afternoon, she was chilled. She would walk the circuit, under the lid. A circumlocution. She turned right, passed the living room window, looked in, walked on. Turned the corner—Leaning against the house, what looked like a crowbar. Except it had a double head. She reached for it, picked it up. Heavy. A weapon to demolish the house? She set it back. On the deck of the veranda, some splinters of wood. She bent down and took one between her fingers. It had paint on the flat side, the rest was raw wood. Same colour white as the house. Her eyes glanced over the clapboard. There, it had come from just there. She placed the splinter in that spot. It didn't fit. For a moment she felt a wash of relief. More gouges maybe half a metre away. She tried there. Nonono! Perfect fit. She felt her eyes well up. Sam and Hannah's house. Maureen's house. Jack's house, goddamn it! She found a tissue in her jeans, let it soak up the beginnings of tears. Now he was looking for a chainsaw—

The garage door stood open but neither he nor Justine were there. She ran down the drive to the woods and around the curve. She found Jack taking measure of the tree. No chainsaw as far as she could see. Justine coming from behind the tree's roots manoeuvring her cello case.

"I'll have to borrow a chainsaw," said Jack.

"Where? How?"

"Luckily your car's on the other side. Can I use it?"

"I'll drive you." She had to talk to him, soon as possible.

"Okay, sure."

Natalia turned to Justine. "Want to stay or come?"

"I'll be fine. He won't talk to me anyway." She marched up the drive toward the house.

Jack and Natalia passed through undergrowth, rounded the tree, and got in the car. "There's a place a bit farther along where you can turn."

Natalia backed slowly, found the turn around, and drove out to the road.

"Left," said Jack.

"What did she mean, you won't talk to her?"

"Best way to keep her from getting frantic. I told her I wouldn't talk about the house and she lit into me. Verbally. But if I'd said anything, she might've done worse. So I clammed up." He grinned. "She didn't like that."

Natalia should have kept Justine from coming over to Crab. Too late. Right now it was time to confront her brother. Just say it. "Jack. You've started on the house."

"Not really."

"That wood chip out of the clapboard—"

"A few chips. And all I'm able to do. For now."

"Promise?"

"To you, and to the small man."

"Who?"

"I need a demolition licence. From the Islands Trust. Run by the small man."

"Oh," said Natalia softly. "And will he give it to you?"

"Maybe by Monday."

"Oh," she said again and drove for a while in silence.

"Just ahead, at that drive, turn left."

Natalia turned. "The Rixtons?"

"Remember Madge and Rick Rixton? And a daughter. Ginny."

"Vaguely."

"He died. The mother and the daughter live there together."

"Wait a minute, that really beautiful girl? She was in high school—"

"She's aged." He sniffed a laugh. "We all have. I've become an old, old man." A smile took his face. "There, stop ahead. By the shed."

"You know this place?"

"I just met the daughter." He got out, headed for the house, and walked up some steps.

She watched as the door opened. A woman in jeans and a plaid shirt appeared. Jack spoke to her and she smiled. She turned back into the house as Jack came down the stairs and headed over to the shed. He opened the door and stepped inside as the woman came striding toward him. She followed Jack into the shed. Natalia waited. Waited. What the hell was taking so long? Two-three-four minutes. She got out of the car. The trees, back from the house on all sides, whined in the wind. Jack appeared carrying a chainsaw with a long blade. Natalia unlatched the trunk. He set the saw down gently. The woman followed him. She had immense eyes.

"My sister, Natalia Golden, Ginny Rixton."

Exchange of Hi, how are you, pleased, and so on.

"Thanks for this, Ginny. I'll get it back to you quick as I can."

"We don't have any trees down. That I know of. But do bring it back."

"I will. See you soon."

Goodbyes. Natalia headed the car down the drive. See you soon. To return the saw. Something more? "I'll drop you and the saw at the house. I want to go see Don. And Frank."

Jack raised his eyebrows. "And leave me alone with Justine and her ghosts."

"Maybe—just let her work it out."

"Sure."

They drove on in silence. As if everything had been settled. For the moment. Jack and Justine. Jack and the house. She turned into the Tartarus drive.

"I'll get out at the turn around."

She raised her eyebrows. "You can walk the rest of the way?"

He gave her a smile. "They'll be at the clinic. Remember where it is?" She nodded, stopped, once more unlatched the trunk. He got out,

207

grabbed the saw, and slammed the trunk shut. "Be back in time for supper, okay?"

"That's why I came. To have supper with you." She waved, turned the car around, and headed for the village. She parked in front of the clinic beside a big Mercury that had to be Frank's. She opened the clinic door and stepped into a waiting room. An argument, at least a heavy-duty exchange, was in progress. Don, a woman, another man. They turned to her.

"Natalia!" Don came to her with open arms and hugged her. She hugged him back. They drew apart. Don said, "Natalia, this is Dr. Bandeen. And my friend Etain." To the others: "Natalia Tartarus and her brother, Jack, are just about my two oldest friends."

How-do-you-dos, preliminary appraisals. "Sorry, I've interrupted your—discussion."

"Dr. Bandeen is Frank's primary care physician and . . ."

"Only physician. At this point." Bandeen, a short, round man with fine features on a middle-dark face, displayed agitation.

"That's what we were talking about," Don explained. "Dr. Bandeen thinks Frank should be sent down to Victoria. First thing tomorrow."

"First thing," repeated Bandeen.

"Is he very bad?"

"Very bad. Very. I cannot help him further."

"So?"

"Frank refuses to allow it." Don let out a breath of flinty exasperation.

"He's conscious, then? Jack said he might not be."

"In and out."

"Can't you convince him? Either of you?" And where did this woman Etain fit in?

"He is the master of his fate," said Don. "Legally, I mean."

"He is about to become the master of his demise," said Bandeen, his scowl pronounced.

"But why won't he let you move him?"

"He's going to die, he says. He knows it. If he's going to die, he'll die here on Crab."

Natalia glanced from Don to the doctor. "And is he going to die?"

"If he stays here," said Bandeen, "yes. And soon."

"And if he's moved?"

Bandeen shrugged.

Natalia couldn't tell, was Bandeen's concern mainly for Frank? Or was the doctor worried that someone, afterward, might think he'd not done all he could? "May I see him?"

Don glanced at Bandeen, who nodded. "You should wear a mask."

Bandeen found the package of masks and handed her one. She placed it over her mouth and nose and adjusted the elastic behind her head. Bandeen opened the door. Natalia stepped into the intensive care unit and closed the door behind her. Frank's head and chest lay propped against pillows on the bed, his eyes closed. A nurse in white sat beside the bed. Natalia heard Bandeen say, "This is Tamara. Tamara, Natalia. An old family friend." Tamara got up so Natalia could take the seat. She reached out to Frank's hand. Plastic tubing fed in under his skin. She stroked his fingers. He opened his eyes. "Hello, Frank. It's Natalia." She heard a small grunt from him, possibly recognition. "I'm here to see Jack," she said. Best not for Don, not now. "Can I get you anything?" No idea what to say to him. He didn't respond. Ask him if he wanted to go somewhere else, where they could take care of him? "Frank. You know how nice it is down in Victoria. There's a wonderful hospital there and you could . . ." She felt his hand withdraw and the sound he made was closer to No than anything she could imagine. He shut his eyes again. Damn! She heard Bandeen from the doorway telling her to come out now. She got up. "I'm going, Frank. I'll be back. I won't talk about Victoria again, I promise." No reaction from Frank. She backed out of the room, turned, started to speak to Don . . .

"I know. I saw. He's adamant. He wants to die on Crab."

"I can understand that."

"I can't. He says he loves this island, doesn't want to die anywhere else. Except for the last half-dozen years, he's gone on about how much he hated it."

The woman, Etain, spoke for the first time. "And you believe everything he says."

"He's been very convincing about his dislike."

"Don, he has nothing except this island. Even if he said he hated it, he felt something about it. He doesn't feel anything about anywhere else. So he has to love this place, it's all he's got. The island and you. And you are here."

Well said, Natalia thought. "Makes sense to me."

Bandeen shook his head. "You people are impossible." To Don he added, "Tamara will call me if necessary." Adding grimly, "When necessary." He spoke a word to Tamara and left.

"I'll go too," Etain said to Don. "Terry can't come in till six. I'll be back. And you, you should go home. You need a little sleep." To Natalia, "A pleasure meeting you."

Natalia nodded. "Yes." A lot going on here. Etain left. "Are you sort of okay, Don?"

"I don't know." He shook his head. "I think I'm the one who has to decide. I think I have to overrule him. I think he has to go to Victoria. That's how I am."

"Plus exhausted."

"Pretty weary. I think I'll sit down." He did, and Natalia too. "And you?"

"Same as ever." Not the same, not now. Suddenly she had nothing to say. And neither did Don. He certainly looked wiped. "Did you sleep last night?"

"In that chair." He gestured with his chin. "On and off."

Again their silence, till Natalia said, "Etain seems insightful."

"She is, yes."

"You've known her long?"

"Couple of years."

"I think we ate at her restaurant. I thought I recognized her."

"Yes, we did. Frank liked—likes to eat there. He likes Etain too."

Natalia's eyebrows went up, but she grinned. "Dirty old man?"

Don smiled sadly. "He'd love to be, I think. But no. He admires Etain."

"How so?" And do you admire her, Don?

"She's a self-made woman, out of very little."

"Yeah?"

"She's Québecoise, and she came out here on her own, long ago.

For work but also for sex and drugs and all the rest. She was a fruit-picker and tree planter." So Don told Natalia about Etain. That when Etain turned twenty-five she knew she had to start to stabilize her life. Drugs, sex, and dreary small-town bands wasn't the way she wanted to spend her second quarter-century.

Natalia thought, He's telling me too much. Or is he? Weariness. Nervousness?

Etain visited a friend on Crab. She heard about a job serving, cleaning, cooking, and everything else at a small restaurant, Eating Thyme, and she took it. The owner was more interested in her lesbian lovers than running the place. Over the next four years the Thyme was rescued from bankruptcy twice while Etain worked there. Then it did go under. Etain had watched the slow demise, saving every dollar she could, and had planned.

He's proud of her! Like she's his discovery. Natalia couldn't stand it. It was inevitable, all Natalia's fault, how long did she think they could continue their parallel distant lives and not have anyone intrude? Damn, damn! Natalia could not bear to hear him talking about her, so pleased with her. And himself.

"So Etain took advice from Tom Elderson, a lawyer who ate at the Thyme two-three lunches a week," Don was saying. "Tom went with her to the Credit Union, they convinced Connie who runs it to accept a tiny down payment on a mortgage amortized over thirty years. Etain paid off the Thyme's few creditors at fifteen cents on the dollar and became a businesswoman. A clever, hardworking businesswoman. In the last thirteen years she's paid down three-quarters of the mortgage."

"Very impressive," said Natalia. So there it is. Too late. Don is in love. Does the poor chump not realize that? Or had his devotion to Frank blinded him even to this. If Frank dies, then Justine will have been right: there goes the opposition. And wrong: only the ancient opposition. Hell of a lot of good it did Natalia. She marvelled at herself, though not in a pleasant way. That she could be so upset. When it was she who had gone away. But Etain had been near. And gotten what she could. Which, given Don, was a lot of good. "Very."

"Yes, she is." But his eyes were nearly closed.

"Don, you should get some sleep. Really," as he shook his head hard, "you should. I could stay here if you'd like."

His head continued to shake. "You go back. Spend time with Jack, get him to give up that folly, tearing down the house. He really can be an ass."

"Yes. He can." She got up, leaned down, kissed his cheek. "I'll see you."

"Nat. Thank you. For coming." He shook his head. "I think I have to call Bandy. Make arrangements for an ambulance. Get Frank down to Victoria."

She nodded, turned, and left. For the second time today her eyes filled with water.

TEN: Jack

Tartarus had lugged Ginny's chainsaw around the tree and headed for the house—the garage, actually. There he mixed some of the new gasoline with oil, fifty to one, and poured the blend into the tank. And chain oil, a can from the garage. No idea how old that stuff was, but it flowed nicely red and viscous. He left the saw on the veranda in the shade, opened the door, went in. Except for the dim distant roar of the generator, all was silent. "Justine!"

After several seconds he heard, from upstairs, "Hello."

No further sound, no movement. He called again, "Just wanted to tell you, I'm back. I'm going to deal with the tree." No answer. "Want to help?" He waited.

A small response, "I'm fine here."

In her teens she'd seemed to him a contained, even selfish, young woman. How much had she changed? He headed for the kitchen and made himself a sandwich. A beer—no, not before handling the saw. He finished the sandwich, took a bottle of water, and headed out to the tree. The wind had died down a bit, its absence intensifying the afternoon heat. He sat on a boulder. No hurry. If Don wasn't at the clinic, Natalia would be back earliest in half an hour, longer if she did find him there. Jack set down the saw. Old but as Ginny'd said trusty, a Husqvarna. She had then kissed him for a long moment and he'd kissed her back, enjoying the pleasure of her.

He did enjoy her: sparring with her second only to sex with her. She aroused in him a passion he'd not felt for a long time. There'd been women wherever he'd worked, attractive women, sensuous, available, often remarkable in bed, pleasant to be with for a day or a night, even a week. But none had caught him so off-guard, gotten to his insides so quickly, the way this girl—this woman—Ginny had. Would she too be a passing whim? Could be. He knew he wanted to find out. Maybe ask when he returned the saw, "Ginny, are you a whim?" Not a waif. He'd ask her when he went shopping. Again. Natalia should have told him Justine was coming over. Or he should have told his sister to pick up another steak, and more broccoli. He ought to have bought extra food altogether because it looked more and more like he'd moved in. Till the demolition permit came through. He wasn't thinking ahead. Wine too. Justine, he remembered, enjoyed a glass of wine. Ginny drank so little wine last night. Ginny the more-than-waif.

He slipped the mufflers over his ears and goggles to protect his eyes. He slid the switch to on, pulled out the choke, thumbed gasoline into the machine, latched the throttle open, and yanked the starter cord. The motor caught, sputtered, died. Once more. It caught and roared. He released the throttle latch, closed the choke, and the motor slowed to idle. Indeed trusty. He squeezed the trigger and the chain whirred around. Utmost care. He limbed the trunk first, that section over the road. The rest could wait for cooler weather. He sweated now from every pore, and the saw was hot. He felt good, strong. He drank the water bottle dry. He bucked the trunk into fourteen-inch lengths—strange how he always thought of logs in feet and inches, like human height and house dimensions, almost all else making more sense metric—and let them drop in place. Somebody else could split them, good dry firewood the winter after this. He closed up the saw. He stacked the logs at the side of the drive and threw the branches in among the trees. The needles and twigs would compost in the next couple of years, the branches over the next half dozen, a new layer of forest floor. He stood back and admired his handiwork.

He set the saw in the trunk of the car. In the house he heard the long, rich sound of the cello flowing down the stairs. He listened for a couple of minutes, something soft and lovely he knew but couldn't place. He took another bottle of water from the fridge and drank half of it.

The sweat on him had mostly dried. A shower before, uhmm, taking the saw back to Ginny. He headed for the stairs. The cello had stopped. Then from above, a voice. Words he couldn't make out. Quiet words, Justine but clearly not calling down to him. What the hell was with that girl? He waited. The cello began again, deep, languorous sound. Full, it seemed to him right then, of longing. Or pain? A shower up there now felt like an intrusion, despite her self-absorption. He flipped his shoes off and climbed the stairs, silent but for a couple of old-house squeaks. From his room he took a change of clothes and brought them to the downstairs shower. The music, the cello now lighter in tone, followed him.

Clean and dressed, he stuck a note on the bathroom door, *Gone to give saw back. I'm turning the generator off till I get back. Don't flush any toilets.* He headed for the front door and heard her speaking again, quietly as before. When he returned he'd ask her . . . What?

He closed down the generator and reached the car just as another vehicle approached. It stopped ten metres from his. Natalia got out. "Hi," he called.

"Hi."

"I've turned off the generator. Saving gas. Know how to turn it back on if you need it?"

"Of course." Her words came out muted.

"You okay?"

"Yeah, I'm fine."

Frank, worse than before? "Did you see Don?"

"Don, and Frank, and the doctor and a nurse."

"And Frank?"

"He's pretty much out of it. Pretty much same as yesterday, Don said. Pretty close to gone, the doctor implied. And he won't let himself be taken down to Victoria."

"Yeah."

"They could help him down there, the doctor said. Or maybe not. And Frank is, well, Frank. Even though he's heavily doped up."

"You talk to him?"

She described the conversation. "He looks awful. I have no idea if he's going to make it." She shrugged. "But what do I know. About anything."

Something more than Frank going on here. "And how's Don coping?"

"He's wiped. But he's got—lots of inner strength." A rueful smile. "And external support."

215

"A good doctor, nurses . . ." He walked toward her.

"And friends. You. Another friend too."

"Oh?"

"A woman. Other than the nurse. A good friend of Don's. Someone he admires a lot."

"Ah. You met Etain."

"I did." She leaned against her car. "You know her?"

"She's the one who came to tell me about Frank's accident. And I saw her at her restaurant. Don picks up food from there at the end of the day. Some days." He was talking too much. Natalia wouldn't care. "For the Island Kitchen. It's a kind of food bank."

"Ah." Her eyes had suddenly gone damp. She stepped away from the car. He reached out for her, put his arms around her. She hugged him back for a moment, then let her arms drop.

"Nat . . ."

"Everything is of my own doing. I think I want to go lie down."

She started to walk past him. He caught her by the wrist. "Look, I'm going into town, pick up some food. I'll stop by, maybe see Don. And return the saw." He dropped her arm.

"Yes. I know. You promised." She walked toward the house, turned. "See you later."

He watched her; as she entered the house he called, "We'll have a beer and . . ." but she was inside. Poor Nat. Maybe talk to Don. At the clinic or his house. Don and Frank's house. No, probably not likely again. Though, given Frank, hard to tell.

Dinner tonight would be less than fun. But given what Nat had come to Crab for, it wouldn't have been a pleasure anyway. And talk would come around to their parents, and how they died. Did Nat know Ginny had found Sam half out of the car? He started his engine and headed down the drive, pleased he'd cleared the route. To the market. He grabbed a shopping basket. Another steak. In case they stayed Saturday night, chicken breasts. Sure, or he could eat them later. With Ginny? Maybe. Potatoes. Tonight he'd start earlier, bake them in the hibachi coals. Broccoli, carrots. Apple pie? Maybe the women would be hungry. Pie it was.

"Good pie," said a voice beside him.

He turned. The hardware store guy. Turtle. Pushing a shopping cart. "Good to know."

"Got company, then."

A question or a comment? With this guy, hard to tell. "In a way."

The clerk nodded. "That's right."

"Yep."

"Ice cream goes good with it. Vanilla."

"With the pie?"

"Worth moving in for."

"I'm sorry?"

"It'll be okay."

"What'd you say?"

"You'll see."

"I don't understand . . ."

"See you 'round." He walked away, pushing his cart.

And what was that all about? He'd ask Don if he knew the man. Or Ginny. Did he have enough bread? Get more tomorrow, fresh. He lay the food on the back seat of his car—too hot, into the trunk, cover it with a tarp—and headed for the clinic. Odd character, that hardware store guy. An empty waiting room. The door to the intensive care unit was shut tight. Knock? He did. It opened, a woman, a different nurse. "Hi, I'm a friend of Don Bonner and his father and . . ."

"Don's not here and Mr. Bonner's asleep."

"How is he?"

"About the same. Don went for a bite to eat."

"Home?"

"I don't know."

"Thank you." He left. To the wine store, couple of bottles of yesterday's Merlot, and a mickey of whisky. Natalia could probably handle some of that and it wouldn't hurt him any. Down to Don's house. But he wasn't there either. With Etain? Go find out. But his watch said nearly four o'clock and her restaurant was across the island. He would check in with Don and Frank tomorrow. He passed his drive and continued on to Ginny's. He stopped in front of the shed. A jazzy little red convertible stood beside the beater. Ginny has company. Well damn. He returned the saw and ear protectors to the shed. He'd go to the door, tell Ginny the saw was back, thanks, and no he wouldn't stay. A curious tingle of trepidation—jealousy?—took him. He'd say Natalia and Justine were waiting, he was cooking them supper . . . The door opened. Ginny came out, waved, sat on the steps. He joined her. "Hi."

She leaned toward him, kissed his mouth, quickly drew away. "My mother's home."

"Her car?"

"Yes. She's upstairs resting. She had a good time with her friend. But it tired her."

"Nice car."

"She loves it. It's right for her." She put her hand on his thigh. "Glad you came by. I wanted to say something."

"Say away."

"About your father. How I found him."

Again a bit uncanny, with him thinking of this a few minutes ago. "Go on."

"There could be any number of reasons why the door was open."

"Like?"

"I don't know. Whatever they were, they died with Sam and Hannah."

"Did . . ." How to ask this . . . "Did they ever talk about—about suicide?"

"Not in front of me. No. Never." She stared out across the field and put her arm about his waist. "They did talk about death. About their dying."

He covered her hand with his. "What?"

"It was a long time ago, Jack."

"But you remember? Any of it?"

"Sometimes the occasional comment, sometimes jokes." She closed her eyes. "Once when I was there, I'd just arrived, I heard them talking. They didn't know I was there yet. I heard Sam say, 'You know, it's going to be either you or me.' And Hannah asked him what he meant, and he said, 'The one who dies first.' Then neither of them said anything, and I waited for a couple of minutes before I called to tell them I'd arrived."

The one who dies first. And Sam's note: *There is no more.* Jack didn't understand. "Ginny, why do you think they did it? Killed themselves?"

"You mean, more than that she'd lost her mind."

"Had she, by then? So fully as to . . . as to die."

Ginny turned to him, her large eyes squinted, shining, the green dominant. "I think Sam knew her moment had come. She was dying in tiny increments, even I could see that. I think she wanted to die quickly, to simply no longer be, not for one day more. Maybe it was her last day. And likely he helped her, and knew he had to die with her. That without her he had no life."

If Jack had been on Crab, would he have seen that his mother was dying—what were Ginny's words?—in tiny increments? Would he have been able to do anything about it? What in her misfiring imagination did the house really have to do with it. "It must have been hard, very hard. For both of them."

She released his waist, took his hand, and intertwined her fingers with his. "Her death had been inside her for a while, I think. It covered all of her, inside. Then it began coming out, it started spreading over her outside too. When it was just about all out, that was her day. So Sam took her to the garage. To be—well, with her again. I think that's all."

"Is it?"

"There was no one to blame. And nothing to blame. And Jack?" She brushed his lips with hers. "I mean this. Nothing to blame. The house is not to blame. Don't take it out on the house."

He laughed, a grim little laugh. "Is this your game? Seducing me to save the house."

"No game. I like you very much, Jack. Very, very much. Believe me, it's no game. I don't want you to destroy the house, but that has nothing to do with me and you."

"We barely know each other . . ."

"Do you like me?"

"You have to know that. Yes. Immensely."

"Good. It makes our—mutual seduction much more lovely. But I wouldn't be participating in anything with you if I didn't like you very, very much. The seduction has nothing to do with the house. I still don't want you to tear it down. But that's like something different altogether."

He said nothing for a while. Then he released a long, loud sigh. "I have to go back."

"Yes, your sister."

"And her daughter, she came along. Both of them are on your side. About the house."

"Listen to them, Jack."

"Can I tell you something a little crazy."

"Crazy or sane, anything you want."

"Justine, that's my niece, she's a cellist. She brought her cello along. When I left the house she was in Sam and Hannah's room, playing the cello. For them."

"I wouldn't call that crazy. That's kind of nice."

"Yeah, except she talks to them too."

"Don't you sometimes talk to dead people? In your head?"

"Yeah, but she talks out loud. Here's the kicker—she's told Natalia they talk back to her."

"Oh my."

"Exactly."

"Then either she is in fact crazy or she's very lucky."

"Lucky?"

"I wish they'd talk to me."

He dropped her hand and took her by the shoulders. "Ginny. This is one self-centred young woman. There's no one there. The ghosts of my parents are not in that house."

She crossed her arms and took his hands. An X of arms. "How can you be so sure?"

"I do not believe in ghosts is how."

"Remember I told you I could feel their presence?"

"And I can feel their presence too. In my mind. It's the same as feeling their absence. I wish they were still there. But they're not."

220

She looked at his face, her eyeballs flicking her focus from left to right and back again, up and down, as if to keep forever the image of his eyes, his nose and mouth, his chin. "Okay."

"And I really have to go cook supper." He let go of her shoulders and stood.

She got up too. "I wish I could be with you tonight. I very much want your presence tonight. I know it's not possible. But you are the presence I want."

He put his arms around her back, hers went around his neck. They held each other, a long embrace, holding each other as if magnetized. They drew their heads back, they kissed.

She pulled away first. "You're right, you better go. Or it'll be too late."

A quick kiss. She took his hand and they walked to the car. A final kiss, he got in and started the engine. She blew him a kiss as he drove away.

His sister would be sad, his niece furious. And what would it do to Ginny? To Ginny and himself. Was there truly already a Ginny and himself? Would she feel the same after the house was down? Damn.

But why did he care? Surely he wasn't falling in love with her. What they had between them, long ago, was lust. Rich, bawdy lust. Wasn't this a version of that lust, an older lust, less manic, but lust all the same? A desire, a craving for the pleasure of her. Hardly love.

He parked, brought in the groceries, put the ice cream into the freezer, opened a beer, and poured it into a mug. No cello playing, no obvious chat upstairs. He called, "I'm back."

"Be right there," called Natalia. No response from Justine.

He lit the coals in the hibachi, set the grill above them, washed vegetables, wrapped potatoes in foil, and laid them at the edge of the coals. Suddenly he stopped himself. He was normalizing the house. He was turning it into his household. He was becoming master of the house. The cupboards were full of his housewares, the bedrooms full of his house guests. Stop!

Natalia appeared from the hall. She noted his beer. "That looks good." She opened a bottle, found another mug, and poured. "Did you see Don?"

"Wasn't there." He scrubbed a carrot. "Justine around?"

"Napping."

"Supper in an hour?"

"Great."

They chatted as Jack prepared the meal, refusing help from Natalia. Both studiously kept off the subject of Don. Or the house. Jack checked the glowing coals and turned the potatoes. "Tell Justine twenty minutes." Natalia headed upstairs. Jack set the table, himself at the head. He was doing it again. Still. Everything, everyone, taking their places. As it had been. As it was no longer supposed to be. He had done this as if all were normal again. All is not normal.

He took the steaks out to the hibachi and tested the potatoes. Almost. He lay the steaks on the grill. They sizzled instantly. He'd forgotten the dousing water for after and came back from the kitchen with a potful. He turned the steaks. He poked a potato with a sharp knife. Done.

Justine appeared at the door. "Smells good."

"Can you get me a plate for the potatoes?" He saw her turn and head into the house. Normal also to ask for a little help. Today at least. Not after the demolition order. Justine was wearing a sundress, shoulders bare. Rare to see a woman in a dress on Crab. Except Ginny wore a sundress too. Was that normal?

He brought food and wine to the table. Water too. They sat, the women on either side facing each other. Jack served. They tasted their steaks. "Yummy" and "Delicious" from his niece and his sister, Justine adding, "It's great, Jack. Like when I was a kid."

"What is?" Natalia asked.

"Eating. Together. All of us."

"Well," said Jack, "not quite."

A quick tinge of red sped down Justine's cheeks and bare neck. "Oh. Jack. I'm sorry."

He shrugged and gave her a wry smile. He said, "Hunnhh" without opening his mouth. He felt a sudden strong irritation at Justine, sharp little fingers of anger.

"I just meant . . . No. Sorry."

"You meant the two of you, and me, and maybe Maureen, and your grandparents, all here in the house. Together. And you think we're all still here." He could feel himself controlling the anger though it burned through him like flames, like a fire he could capture and hold only with a camera lens. "They're not here, Justine. None of them. Not your grandparents. Not Maureen."

"I didn't . . ."

"You say you talk to them. Well, two of them. Not the third. She's definitely not here."

"Jack. It was dumb of me to—"

"Yes." He had to contain this fury, catch it and bind it down. But fire can't be caught, fire has to be doused. He took a careful sip of water. Another. A third.

"I only said it because I was feeling happy." Justine spoke in little more than a whisper.

Jack could feel she was telling her own truth. But her self-centred comment, even if it arose out of whatever she called happiness, had flared through him with lightning rapidity. Deeply unlike him. And thinking this, his fury, not yet extinguished, reduced to a smoulder. That was better. Cinders, hot as they were, he could contain. "I understand."

"May I have more wine?" Natalia raised her empty glass.

"Thirsty," said Jack, pouring. They ate in silence for more than a minute. He sensed Justine at some kind of bursting point, wanting to speak. He would not ease her progress.

"It's been a long time since I had steak cooked on coals. It's as good as I remember." Natalia smiled at her brother.

A careful smile, he noted.

"It's no use, Jack. I have to say it again. I have to beg you. Please. Don't tear down the house. Please!" In Justine's eyes, welling tears. "Please don't."

He put down his cutlery. He patted his lips with his napkin. "I have to. I have no choice."

"But why?"

Should he simply say it? Suddenly it now seemed fair that she should know. "Vengeance," he said.

Both of the women stared at him. Natalia repeated, "Vengeance."

"Vengeance."

"For?"

"For killing our parents. Justine's grandparents."

Justine said, "Uh—I don't understand."

"There's nothing complicated here. The house killed Sam and Hannah Tartarus."

"Oh stop it, Jack," said Natalia.

He shrugged. "That's how it is."

Justine said, "Jack, you've gone loony."

"If they hadn't been living in this house, they wouldn't have killed themselves."

"Stop, Jack."

He glanced at Natalia. She had withdrawn. Justine's hand to play. "It is the case."

"The house made them kill themselves. Right. And how do you know that?"

"I know."

"Because you were here? Because you were around for them? Or because, really, you were far away. Taking pictures of fires. That's how you know."

She would not draw him in. "The house drove them to killing themselves. An early death. I know this."

"And if you raze the house?"

"I can at least rebalance the disorder."

"In you. Not in them. Or in the house."

He felt as if Justine had slapped him. She was right, she was wrong, she was wrong. "In all three." In himself. Razing the house was vengeance against himself as well. He hid a shiver. Why had he never considered that?

Natalia leaned toward him, took his forearm. "Jack, let's say you really believe the house was somehow—what? responsible?—for their deaths. Just because you tear down the house, even if you sell the land, you won't get rid of its responsibilities. Or yours. They'll still be out there."

But damned if he'd admit to vengeance against himself. Not now. He had to think this through. In this shifted context. "I have to try." He poured himself more wine, and more for Natalia. Justine's glass remained full. "If I didn't, it'd be unfair to my memory of them."

"You are crazy, Jack." Justine glared at him. "You really are. What's happened to you?"

"More than ten years has happened. And it's a conclusion I've come to."

"First of all, you're loony-tunes. And second, you're wrong."

No one spoke for ten confused seconds, till Natalia said, "Wrong?"

"Completely wrong. If the house had been responsible they'd have told me. They wouldn't have gone on hoping I'd keep coming back here."

"What?"

A small, sad smile on Justine's lips. "It was their home, and they loved it."

"For a while, yes. But not later."

"All the time."

"And what lets you say that?"

"They told me."

"What, when you were nine, ten? Come on."

"Last month. Last year."

"Okay, that's it." He shook his head. "There are no ghosts in this house. And if there are, all the more reason to tear it down." He had to leave the table. Soon as he could. "I'm going to do it, Justine. As soon as I get the demolition order."

Justine sighed and spoke in a small, suddenly respectful voice. "If I can prove to you that they loved their house?"

"How?"

"By asking them. With you and Mom right there by me."

He laughed. "And only you can talk to them, so you can have them 'say' anything you want. Right?"

"I'll think of a way."

"Ask them something you couldn't know about," Natalia said.

He smiled gently at his sister. "Good." Natalia didn't want the

225

house destroyed. But even more she needed to prove to Justine that she spoke to her grandparents only in her imagination. "Let's do that. Right now." He pushed back from the table.

"No, no." Justine's head shook sharply, as if something had frightened her.

"Why not?" Jack stood.

"Because—because they're—they're not around now."

"They've left the house."

"No, no, they're here. But just not—around."

"Ah, around but not around. Okay. And when will they be the other around?"

"Later. Maybe later, after it's dark."

"That's true," he said. "Ghosts like it better in the dark."

"They aren't ghosts, Jack."

"Then what are they?" The conversation had gone beyond goofiness.

"They're just—Sam and Hannah Tartarus. And they're dead. And they'll be around later."

Jack sat down and reached for the wine bottle. It was empty. He didn't remember finishing it. "Okay. Later." Maybe Sam had finished it. A ghost with a thirst for wine. Right. He located the corkscrew, reached for the second bottle, uncorked it, poured for himself and Natalia. To Justine he said, "You're not drinking tonight?"

Justine stared at her glass of wine as if seeing it for the first time. She took it and sipped. "I've been distracted."

This made Natalia giggle. The giggle turned into a laugh. Justine too whooped out a laugh. Mother and daughter, laughing, harder, more, near out of control. Tartarus discovered he was smiling. He didn't want to smile. He couldn't stop.

Natalia between breaths, between laughs, blurted, "Justine—is dis—dis—tracted! And Jack is—is loony—loony—tunes!"

Jack Tartarus couldn't join them, couldn't withdraw. He said, "And so is Justine."

Which stopped Justine's laughter. Now she merely wheezed for breath. She said as soon as she could, "I'm not."

Natalia wiped her eyes, Justine sipped her wine and cut into the last of her steak. "There's dessert if anybody wants it. Apple pie. And ice cream. I'm going for a walk."

"You haven't finished your supper." Natalia, her practical self.

"I'll put it in the fridge. For later. After the seance." He got up, taking his plate with him.

Natalia followed, her unfinished plate in hand as well. "Want company?"

He didn't. He had to think. He had to wonder, Can one avenge oneself? One's own acts. Or the lack of them. But she had come here to be with him. And today she had lost Don, maybe this time for good. "Sure," he said.

She popped back to the dining room, told Justine she was going with Jack. Certain she'd be refused, she asked if Justine wanted to come along.

"I'll play my cello. Maybe they'll come around sooner."

Her daughter's smile, Natalia realized, reeked of superiority. But for the moment her concern was Jack. This scenario of his, that the house was responsible for their parents' deaths, had alarmed her more than she wanted to admit. Something had happened to Jack in the last years. How very little she knew about what he'd done and thought over that time. Was Justine in some way right, that Jack was maybe crazy, possibly in a clinical way? Had his fascination with fire burned something in his brain? She returned to the kitchen. "I'm ready." They went out.

"Want to walk up the stream?"

"Haven't been there for a long time."

"To the spring?"

"Sure."

From the angle of the house the sun floated six or seven of its diameters above the treetops. The path along the stream was overgrown with grasses, Oregon grape, salal, but wide enough to walk side by side. The stream below was down to a trickle between occasional pools. He remembered it as wide, deep, much wetter. His father would have said that today the life had been drawn from the land. Jack knew better. Water would return here. And someone might one day build that pond his father had projected but never began.

They talked about Justine, her pretended relationship to some chimerical memory of Hannah and Sam, Natalia's frustration with it, her fear for Justine's recent aberrant behaviour altogether, her so-called decision of taking up plumbing. Covering old ground.

"You know," Natalia said, "it's been strange for me too. These last few days."

"Strange how."

"Things ending. Assumptions no longer valid."

"Are we still talking about Justine?"

Natalia nodded. "I've long presumed I'd be the mother of a world-class virtuoso. Over the years I've built scenarios about the two of us, fears of Justine going away on long concert tours, losing her to music." A grim sniff. "At least copper piping can be local."

"Has it really been her desire to become a great cellist, or is it your fantasy?"

Natalia smiled. "A lot of both, I think."

"She'll come back to her music. It'll always be there."

"Not if she let's it go for a while." A bitter little laugh. "Comes a point along the way when it's too late."

They walked in silence. The path started up the incline toward the spring. The stream bed was barely damp here. "You've just gone beyond Justine."

Natalia stopped. She stared at the ground. "It seemed like he'd be there forever. Like he always has been." She shook her head. "Like I'd always been. Since Stan died."

"Don's still there, Nat."

"But not for me."

Jack put his arm around her shoulder, squeezed a little. "You could make a battle of it."

"I think the battle's lost. She's there for Don. I'm just there. Simple as that."

He pulled her shoulder against his and leaned on it tight. "Come on, let's find the spring." She was right. Nothing else to say.

The sunlight was muted now. They found the source, little more than humidity, oozing from between mossy rocks. He had never seen it producing so little water. It might have been as dry for years, but he'd not been up to this place since before Maureen died. Maybe it had dried up then. "Wonder how long it's been like this."

"Maybe just this summer."

He felt he had to say it aloud: "Haven't been here since before Maureen died."

She took his hand. "She's still there? With you."

He laughed a little. "In a way she'll always be. But I can do as much about that as . . ."

She squeezed his fingers. "I know."

"Sorry, Nat."

"Nobody to blame but me."

"But you know, in a far stronger way, Maureen is gone. I did *FIRE AND THE PHOENIX* for her. When I finished, Maureen just wasn't there anymore. As if somewhere deep in my mind she'd been looking out for me, to make sure I finished up. And I did. It somehow released her."

Natalia dropped his fingers, took his arm, and they started walking back slowly. After some seconds of silence, she said, "I want to ask you something. Please don't be angry with me."

"It's very hard for me to get angry with you."

"You get angry with Justine because she says she talks with Mom and Pop. Are you—I don't quite know what to call it. Jealous? Jealous of her because she says she can speak to them, and you can't speak with Maureen? If such things were possible, Maureen would speak to you?"

Jack felt his cheeks and neck grow hot. Could Natalia be right, even in a little way? Jealous? No chance. Not possible. "Impossible."

"What? That you couldn't be jealous?"

"That I could ever talk to Maureen again. That she could talk to me."

"You did say she was looking out for you. Till you finished *FIRE AND THE PHOENIX*."

"In my mind, I said. Far back there." His face still felt hot. Jealous of Justine? Not damn likely. "All in my mind."

Natalia nodded, stopped walking, loosed her hold on his arm, looked him in the eyes, right, left. "I wonder."

Jack could think of nothing to say. He shook his head. Now he felt embarrassed. Why? Now he took her arm and guided them into walking again. "Shall we go back?"

"Good." After more than a minute of silence she said, "Will you show me the DVD tonight? We could bring the TV into the kitchen, play it off one of the generator plugs."

"Before or after the seance?"

"Oh yes. Oh dear."

"Shall we see if they're 'around'?"

"I suppose." She stopped and stared at the damp moss. "Not much water, is there."

"No." His ears still burned a bit. Jealous of Justine . . .

"Will you tell me? About you and—and fire."

"Tell." What could he tell her that he hadn't already done. "The DVD can tell it better."

"The show, the performance, it'll always be there—" she caught herself "—it will, Jack. From everything I've read about it. But I want to hear about fire from you."

"From me." He considered that. "What from me?"

"What fire is. Right now. For you."

In truth, he had kept himself from thinking much about fire since he'd finished the film. Once burned onto the DVD, it would not change. And he wasn't ready for the sequel. Not ready for anything until he dealt with the house. Until he dealt with himself. And with Ginny, whatever all that was.

"Jack?"

Fire. She wanted to know about fire. What in fact did he think about fire? Right now. "Fire," he said.

They walked through the light underbrush.

"Well, I make fires. I set them. I burn things, wood, paper, plastic, cloth, hair, whatever can catch. I structure my burn. I photograph it. Still and video photography. Then I edit, structuring larger units." He stopped and turned to her. "That's it."

"I don't think so," she said. "What is fire?"

Did he want to go here? He wanted mainly to avoid her question.

But maybe she deserved more. "Fire is fleeting. I capture it. In its infinite moments. For some when they see these moments..." He stopped himself, his words and his feet. "There are two different kinds of moments. Moments as I've witnessed them. And moments as I've patched them together. Some people see them as display. Colour and shape. I heard people say it was like fireworks. At first I thought that was intriguing. But it's wrong. I don't use explosives. I'm much more interested in the constancy of change. In the mutating patterns."

She had been nodding as he spoke. "Why?" she asked and led him into walking again.

Why. "I think ... because fire patterns are familiar. To anybody. Fire is a piece of popular knowledge. Popular activity. Popular culture even. Anybody can make a fire. Everybody knows what fire is. Or think they do. So what I've been doing, I've been taking fire from the level of fact. I've tried to give it a newer force. A kind of shape. If you can ever talk about the shape of fire." As hard as talking about the movement of the mind.

"So that people stop taking it for granted?"

"It's an important human thing, fire. It gives off heat. Heat keeps people's bodies warm, it keeps them alive."

She smiled. "Literally."

"But it's more than that. The image of fire, it can burn into your imagination. As if it's kindling your spirit."

She squeezed his arm against her side. "Careful or you'll soon be talking to ghosts."

"Not even close."

They walked on in silence. Out again in the open they saw the low light against the side of the house, turning the white siding golden as if it itself were the source of fire. Both noted this. Neither commented. Should he mention Don again, before they went back inside. Maybe with Don receding from her life—receded?—she would give Jack less of a hard time about the house. If Don was out of her life—out of her imagination—maybe the house would no longer be a place worth returning to. Cold thought. Except on the other hand the house might now become all-important, the centre of her future life on Crab. But hell, what did it matter, what she thought. No, not the moment to mention Don again.

"Jack? Promise me. If we go ahead with Justine's, well, charade, lay off her, okay? Just let her hang herself. Without you yanking the rope."

They found Justine in the living room, four candles burning above the fireplace, another eight on the windowsills, three on the table in front of the couch. The candles on the sills reflected in the glass, in the double panes two little flames for each candle, a multiplication of tiny fire. She was sitting on the chair beside the side window. As if to protect the wall I've been hacking at, Tartarus thought. He spoke lightly. "So. They 'around'?"

Justine said quietly, "Yes."

"Oh." He sat on the chair nearest the fireplace. "Hello, Mom. Hello, Pop."

"Stop, Jack," she said.

"Okay. Sorry."

"But they say hello to you too."

"Justine—"

"And to you, Mom."

Natalia said nothing. She stood by the open sliding door to the dining room.

"I've asked them," Justine said to Jack, "how they feel about you razing the house. "They say please, please, don't."

"Tell them I have to. And I will."

"I don't have to tell them. They can hear you."

Natalia said, "Okay, Justine, let's get to it."

Justine stared at the couch, as if her grandparents sat there. "Tell me something about my mom that I don't know."

Silence. Natalia too stared at the couch, Jack at his niece. He saw her yank her hand to her bosom as a blush of bright red spread from her ears to the tops of her breasts.

"Justine, are you—" But she held up a finger, silencing him. The blush slowly dimmed. Justine looked as if she were continuing to listen. At last she nodded. And smiled. And giggled, just a little.

"Yes?" said Natalia.

"Sorry, Mom. But you asked. And this is what they said I should tell you." She stopped, waited . . .

Natalia repeated, "Yes?"

"The couch—the one they're sitting on, right there. That's the couch you lost your virginity on. With Don. Long ago."

For seconds Natalia said nothing. Then she whispered, "Good god."

"Something I never knew, Mom." She giggled again.

"How did they—we were completely alone—how could—they weren't even on the island—how—?"

"You want them to answer all that?"

"No," said Natalia.

"Okay," said Jack, "pretty fancy. But you've always known your mother and Don were lovers, long ago. And they still care for each other."

"Sure. But this couch?"

"Why not? Where else? Not in her own bed, Nat's room was her private place. She didn't let others in. Let Don in? No way. Her parents' bed? That'd be an abomination. My bed? I'd've been able to smell them. That leaves the couch."

"Or the woods, or Don's place, or anywhere."

"A good guess, Justine. I don't deny you're smart."

"Okay, Jack." She turned to the couch. "Tell me something I don't know about my Uncle Jack." She waited. She listened. Her mouth dropped open, a centimetre, two. She listened longer. At last she said, "Wow."

"Okay. What did they tell you now."

"Years ago you and a young woman half your age screwed in every corner of this house."

A wild chill took him. With the low candlelight, could they see him quiver? He kept his voice level. "I never knew my parents had such an overweening sexual imagination. Two so-called secrets, both involving fornication." But he was rattled.

"You deny it."

"I won't honour it with a response." His mind whirred. How the hell—He'd never told anyone. Ginny must have told someone. Who? Someone she could brag to. I've made it with an old guy—Someone at

233

her school. Couldn't have been Justine, least not then, she'd have been barely more than a baby. And Ginny left here—right after. Who could Ginny have told, who told Justine? Someone. And Justine had saved that little prize till this moment. Damn her.

Natalia said only, "Ginny?"

"It's all ridiculous, Nat." Not that he wouldn't tell Nat it was true. But he couldn't allow the least credit to the impossible scenario Justine was building. His parents were dead. Justine had learned this piece of information from someone Ginny had told and now had played her card. Had to be something like that. "Justine hasn't proven a thing. And this whole bit of psychodrama is stupid."

Justine merely smiled. "Want me to try again?"

Jack stood so he could look down at Justine, a little chunk of control. "I'm impressed with the tableau you've concocted here. A fine little monologue. Pretending to listen, pretending to hear. But there is no way you're talking to my parents' ghosts. I don't know why you're doing this, making all this up." He marched toward the hallway, stopped, turned to her. "And I don't like it. You're making a mockery of your grandparents. So stop." He left the house. He was furious at her. And, he realized, with himself. For letting her get to him? Or because he was, indeed, jealous of her, of this—ability of hers?

Natalia waited till she heard the door close before she said, "Oh Justine . . ."

"I'm sorry, Mom, I'm sorry I upset him, I really am. But—but . . ."

"But?"

"But to not tell him what they were telling me—I mean, he said he wanted to know."

"He did," said Natalia. "You're right, he did."

ELEVEN: Don and Etain, Ginny and Jack

Etain said, "Nothing you can do."

"I can be with him," said Don.

"He's so doped up he doesn't have the first idea who's here. Or where he is."

"He might come out of it."

"Don. Tomorrow he's going to Victoria. You'll go with him, you'll stay with him as long as you think he needs you. Now come back with me, get some sleep."

"I don't know if . . ."

"In a real bed. You're so wiped out all you're good for is sleeping." She took his hand.

He still resisted. "They should've tried to deal with him in Nanaimo."

"He needs special treatment. Dr. Bandeen said so. He can't get it in Nanaimo. And certainly not here. Be grateful. And you with him right now isn't helping. Just exhausting you even more. Come on." She tugged at his hand.

He released his fingers from hers, opened the door, and glanced in. Tamara was reading entries on her clipboard, pen in hand. His father lay flat on the bed, his face near as white as the sheets. Don could see it clearly: Frank would not make it to Victoria. "Tamara, I'm going to get some sleep." He gave her his cellphone number. "If there's anything, call right away."

"Sleep'll do you good. Tomorrow'll be long."

"Thanks for being here." She smiled, and he appreciated her the more for that. "Okay, let's go," he said to Etain. They stepped out into the warm evening air, the sun just down.

"Leave your car," Etain said. "If you have to come back, I'll drive you."

He knew she thought he was too tired to drive but said nothing. He sat in the passenger seat. He felt his head drooping so he pulled it back, the headrest his support. He closed his eyes. He heard the door open, Etain speaking. "Hunghh. What?"

"We're here." She leaned over and helped him out. She took his arm.

"Thank you." He let her lead him to Eating Thyme's back door. He already felt better. Not rested. Less weary for the tiny sleep. A restorative nap.

"Hungry?"

He considered that. "I could eat something. Soup maybe."

"We might just have some. Go up. I'll see what's left." She opened the door to the restaurant. A low rumble of voices came from the far side, and the clank of dishes being stacked. "Hi, Terry." She closed the door behind her.

Don checked his watch. 9:35. Past closing time. Etain had finished serving the last customers an hour ago, left the cleaning up for Terry, came over to the clinic. And tried to hustle him out from the moment she arrived. He climbed the stairs slowly. On the landing he opened the door and stepped into the living room. The dog Batiste rose to his feet and ambled over. Don lowered his hand. Batiste licked it. Don stroked his head. The ritual done, Batiste returned to his place on the floor. Don noted Patrick's door stood ajar. He glanced into the boy's room. Patrick lay fast asleep in underpants and T-shirt, the sheet pulled away, his flat hair covering his head like a helmet. Don thought, What a fine kid. Etain's fine kid. The father, he knew, had never been a factor. A passing donor. He pulled the door closed, sat on the couch, kicked off his sandals, and pulled up his feet. He wanted a drink. Wine? If he took out a bottle, would she misunderstand? He was incapable of making love tonight. Just to lie next to her, hold her, kiss her neck, that'd be fine. Let Frank be okay overnight, so Don could stay unconscious all night long.

A beer, that's what Frank would say. Don could use a beer. He got up, took one from the fridge, opened it, drank from the bottle. Cold. Good. Bet Frank would like a cold beer right now.

His father was about to die, Don could feel it. They remove him from Crab, he dies. And what could Don do about that? Frank wasn't in good enough shape to stay on the island. So he'd die. And if they took the island away from him, he'd die too. An awful, terrible quandary.

Frank, the final buffer between Don and his own departure. Etain's mother too, far away, growing weaker, increasingly incapable. Don took a swallow of beer and sat again on the couch. And how, he wondered again, did Natalia see her parents? Lots of people think about suicide. Don had been there for her after, at the funeral. She'd seemed somehow—what?—away. Distant. From him, from other people. From herself too, maybe. Dealing with the suicides by not dealing. He hoped she would understand. About Etain.

He still adored Natalia, a grand friend, a fine companion. He would talk to her—when? Not likely tomorrow, tomorrow was for an ambulance. Please, do not let the departure, the trip, kill Frank. He could talk to Natalia later, on the phone.

The door from downstairs opened. Etain. She reached to her side and brought in a tray—soup tureen with steaming liquid, bowl, bread, cutlery. She set it on the table. "Minestrone," she said. "Bottom of the pot. Very thick." She scooped soup from the tureen into the bowl.

He walked over and put both arms around her. "Thank you." He held her. "Smells great."

"Sit." She pulled her head back and kissed him. Felt him let go. Watched him sit.

He set his spoon against the inside of the bowl and let the liquid flow in, raised it, blew on it, put it in his mouth, swallowed. "Perfect."

From the fridge she took another beer, opened it, clicked his. "To your father."

Don nodded. "And your mother." They both sipped. "I've been thinking about them. Our parental generation. A kind of cohort. Leaving us behind."

"I heard from my sisters, by the way. They're actively looking for a place for her now."

A spoonful, another blow, another swallow. "Maybe Jack's parents did the right thing."

"The suicide?" She squinted at him.

"Yeah."

"Never."

"Ending the suffering."

"Could you? For yourself?"

He thought for a long moment and took her hand. "I don't know."

"I do. Whatever the pain. Life happens only once. I want as much as I can get."

He said it for the first time, without thinking. "I think that's why I love you." Her smile then, tiny, was the loveliest and most perfect image he had ever known.

"I'm glad." She squeezed his hand. "And I think I love you because you will admit you don't know something when it's true that you don't."

"You do? Love me?"

"Don't you know that?"

"I—I've not been sure." He grinned. "I guess I should have asked earlier."

"No. We say things aloud when we're ready to. And think the listener is ready to hear."

"I do, you know. Love you."

"Should we celebrate that?"

"We've been celebrating that. For quite a while now."

"You are remarkable."

"We both are." She laughed. "We are as we should be."

"I hope I can be. With you."

"You have been. Since I've known you. Even before we knew each other well." She leaned over and kissed him lightly on the lips and sat back. "Do you think we can do a better job of it, love I mean, than my parents?"

"What kind of question is that?"

"My question. I think that with you, I can do better than my parents did."

"But your father died when you were very young." He took more soup.

"Thirteen. Old enough to see there wasn't a lot between them. Frank was kind to your mother. At least in public. I don't know more than that."

"You met them? You never told me."

"Met is too strong. They'd come in here for lunch once or twice a week. Long before I bought the place. End of the eighties."

"She died in nineteen-ninety. In the spring."

"He'd help her walk, help her sit down. Even laid out her napkin on her lap, I remember that so clearly. He'd even cut up her vegetables."

Frank, selecting Eating Thyme on his own volition? The fight Don had had to get him here. Till he met Etain. "I wouldn't have guessed he'd choose to eat here."

"Your mother must've been pretty ill. They liked coming in, for the organic food. Somebody must have told Frank it'd be good for your mother." Etain smiled again, sad but content. "She seemed like a charming woman."

Don's sense of his mother came from what he found in his memories. He didn't know how others had seen her, interacted with her—had never thought to ask. Now even Etain's few words were a revelation. "I think she was a good woman." And, he now wondered, what had his father been to his mother. And she to him.

"They sometimes ate here with your friend Jack's parents. And later Hannah and Sam would come, just the two of them. I can't remember if Frank was ever with them after your mother died." She took a sip of beer. "Those two, Hannah and Sam Tartarus, now there was a grand love. I didn't know them. But I could see it, every time."

"How could you tell that?"

She shrugged. "Because they looked together like I'm feeling right now. About you."

He pushed the half-empty bowl away and reached out both his hands for hers. She took them. They studied each other's faces, a magnificent need to memorize every detail from hair to brow to eyes and nose to lips and chin, ears and cheeks and neck as well. He reached up and lay his fingers and palm against her cheek. His hand had never touched anything so enchanting

They went to bed. Despite each of their unspoken vows to let Don sleep, their bodies had minds of their own. Later they lay face to face on their sides, holding each other. "I am so tired." Don said, "But I have to tell you something."

"Tell me everything."

He thought, How do I say this? And answered, straight. "I once thought I was in love."

"With Natalia."

He drew back. "How did you know?"

She pulled him to her, kissed him lightly. "You've talked about her."

"Like I've talked about Jack. Or—well—anybody."

"You've talked about her like you cared for her a lot. More than a lot."

"I did. I still do. She's a good woman."

"Don. That's what you said earlier. About your mother."

Oh dear. He'd better mock being indignant. "And you think I didn't love my mother."

"I think you loved your mother. And I think you loved Natalia. Loved. Past tense." She tweaked his right nipple.

"Ouch!" He squeezed her tight to him as if to keep her from doing that again. "But even that past-tense love isn't the same as now."

"She was your first love." A question without being a question.

"She was. First."

"That's a special thing. And you've known her for many years."

"A long time."

"You'd see her when she came to Crab."

"When she came to live, mostly. Sometimes—sometimes she'd come for a weekend and not tell me."

"Because she knew you were busy." She pulled back to see his face. "With Frank."

"I—guess. We sort of took each other for granted. A bit."

"A habit." She suddenly turned from him and lay on her back.

"What?"

"I think it's often better to leave the place where you grew up. Start somewhere new."

"I didn't."

"You did, a bit. From Vancouver to Crab."

"Not very far."

She reached her arm across her body and pulled herself against him. "It's the old patterns. Habits. The adult in us gets drawn into old ways when the adult lives in the child's place. Ways that might have been splendid the first time, the second, but ways that don't fit anymore."

A sudden sadness took his gut. Natalia? Yes, in a way. But not a sense of loss. Natalia was to have been—was?—a great love. What he'd been nursing was a conscious responsibility to his love for Natalia. Yet all the while the sinew of that love was weakening, had been for years, maybe decades. He'd not noticed. What was left of it had faded just as this other had grown large, his coming to know and, equally unverbalized, to love Etain. He felt his thoughts thicken. He felt himself falling asleep. "Good night."

Dinner with Madge was usually pleasant. Ginny and she would exchange thoughts from the morning, incidents of the day, small plans for the week. Madge cooked well. Nearly eight decades of eating, so she knew what she liked. And Ginny had a knack of her own in the kitchen. Meals were tasty. But this evening their talk had been forced, the food overcooked, mismatched. Honey-glazed chicken? It'd been delicious when Charles made it for Madge on Tuesday down in Victoria. Tonight Madge had gone to bed early. Still tired, she said. Charles was demanding.

Okay with Ginny. She'd not been able to concentrate on her mother's stories. The flowers in which garden? The deal for some blouse where? In her mind was Jack Jack Jack, tonight with his sister and her daughter. She figured she'd recognize Natalia from the old photo. Justine was an unknown. She smiled to herself. Go over, introduce herself? Hi, I'm your brother's, uncle's, what? mistress? paramour? wench? She liked that. Jack's wench. Felt good, to wench. Boyoboy good. Boyoboy? She hadn't thought boyoboy, not in years. If ever. Something new going on here. For her wench-self. But her wench-self was not having a good time at home with her aged mother, and no Jack. Nine-thirty at night, no Jack.

Talk about not having a good time, Jack must be having a hell of a time. Tomorrow she would talk to him about them. Not tonight.

241

His sister, his niece, and Jack having a fine time getting reacquainted. Convincing him not to tear the house down. She'd leave them to it. They'd get to him.

On the other hand. On the other hand if Ginny were there too, that'd be three against one. He couldn't stand his ground against her and his family. The house would be spared. For the sake of the Tartarus family. The living and the dead. So the niece played the cello for Hannah and Sam. As if they were right there in front of her. Was the girl deep into that sort of thing? Or nuts? Be kinda interesting to find out. Just go to bed, Ginny. What, like Madge? It wasn't even dark out. Bed? This early? By herself? Wenches don't go to bed early. Wenches don't go to bed alone. A long time since she'd last felt wench-like, so long a time. Don't waste it.

So she climbed the stairs to her room. She changed from jeans and tank top to a sundress, dark blue, appropriate for evening after the sun had gone down, loose skirt, spaghetti straps to show off bare shoulders. She combed the tangles from her hair. Caught her face in the mirror. Her eyes had gotten overlarge again. Her high cheekbones were good. What would her eyes look like without such high cheekbones? She drank water. Sandals. Purse. Eye drops. New water bottle. Car keys. Or maybe walk over. No. Outside to her beater. Or borrow her mother's convertible. Just right for a wench.

She nearly laughed aloud. She had just equated her mother to a fornicatress. Well, why not. Madge with her Charles. The convertible, a sexmobile. For one more moment she considered taking it. No. She'd driven it a couple of times but it was too light in action, had too much power, she'd not felt full control. Not to be tried at night.

She backed her trusty beater away from the house, turned, and headed down the drive. The half-kilometre to Jack's. She slowed. Pulled to the shoulder. Stopped. Not a good idea, Ginny. How would she explain herself. Wench was out, or anything like it. What definition did she have in Jack's world? Neighbour. Neighbour showing up at quarter to ten? She got out of the car and stared at the drive. Silence. She took the flashlight from under the seat, switched it on. Played the beam across the front of the drive. Walk down, see. Maybe they weren't even awake.

Her steps followed the beam. A three-minute walk. The house loomed dark. Maybe they're not asleep. Impossible to tell. Unless she knocked. Hi, it's Jack's wench come to call. She switched off the lamp. Squeezed her eyes closed. Opened them. Nothing had changed. Nothing would change. Her eyes had adjusted to the dark. She couldn't see the drive but knew its route from the trees overhead, and through the cut in the woods she saw stars. She walked back slowly. She felt the warm air on her bare shoulders. On her bare legs up to her thighs. She felt ultra-wenchy. All dressed up, nowhere to go.

Only place worth going was to Jack. Would she have a chance now, with Jack? Could it be with Jack? Did he want her? Nearly fifteen years alone. The occasional fling. With nobodies. Well, bodies, but that was it. Nobody since her engagement, no one since Lincoln. Who had opted out soon as she got sick. So he was nobody too. No life since then, what she once had thought was a life. Jobs clerking was no life, pet grooming not a life. She never wanted to smell a dog, cat, gerbil ever again. Forever the fear, at a right moment with someone special that her syndrome—no, fuck syndrome: her disease—would grab her, hold her, take her away. And the special person would follow the route of Lincoln. But with Jack she had the sense that possibly, really, whatever happened to her, he'd be okay with it. And maybe—no, more, surely—she would be good for Jack too.

Yeah, except what gave her the right to think such thoughts? Nothing, nothing gave her that. Except, because she'd thought it, she almost believed it. It made her feel wenchy again. Capable of every and any thing. For Jack.

She was alone this evening. She could do whatever she wanted. Except be with Jack. So she'd be herself. Head down to the Dock Pub, order a glass of wine, look down at the tourists, say hello to someone she knew. Unusual for her, this yen for company. Then come home. Start up again tomorrow. And the day after that. Would Jack remain here, the day after destroying his house? Would there always be a day after and a day after? What was her definition in Jack's world anyway. Damn, and just a moment ago she'd felt so good. Damn, damn, damn. Back at her car. Get in, turn around, go home. Or drive to The Pub. No, what good would it do, she wasn't meeting a friend, didn't want to get picked up. Let alone pick up someone. Nothing good to be found at The Pub. But maybe something better than heading home, dropping into bed. A night of sleeplessness. Didn't sound like a good idea. She drove straight to the village. Parked close to The Pub, another car had just pulled out. Good omen. Purse, and up the stairs, and in.

The place was crowded. Noisy. Sweaty. At least not smoky, her eyes couldn't stand smoke. She worked her way between and around people, older, younger, holding wineglasses, beer glasses. Like the car unparking as she arrived, someone got off a stool as she approached the bar. She knew the woman filling a pitcher of draft beer, the owner, Shelagh, only by sight. Shelagh handed the pitcher to a customer who paid and took it away.

Shelagh's eye must note newcomers out of work habit because she came right over to Ginny and said, "Hi, hon, what'll it be?"

"Glass of Chardonnay, please."

A bottle of Chardonnay appeared in Shelagh's hand, a glass out from under the counter, Shelagh poured. "Run a tab?"

Not a good idea. One glass would do her. But she said, "Okay."

Shelagh spotted a dry drinker and was gone. The man next to her turned and raised his beer glass. "Cheers."

"Uh—cheers." She sipped from her glass. In for half a minute and the pick-up process had begun. One glass, she was outta here.

"You sure you want to have more after this one?"

"Uh—I don't know." Weird pick-up line. Had she seen him before?

"Probably not a good idea."

Did this guy read minds? "Why do you say that?"

"You shouldn't be drinking."

"Is that any of your business?"

"Nope." He sipped his beer. "Name's Dennis, but people call me Turtle."

She laughed. "Why? D'you hide in your shell?"

"Not usually."

"Okay, Turtle." She sipped. In five sips the glass would be empty, it'd be time to go. "You live on the island?"

"Yep."

"Work?"

"Yep. At the hardware store."

That's where she'd seen him. "Ah."

"I recognize you too. Came in with the fella bought himself the wrecking bar. A Fulton."

"You have an excellent memory."

"Pride myself on it. I remember lots of things."

"Yes? Like?"

"That Fulton. It's double-headed. Bites left, bites right."

What was this guy on about. "So?"

"That's good sometimes. Not so good other times. Depends on the job." Turtle sipped beer. "He making progress?"

Did this guy—Turtle—did he remember something Jack had told him? "He started. But he had to stop."

Turtle nodded. "That's good."

"Why do you say it's good?"

"'Cause the job's not good. As I see it."

At least he was on the right side. Bizarre. "Is that any business of yours?" She sipped.

"Nope. Not really. Except, in a way . . ."

"What?"

"We all like living on the island."

From intrusion to generalization. "We do."

"Like living in our own homes. You too?"

"I do." Where the hell was he headed? If anywhere.

"Way you get to know a house, you live in it. When you live in it, it's yours."

She had to agree. "That's right." She sipped. A couple of sips left. Too much?

"And a house needs living in. A house empty, that's no good."

He was making such complete sense a chill took her. Eerie. Shift the direction. "Except there's a lot of vacation homes here. Summer homes. Empty most of the year. Still good houses."

He sipped beer, stayed silent for a few seconds. "Not what I'm talking about."

"No," and found herself adding, "I didn't think so."

He smiled at her. "Good."

"And—what are you talking about?"

"You know."

"I think I do." Preposterous, such clarity about the Tartarus house. "But how do you?"

"It's obvious. He bought the Fulton."

Instantly she knew she had to defend Jack. "He's living in the house now. Sleeping there." She knew this for a happy fact.

Turtle raised his eyebrows. "How 'bout that. Well well well."

"Since last night." She sipped wine. "His sister's there too. In the house. And his niece."

Turtle said, "Good." He drank the last of his beer. "Now he's got to be careful."

"Careful. About?"

"What happens next."

"Which is?"

Turtle laughed. "You think I can see the future?"

She wanted to say, Yes. Instead she smiled. "Thank you." She took a last sip. "I agree."

"But I think it's going to be okay."

For a moment everything surrounding her stood out in the sharpest detail, as if she were seeing the bar, the bottles, the woman Shelagh, this man Turtle, the beer spigots, for the first time. "I hope you're right." Objects and people had taken on the brightest, clearest colours. It felt wondrous, staring at them. "I really do." She brought her glass to her lips. She realized it was empty. His was too. She wanted him to continue talking. To continue saying important things. She tried to catch Shelagh's eye but found only the back of her head. "Can I buy you a drink?"

"You going to have another glass of wine?"

"I . . . Yes."

"Don't think you should."

She stared at her hands. "You're right." Second glass of wine in two days. She stood, hoping Shelagh would see the move. Her hands fidgeted with her purse. She found a ten-dollar bill. The colours in The Pub had gone dull, browns and pastels. She either had to stay and talk some more with this Turtle or get out of here quickly. She heard Shelagh laughing somewhere.

"It's on me."

"No—I can't—Here." She thrust the money at him.

He folded her fingers over the bill. "Go home. Where you should be."

The smile that came to her lips must have shown both relief and a touch of fear. What could Turtle know about the Tartarus house? And what was the house to him? She turned and pushed through the drinkers as if she were fleeing from The Pub. Possibly she was.

Outside the dark air had cooled a little. Wind blew across her bare shoulders and chilled her. She stood beside the old Pontiac and touched its hood with the relief of meeting an old friend who'd stand by her in any distress. She got in, opened the window, sat still. Suddenly her eyelids felt as if they were rasping her eyeballs. She closed her eyes. That felt better. In a minute she would put the drops in. Her heart had been pounding. Now it was only thumping. The wine—A voice said, "Excuse me?" She opened her eyes. Outside the window, a woman's face, her lips saying, "You leaving?" Ginny could only shake her head and close her eyes again. The woman said, "Are you all right?" and Ginny found herself nodding hard. "Take care."

She opened her eyes. She found her purse and the medication, unscrewed the top, leaned back, pulled her lower lid back, and dripped the liquid into the lid pocket, right first, then left. She closed her eyes and fumbled in her purse for the packet of tissues, pulled one loose, and swabbed the overflow dry. Turtle. Strange conversation. She was feeling better. What had so overcome her? Not what Turtle had said. His stance. As if he knew things he couldn't know. More of a pub encounter than she'd figured on. She was feeling better. Time to go home. Like Turtle had said.

She opened her eyes. They felt normal. Best damn medication in the world, couldn't have made it through the last dozen years without it. Stay down, damn Sjögren's! Down! She took out her water bottle and drank. She started the engine and drove home, past Jack's with not a thought of stopping, down her drive to the house. Where her headlight picked out a second car, parked. And on the steps to the house, a man. My house. Where I have to be.

She turned off the engine, got out, and in the dark walked slowly toward him. Despite the wind, blowing harder up here, she could feel him moving toward her. They met, they embraced.

After a minute or more Jack said, "Is it okay? That I'm here."

"It's grand. How long were you sitting like that?"

"Oh, half an hour maybe. Ginny, I need—I need to talk with you."

She drew back to see his face. "Are you okay?"

"Nothing wrong." He made himself smile, a relaxed grin. "Nothing serious."

"You want to come in?"

"I want to talk with you. In private."

"My mother's asleep. But she wakes a lot." She took his hand. "Let's go out back. Our campfire site." She led him around the house. "I have to tell you, I almost came to your house this evening. But I decided I better not. I went to the village and had a glass of wine." She told him quickly about her conversation with Turtle.

"Weird is right," said Tartarus.

They sat on a bench. Their eyes, accustomed to the dark, now could see in the starlight the outlines of a campfire site and an outbuilding of some sort. "Jack? We could make a fire. Watch the flames and you can tell me about them."

"I don't think we should. There's no open burning."

"It's in a pit, it's contained. It'd be out of the wind. We wouldn't let the sparks escape."

He put his arm around her shoulder. "I can talk about flames without seeing them."

They stared at the dark fire pit in silence till she said, "Okay. Talk."

First he told her about his evening with Natalia and Justine, all the moments leading to Justine's set piece, the burlesqued conversations with an ostensible Sam and Hannah that dealt with material Justine purportedly couldn't know. Natalia and Don losing their virginities with the other on the living room couch. And the wild four days Jack and Ginny had together before Ginny left for university. "I have to say, the whole of her—her recitation, it shook me. She played it through with great aplomb. She shouldn't be a cellist, she's too great an actress. She's missing her calling. As if the most natural thing in the world is chatting with your dead grandparents."

Ginny had set her head against Jack's shoulder and stared at the dark fire pit, spark-free. "You're right, very strange. But, and I've said this before, in a curious way I do envy her."

"Even if she's crazy." Should he tell Ginny? "My sister said something to me this evening, that maybe I was jealous of Justine. That she could speak to the dead, and I couldn't." There. He'd told her. He must trust her completely. He hadn't known this.

It took a few seconds before she said, "Are you? Jealous?"

"I don't usually get angry at people, and when I do I know why. What Justine is doing I don't approve of, but I don't need to be so mad. I don't know where the anger comes from." He laughed, without humour. "Jealousy? I'd just never thought about it till Natalia said it."

"And Justine believes what she's doing? What she's saying."

"Yeah. And when I was there, when I was listening, at moments I didn't know whether to accept it all and simply have a pleasant indirect make-believe conversation with my parents or be completely openly furious with her for—for—for using her memory of them like that."

"Like when I went into the house when it was empty. I'd talk to them aloud." She laughed a little. "They never answered. Or not so as I could hear." She took his hand. "Maybe she talks to them like that to keep them from being so completely dead."

He said nothing for a few seconds. Then he interlaced her fingers with his. "Maybe."

"She remembers them by remaking them. I think lots of us do versions of that."

He laughed, a dry, short outbreath. "Remembering." He shook his head. "There's something no one could remember. No one except you and me."

"The four days."

He nodded. "I have to ask you. Did you ever tell anyone? About those four days."

"Someone who could have told Justine?" She shook her head. "Not possible."

"Anyone. No one at all?"

"For a long time, no. It had to be our secret. Such a perfect four days, I couldn't talk about it, telling anyone would make our time together something, I don't know, dishonourable."

"I thought it was just you testing yourself."

"It came to be way more. So special. In my imagination."

"Okay." How to think about that—what? revelation? "But you did. Tell someone."

She nodded. "But no way could any of that have gotten to Justine."

"Who?"

She waited, then laughed. "I was about to say, Does it matter? But I'm feeling it does."

"Yes."

"I told you I was going to be married. About a year after I graduated. Three months before the wedding, my best girlfriend, her name was Jane, she said after I was married I'd do everything with Lincoln, I'd only be there for him. I could never be free and uncaring again. Whatever I wanted to try I had to do it before. So we went off together for a week, Jane and me, and we drank and smoked and tried a whole assortment of drugs. And we talked. We told each other everything we'd ever done. Swore to keep each other's secrets forever. The four days was part of what I told her about. We came home and our lives were supposed to go back to normal. Except somehow I got sick, nobody knew what it was but I was out of it, and it turned into this Sjögren's syndrome. And Linc couldn't handle it and backed out of the engagement."

"He broke the engagement? Because you were sick?"

"Right."

"Damn good thing you found out about his loyalty early on."

"Yeah. I've come to realize that."

"Ginny. Why did you and Jane go on that binge? I mean, really?"

"I told you. My last chance to . . ."

"A last chance. After that a piece of your life would be over."

"Well, sort of. Yeah, I guess."

"Did you ever think you took that week away from your normal life, away from Linc, because you didn't want to marry him?"

"Why—why do you ask that?"

"Maybe you dropped him as much as he dropped you."

She took both his hands in hers. "In the last years, I've wondered something like that." She sighed. "I don't know. It's possible."

"You've been blaming him. Not yourself."

"Like I said, I don't know. And after all these years, it doesn't much matter to me."

Jack nodded.

"Wherever that blame belongs, when Linc left me, I wasn't much interested in romance any longer. I just felt always at the depths of shitty. But my point is Jane. She cast blame. On herself. She insisted it was her fault, what happened to me. She got depressed. Stayed depressed. She'd always been a bit dramatic, great highs and dirty lows." A grim laugh. "I guess it wasn't such a terrific idea, our binge. Then one day maybe half a year later my father sat me down and told me Jane had killed herself. Overdosed. So she died with all my secrets inside her, Jack. She couldn't have told anyone."

He would not challenge Ginny on this. But the four days he and she had together now appeared to be less than a total and pristine secret. Jane could have told someone, who told someone else, who one day told Justine. Unlikely, yes. Not impossible. Why would anyone who didn't know Ginny care? No one would. Still. Maybe Jane wrote down some of Ginny's secrets. But how would they get to Justine. What possible connection could there be between Jane and Justine. "That's terrible about Jane," he said.

"For a long time it got me depressed as well. And of course I thought about suicide too. But one day I woke up and knew something had

251

shifted. Like, how dumb it would be if I killed myself." She stopped and concentrated on their non-fire. "I think it's what angered me most about your parents. Your father, mainly."

"What?"

"That he hadn't figured out suicide was dumb. I could've told him. But he never asked. He'd have thought it was none of my business. But it was. Because I liked him. Both of them. But by then your mother wasn't able to figure out how dumb suicide was either. But he could have worked that out for her." She stood and walked slowly around the fire pit. "That's why I wish I could talk to them. Like maybe Justine can. To sort of apologize for not telling him suicide was really truly dumb. Even if he didn't ask me."

"Asking can be hard."

"The hardest."

Jack nodded. "Something I've wanted to ask you too. Did you go to their funeral? Till now I never thought of you and them as part of the same world."

"I didn't go."

"Because you were angry? Because suicide is dumb."

"No." She shook her head. "I didn't go because I didn't want to meet up with you."

"What?" She'd rejected the chance to see him again? "Why?"

"I told you. Our time was special. It's frozen back in time. It's why I didn't recognize you when you were swinging that crowbar. Not to mention the beard. You were a different person, had to be. I couldn't go to the funeral. How could I stand near you? It'd contaminate that memory." She sat beside him again. "And if you recognized me, what were we going to do about it? Leap back eight years and start over? The day of your parents' funeral? Come on, Jack."

"So you stayed away." And if she had appeared then? "You could have come but . . ."

"But I actively, consciously decided not to."

"Those four days were, you know, special, very special for me too. Time out of time. All those circumstances coming together."

"Yes."

"My first island photography show. The empty house. Maureen's absence."

"A lot of electricity in the house, Jack. It couldn't have happened anywhere else."

"It was a different house. I remember. The same building. But a different house."

"Maybe. Maybe."

"It was our setting. In the house that caused Sam and Hannah to kill themselves."

"You really blame the house."

"I do. It's irrational to think that, I know. But it destroyed them, in a full, real way." He thought for a moment. "Yes, I'm looking for vengeance. For them. But I've started to wonder, have I maybe been looking for vengeance in another way." He turned away from the stars, to her. "Almost like—vengeance against myself."

"I don't think I understand."

"I don't know if I do either. I wasn't there for them, Ginny. I don't think I feel guilty about that, I mean, it's not a blaming issue. But . . ."

"But?"

"I did what I did, didn't do what I didn't do. I have to avoid distorting and denying what did and what didn't happen. Both are part of my history. You understand that?"

"In a messy sort of way."

"Yeah. It is messy. The whole idea of vengeance against oneself. I don't know if such a thing can happen."

"Why would you want it to?"

"It's like razing the house. The same kind of revenge."

She drew him to her, and held him. She closed her eyes.

"As if it's my responsibility. Mine alone. Just as our four days are my responsibility."

"Hey! And mine."

"Yours less. It's my house."

"Your house . . ." For a few seconds she said nothing, then stared at him. "Oh dear."

"What?"

"I just had a clear thought. I mean, a very unmessy thought."

"What?"

"You want to destroy the house. Not because it caused your parents' suicide."

"Then why?"

"Because—because of what we did there over those four days."

"No. That's ridiculous."

"It may sound ridiculous. But I think I'm right. It's why you say that for those four days it was a different house. Not your parents' house. Our house."

"The place where we . . ."

She set a finger to his lips, took his hand, and stared at him.

"What, you're saying I want to destroy the house out of—out of some kind of—what? guilt? Stepping out on Maureen or something?"

"Some kind of something. Destroy it so no one who didn't have our four days can live in it. Because those four days were so important to you too. Other people's lives in the house would be some kind of sacrilege." She laughed. "That's not vengeance, Jack. That's just some creepy kind of ownership."

"Come on. I rented it out. People lived in it. I arranged for people to live there."

"Then two years ago something changed. You realized it. It took you a while to figure out, but soon as you did you stopped renting. Kept anyone else from living there."

"You're nuts. This is psychoanalytic nuttery."

She shrugged. "And wanting to raze the house because it 'killed' your parents is sociological nuttery."

"What are we playing here, My theory is bigger than yours?"

She brought his hands to her shoulders and took his shoulders in hers. She leaned her head to his. "We're not playing anything. We're looking at possibilities." She grinned. "Okay?"

"Okay."

"And we're out on a long tangent." But, she thought, a useful tangent. A very important tangent. "I don't know how Justine knew about you and me, back then."

"Yeah. A tangent. But, damn it, how could she have known?"

She took his hands from her shoulders, held his right, and brought it to her lips. She kissed his fingers. "Maybe your parents did tell her."

"First I want to tear the house down so that we can have it live only in memory as a shrine to our four days, and then . . ."

"Come on, I didn't say that, I said . . ."

"You came pretty close. And then you concede Justine's ploy."

"No." She brought his hand to her cheek and closed her eyes.

"Okay. Let's for a moment consider the impossible. Justine talked with Sam and Hannah's ghosts. How in hell could my parents have known about you and me?"

Ginny shrugged. "Maybe the house told them."

Which is what Natalia had said: the house told Hannah she was useless. But this he wouldn't repeat to Ginny. Because he didn't trust her that much? "So now the house is an animate being."

"You said it caused their deaths. You can't have cause without some kind of power."

"Let's not go there."

She looked at him, hard. "If houses could talk . . ."

Another thought. He took his hand from her face. "Ginny. Listen to me. Did you—did you tell your good friends Sam and Hannah about our spree?"

"Are you crazy? How can you even ask?"

"Yeah. Ridiculous." He shook his head. "Could they have guessed?"

"How?"

"You might have said something. Did you . . . ever talk to them about me?"

"Sometimes they talked about you to me. About your work. But we mostly didn't talk about you at all." She sighed. "And certainly not about you and me."

"And if you had it's impossible for them to tell anyone now. Because, and right now this bears saying clearly, they are dead."

"And now can we just sit here and stare at the stars and say nothing?"

"We can." He brought his arm around her shoulder. She lay her hand on his chest. They stared at the blackness above them, blackness perforated with dots of light, in silence.

At last Ginny said, "What do you see?"

"Up there?"

"Yep."

"Right now not so much what I see. More what I feel. It's a kind of deep pleasure. A pleasure beyond."

"Beyond."

"Beyond what I rarely experience with people." He felt her tighten. "And I wouldn't have said that if you weren't an exceptional rarity."

"Oh," she said, her voice near to a whisper.

"It's when I'm by myself, working with fire, in my photos I'm part of the fire. I've stepped into the flicker of the flame."

"Like you're . . . burning?"

"Sometimes. Whatever it is, I feel myself moving to completion."

"Because . . ."

"Because the flame is transforming what it burns. And I'm part of that transformation."

"And that's why you make photos of fire. For that transformation?"

"It's been the only way." He needed to add, so did: "Till now."

"Now is . . ."

"Here. With you."

"Oh."

TWELVE: Jack and Ginny, and the Phoenix

Jack Tartarus dreamt of his father. They sat side by side on the front seat of Sam Tartarus's new 1975 Oldsmobile Ninety-Eight. Sam, then in his mid-fifties, stared straight ahead. Jack, at his present age, also mid-fifties, wondered when his father would put the car in gear and drive away. But Sam remained motionless. Jack wanted to ask his father what they were waiting for. Didn't matter, it felt right sitting here, the silence amicable. Beyond the windshield, the late-afternoon sun glowed golden white on the wall of their house on Crab Island. The shutters outlined the windows, sharp and green against the gilded siding. Jack thought, Damn good paint job on those shutters. Why, since Jack had painted them, had his father never told him how good the house looked? He could ask his father right now. But that would disturb him. The sun sank lower. Tree shadows climbed up the side of the house, a grey blanket sliding up the wall. Jack had grown sleepy. He lay his head on his father's shoulder. Still Sam Tartarus didn't move. Jack slid over to his father's side. They sat touching. He put his arm around his father's shoulder and closed his eyes. He hadn't cuddled with his father in years. In his dream he remembered a time when young Jack was sick, the flu, and his father took him from his bed wrapped in a blanket and brought him to the living room in front of the fireplace where they sat together, Jack on his father's lap, wrapped and warm, and his father read to him long stories as the fire crackled and spat bright flames up the chimney, a beautiful thing to see. Now in the dream they sat together in this close manner for a long time. It was a fine way to be. Then Sam Tartarus's left shoulder slid slowly toward the door, which now stood open. Sam Tartarus's head and left arm hung from the car. Jack too leaned farther left, to be close to his father. Then in his dream he fell asleep.

He awoke simultaneously from his real and dreamt sleep. Early silver light gleamed in from beyond the window. He lay still. He'd had a dream about his father. They'd sat and waited for something. He couldn't remember what.

But he knew it would be a good day, this Sunday. He'd invited Ginny to lunch. She'd said she looked forward to that. To meet Natalia. And Justine. His niece's seance scene yesterday had gotten to him then and it still haunted him. Would he tell Natalia about Ginny and himself, years ago? She probably needed to understand how close Justine had come to the fact of the matter. Would she repeat his admission to Justine?

Not yet the getting-up hour but he would anyway. He put on jeans and a T-shirt and went outside to start the generator. It sprang to life with a hellish roar. He glanced eastward and watched the sun rise from behind fir and alder tips. The rays caught the house side-on and gave it a comforting glow. The posts on the veranda cast sharp shadows that stretched to the stream bed. Light wind coming up again, he noted, today from the southeast, already hot. He walked around the house on the veranda. He passed the Fulton and picked it up. Hefted it. Stepped back, took a swing toward the house, missing contact by ten inches. He set the bar down. With the generator running, the pump worked and water flowed. Ablutions. He made coffee, cut bread for toast.

Natalia appeared, wearing shorts and a tank top. "Morning."

"Hi. Coffee?"

"Please. Going to be a hot one."

"Looks that way."

She sat. "You got back late." Not a question.

"Not that late." He poured her a cupful.

She cocked her head slightly. "You okay?"

As good a moment as any other. A Justine-free moment. "Look, I need to tell you something. Couple of things."

She sipped her coffee. "Good." She smiled at him. "Yes?"

"That scenario Justine made up, about me and a young woman, the wild screwing? It comes close to something that did happen here." He explained about Maureen's absence, the reasons for it, the sex just happening. "Her name's Ginny. Ginny Rixton."

"The Rixtons who own the chainsaw."

"Those Rixtons."

"My my."

"I'm not ashamed of it. Nor guilty. Just the opposite. It was a remarkable few days."

"Days."

He shrugged. "It was out of time. And it was that brief. I never saw her again." He sniffed a laugh. "Till Wednesday. And Nat? I like her immensely."

"You do work fast."

"I want you to meet her. I've invited her to lunch."

Natalia chuckled. "I can hardly wait."

"So it means I can't refuse Justine's—scenario out of hand. I know there's an explanation for her coming up with it. What, I have no idea. A real chat with our parents, I reject that."

Natalia nodded and sipped coffee. "I've been mulling over last evening."

"And?"

"I do think she made it up. Both so-called conversations. I think your explanation about Don and me makes a lot of sense. I think the time she took when she said the ghosts weren't around was time she needed to invent the two conversations."

He poured himself more coffee. "And how do you explain the one about me?"

Natalia sipped coffee, as if collecting her thoughts. "Let's go out on the veranda."

He followed her out. They sat on the steps.

Natalia said, "You know Justine, you've known her all your life." She waited. Jack said nothing. "When she was young she loved being with you. You remember that."

"Sure. I liked playing with her, taking her places."

"And you liked her stories. Her fantasy life."

"An imposing imagination. She . . . Wait. You're saying she fantasized me with some woman?"

"Some young woman. All that adolescent business from her with you? You must know she had a wild crush on you."

259

"Come on, Nat..."

"I think she fantasized sex with you. Maybe consciously, maybe more hidden. She'd never let it happen—hell, neither would you. But the desire maybe lived with her for a long time."

"Thank you, Mrs. Freud."

"It wouldn't be unusual, I don't think. Young girls fantasize in many ways." She grinned. "Young boys too, I'd bet."

"But what's that got to do with yesterday, her scenario?"

"She was playing out a fantasy, I think. From years ago. The young woman Jack Tartarus was screwing in every corner of the house would have been Justine."

"That's pretty weird."

"But way less weird than the chat-with-our-parents scenario."

"Yeah..."

"We didn't talk last night, after you left. She helped clean up and went to bed. You want me to have a casual chat with her, try to get her to admit she made up both 'conversations'?"

"It'd clear a lot of air." He breathed a sigh. "But maybe it's something she has to do, these conversations. If it takes 'talking' to our parents to remember them, maybe just let her."

"Maybe." Natalia nodded. "Can we have some breakfast now?"

"Course." He got up from the stair and headed back to the kitchen. He put bread in the toaster, poured them more coffee.

Justine appeared, still in her nightgown, a dry bath towel wrapped around her shoulders. "I think—I think Mr. Bonner, Frank... something's happened to him."

They both stared at her. Jack spoke first. "Of course something happened to him. He had a car accident, he's in intensive care."

"No, no. I mean something—more."

Natalia said what Jack had been thinking. "Are you suggesting the ghosts of your grandparents have told you something about Frank?"

"No, Mom!"

"Well then?"

"I can just feel it! Call wherever he is! They'll tell you."

"Easy enough." Jack found his cellphone and pressed in the clinic number. It rang five times. A voice answered. It sounded a little like Don. "Don? That you?"

On the other end, Don said softly, "Yes. Jack?"

"Hey, are you okay?"

"Yes. No."

"Don. Your father. How's Frank?"

For maybe five seconds, silence. Then Don said, "He's dead, Jack. He just—died."

"Oh god..." Jack stared at his sister and his niece. He said to them, "Frank just died." Justine shuddered. Natalia brought her arms about her daughter and held her tight. "Don. Are you alone? Anybody there with you."

"Etain. And Bandy."

"Okay. Just stay there. I'll be down right away."

"You don't have..." was as far as Don got.

Jack had cut the connection. "Going to see if I can help." To Justine he added, "How the hell did you know that?"

"I told you. I didn't know."

"Then how?"

"Jack." She pulled herself loose from her mother's embrace. "Listen to me. I didn't know. But something came over me, just as I woke up." She shook her head. "I feel things here. In this house. I did often, all those times I came over here alone. Is that so hard to understand?"

Tartarus stared at her for a long moment before saying, "For me, yes. But if it's how you work..." He shrugged, turned, and headed for the door.

Natalia said, "I'm coming with you. Wait for me. Just a minute."

Justine rushed up the stairs. Her mother disappeared into her bedroom. Poor Don. Or maybe lucky Don. He had Etain. Don had understood his father and, whatever crankiness there was in the old man, had cared for him deeply. One cares for one's father, one loves one's father. Tartarus remembered he'd had a dream about his father, just overnight. He wished he could remember what he'd dreamt...

If Natalia and Justine didn't get here in two minutes, he'd leave by himself. He checked his watch. They appeared with fifteen seconds to spare, each wearing slacks and a shirt.

At the clinic Frank's big Mercury, angled across a couple of parking spaces, gave evidence of the speed of Don's arrival. An RCMP patrol car was parked beside it, and several other vehicles in a row. An ambulance was backed to the side door. Jack and the two women hustled up the steps.

Jack opened the door. Don, Etain, an RCMP officer, Dr. Bandeen, Tamara the nurse, two men Jack didn't know. Don came toward him, paused, then hugged Jack hard. Jack returned the hug. They held on to each other for several seconds. "Donnie. I'm very sorry."

"Thanks for coming." He stepped out of the room. "There's no space in there," he said, as if he were responsible for the square footage and the people.

Natalia put her arms around him. "Oh Don."

He hugged her back. "It'll be . . . strange. Without him."

"Yes."

He let out a sad little laugh. "He made it clear, he wouldn't leave the island alive."

Justine too gave Don a hug. "Don, I'm really sorry."

"Yes." He held on to her for a moment.

Jack said, "What happened? Not stable enough for the ambulance?"

"He—seemed to be. Tamara was with him all night. She went out to get coffee at about seven-thirty and stopped off for a bathroom break. Then she went back into his room. He'd pulled all the tubes out, and he was dead. She's very upset."

"But would that have killed him?"

"They're trying to figure it out. But I don't think so."

"Then what?"

"I think he willed himself to death." Said in Don's usual matter-of-fact voice. "He was close enough. Then he let himself slide over the edge."

"Look, I know he had a strong resolve and all that, but . . ." A morning of improbable psychic explanations.

"I can't figure anything else."

Natalia said, "What can we do, Don? Anything."

His head shook slowly. "I've got to deal with it. He wanted to be cremated, like my mother." Tears overflowed his bottom lids. With his head he gestured at the ambulance. "Got to get rid of it, bring in the one to take him to the funeral parlour. Sign a bunch of papers. Make Tamara realize it's not her fault." He wiped his eyes with the backs of his hands. "It's going take a few hours. The business of death. When everybody's gone I'll sit with him till the other ambulance gets here. Tell him things he won't hear. Some last things to say. Tell him I loved him in spite of how much he sometimes pissed me off."

Natalia hugged him again. "Don, whatever you need, let us know."

"Want us to come by your place later?" Jack asked.

"Thanks. I'll call you. Don't know when I'll be done with—with everything." He went back into the clinic.

They watched him close the door. "Hard," Natalia said. "But he'll be okay." No one responded. "Well, as long as we're at the village, anyone for being served breakfast?"

They walked toward the centre. Swirls of warm wind brushed the skin on their arms and faces, pleasant enough. Natalia said, "Strange he just died, just like that."

"I think Don is right," said Justine.

"That he willed himself to die?"

Justine nodded.

Jack kept himself from commenting.

It might be possible, it might be possible. In Ginny's mind the mantra kept repeating itself, like a line from a song she couldn't shake. Jack and her, it might be possible. She would meet his family. Today at lunch. It might be possible. The Tartarus house. With Jack. Their house. Jack's and Ginny's house. Like once before.

They had gotten up from the bench and were lying on their backs on the dry grass, an arm of each behind the other's head, staring up at the stars. Jack spoke to her about fire and flame, and his photography. That using photography to show things as they are was for him not sufficient, he used to do that. The show the evening they met had shouted out what he knew, what he could see, what he brought out for others to see. Not enough, Jack said. And attempting to transform his realm into a better world, using photography to build improved models for

263

a happier future, that doesn't work. He knew this too, he'd tried it, for four years he'd tried. No, he'd at last learned that photography becomes consequential, valuable, some might say art, when it turns into a process of eliminating, of cleansing. Fire cleanses the world, fire on film cleanses the viewer. Such cleansing had become the purpose of Tartarus's work. Cleansing, like water? she'd asked. Yes. Water was a possibility. Some day he might work with water. But he wasn't finished with fire.

It might be possible. Now she took a long swallow of water. She put the drops in her eyes. She slipped on her cream silk blouse and buttoned it, wrapped her long white Mexican skirt about her waist and tied it in place. Sandals. She opened her front door and heard a small roar, like distant thunder. She felt the hot windy air on her arms and face. Last night they had watched the black universe above them with its pinpricks of fire, had seen two shooting stars, had talked of anything that entered their minds. She could, she knew, continue to do this forever. They did not fuck, they didn't need to, they were making love at every moment.

She breathed in deeply. The air was heavy with dryness. Like smoke. She sniffed. A light but definite smell of smoke. They hadn't made a fire last night. Wood coals in the fire pit. Was the wind blowing old ashes around? She strode quickly around and to the back. In the pit, only the ancient coals. But a definite smell of smoke. Back into the house she took the stairs two at a time and out to the little balcony. A stronger smell here. She saw it then, a dark swirl, to the east. Not far away. In the direction of the Tartarus house! A sense of panic took her, for a moment she froze, then she flew down the stairs, out the door, to her beater, in, away.

At Fisherman's Rest-or-Rant, the first open eatery they found, Jack said, "This place is okay."

They were seated, they ordered. Jack again asked for the Rant, "It's not bad." The women took him at his word. He glanced about the room. That man was there again, the hardware store clerk. The man Ginny had talked to at the bar. The man who was everywhere. Turtle.

They talked of Don, would his life change. Justine said, "Don's a free man now, Mom."

Natalia said, "Less than before, I'd guess."

"No way! Why?"

"Let's just say it's something I can . . . feel in my bones."

Justine pushed: "You could call your students, stay here with him for a few days."

"We're going back to Vancouver this evening."

"I think you should try to . . ."

"I think you should butt out. Anyway, we've got a reservation for the car on the ferry."

"That doesn't . . ."

"I'm going back. You can stay."

She glared at Jack. The glare turned into a flirting grin. "I'll stay until I convince Jack to leave the house alone. To give up on this silly notion of tearing it down." A controlling smile now. "I'll do everything I have to to save the house."

Tartarus thought, No, Justine. No. Even if Natalia's judgement had been wrong, he was not interested in having Justine at his house. So the easiest thing to say—which he was going to tell them later anyway—was, "I've already decided. I'm not going to tear the house down."

Natalia frowned. "At all? Ever?"

"The house stays."

"Oh Jack!" Natalia stood and leaned over her brother, to hug him.

Justine hugged him from the other side. "Oh thank you, Jack, thank you."

"What changed your mind?"

He raised his eyebrows at them as they sat again. "Well, two things. First, you're both so very convincing." He suddenly stared past them, into the middle distance."

Natalia said, "And?"

"And?" He came back. "Oh, second. There are some kinds of vengeance it's impossible to wreak."

"Like?"

He shook his head. "It's stopped mattering."

The food came. They ate. They kept talking about their relief, their pleasure, that he wouldn't harm the house. He told them about his restaurant theory, the law of ten percent, eight percent, ten percent, how it had grown from much empirical evidence—the best kind—from being on the road, when ten percent of all breakfasts are great, another ten percent are awful, the rest adequate to the job.

And slowly they felt it dissipate, the sadness in each of them about Frank's death. Their moods lightened. Natalia, Justine, and Jack had returned to Crab.

A voice at Jack's side said, "Excuse me."

Tartarus turned. Turtle. "Yes?"

"I don't know exactly how to say this but, well, I think there's a fire on your land."

"What?"

"I said I think there's a fire—"

"What are you talking about?"

"Your land, man, your house."

"How do you know?"

"I don't know. I said I think. I think."

Justine jumped up. "Come on, Jack, quick!"

Natalia stood also. "We'll go check. Come on."

Jack dropped fifty dollars on the table. He could hear its echo: the third psychic shoe of the day had just dropped hard. "Thanks. I hope you're wrong." They dashed to the Buick, leapt in, passed quickly through the village, and barrelled up Arbutus, at the straightaways hitting a hundred kilometres an hour.

Justine whispered, "Do either of you have a cellphone?"

Natalia said, "Cellphone?"

"To call 911."

Jack said, "Shit. No. Natalia?"

"Mine's at the house."

Onto Scott, to the drive. They could smell smoke now, immediately they saw it. The garage. Collapsed in on itself, charred, unidentifiable blackened chunks of metal sticking through once-brown roofing. And thirty-forty metres from it, Ginny's ancient automobile.

They leapt from the Buick. The house seemed untouched by the fire. No, the house hadn't burned. Between the garage and the house the grass had burned, from the garage toward the house. Jack saw blankets, recognized them, from the house, unused this summer, charred and burned, bundles of material. And then one of the blankets moved, a dirty white one. He ran to it, it started to rise, it stumbled and fell. He caught it, pulled the scorched covering from Ginny, and held her to him. She winced, and cried out, and opened her eyes, large and white, small green irises, scared. She was shivering. Shock? Bits of her hair had frizzled away, turned to ash where sparks must have touched it, and her right eyebrow was seared. "Ginny. Ginny." He saw now she wore a skirt. Once it was white. The right side of it had caught fire and the hole was fringed with ash. "Ginny. I'm going to support you." He saw Justine at the edge of his vision, turned, said "Get her other side." And to Ginny, "Can you walk? Far as the veranda?"

She whispered, "Yes," and added, "Cold."

They half-carried, half-lunged her to the shade of the veranda. Natalia appeared carrying bath towels and dishtowels, another blanket, a pillow. They lay Ginny flat. Jack said to Natalia, "Get water." And to Justine, "In the trunk of the Buick. With my cameras. There's an emergency kit. Bring it." He wrapped the blanket around the back of Ginny's head and over her shoulders.

Ginny said, "No—water, no pressure, generator's gone, blew, must've started—fire."

"Nat. The bucket. Open the cistern, remember how we used to do it? Get a bucketful." And to Ginny, "Now I'm going to take your blouse and skirt off . . ." he saw the weak grin that came to her lips, "to see what you've done to yourself."

"My leg . . ."

"Okay, don't talk, let me see," and he untied the waist of the skirt and unwrapped the material, let it fall to the side. She whimpered once, twice. Yes, on her right shin the skin was both lightly burned and badly scraped, about ten centimetres down from the knee, three-four centimetres long, bit more than a centimetre wide. Blood oozed. Ugly but not a disaster. Despite the circumstances, he couldn't help but notice the elegant shape of buttocks, thighs, legs. He covered her lower torso with a bath towel, careful to keep it from touching the burnt shin. He reached for the top button of her blouse—

She said, "Okay, no fire . . ."
"I should look—"
"Others here . . ."
He grinned. "Modesty?"
"You—know me . . ."
"A little better all the time."

Justine returned with the emergency medical kit. "Thanks." Jack took out a bottle of aloe vera and some scissors. He cut two dishtowels in half, glanced up and saw Natalia approaching with the bucket. Good. He took it from her, soaked a half towel in water and rang it out, removed the towel from Ginny's leg, and washed the skin around the scrape and burn. He soaked the other half towel and said, "This may sting," as he squeezed the water-laden towel above the shin. He saw Ginny bite her lower lip. No sound came from her. He repeated the wound-cleansing three times, with another half dishtowel he patted the water away. He spread aloe on the burn. Again Ginny didn't cry out. The cool contact on raw flesh must have been painful. Plucky woman.

She said, "Something burning—flew at me, hit me . . . my leg."
"I can see." With the wet dishtowel he wiped flecks of ash from her cheek and chin.
"Jack?" Natalia speaking. "Can we move her? Bring her inside?"
"I think so." To Ginny: "You okay for a little light walking?"
"I think so . . ."

Justine again on one side, Jack on the other, they walked her to the house and into the room Natalia had slept in. They lay her on top of the sheet, the blanket still around her. Natalia found another sheet. They spread it over her, avoiding contact with her shin.

Jack said, "You warmer now?"
"Getting warmer."
"A touch of shock."
"I know. Jack . . . Sorry."
"For?" He sensed Justine backing away, and then Natalia.
"Lousy gen-generator."
"Generator?"
"Where the fire must've—must've started."

"No sorry, please." He heard the door shut. "Only thank you from me. Us."

"Why thank you?"

"You saved the Tartarus house."

"So you can—raze it."

"Won't happen. I won't be doing that."

"No?"

"No."

"Good. Glad I—saved it. Not the garage."

"A sacrifice. For the greater good." He saw her smile. Her singed eyebrow, her burnt hair. No permanent damage. A house on an island shouldn't have a garage anyway. A carport maybe. The garage had been wrong from the start. Not even used as a garage. "Close your eyes, okay? Try to sleep a little. You'll be practically perfect when you wake up."

"Never never perfect. People with—syndromes—aren't perfect."

"Hey, I said practically. Couldn't stand it if you were perfect."

"Okay." She closed her eyes. "Eyes are closed."

"Good." He sat on the mattress, at her side. She whimpered a couple of times. He let her be. Five minutes and her light breathing told him she was asleep. Brave. And clever. No water. She'd beaten the grass fire away from the house with blankets. She'd saved the house. He wondered what had brought her here. Same as the first time, her love of the house?

He stood, silently walked to the door, looked back. No reaction from Ginny. Quiet as he could he turned the handle and pulled the door open. Still no movement on the bed. He closed the door behind him. No one in the kitchen. From the living room, Justine's voice, then Natalia's. He joined them.

Natalia said, "How is she?"

"Resting. Sleeping."

"Should we bring her to the clinic?"

"I think she'll be okay. But we can ask her. When she wakes up."

Justine said, "I take it that's Ginny?"

"Ginny," said Jack.

"Ah."

Natalia would have told Justine the whole story. It made no difference. "I'm going out. Check the damage." Natalia said nothing. Neither did Justine.

On the veranda he noted the burned grass. The wind had blown the flames to within three metres of the house. A little more time and the house would've caught. She'd simply have used blankets to beat the flames. Yeah, simply.

He walked the thirty metres to the ex-garage. His hand in his right pocket played with the House Keys. He brought them out. Here was one key he'd never use again. He scanned the destruction site. Done without a permit. Would the small man believe it was an accident? Who cared. The sheets of metal that had comprised the roof, though bent and folded, were individually near to intact. The screws that once held them together had given at most joins and much of the mess beneath was visible. Smoke still rose from the jumble. Though the fire had burned itself out, cinders continued to generate heat. The whole inferno would have been over in fifteen-twenty minutes. How in hell did that fellow Turtle know there was a fire here? No arrival of the Volunteer Fire Department. Had only Ginny seen smoke?

The generator, the apparent cause, was a skeleton, body twisted, legs contorted. Didn't look like it had exploded, more as if it flashed into flame. From the drips? What would have sparked it he'd never know. A generator from hell. There'd be no inquiry since he wasn't signed with any insurance company. No report to file. For a moment he envied Ginny, if she'd been here to see the garage flare up . . . Though he doubted she'd have watched with an aesthetic eye.

The binding for a ski caught his glance, and the bar of a chainsaw, one of those that hadn't worked in decades. And what looked like the cover to the barbecue. Maybe the present he and Natalia gave Sam for his birthday the year after the house was built. The toboggan and old bookshelves, never-used lumber, crab traps, just so much helpful fuel. Pieces of the past, gone forever. Memories that wouldn't live without the objects they were attached to, all gone. What had he said to Ginny, a sacrifice? Not merely for a house held at ransom by a fire. Jack Tartarus, sacrificing tatters of memories that were unnecessary anyway, so gaining new life. Maybe.

Sacrifice, short of vengeance. And a mess. It'd take days to clean it up and haul it away. Though likely not as long as tearing down a house, board by board. He'd rent a truck and do it himself. Not necessary for a lot of people to bother themselves about this fire.

No, he wouldn't raze the house. He'd promised this to three women. Each for their reasons was delighted. Was he delighted? Too strong. Merely, now he didn't need to tear it down. The garage had been ravaged. That was enough revenge. Against one and all. Another moment in the history of the Tartarus house. To be lived with, just as he would have to live with not being there to keep his mother and his father from killing themselves. The house would be his constant reminder. Which was okay.

He went back inside, heard voices in the living room. Natalia and Justine, and Ginny. He stepped through the arch into the room. The talk stopped. Ginny, sitting on the couch, the sheet wrapped about her shoulders to knee. The burn-scrape below shone red but less raw. He'd dress it again later. "I see you've been introduced." He turned to Ginny. "How you feeling?" It felt strange, she there with them. She looked different, in some way. Natalia stood behind the couch. Justine sat on the chair by the sliding doors. The configuration seemed less than natural.

"I'll be okay. They said did I want a doctor to look at it. I said you'd dealt with it fine." She smiled at him. "Thank you."

"You're the one who deserves thanks."

"We were just saying we're so happy the house is still here." Ginny turned to Justine. "And Justine believes her grandparents are appreciative beyond anything."

"Jack said you talk with them."

"She does talk to them," Jack said. And was going to add, But they don't talk to her, then didn't. Was Ginny pushing for some sort of confrontation?

Justine stared at him. "You finally believe me."

"It's your way of remembering them. I'm learning to be okay about that." He tried a grin at her. "Just don't push it."

"I did talk to them. Just before, while you were in with Ginny. They said they care, they care, they're glad they still have their house."

Ginny asked, in a whisper, "Do they talk—do they want to talk—with others too?"

"I think, with a few others."

"Would they—talk to me?"

Justine dropped her head. "I think they . . . They've tried."

"I haven't heard them?"

Justine shook her head.

"Oh," said Ginny.

She was getting to him again, right under the skin. Did he have to say, one last time, There are no ghosts in this house? He stepped over behind Ginny on the couch and lay his hand on her shoulder. "Natalia and I were very close to them. That was then . . ."

"What?" Justine's head jerked to the right.

Jack said, "But now they're . . ."

"What, Granpop?" Justine paid no attention to Jack.

They stared at her. She stared toward the fireplace. She was listening, hard. Or pretending to. Her breath suddenly came fast and shallow. Ginny reached up and set her hand on Jack's. Her hand felt cold. Limp. They watched as Justine's fingers came to her mouth. He saw Justine's eyes water. He watched as her head slumped, as she wiped her eyes.

She took a very deep breath. And sat straight. "Mom. Jack. You might want to sit down."

He believed not a moment of her drama. He remained standing. Natalia sat.

"This is . . . this is how Gran and Granpop died."

Jack caught Natalia's glance. She clasped her hands. He felt the sudden pressure of Ginny's hand. He turned back to Justine.

"He couldn't stand living with her any longer. Her pain was too great. Watching her die became more and more impossible." Justine wiped her eyes with her fingers. "She didn't want to go, despite the pain. Not yet. But he knew it'd be better for her, to end her suffering." Justine stopped again, swallowed hard. "So he killed her. Took her to the car."

"Stop it! My father did not kill my mother."

"Told her they were going for a long, long drive. He . . . he belted her in, he started the engine. He closed the garage door." Justine sniffed, and wiped her nose, and her eyes. "He went back into the house. After a while he went back to the car and turned off the engine. Gran was dead. He was, he wants me to say he—he understood this completely, a murderer."

"Justine! Stop!"

"Later, in the evening—he went back to the garage. He turned the engine on again. He had to go too. He belted himself in. He smelled nothing. He got sleepy. And he panicked. He knew he was killing himself. He didn't want to die. He couldn't live as a murderer. He was, uhm, undecided." She smiled a tiny smile, but it turned into a sob. "Then he decided. He had to get out of the garage. But he felt light. And the seat belt wouldn't let go. He fell partly out of the car. Hooked in. At the waist." She waited, as if listening again. "He says his last living thought was, What a clumsy way to die." She leaned against the back of her chair.

A scenario to fit the facts. As they were known. But she'd added very little to the general knowledge. The murderer bit was sheer invention. Ginny had told him most of the rest of it. But the last part, Sam Tartarus half falling out of the car, how could she have guessed that? He fought back the fury building in him. He spoke calmly. "Okay, and now you'll tell us one thing more. What you just said, what you just told us, we knew all that. Except for my father's good exit line. A deft final touch. Admit that and we'll take the whole of your show for what it was, a masterly piece of drama."

Justine stared up at her uncle. "Jack, I'm sorry, sorry . . ."

"Say it: I made up that exit line."

"You really want me to . . ."

"Yes."

"I made up . . . Granpop's exit line."

The silent anger fell from him. "Thank you. That's the end to it." He had to leave the room, get out of the door. Ginny stood and limped after him.

Natalia said, "You shouldn't have started again."

Justine said, "I know. But I couldn't help it."

"At least you admitted to him you made it up."

Justine stared at the floor. "I lied. I didn't make it up."

Ginny found him picking up a burnt blanket, missed before. "Jack."

"Hi."

"You okay?"

"Better when I'm not listening to Justine making up her stories. I took to heart what you said yesterday, that it's her way of remembering. But all that was too much."

"Eerie how close she came to what might have happened to them. I'm the only person who saw Sam. And I've never told anyone. Except you."

"How perfectly did you push my father back onto the seat?"

"Perfectly?"

"Make him look like he was sitting there naturally."

"I don't remember. I just didn't want him half out."

"Could he have . . . No, never mind."

"Could he have what?"

"Could he have fallen again, after you put him back in? Before the police came? Did you go back to look at him?"

"No. No, I went to the house . . ." she closed her eyes, envisioning, "I unlocked the door and went in. Everything seemed so—normal. Quiet. I found the phone and called 911, to get the Mounties here." She looked up at Jack. "And I waited till they came."

"Did you close the car door?" There was definitely something different about her.

She waited a moment before saying, "I don't remember. Why?"

"I don't know."

"Is it important?"

He realized she was still grasping at the sheet about her. "Ginny. I'm sorry. The sheet does make a fetching dress, but I'll drive you home."

"Thank you. I was just about to ask."

He took the aloe vera with him. He met Madge Rixton, explained how Ginny had fought off the fire, left her with her mother and the aloe.

He didn't feel like going home. He didn't want to see Justine, not now anyway. He drove to Don and Frank's... To Don's home. He wasn't there. To the clinic? Closed tight. He'd likely be at Eating Thyme. And Jack would be interrupting.

He drove out to Lighthouse Point. Maureen's favourite place on Crab. He clambered over rocks down to the water. He walked along the beach, around the point. He had loved Maureen, loved as he had never expected to love. She was gone. And that love was gone. And this with Ginny? Lust, certainly. But more. He wanted to be with her. No lust necessary. And it felt right. So maybe love was not exactly found again, love as he'd known it with Maureen had died with Maureen. He sat on a rock, closed his eyes, listened. No one, no sound. What, Maureen speaking to him? Telling him it was okay for him to love a woman again? Nothing. What then? Was this new love? Reborn love? Love at all? He would wait to find out.

Tomorrow he'd buy the Rixton women a new generator. One for himself too. He'd need an electrician to wire it into the house since the patch board had been in the garage. In fact better, tomorrow he'd call Hydro and have his power turned back on. And the phone company. And the insurance company. It seemed he was planning to live in the Tartarus house. He drove back.

In the kitchen, he found a note from Natalia: *Thank you, Jack, for keeping the house intact. We decided to take the earlier ferry. I'll call you tomorrow. Sorry to leave you with so many dirty sheets. Let me know when the memorial service for Frank will be and I'll try to come over. Nat.* Beneath it Justine had written: *Jack—Sorry to have upset you so. Justine.*

He called Ginny. Feeling better? A little. Strong enough to have dinner with him? No, maybe not, but she'd like to be with him. Would she go with him to see Don? Of course.

Don had told Jack he'd be at Eating Thyme. He washed as best he could, dipping the pail into the cistern for cold water. He picked her up at seven. She wore a knee-length blue dress with a loose skirt and clutched a purse. The burn glared out below the hem. Yes it hurt, when she thought about it. Somehow she seemed changed. Something different. The dress? But he'd seen her in a dress before. Just that charred white skirt.

Etain saw them as they came in the door. "Upstairs. Don's playing with Patrick." She took them up to her little apartment. He introduced Ginny to Don and Patrick. Etain mentioned she thought she'd seen Ginny around the village.

Patrick said, pointing to the candle-glitter on the ceiling, "See the pretty lights up there?"

They opened a bottle of wine, a tiny sip for Ginny, and toasted Frank. "Should be high-quality beer, but this'll have to do," said Don.

"Will there be a service at the cremation?"

Don shook his head. "Just me and Etain as witnesses. For later I'm thinking about some kind of memorial service. Maybe in a couple of months."

"Natalia would like to come over for it."

His eyes connected with Etain's. "That's good of her."

Etain had to go back to the restaurant. Did Don need anything? Just a little quiet time, he'd stay here tonight, play with Patrick till Etain was done downstairs. This pleased Patrick, who said, "Don's a ceiling uncle."

Don laughed.

Jack and Ginny left and drove to the cliffs. They sat in the car, staring out at the ocean.

Something definitely different about her. "How's the leg?"

Ginny turned to him. "Healing."

He took her hand and searched her face. Suddenly he knew. "Your eyes."

"My eyes?"

"They're blinking less. What's happened?"

"I don't know."

"Did you take some new prescription? Do something different? Feel any different?"

She shook her head slowly. "Don't think so. I feel the same. No new prescription, no."

"Or done something unusual?"

"No, not that I know . . ." She caught herself and started to giggle.

"What?"

"I fought a fire."

In mock shame he lowered his eyes. "You did."

"How quickly they forget." She squinted at him, her own eyes near to hidden behind inquisitive slits.

"Do they feel dry? Your eyes."

Not a blink, not for ten long testing seconds. "A little. Just a little."

"Did you put the drops in?"

"Of course. Before I left. I always do." She checked in her purse. "The bottle's here." She blinked, just once. "Right now I don't need them. My eyes feel like I've just used the drops. Damp." She laughed.

"Hmm," said Jack. He squeezed her hands.

"Hmm, what?"

"Hmm, you know what."

"Hmm, I think I do." She considered this. "Shall we find out?"

"If you'd like to."

"Soon, Jack. Maybe even tomorrow. Okay?"

"Okay." He touched her cheek. "We'll have time."

"Time?"

"I'm moving in. To my house."

"You're—staying. For a while."

"For a long while. It'll be my base camp. I'll build a studio."

"Oh Jack. We'll celebrate."

"We're celebrating now."

"We are. Yes."

In the morning, Monday, he called to see how she was doing. Better, she thought. Could he make supper for her tonight? That would be wonderful. Once again he drove to Lighthouse Point and parked. He sat on the hood of his Buick and stared out to sea. Natalia and Justine. Ginny. The three of them, their passion for the house. Each for their reasons. But he could feel a similarity among these. Three women, each in her manner, alone. As if each of them has used the house as a withdrawal space. As if, in their separate ways they each united with the house? Had it allowed them to deny their private isolations? The draw of the house he couldn't contradict; he too had succumbed to it often enough. Out of loneliness? He didn't know.

He headed back to the village, the Islands Trust office. Time now to bluff. No, not a bluff—he knew what Justine had done. Time now to confirm it.

"Yes, Mr. Toussaint is in, but the papers haven't yet been . . ." said Ms. Chance.

Tartarus was already past her desk and through the Allholy door. "Dominic. I have a question for you."

"There hasn't been time to process your request, Jack. Middle of the week, we said."

The small man's bow-tie quivered.

"Cancel the request. I'm not going to tear down the house after all. I need to know about the young woman who came asking about the coroner's report."

"Coroner's report?"

"Of my parents' deaths."

"Ah, that young woman."

"Early twenties." He described Justine.

"As near as I remember, yes that could be her. You don't have a photograph?"

No, he didn't. He thanked Allholy and drove to RCMP headquarters. Yes, they had such reports. But one that old it would be filed in storage. Of course Mr. Tartarus could see it, someone would bring it up. Could Mr. Tartarus come back in the afternoon?

Tartarus made arrangements for electricity, phone, and cable. He bought two shiny new generators, one to be picked up later, one to be delivered to the Rixton house. He took himself out for lunch. He bought the makings of a supper that could be cooked on a hibachi and a camp stove. He went to the hardware store and bought several items he needed for the house. He bought another large sack of ice. He found Turtle and thanked him for the warning that there might be a fire at the Tartarus house.

"But how did you know?" Turtle reminded him that he didn't know. But sometimes he got to feeling things.

Tartarus returned in the afternoon. He read the coroner's report. Sam and Hannah Tartarus had died of self-afflicted carbon monoxide poisoning. The bodies were found about forty-eight hours after the couple had died. Both were sitting in the family car at time of death, Hannah Tartarus upright, Sam Tartarus slumped to his left side. The driver's door was open. Next of kin had been notified.

Natalia reached Jack on his cellphone just after he returned to his house. "Jack. On the ferry going home. Justine, she told me she was taking the scholarship. I cried. She's not going to become a plumber."

"I thought she'd already turned it down."

"No, no . . ."

"She changed her mind."

"No again. She'd always decided to accept it."

"So she lied to you?"

"I asked her, about just that. She said no, not a lie, she just had to try thinking of herself in another way. What would it be like, becoming a plumber."

"Another story she made up, you mean."

"I—guess."

"Oh dear."

"Yes."

"Sorry, Nat. But listen . . ." He told her about the coroner's report. "Justine read it, Nat."

A pause at the other end of the line. "She has a large imagination."

Jack Tartarus would leave it there. Justine had created her Sam and Hannah conversations. Invented them, not out of whole cloth but from shards and threads of what she knew, woven them together to project what might have happened. If Nat was correct, that Justine had constructed fantasies about her Uncle Jack, then it made equal sense that it had been Jack's fault, and Jack had to be punished. How? By showing Jack she was superior to him. She can speak to his parents while he cannot. Was this only tomfoolery? Or something more. Here could be a worry. He found himself wondering how he could be of help to her. And thereby he realized how fully he had come back to Crab.

Something he wanted to do. He removed his camera equipment and sleeping bag from the trunk and brought them into the house, returned to the car and headed out the drive. He stopped where the tree had come down and lifted the bucked-up logs into the emptied trunk. Way too many for one trip. He drove a first load around to the back of the house, the woodshed across from the kitchen door, then the second. He set up the largest round as a chopping block, placed a smaller log on top, took the maul from the shed and began splitting. Good tool, a maul. Not as classy as a Fulton bar but it did its job well. After an hour, his shirt dripping with sweat, he had nearly half a cord piled in the shed, starting to dry. Hard today to imagine winter, but it would come.

Perfect thing to do right now, go for a swim. But, despite the Tartarus land being surrounded by water, it meant getting in the car. Too much. Now if his father had dug that pond—Maybe later when the fire danger was over and heavy machinery could do its work again, he'd get an excavator in, dig out the stream bed, dam its outflow. Make himself a pond.

He poured a beer into a glass. In a few minutes he would wash, maybe even heat some water, prepare supper for Ginny and himself. First, one more task. He found the glue he'd bought at the hardware store and took it out to the veranda. The Fulton bar still leaned against the white siding. Beside it lay the splinters he'd hacked out of the wall. He slid the first into its space. Not a total fit, but pretty close. He tried the others. About the same. He removed them each, smeared them with glue, and slipped them back in place. With the handle of the bar, he tamped them tight as he could.

The Tartarus house, two storeys high. Shiny white clapboard siding, pea-green shutters beside the windows. A grass-green metal roof, pitched front and back. Facing the drive in, two dormer windows extrude through the roof-line, two more adorn the back. A covered veranda skirts the house. Pillars, four to a side, wood painted white, support the veranda roof. Wooden arabesque lacework softens the corners where pillar meets overhang. Along the west side a thin stream leads to a small pond. To the east, thirty metres away, a studio, white clapboard, green shutters. The land about the buildings has been cleared, fifty metres on three sides. The meadow to the east extends a hundred-eighty metres. Beyond the clearing, dense woods. The house dominates the land.

Acknowledgements

My great thanks to Ruth Linka for her continued faith in my writing, Lynne Van Luven for her insightful editing, and Tara Saracuse for her efforts. In addition, deep thanks to my reader-critics, Sandy Frances Duncan, David Szanto and Kit Szanto for their suggestions and critiques—which I mostly accepted.

A National Magazine Award recipient and winner of the Hugh MacLennan Prize for fiction, **George Szanto** is the author of several books of essays and half a dozen novels, the most recent being his Conquests of Mexico trilogy: *The Underside of Stones, Second Sight*, and *The Condesa of M*. He is also the co-author of the popular Islands Investigations International Mystery series, which includes the titles *Never Sleep with a Suspect on Gabriola Island* and *Always Kiss the Corpse on Whidbey Island*. Szanto is a Fellow of the Royal Society of Canada. Please visit georgeszanto.com.

ALSO BY GEORGE SZANTO

Islands Investigations International Mystery series
(co-authored with Sandy Frances Duncan):
Never Sleep with a Suspect on Gabriola Island
Always Kiss the Corpse on Whidbey Island

Conquests of Mexico Trilogy:
The Underside of Stones
Second Sight
The Condesa of M.

OTHER FICTION:
Friends & Marriages
Duets
The Great Chinchilla War
Not Working
The New Black Crook
The Next Move
After the Ceremony
Sixteen Ways to Skin a Cat